BLACKCOCK'S FEATHER

by Maurice Walsh

The Key Above the Door
The Small Dark Man
Trouble in the Glen
Blackcock's Feather
While Rivers Run
Danger Under the Moon
The Road to Nowhere
And No Quarter
The Spanish Lady
The Hill is Mine
The Man in Brown
Thomasheen James, Man-of-no-Work
Castle Gillian
Green Rushes
Son of a Tinker and Other Tales
The Honest Fisherman and Other Tales
Son of Apple
Sons of the Swordmaker
The Smart Fellow
A Strange Woman's Daughter

BLACKCOCK'S FEATHER

Maurice Walsh

CHAMBERS

This edition

Printed in Great Britain
by T & A Constable Ltd, Edinburgh

ISBN 0 550 20414 8

TO MY FATHER
JOHN WALSH
OF
BALLYDONOGHUE

PART I: DUNGIVEN

CHAPTER I

I

THIS is the story of me, David Gordon, and I will begin it on that day in May that I walked down the quay-wall at Mouth of Avon, below Bristol, and held discourse with one Diggory, sailing-master of the *Speckled Hind*. I begin it on that day because it was on that day Life began for me.

The sailing-master stood wide-leg on his poop-deck, a short square fellow with a spade-beard below a leather basnet. The grey-green waters of the Bristol sea shimmered and ran behind his wide shoulders; and the wing of a gull, white-flashing in the sun, flicked and dipped across the green, and the uncanny cry of the bird made mock of me and of all men. The sailing-master was in converse with a tall springald of a gallant, who leant in a carelessly elegant pose against one of the caryatids, slim rose-hosed legs ankle-crossed, and a gauntleted hand in the silken folds of slashed trunks.

The shipmen were rolling casks of Spain wine on board, and the roll of the casks on the wooden shell of the quay had the quivering deep boom of a drum. I picked a road between them, and stood on the edge of the wharf within a long stride of the wide rail of the poop.

The shipmaster glanced up at me from under his black brows, and went on talking. I waited until he looked again. "Master," I called then, "a word with you!"

The gallant facing him turned, and his countenance surprised me. His back was the back of a court popinjay, but his face was the face of a man. Below the brim of a high, plumed hat a bold blue eye looked out at each side of a strong, bony nose, and lip and chin carried a manly amber beard.

"Yourself it is?" greeted the shipmaster in his Cornish tongue. "You come early."

"A week past," I explained, "I engaged with you a passage for two men to Dublin town in Ireland."

"Ay! an' if you be aboard at run of tide come seven of the clock, in Dublin town you will be in three days, in spite of the king o' Spain and the Waterford pirates."

"Now I need a passage for but one man."

"One let it be," said he, "and no questions asked."

"I paid you an English pound for each passage, and would claim one back, if I might."

And at that the silken gallant threw up his head and laughed a gay laugh, a laugh with a fine ring.

"You laugh easily, sir," said I mildly, turning an eye on him.

"The only way to laugh." His was the light, mincing tone of London court. "I think, sir, that your nation is known to me."

"It is not, sir," said I. "I have no nation."

"An you please. Many of that breed there be, and most of them finish in the same way—head on spike over a town gate."

"From hurting men in silk doublets."

"Touch, sir!" He threw up his gauntleted hand in the fencer's gesture. "Silk doublet I wear, and hurt

8

I avoid without good reason.—Well, Master Diggory?"

Diggory, the shipmaster, looked at me, a gleam in his eye, and shook his head. "'Tis against the rule."

I was as reasonable as any man. "If 'tis so, it cannot be helped," I said. "But your rule is a dishonest one, whoever made it."

He mocked me with his great bellow of a laugh. "To tell truth," said he, "I made that rule myself this very minute."

I looked him over carefully. Though his eyes were merry there was a hot spark behind them. Now, a pound is a pound, and I had not many left in my purse, but, half Scot though I might be, it was not the gold coin that urged me on. It was the Highlands in me that hated to be laughed at. "A rule made by one man," said I, "should be in the keeping of that man. If you are honest as well as Cornish you will be putting an addendum to it." That was a long speech for me.

"I might," said he, "if I could remember it."

"That any man who could get the unused fare back from you would be welcome to it."

"Surely," he cried. "That goes without saying."

The hot spark in his black eyes had not belied him. His type was known to me. In Picardy and the Walloons I had met many of his kidney; squat fellows with great girth of chest, vain of their sheer strength, and despising and disliking tall men. Small hardy men I had met, too, who were always in the company of tall men and liked by them. Tall enough was I, and, at that time, I did not think any man drawing breath was much stronger. At the back of my mind

9

I was sorry to be taking advantage of this fellow's vanity and dislike.

He thrust a stained brown paw into his leather trunks and displayed a fat skin purse; he shook it, and it clinked richly. "Your coin is in there with two-three others," he taunted. "Come and get it if you have the guts, long-shanks!"

In two strides I was over the rail and on the poop. He was surprised at this readiness. With a ludicrous hurry he fumbled his purse into its hiding-place and backed away, one shoulder hunched forward and an elbow crooked, like a man used to wrestling.

I turned to the gallant, still aslouch against the caryatid, and took off my fine Highland bonnet. "If it please you," I requested, holding it out to him. "I would not like that blackcock's feather broken."

He took the bonnet in the tips of his gauntleted fingers. "Better it than the broken head you will have in a trice," he warned. "Cornish men start wrestling with mother's pap. Guard you!"

Suddenly everything was quiet all round us. The rumble of the wine casks ceased, and from the distance came the faint clang of chains on board one of William de Burgh's transport ships. And then the gull's cry again mocked us.

It was as I turned from the gallant that the ship-master made his rush, head down like a bull. I slipped a bare step aside, and as he went by dealt him a single thrust of hand and foot. He fell flat on his face, my knee was in his back—and before he could twist I had his purse in one hand and my pound in the other. And before he was on his feet I was over the rail and on the quay-wall. In sword-play, in wrestling—in Life—one has to be quick or eat dust, and in this small tulzie [1] slowness might mean mauling and blood-letting.

I held up the coin for him to see, whereat he swore mightily and made a rush for the rail. I threw his purse in his face, and, shut-eyed, he clutched at it. And there was my fine gallant facing him. "Your rule settled for you, my Diggory," he said.

The shipmaster tried to get by, but the gallant brought gauntleted hand clap on shoulder, and his voice, no longer mincing, was sharp as hand-clap. "Enough, Master Diggory! One addendum at a time. Enough, I say!"

Diggory drew back, agrowl; on the wharf-wall a man laughed; and the rumbling of the casks again made the air hollow. It was but a small incident after all, and it was finished.

The gallant came over the rail with easy grace and was facing me on the quay, holding my bonnet out in his finger-tips. "Your cock's feather would have run no risk," he said. "Might I have a word with you?"

"If your road is mine," said I, who had no desire further to bandy words with him or with the irate shipmaster.

And so we went up the quay-wall, side by side.

II

By habit I am a leisurely, long-striding walker, as one is who has spent years aimlessly, and this courtier-gallant had the light carriage of one used to picking his steps across polished floors. We were, indeed, no matched pair. He was tall and lithely slim; I was

[1] Struggle.

taller, and heavy shouldered above lean stomach. His silk hose and orange buskins, his slashed trunks and lace ruff, his short scarlet-lined cloak with rapier acock below it were a complete contrast to my sober cloth and leather, and plain black-hafted knife at hip. But I do think that my bonnet with blackcock's tail over one ear was a more gallant headgear than his high-crowned hat.

Also, he was handsome and bearded, while I was clean-shaven and ugly. Ugly! Ay! Ugly I was, and ugly I am: a dangerous, sullen fellow to outward seeming, though, in truth, I was, even then, of mild and reasonable habit. My face belied me. It was a long hatchet face, a bony dour face, with red-brown eyes deep-set close to a lean nose, and dark-red hair waving back from a high jut of brow. No maid might look at me twice; and men might count me dangerous, a man too ready for bare steel. Yet in all my twenty-eight years I had never drawn sword in anger, never shed blood with point or edge, never sought a quarrel or made one. I was but a plain Highland clansman, with a clansman's loyalty, used to following my father here and there in strange places and biding my time patiently.

This tall gallant gave me a sideways look. "What I would ask," said he, courteously enough, "is why you seek passage to Ireland?"

I considered that question. "If you have the right to ask that," I told him at last, "I will answer you with truth—or lie."

"As seems best to you. I am Francis Vaughan, Knight and Queen's Captain, brother-in-law to William de Burgh, the new Lord Deputy of Ireland—that prudent veteran! and any man who would set foot in Dublin these days must bear with his questioning."

"In that case, Sir Francis Vaughan," said I, "I will tell you that my name is David Gordon, out of Scotland, and that I go to Ireland to seek my fortune."

At that he halted his light stride and, with that gay habit of his, threw back his head and laughed pleasantly. And this time I halted with him and patiently let him have his laugh out.

"Your pardon," he excused. "But it is droll that a man should seek Ireland and a fortune at the same time." He let his eyes rove over me from heel to crown. "The only plenty in wild Ireland these days that might suit you is a plenitude of blows." He paused for a reply.

"I am no dealer in blows," I told him.

I saw by his smile that he did not believe me.

"In my Queen's Ireland you will deal or be dealt them. Quit me of offence, Master David Gordon, but back there on the *Speckled Hind* your treatment of hot Diggory was so featly managed that I am prompted to think you a dangerous man behind a sword—if you carry one."

"An Andrea Ferrara, but——"

"And it is well worth inquiring on which side you might use it."

"Sir," said I, "three days ago I could have answered your inquiry if I had had a mind. But now I cannot."

He looked at me with puzzled scrutiny, and then shrugged his shoulders. "Ah well! Let it be! Your answer can wait. One other question. Who was the other for whom you had passage engaged?"

"My father. I buried him yesterday in St Werburgh's churchyard."

And that is why I begin my story on this day. For until my father died I was not the entity that is David Gordon. I was only my father's son, following him about in strange and lonely towns in France and the Netherlands.

III

My father was aye a wandering man, and a wandering man he died. He was younger son of Gordon of Auchindoun in Scotland, sept of Huntly, and he had two loves in all his life: my mother, who died in his arms at Auchindoun, and his sovereign, Mary Queen, whose headless body he saw in the Castle of Fotheringay. And that last love ruined his life and left me without a career.

In his early manhood he had gone adventuring with one of the MacNeill hired fighting-men into Dalriada and Claneboy, across the Irish Sea, and as far as the wild, half-royal, open-handed court kept by Shane O'Neill, Prince of Ulster, at Dungannon. It was there that he met and became friendly with Donal O'Cahan, Chief of Ciannachta, and accepted an invitation to a feasting at the O'Cahan stronghold of Dungiven on the Roe. And there, at Dungiven, he saw Fionuala, daughter of the house, and his heart became entangled in the meshes of her red hair.

He was only a penniless younger son, and she the daughter of a chief who counted ten thousand head of kine and led five hundred gallowglasses into battle. But love does not calculate by beeves or battle-axes, and the two were secretly wed by a young Austin monk out of Arachty, and fled to the protection of Sorley Boy MacDonnell in the Antrim Fastnesses.

My father was at that last grim feast that Sorley Boy and his Scots gave the great Shane O'Neill in the Glens, a feast that began with boiled ox-blood and ended with daggers. Twenty black-*sgian* strokes went to the killing of the O'Neill, and the blood spilled that night was the first of an ocean. But for that long spilling my father did not tarry. He was one of the few who stood at the O'Neill's side that night, and again he had to flee. This time he brought his young wife home to Auchindoun.

There at Auchindoun was I born, and there my Irish mother died before ever I knew her. And yet, dimly, I remember a tall white woman, with sunny red hair, that, I think, was she; but sometimes memory grows confused, and the woman with sun in her hair might have been Mary of Scotland. That time she journeyed into the Highlands to make the Gael her own, my father, tall and handsome Iain Gordon, saw the Queen at Balvenie Castle, and talked with her, and sat at her right hand, and thereafter, Gordon or no Gordon, he was the Queen's man in victory and in defeat.

He was on her side against John Knox, who, I think, longed overmuch to be at her side, and against the Lords Regent and Elizabeth of England and the world. He helped George Douglas to smuggle her across Loch Leven; he drew blood for her at Langside; he followed her into English exile; and was in all the conspiracies to set her on one throne or on two —at Sheffield, Wingfield, Tutbury, and that final fatal one of Babington's that cost Mary her head.

It nigh cost him his own. With the net closing on

him, he barely managed to wriggle through and get away in a coastwise boat out of Whitby; landing at Stanehive, and making his way through the Deeside passes to Auchindoun, where I was—where I had always been—I a lad close on twenty and coming to my many inches and shoulder-spread, as well I might in that clean Highland air.

The grey tower of Auchindoun, within its four-square grey wall, stands high above the clear-running water of the Fiddich River, its back to the brown hills of heather, and looking across the wide, hollow green bowl of valley to the smooth breasts of the Convals and the high tilted cap of big Ben Rinnes; a sunny and a windy place, peopled by a strong and kindly people, not yet made stern and silent by the austere urges of Calvinism—that strange faith evolved in a land in no way kin to Scotland. There for twenty years I had lived the life of a Highland youth, learning little in book-lore but a goodly store from Nature. A Benedictine Father out of Pluscarden taught my cousins and myself a little Latin and some English and a fair theory of Christianity, but his lessons we were aye ready to forsake for a turn at the Fiddich trout or at Huntly's deer away up in Corryhabbie, or for a bout of wrestling or claymore down below at the Kirkton of Mortlach. A splendid fine youth, that of mine, if only I had realised the fact! Youth never does. My hero-father was away in a fairy-world playing gallant adventures, risking but never losing life in a Queen's cause, throwing a bold game against the English. And I would be with him in that romantic realm. How I used long to be with him! And with him I would be as soon as beard stood up to razor's edge—as soon as I could swing broadsword in double-cross. I was with him soon enough, and I was to be with him many weary days.

For Edinburgh and the new Church in Scotland had a long reach, and my popish-plotting father was none too safe even in the remote glen of the Fiddich. Moreover, his elder brother, Alistair, now Laird of Auchindoun, was a prudent man who wanted no trouble, and, saying few words, he nevertheless made plain that a long visit was not expected, and that any help that might be given must be given at a distance. My father took the hint and umbrage at the same time. Within a month he was out of Auchindoun and I with him, and a week after that, both of us were at sea, and came to land at Dunkirk in France.

I was a happy and excited lad. For was I not at my gallant father's right hand with life opening out before me. My grief! Instead, life shut down before my long nose, and all prospects were at the other side of a high wall. Even at this day I do not like to think or talk of the time that ensued, and I will say as little about it as I may.

IV

My father was a loyal man to a single cause, and a man of principle; that is, he was something of a fanatic. He hated the English. No, not the English, but Elizabeth their Queen, who had wronged his own. He would take service against her, given the chance; but there his principle intervened. To fight Elizabeth he would have to serve against the Netherlands, and that he would not do, for the Netherlands was a small nation, like his own, fighting dourly for freedom against the might of Spain. And neither could he take service with France, for France was playing a game with Spain and carefully biding her time. He was a fighting-man who could not sell his sword, moving here and there across Picardy and the Walloon and Flemish provinces, waiting for a change of wind and a shuffle among alliances. And change and shuffle were long in coming—too long in coming for us.

We were driven to many shifts. Aid from Auchindoun was tardy and never princely. It did no more than eke out what we earned precariously by our swords and our sinew. By our swords? So. I, that was so keen to wield a soldier's blade, never wielded any but the sham one of the fencer. My father, a skilled swordsman, taught fencing and wrestling in small towns on the skirts of campaigning armies, and I was his foil. Broadsword, broadsword and targe, rapier, rapier and cloak, rapier and dagger in the new Italian mode—I acquired some knowledge of them all, and helped to teach them in garrison towns. I had strength of wrist and weight of shoulder-drive, but my father said I was clumsy, and might be clumsier if the buttons were off or edge keened for blood as it sheared. And, indeed, I met no real sworders to test my skill. We moved only on the fringes of armies, and lived amongst and on that sad and sordid tribe : the camp-followers of armies, that ape and pander to soldiers.

Of life and its sordidness I learned my share in that sorry crew. All my illusions went, but I gained a certain balance of mind. Evil I knew and good I knew, and I met much of good in many that were evil. And always my greying father watched over me and kept some loyalty and cleanliness alive in me—even at the end, when a growing fondness for the sour country wine was sapping him.

I never once thought of forsaking him and offering my sword where it might be accepted. In pride I say it. For I was a clansman, too, with a clansman's loyalty, and, being young, believed that a place was waiting for me amongst soldierly men.

Then there filtered to us, up from Spain or down from Scotland, rumours of the new fight the united Irish chiefs were waging against Elizabeth. At first my father laughed his grim unbelief. He admitted the fight, but was sceptical of any unity of purpose. He had in mind the days of Shane the Proud, when O'Neill fought the O'Donnells, the Maguires, the Scots of Claneboy, anyone, while the wily Sassenach took this side and that side to ensure harmlessness by a general ruin. Clan warfare was never done in Erin, and clan warfare made no longer any appeal to a man who had plotted for a queen.

But in time there could be no doubt that this new fight was very nearly a national one. Hugh O'Neill, the queen-made Earl of Tirowen, and young Hugh Roe O'Donnell of Tirconnail had brought all the north into a confederation of power, had beaten the English in pitched battles, and were threatening the very heart of the Pale—Dublin town.

So my father girded his loins afresh and a new light came into his eyes. "There is work for us over there, David boy," he said. Somehow he still looked upon me as a boy, though I was then in my twenty-eighth year. "Do not believe that the Irish are backward fighters in their own land—as is held. Nothing will stop a charge of gallowglasses but mailed horse, and only mailed horse have beaten them in open fight. This O'Neill is something more than an ordinary cut-and-thrust leader of wild lads; he seems to have learned the arts of Burleigh and Walsingham while he was at Greenwich Court. And it looks to me that there is good chance the fight will not stay in Ireland. The Highland tie is still strong, and, who kens? we might set a Scots king on an English throne without waiting for a dead woman's dancing shoes. Let us up and away. We have kin amongst the O'Cahan of Dungiven and will look in on them."

So we crossed the French sea and by devious ways came to Bristol. And there the first thing we learned was that a truce had been made in Ireland and that there was likelihood of a settlement with the northern chiefs.

My father, used as he was to disappointments, was hit deeply by the blow. Outwardly there was little sign of the wound, but, I think, deep down his last hardihood was sapped. "Well, lad!" he said patiently, "since we are so far on the road, we will not turn back." And then a bitterness came into his tone. "But I might have jaloused that clan chiefs—earls of a bastard queen—would not hold steady on one course."

So we went down to Avon Mouth to seek passage to Dublin. One was easy got. The new Lord Deputy to Ireland, Sir William de Burgh, was there outfitting his expedition, and in addition to the Queen's squadron had impressed every seaworthy boat from Bristol and Bideford. These privateer shipmasters were glad enough to eke out the meagre official fee by a little private trade, and the first man we spoke struck a bargain for a brace of pounds—and lost one, as has been told.

It was the gab o' May, and a cold north wind, blowing down from the Welsh mountains, nipped my father with his vitality at lowest ebb. He took to his bed with a shooting pain across the back, made no struggle, turned his face, with a strange loneliness, from me and the world, and was dead in five days. More than that I will not say.

But there I was at a loose end. No longer had I any living loyalty to uphold me, no hate to spur me, no clearly seen object to strive for. I was only David Gordon out of swaddling clothes, for all that I was a grown man—a big, long-legged, sullen lad, without any of the enthusiasms of youth. And lacking these, life is a terrible thing for youth. What had I, then? A purse of twenty gold coins, a long blade of Ferrara, and—nothing more. Once on a time I would have asked for nothing better than a loose foot and that blade to carve a road. But now I knew too much, or I did not know enough. I had to choose my road, and there was no choice that called me like a trumpet.

I could go back to Auchindoun and live the life of a kinsman to a small laird, with a faint prospect of a small place in Edinburgh, and a still fainter one of following James Stewart, that unnatural son, to London town; I could go back to the walled town of Arras, where a certain colonel of pikes had employ for strong shoulders; or I could, no doubt, get a place in this expedition to Ireland, since this Sir Francis Vaughan might be glad of a volunteer, it being evident that the pressed train-bands of Somerset and Devon had no stomach for the work before them.

What else might I do? Ah well! My father was scarcely cold in his grave, and I would be no traitor to him. Let me be loyal for a little while yet and set foot on the road he had pointed. Very like there were cousins of mine amongst the O'Cahan near Derry Columcill, and, anyway, I could be moving that airt without binding myself to any side in any quarrel. To Dublin town, then, would I go, with a mind not yet made up.

It was in that lax spirit that I took passage for Ireland.

CHAPTER II

I

I WENT down the quay-wall that evening shortly
before seven of the clock, my not-too-heavy travelling-
satchel slung on shoulder, light purse in breast of cloth
doublet, and long Andrea Ferrara at left hip—loneliness in my heart, and none of the hopes of youth to
leaven it. Sir Francis Vaughan was on the poop-deck
with some of his officers. He now wore the sailor's
leather head-piece, and had changed his short scarlet-
lined cloak for a long one of blue cloth. Both suited
his soldierly face. The tide was full in, and he stood
leaning on the rail, looking down at me. "Dublin
town it is, then?" he greeted, gesturing towards the
gangway at the waist of the ship. "Come up this
way!"

The waist was crowded with buff-coated arque-
busiers, and the shipmen were bustling about amongst
them at their duties, of which I am very ignorant.
Already big brown sails were hanging loosely here
and there, and a line of seamen up in the bow were
tailing on a rope and marking time to a sea-song.

I was at the foot of the poop-stairs, when a voice
hailed me. "Hey, master! One-piece passengers in
the mainhouse."

It was Diggory, the ship-captain. His eyes were
black, and he came at me with a power of truculence.
One place was the same as another to me, so I turned
away from the poop.

"This way, Master David Gordon," came Sir Francis Vaughan's voice from the stairhead. "My good Diggory, if you will attend to your business of casting-off I will attend to this gentleman for a little while."

Diggory glowered at him and then at me, a heat in his eyes.

"Man," said I peaceably, "forget yon. A Cornish wrestler should take a fall as it comes."

"That was not fair wrestling."

"No. I was not wrestling that time."

He went off growling, and presently his voice came bellowing from the forepart of his ship.

I mounted the stairs to Vaughan's side. "The mainhouse is packed like salt fish," he said. "Doubtless there will be a corner up here."

I thanked him kindly.

He laughed his pleasant light laugh, and, taking my arm, led me aside to the rail, away from his officers. "Do not flatter me," he said. "My kindness has its own meaning. A tall man who uses his head and wears a long sword has much to commend him—in this business we are embarked on. You are better on my Queen's side than against her."

"I am on no side."

"As you say. But who seeks fortune in Ireland has to be on one side or the other. Look, Master Gordon, and you will see on which side fortune is!"

I looked out to sea, and the sea was crowded with sails—white and black and red sails, with the green English sea between and the gold path of the sun laid down amongst them.

"De Burgh's fleet. Three thousand veteran soldiers, a couple of thousand stout lads of Devon, and a park of culverin."

"And a truce in Ireland?" My tone was a trace quirky.

He laughed. "Of a sort. The wild Irish must have their lesson this time."

"Or teach one!"

"They might—as at Clontibret not so long ago. Here goes our answer to that, if need be. William de Burgh, fresh from fighting Spain, has a trick or two to astonish the O'Neill." He pointed into the waist of the ship. "There be some five standards of fighting-men down there, and you can have your chance of fortune if your mind leans that way."

Here was the direct offer. What would my father have said to that? Nothing. It was not his custom to display his thoughts.

"My Queen is a good mistress," said Vaughan, quietly urging. "She has contended against your Scotland and Spain—and Ireland always, and has beaten them all."

"And men do not trust her."

"Any man that does—for his own ends, not England's—carries a loose head. But, Master Gordon, if you mistrust my Queen take this my offer as personal. To tell truth I was taken with you, and am honestly interested to see how you take to soldiering."

"I am no soldier," I told him.

"You carry a good long blade and a cool head."

"But I am no soldier."

"Be it so. Your attention, Master Gordon. No man like you, sword and habit, may go foot-loose about Dublin and out of it without question. That is only prudence and no threat. Pray consider my offer at your leisure, and let us say no more for the present.

Will you accompany me to the after-house and try a stoup of wine?"

At that we left it.

II

I know nothing about the art of the navigator, and sailing open water does not go well with me. The *Speckled Hind*, rolling and wallowing in that late spring sea, unpleasantly disturbed my internal economy. A short hour after reaching the width of the channel, and during a sideways beat towards the Island of Lundy to clear the Welsh coast, I lost interest in the bonny green sea under the red sunset, and in the fine lift of the Exmoor Forest, the rich colour of the sails and the fluttering of the flags of England—in everything. And no interest revived in me for all of three days. Sir Francis Vaughan, accustomed to the steep short seas off the Lowlands and the long steep seas of the Bay in his filibustering as far as Cadiz, made light of this small jabble and of my ailment. He but dozed me with a dry wine spiced with Guinea pepper, and said it was well to have all green humours cleansed out of me.

I came out on deck on the third afternoon, and there was the Irish coast close at hand. A stiff headland thrust itself out into deep water, and behind it, above thick young-foliaged woods, two conical peaks stood up against the sky; away in the north another heathery headland, ribbed with stone, had the sea beating white against its base; and between the two was a flat curve of shore with the river Life flowing sluggishly between sand-banks—and the sunlight, in a soft haze, shining on the dark green of woods, the bright green of sea grass, and making gold of the barren sands.

Most of the fleet anchored in the bay, but the Lord Deputy's ship and a few others—including the *Speckled Hind*—carrying leaders, ventured the river passage to the Dublin Quays. During the last mile the seamen had to take to the boats and tow, a slow business even with the making tide. It was near sunset before we tied up at Wood Quay, above a strong, double, square tower, and there at last was Dublin town before us on the south bank.

III

I had expected something outlandish and strange in this citadel of the English Pale; but it looked no different from any other town of similar state that I had sojourned in: just a middle-sized place with a shelter-wall to the quays, high roofs behind, and a scatter of houses on the north side of the river. Upstream from us a towered bridge of two arches crossed the water. There was every sign of a thriving sea-trade, comfort, thrift, and a hard-held security. This evening the town was in gala to welcome the new Lord Deputy; flags flew, drums beat, silver trumpets sounded, and the populace was down at the waterside to see the show. The merchant, apprentice, and artisan dress was the same that I had seen at Bristol or Dover, and I realised that this city outside the bounds of wild Ireland was but an English town.

I left the ship as soon as I might, satchel on shoulder and sword at hip. Sir Francis Vaughan was busy, and, moreover, I did not want him yet awhile to order my bestowing. He saw me go, and made no effort to stay me; he but waved a gauntlet and called, "See you again, Master Gordon."

Making my way amongst the crowd, I had my first

surprise and one small twinge for my father's memory, for the tongue that was spoken around me was not English, but the Gaelic—my mother-tongue. My father and I, speaking together, had always used that tongue. Here now in Dublin it was in general use—and, I believe, a cause of some complaint amongst the loyalists—a broader *blas* [1] than I was used to and emphasised differently, but still homely and understandable. And yet it sounded strange to hear a man, attired in hose and jerkin and with the unmistakable round and ruddy face of the Saxon, use the wide vowel and the strong guttural.

I made my way through the press towards a turreted tower above a wide arch giving on a steep street of timbered houses. Close to a buttress on the quayside of the arch was the first man I could put finger on as Irish—a tall lean fellow with clean-shaven face and no head covering. His thick red hair was finely combed down on his neck and cut straight across his brows—brows set in a lower above eyes intent on arquebusier and halberdier disembarking on the quay. A long woollen cloak, with hood fallen on shoulders, was thrown back, and bare sinewy arms were crossed on a crotal [2]-brown tunic that reached knee-cap, after the fashion of our philabeg. He wore finely wrought horse-boots of yellow leather; his woollen cloak was lined with orange silk, and there was gold and silver work on leather belt. A gallant, tall, grim lad! He carried no weapon that I could see, but then no wild Irishman was allowed weapon within Dublin walls.

Sometimes now I wonder if Providence set that man there to wait for me—and for his fate.

I paused at his shoulder and addressed him in the

---

[1] Accent.   [2] A lichen, used for dyeing.

Gaelic. "Would there be an inn up this street, friend?"

He started, and surprise was in the deep-set eye he turned on me. He looked me up and down, and I waited his answer patiently. "Plenty," he said at last, and shortly. And then thought better of it. "This is the street of wine taverns. There is the 'Crane' close at hand, for a full purse——"

"And——"

"The 'Pied Horse,' near King's Gate, is an honest house."

"My thanks. This way?"

For another moment he turned to look loweringly at the Queen's ships, and I saw his jaw muscles ridge and ripple. Then he shrugged his shoulders and turned with me. "I will show you," he said.

We walked up the slope of the nearly empty street side by side, his head short of mine, but his stride as long as my stride. No townsman this. Once I caught his glance turned aside on me in scrutiny. No doubt he was curious about this tall, narrow-eyed, ugly fellow in the feathered bonnet, who spoke a strange Gaelic. I had come off a Queen's ship and wore a long sword, yet I did not seem to be of the ship's company or a Queen's man. Now I know that, running in his mind, was the thought that by careful questionings some of the information he wanted might be won from me. Listen to him, then.

"'Tis said this new Lord Deputy—de Burgh—is a fighting-man."

"The Spaniards held him that, 'tis said."

"Fine judges, by all accounts. And he with ten thousand soldiers in his tail?"

"A good many."

"You would think there was never a truce in Ireland," he said something warmly. "Like enough ye will be for harrying us out of the glens before harvest."

"I am for harrying no one."

"In bad company you were, then."

I did not agree or disagree.

"Good it is to be prudent," he said, a little tartly.

"Surely," I agreed.

"Silence is as good as truth, and sometimes no worse than a lie. That saying might be known where you come from?"

"It is."

"You are no Sassenach, then. Here we are, now."

As we turned under the hanging sign of the "Pied Horse," in the shadow of the King's Gate, I happened to glance down the slope of street. Women and young people were at the windows waiting for the show, but the street itself was empty except for one man, and him I knew. He was Sir Francis Vaughan's body-servant, a big fair fellow out of Essex, named Tom Pybus. He seemed to be in a great hurry, but his hurry had started as I turned my head. He passed by without looking our way, and I followed the Irishman into the wide, low ordinary of the inn.

There were there only the jerkined Anglo-Irish landlord and a saffron-clad man carrying a fine head of flaxen hair. But though the inn was now empty there was not a room to be engaged, and the landlord intimated as much, very bluntly, after a glance at my cloth and leather.

My young conductor flared, but his voice came slow and cold. "That is a lie, my fine fellow."

The landlord did not treat this man rudely. There was respectful fear in his eye, and his hands were apologetic. He protested that the almoner of the Garrison had fore-engaged all his rooms for the officers of the Devon train-bands now disembarking, but the Irishman would not accept that excuse. He had brought me here for lodging, and lodging I would have.

"I dare not," cried the landlord, and then had a bright thought. "Quarters your friend must have if you say it, Lord O'More," he said humbly, "and that is as good as prison-cell for me. But you have my best room, and, with your favour, a pallet——"

"Do not trouble," I stopped him. "I will seek other quarters."

"And not find them," said the landlord, "as long as the Queen's soldiers are in garrison."

This Lord O'More looked at me, and there was that speculation in his eye I had noted before. And then that grim face of his smiled pleasantly. "My name is Colum O'More," said he, "and this is my cousin, Cathal O'Dwyer." The other young Irishman nodded his flaxen head.

I did what was required. "My name is David Gordon," I told him.

"Out of Scotland—the Fifth Province? A long way you are from home, but our race is kin, and you are welcome to share what is going."

The Gael in me responded. And so my very first night in Dublin was spent with two Irish fighting-men —it was plain that fighting-men they were—from beyond the borders of the Pale.

IV

Eight days I spent in Dublin, and then Fate, dim mover of gods and men, set my feet on the road

31

ordained. And in these eight days a friendliness grew between me and the two young Irishmen, or, rather, between the flaxen-haired Cathal O'Dwyer and myself. O'More, with his red hair and grim-face and hot eyes, was not a friendly man. He was a man apart, using me for his own purpose, and his own purpose—his one purpose in life—was to hold his land against the English. No doubt he thought the company of a man who had come off a Queen's ship useful company in the inquiries he was making. He was in Dublin under licence for the apparent purpose of selling native-bred ponies; but though he said little, and I said less, I soon gathered that his main object was to discover the strength and quality of the English reinforcements and their disposal. O'Dwyer and I, shoulder to shoulder, followed him about the city of Dublin, to the lowering Castle with its round bastions, to Greneville Keep, Ostman Gate, the Bull Ring, wherever the soldiers were bestowed, and even I, a stranger, could see that the new army was only in temporary quarters, and that its ultimate disposal meant no good to the doubtful truce that existed.

Young Cathal O'Dwyer was a friendly lad, and got behind my dourness and silent habit; they did not repel him, because he understood them. He took hold of my arm, tossed back his fine flaxen hair, gave me the friendly lustre of his grey eye, and talked gaily and openly. In a day or two he made me free of their camp beyond the wall, where a score or so of light, wiry men guarded a great herd of ponies on the Fair Green, near the ruined abbey of St Francis, outside the Bull Ring Gate. He made it plain that, whatever their secret business might be, they were there to sell ponies; and a very good sale they had, too, for their hardy animals—hairy beasts with good legs, a hand higher in the shoulder than the Highland shelt.

During these eight days I saw nothing of Sir Francis Vaughan, nor did anyone meddle with us or accost us. Once or twice I saw Trooper Tom Pybus, and he, with a certain stupidity, avoided seeing me. I realised that I was keeping company with spies and was being quietly spied on; but, with something of fatalism, I let myself drift, for I could not make up my mind, and waited for something to make it up for me. Poor Colum O'More! with your hot eyes and mind set on war, it might be that Fate in the by-going used you for that purpose before she snapped the string for you.

At no time did O'More or O'Dwyer put me a direct question as to my business in Dublin. No doubt they wondered, but it was against their tradition to show an impertinent curiosity. They waited for me to display my mind, and I had none to display.

So I was being quietly watched by both sides.

CHAPTER III

I

MIDDAY of a Saturday and the three of us at meat in the ordinary of the "Pied Horse."

Truly the tavern was enjoying full custom. The long table and the cross table were crowded, and some small trestle dining-boards had been set in the low window alcoves. The landlord, a prudent fellow, had bestowed us at one of these, for he was none sure that Irish chiefs would thole shoulder-rubbing with English officers. I saw no harm or insolence in these young Englishmen. Fresh-faced boys out of Somerset and Devon, raw to war and the ways of dominance, they were boisterous at table, but never discourteous. Rather were they full of curiosity, and looked with something akin to admiration on these fine, bareheaded young chiefs, who had silk lining to their cloaks, gold bosses on their belts, wrought silver on their finely made horse-boots—and no weapon better than the short black knife.

We were eating our manchets of bread and soup, when a loud, arrogant voice from the floor made us turn head. Two men had just come in. One was Sir Frances Vaughan in his courtier dress; the other was a soldier in the panoply of war—ribbed morion and fluted corselet above long boots—and he was showing his teeth in a laugh. His teeth were more noticeable than the laugh. They were strong white teeth, and there was no chuckle of gaiety in the

34

laughter. A superbly tall fellow he was, with upright carriage of head, great shoulders and flat stomach, flaxen moustaches curling up on his ruddy cheek-bones, and eyes so light that they looked like polished bosses of limestone. A man you would say at a first glance was handsome and merry—and be only a good judge of looks.

"'Sdeath! the place is thick with shavelings." He said that loud enough for the room to hear.

I turned back to my soup. It was not my part to notice Vaughan, and the loud-voiced man did not interest me. I heard their footsteps come across the floor towards us, but there was no room for any others at our table. A heavy stride stopped close behind my chair, and the loud voice spoke again with contempt in it. "Dublin town's come to a nice pass, Vaughan! Wild Irish at meat with English officers! To your feet, dogs!"

He addressed O'More across the board, and O'More took it well. His cheek-bones hardened and his eyes narrowed, but he made no move, and his voice was cold and quiet. "Our table, foul-mouth," he said in the Gaelic.

The man behind me, as I now know, was a veteran of Irish wars and knew the language. "Ho! Ho!" There was no merriment there. "Stop that dog's gibberish and lap your wash in the corner.—You too, leather-jerkin!" His hand clapped my shoulder, and gripped.

O'More was swifter than I was. A mazer [1] of mead was close to his hand, and in one rapid motion he caught and flung it, vessel and liquor, at the fellow's face. The bully, for all his size, must have been as

---

[1] Goblet.

quick as a cat. I felt a few spatters of moisture, and then heard the vessel clank and roll on the floor behind him. And before I heard that I heard the rasp of steel out of scabbard. The soldier was as quick as that. Oh, but he was deadly quick. For he slew the unarmed Irishman then and there. O'More had not time to push back the heavy chair before the sword-point was at his face. The killer knew swording. He feinted quickly at the eyes, brought O'More's arms up, and ran him through the neck—a fierce thrust and recover that sent chair and man over backwards and wrenched blade free.

A great, terrible, wordless cry filled the room. It came from Cathal O'Dwyer. But I had no time to pay any attention to Cathal O'Dwyer. Clumsy my father had dubbed me, but yet Andrea Ferrara was bare in my hand as I twisted to my feet, and the killer's sword was no more than on the recover before I had shortened blade and lunged above the gorget.

He parried it in time and no more. My point ripped his leather collar as he swayed away. "You too," he cried, his teeth agrin, and he was too busy to say more for a space.

I drove in on him, all the will and force, every atom that was of me and in me gathered to a point. The buttons were off the blades and here was killing. "Kill him! Kill him before these Sassenach kill you." Something shouted that through my head loud as thunder, and all that was David Gordon became a point behind a driven sword-point.

A chair fell over, a table slithered, the blades grated

and twisted. I drove him. And there was his throat.
My point pinged on the edge of his steel corselet and
curved half-circle. The shock threw him back on his
heels, and his weapon was only at half-guard. I beat
it aside, twisted in the upper circle, and made sure of
his open mouth. And even as my blade lunged it was
beaten fiercely upward, and Sir Francis Vaughan was
between us.

It was as rapid as that. Not as much as half a
minute—and in another second . . . That second was
over now and he was still alive, but my concentration
still held. I was so sure that I was to die in that room
under the swords of the English that now I swung to
face them, sword on guard and feet set. No one made
any move at all. All these young officers stood or sat
acrouch, shocked surprise and anger in their eyes,
but their eyes were not set on me. They watched that
big brute of their own, and here and there came a
murmur that was on the brink of the fighting growl.
I might have known. It is only the veteran in Ireland,
embittered by endless and very deadly fighting, by
intrigue, by the constant strain of maintaining
supremacy over a breed not at all suppressible, that
acquires an unnatural brutality—a ruthlessness that
has much of fear in it. This war in Ireland was not a
gallant affair.

I turned to Sir Francis Vaughan. His back was
to me as he faced O'More's slayer. Then someone
came at my side and I heard a hard-drawn breath.
Cathal O'Dwyer was crouching at my hip, his
hand in the breast of his saffron tunic and his eyes
on Vaughan. I knew he carried a long *sgian* under
his armpit and was going to kill or be killed. I
caught him at the elbow and pulled him upright

37

against my shoulder. "Not yet," I whispered. "Not now."

He looked upward into my face, a terrible agony in his eyes. "Let me die," he whispered back. "Let me die now."

I shook him. "We will kill him at the World's End."

He relaxed against me, and we heard Vaughan speaking.

"This is not finished, Captain Cosby." His voice was strong. "You will hear of it——"

"Only spawn, Sir Francis!" His voice was as loud as ever, but his cheeks twitched and were ashen.

Vaughan stamped his foot. "You are under arrest. Hold yourself at the Castle until word comes from de Burgh. Go, now."

And Cosby went, thrusting his sword, stained as it was, into sheath and throwing his head up in bravado. Vaughan pivoted so that he was still between us, and the big fellow looked back at me over his shoulder. "Another day, you dog," he threatened.

I said nothing, but at that instant I could have told him out of some strange vision that his life was for my plucking when the time came.

The room was watching me now—Vaughan and me facing each other. We looked each other full in the eye and said no word. So bitterly did I feel that I was ready to cross swords with this gallant and try my best to spit him.

His eyes left mine at last and looked behind me at the floor. "Will you see to your friend, Master Gordon?" he requested quietly.

There was no more to be said and nothing else to do.

Upstairs in our room poor Cathal O'Dwyer, grinding one hand into the other, bent over the couch whereon lay the body of Colum O'More under silken-lined cloak. "O God! O God! O God!" He spoke low and desperately. "What will the clan say? How will I tell the clan?"

"What will your clan do?" I put to him.

A red flame leaped in him for a moment. "A thousand will die for this." But the desperate mood flowed over him again. "But he is dead—dead—and nothing matters. Why did we not die killing, David Gordon?"

"Easy enough to die in Dublin town, brother, but not killing!"

The door behind us opened and shut, and Sir Francis Vaughan was in the room. We turned and faced him. "I am grieved that this happened," he said at once, his high-crowned hat in his hand.

"Why did you beat up the sword at its work, Sassenach?" Cathal cried at him, his hand coming up to his breast.

Vaughan looked at me. "I am sorry for that too," he told me, and seemed anxious that I should know his motive. "What else might I do? I saved Captain Cosby's life, but I saved yours too. This is Dublin town, and if you had killed him, not even de Burgh could have saved your head from Hanging Gate."

This was true enough, but I was not in the mood to acknowledge it. "Who is this man Cosby?" I asked him bluntly.

"Captain Sir William Cosby, Governor of Cong and Hy-Many in Connacht."

Surely. We could tell him the names of all the Connacht loyalists who had hasted to Dublin for a council with the new Lord Deputy: Sir Conyers Clifford, Bingham of Galway, Clanricard, Dunkelin, O'Connor Roe, and the killer Cosby. The dead man had gleaned that knowledge and was beyond all use of it.

"You will forgive me for intruding," Vaughan said then, "but I would warn you that you are no longer safe here." He looked at O'Dwyer and spoke shortly. "You, O'Dwyer, had better be back in your hills with your men and horses—and your chief there. —And for you, Master Gordon." He paused. "You have been keeping unsafe company, but I have three choices to offer you—" He paused again, and I waited patiently. "The first ship out of Dublin, a strong lodging in Bermingham Tower, or—the third choice you know."

Even as he spoke I had made my choice—and it was none of his three. But I had learned to hold my tongue in narrow places, and I but gestured towards the couch. "No place for choosing," said I. "To-morrow——"

"To-morrow I leave for Portmore in the Gap-of-the-North, and Cosby has the ear of de Burgh. To-morrow you may have no choice."

"To-morrow you will know my choice," I said evenly.

He looked at me long and steadily, as if trying to get behind the ugly mask of my face. "Let it be," he said at last, shrugging his shoulders. "You have a strong sword-arm, but it is not as long or as strong as my Queen's. She will hold you within the Pale or thrust you outside it as it pleases her, and I warn you not to be rash. We hold you securely, Master Gordon."

Without another word he turned on his heel and left us. Now I knew where I stood. He had given me my orders. The stakes were on the board and the dice loaded, and I set my dour Scots jaw against compulsion.

III

Next morning I went out of Dublin by the Bull Ring, behind the last of Colum O'More. He lay under his cloak on a bier borne by four men of his clan. Cathal O'Dwyer and his kerns marched behind, and Dublin town looked on, silent and aloof. I brought up the rear. I was without sword or cloak, and carried my feathered bonnet in my hand, for all men to see that I had no other motive in going beyond the walls than respect for a man who had befriended me, a stranger. But Andrea Ferrara, that dumb one that knew only one tune, lay by the dead man under his cloak, and my travelling-satchel was hidden there too. It was well. Near Audoen's Gate I saw the man Pybus out of the tail of an eye, and knew that he would follow as far as he might. With the help of God I would lead him far and hard.

Never did I see men more stricken than the Irish kerns in their camp outside St Francis Abbey. They made no wailings, but their shoulders were shrunken, their heads bowed, and their voices that had been so gay always had a quiet sombre depth more grievous than tears. But, now and then, one and another looked up at Dublin Wall with its Hanging Tower lowering down, and jaw muscles clenched and a long breath lifted sunken shoulders. God help this English town if ever it lay at the mercy of the Glens! Indeed and indeed, war in this land was no gallant thing.

In the short time that had elapsed since the death of the young chief the camp had already been broken, the gear collected, and the pack-ponies loaded. By nightfall these men would be back on the hills; to-morrow all the Glens would know; next day no man of the Pale would be safe south of the Dodder River.

For a space Cathal O'Dwyer was busy with his camp affairs, and I moved about by myself. I loitered back by the Fair Green, keeping an eye lifting, and saw no sign of Tom Pybus or any man I could put down as English. But as I watched behind a booth a small troop of horse came clattering out of the Bull Ring Gate and took the south road towards the first green lift of the hills. I stood looking after them. That was the kerns' road too. These soldiers might have no concern with me, but they were on one of the roads I might go, and must be considered along with another road that might be guarded. So considering, I walked back to the camp and found Cathal O'Dwyer waiting for me.

Already he was a changed man. The killing had shocked his soul off balance. He was no longer the gay lad with the flaxen locks atoss and the laughing grey eye. There was no colour in his face and his eyes were sunken; life seemed to have receded deep down in him. "We are ready now, David Gordon," he said, his voice drawing slow and toneless. "You will come with us?"

"No, Cathal," I told him. "I go another road."
He looked towards Dublin.

"I am not going back," I told him. "I go north."

"North!" He livened a little at the word. "Where Freedom is. Ah! but it is a long road, and the Gap is well guarded."

"It is the road I go. I will tell you now that I am half Irish. My mother was an O'Cahan of Dungiven. I go there."

"A strong clan. Young Donal Ballagh the chief is a namely man. Always I knew that you were one of our own. Listen, a friend! My life hangs by a thread. I should have died back there. See the men's eyes when they look at me. This night my life may be asked and given. Given—that is easy!"

I put my hand on his shoulder. "Come with me, then."

"No, I must face the clan. It is the law. If I do not die I will be a wandering man till I kill Cosby. That is the law too." He looked close into my eyes. "If you meet him, do not kill him unless you are pressed and I am dead. Word will come to you wherever you are, and if my work is undone I put it on you, blood brother."

"I take it," I said firmly, and went on. "I want you to arrange the payment of my reckoning at the 'Pied Horse,' and I want you to sell me a horse and a cloak——"

"Anything the clan owns is yours. . . . If fair play was given you—O Mary! only another second and you had him. What is the good—what is the good? He is dead and my heart withered. Come, brother!"

He chose me a chestnut-red mare, five years old and

43

fifteen-and-a-half hands at the shoulder, a broad-backed lady with good legs.

"Her name is Benmee," he told me, his hand in her black mane, "cross-bred out of a Norman stallion, and she is trained to arms. The longest day she will carry you and the spark not quenched in her. Ride her with the knee only and use her mouth softly. I trained her that way to leave a man's hands free for hilt. You will grow fond of her."

Fond and fond of her I grew, many a long day.

And then he fitted me with the dead man's travelling-cloak. Alas! the yellow-lined one that covered him had his life-blood stains on it. The travelling-cloak of the Irish is the finest campaigning-cloak I know. This one of mine was of close-woven wool, dyed crotal brown and lined with marten skins. Tall as I was, it fell from neck to heel, was of generous width, and carried a hood to pull over the head in night camp.

Cathal would take no money other than what was required to pay my tavern reckoning, and I dared not press it on him. And at the end he led me to the edge of the camp, and, as I sat on Benmee, placed his hand on my thigh and looked into my eyes. "The knowledge is in me that we will meet again, David Gordon," he said. "Where or how, I do not know. Listen, now. Make your own road north, keeping to the byways and wood-paths." And thereupon he advised me closely on the long way I must go and the dangers to be faced. At the end he pressed my thigh. "Trust no man who lives in a stone dun," he said; "but men who sleep in *bothans* [1] you can trust for one night or for longer—if they are on the right side. Once across the ford at Portmore you are in O'Neill's

[1] Huts.

44

country and may ride openly any road, and no one to challenge you, and you riding in peace. That is all I can tell you, David Gordon—and if God is good to me we will meet across the Shannon."

His was the wine of advice.

CHAPTER IV

I

BEHOLD me, then, that pleasant afternoon in May weather, riding my chestnut-red Benmee westwards through the open woods along the Esker ridge outside Dublin, my knees agrip back of her elbow and my long shanks wagging. I rode the Irish saddle, which is stirrupless and no more than a felted pad girthed behind the withers. I was at home on such a saddle. All my youth I had ridden the Highland shelt bare-backed, and knew the art of leaning-back balance on easy roads, and the grip of knee that gives the arms free play.

Yesterday I had seen a man die, had felt the nerve-loosening desire to kill, had looked on the broken grief of a man I liked, and was myself come into the narrow ways of danger. Yet for the first time in my life I knew the content of a definite purpose. At last I was my own man going my own road, a good mare between my knees, a fine sword yet to blood, money in my purse, a long cloak against the night, food for two days—oaten bannock and collops of veal—and adventure beckoning me on. I might die on that road; I might die at the end of it; but it was the road I myself had chosen. I tugged the hilt of my sword to the front. I was on the road—to fortune or the World's End. I was in tune with the sun and the spring, and my heart lifted with the blackbird's song.

All the half-dozen miles to Leamcan I kept within

46

the fringes of the woods—oak trees in early leafage mixed with the dark plumes of pine and the still budding boughs of ash. When, at last, the Esker slanted to the river I went still more warily, for here the risk began. Where the Life curved was the long slant of a mill-weir, and some distance below rose the stone face of the mill with the big wheel hanging idle over the lade. I could hear the soft rush of water over the weir, and in the still, sunny afternoon it was a pleasant and sleepy sound, and somehow at the same time a little lonesome.

From the lift of ground I judged the crossing higher up, and edged along the flank of the ridge, out of sight of a strong tower close to the river, until I saw the broken water of the ford gleaming between the branches. From the shelter of the trees I examined the ground I had to go over. A slope of grass ran down to the ford, and beyond it a thick clump of sallies grew down to the edge of the water. Behind that the brae, heavily wooded, rose steeply, and the green solid curves of the tree-tops fringed the blue of the sky.

I looked upstream and down. There was no one in view. Now was the time. I gave Benmee a touch of knee, rode boldly down the slope, and splashed into the water.

II

And as I splashed out on the other side a big man on a big horse came out from behind the sallies directly in my path. And the big man was Trooper Tom Pybus, dressed for war—buff coat, peaked casque, and long sword—but the sword was still in scabbard. And as I brought Benmee to a halt two more troopers edged out of the clump. Three to one! Vaughan had given me good measure. Three to one, and back to Dublin city and worse! It looked like that.

Pybus was a plain Saxon man and not given to heroics. He saluted me with a decent show of respect. "My master, Sir Francis Vaughan," said he, "wants word with you, Master Gordon, in Dublin town."

I kept my hands still, though my heart beat, and looked about me. There were no more than the three. Three were enough surely; yet it was well for me that Vaughan was not come himself. My plight was desperate enough, but the notion of being led back to Dublin like a sheep did not enter my head. I think that I was, somehow, glad that the test had come. For eight years I had been moribund, and now I was alive, and life was worth a risk. Here was the risk surely.

One thing I had learned in eight years' wandering: that a man does not go far if action lags behind decision. I said no word at all. Tom Pybus, towering above me on the slope, a slow man on a heavy English horse, waited patiently for my answer, already sure of it. He got it, and it surprised him.

My blade was out of scabbard and poised in one long draw that had the song of steel in it. My knees pressed Benmee, and gallantly she responded, ears back and neck forward. She charged up the slope directly at the big horse, and Pybus had no time even to yell. Instinctively he pulled his off-rein and clawed for his hilt, and he was still clawing as I brushed by him. My blade was up and on the swing, back-hand— that savage late cut that has no guard and shears heads like a lad shearing thistles—but I did not shear the head of Tom Pybus. Instead, I brought the flat of the blade across his buff shoulders, and flattened him over his saddle bow.   I rode on.

I heard a bark of laughter from one of the troopers, and looked back over the curve of a shoulder. One was laughing indeed as he swung his horse awkwardly, but the other was wrestling with the lock of an arquebus. I crouched over Benmee's withers and gave her voice and rein, and she took the slope like a bird. We were near the head of it when the shot roared amongst the trees. It was badly aimed, for I did not hear the whistle of the lead, and not even a leaf fell.

And that finished that small adventure.

III

Benmee and I had no difficulty in evading the pursuit, if pursuit there was. We were westwards of the cultivated lands round Dublin, and all that Meath border was thickly wooded and in places marshy. The heavy English horses lacked pace in such a country, and we soon got beyond sight and sound of them. Still we hurried, with the sun at my left shoulder, and never slackened till we got down on the soldiers' road to Trim. That we crossed safely, after a careful scrutiny. By then the sun was behind the trees; and the sky was red with the death of the day when we came to a strong stream gurgling between low banks of grass and iris. This, I judged, was the Tolka, and we crossed it and followed it up in the airt we were going till we came to a clump of larch in young foliage. We were now well away from all roads, and here I decided to camp.

First I unsaddled and unbridled Benmee, and let her roll herself fresh on a patch of dry soil. Then I

49

tied her out to nibble a patch of short grass near the water, while I sat down on the bank to eat my supper frugally—one bannock and a rib of veal. As I ate I watched her mouth the grass daintily and switch her long black tail. I must be kind to this bonny mare of mine. She was a generous little lady, and never failed to answer knee and voice. The black points to her chestnut-red looked well, and her eyes were wide-set on a small head. As she nibbled she kept edging nearer to me, as if she liked my company. In a day or two now she would come to know me and lip a bannock out of my hand, and we would talk to each other as we went along the road to far Dungiven, the dun of Donal Ballagh O'Cahan, my cousin.

After supper I groomed her and, now that she was cool, led her to drink, and thereafter plucked fresh herbage for her. By then it was full dusk, and I tied her out on the fringe of the larches and myself went in amongst the trees. Wrapped from neck to heel in my fine cloak and with the hood drawn up, I lay on my back in the crotch of a root and looked up along the lean trunk at the dim crown of the tree, through which a star glinted down from a far-away pale sky. And I reviewed my day. Life had begun for me at last. Twice that day I had drawn sword—and my sword was still clean. I was not sorry for that now. All my old weary life—or lack of life—was behind me, and to-morrow I would start life afresh, facing strange and twisty roads with I-knew-not-what at the end of them. But if there was fight against the English, in that fight would I be; and if fortune came my way, I would take it; and if death took me, I would hope to be no craven, for death is a soldier's part and his meed, and no soldier should hope to draw old breath.

50

David Gordon, fighting-man! That was I. Of love I did not think at all. There I was cynical and wary, for the women that follow armies do not feed romance, and these were the only women I knew—or did not know.

There was no breath of air, yet the fronds of larch sighed to themselves, and here and there in the wood were small sounds of the life of small things—a quiet sigh, a quiet rustle—and quietly I fell asleep.

I wakened in the late dawn to the blackbird's song, a clear strong whistle that drowned the finches' chatter. Long unused to camping in the open, I was stiff and chilled, and the wan light of day-before-the-sun put something of sombreness on me. But the blackbird's song had a stir to it, and in a minute the mavis came trilling, and I was heartened to take the drastic course to make blood run freely. I stripped and plunged into a pool, let the runnel of a small cascade pour over me, and came out to run along the bank and slap myself till I was dry and glowing. Breakfast then, and the saddling of Benmee, who was lively and already beginning to know me. And so I turned head northward and away.

IV

I took all of eight days to reach the Ulster Border— O'Neill's line—on the Blackwater beyond Armagh. By the soldiers' road to Dundalk and the Gap-of-the-North it might be done in three, but following O'Dwyer's advice, I kept well wide of all made roads and steered a course of my own by the sun. I was in no great hurry, and canny going was safe going. Moreover, the line I took was no easy one. Mostly it lay through a wilderness of heavy woods, thick under-growth, and dangerous green marshes. Here was a land that was fast going back to a wild state after forty years of ravage by raid and counter-raid. Time and again, following a faint track, I came on the ruins of townships sinking down into the clay and grown over with brambles. In no place at all did I come on any real sign of husbandry. Like all races who live hardly and in constant peril of war, the clans had become pastoral. They lived by their herds and on their herds and on the game produce of the woods.

I avoided all habitations until my store of pro-visions was finished, for it was well to get as far as I might from Dublin before putting my kind to the test of hospitality. On the forenoon of the third day, in a lumpy country of bare knolls and marshy hollows, somewhere on the borders of Uriel, I made my first venture. I struck a narrow kine-trodden track with peat-hags on one side and stunted pine-woods on the other, and followed it up. It wound in and out on sound ground among quaggy marshes, and in time rose up over the shoulder of a stony knowe. And from there I looked into a small cup of a valley with pasturage on the brae-side and cultivated patches in the hollow—a quiet and pleasant small valley, sleepy under the midday sun. At the far end, under a beetle of rocks, was a township of, maybe, a score of bothies, strung out in one straggling line.

Any stranger coming into that valley had to come by road, and could be seen in good time by watchful eyes. Even as I came over the knowe a man came out before the *straid* [1] and stood watching, and here and there women and children disappeared into black

[1] Street.

doorways. I rode down quietly and peacefully, but I was careful to pull forward hilt under the cover of my cloak, for I had no inkling how these wild Irish might act towards a lone stranger. And yet it was so like a Highland scene that confidence did not altogether leave me. Hill-side and haugh, long-horned cattle grazing, the smoke oozing from the vents of the clay bothies—I might be at home in a little Highland glen; and when I came nearer there was the same reek of peat and the same not unpleasant odour of cow-byre, and a big hound came forward barking, and he was very twin to a brindled deer-hound I owned as a boy.

The man waited for me, and he was the only man in sight. A tall old fellow he was, wearing a crotal tunic, cross-strapped trews, and rawhide brogans; with a lined, worn face below shaggy grey hair, and one of his ears split in two by an old wound. He stood looking up at me, and, sitting at ease—yet warily—on Benmee's broad back, I looked down at him. I gave him good-day, and in return he gave me God and Mary's blessing.

"A friend," said he, then. "Is there any news with you?"

"Not a word," said I. "Is there any with yourself?"

"Indeed no. Maybe you could tell us if they have struck in at the fighting—the Sassenach."

"The truce still holds."

"But not for long, by all signs." He threw his hand back towards the bothies. "There is not a man left in the street—if it is men you are looking for."

"I am looking only for my dinner, father."

"To that you are welcome, surely," he said readily.

"There is the hind-quarter of a late-dropped bull-calf in the pot, and a man's share and a guest's share is yours and welcome. Come down off your fine mare, tall hero."

So I lighted down, keeping an eye on the house doors. Here and there women peeped out, and children looked round their hips. No men, not even old men, did I glimpse.

"We will put the mare in the park," said my host.

The park was one of two stone-fenced fields in the bottom of the valley. It grew a short green herbage, and Benmee whinnied as she saw it. As I unsaddled her she made a playful nip at me and, when head-free, kicked up her heels, galloped half-circle to the end of the field, and began cropping busily. Leaving saddle and bridle slung on the fence, we walked back to the old man's house. It was no larger than any of the others, though I gathered he was chief man and Brehon-judge of the village.

I bent head under the low lintel behind him. I did not know what I might be entering into in the half-light. Back in Dublin there was talk that Ireland outside the Pale was full of brigands, and that a stranger's throat was cut oftener than not. But I had no reason yet to mistrust this old man, and if one must venture, one must venture to the full. The risk of being set on in the half-dusk inside was the risk I had to take for my dinner, and dinner I must have—and there was an end to it.

I ran no risk at all. There was a peat-fire in the middle of the floor, with a big black skillet abubble on a crook over it, and a fine odour of veal and peat. There was a layer of smoke four feet off the ground, and a trickle of it came through the doorway, and a small trickle of it went up through the black-edged vent in the roof. There were a trestle-bench, a few creepie-stools, a round boss of stone, a block of bog-oak, and no other furnishing that I could see. And of people there were an old crone, a young pleasant-faced woman, and three sturdy half-naked children. They sat acrouch out of the smoke, and I did likewise as soon as I might. And they made me welcome. I might be back in a bothy in Glenfiddich with a side of venison acooking.

Into a big wooden ashet on the trestle-bench the young woman poured the smoking contents of the black skillet, and there was, not one, but two quarters of veal. And we all sat round and ate, and sopped the gravy with bannocks of bread. The guest got first choice, and took it as a guest must, cutting off a browned slice high up on the thigh with his short *sgian*, and passing the knife to the old man, who chose the next best cut judiciously. And in a short while there was nothing left but two long bones, and these the brindled hound took out of doors, where presently we heard him fight furiously with a brother.

We Gaels were always famous eaters of meat. At that time, and for a few years after, there was plenty in Ireland, and that plenty was used lavishly. Milk, meat, strong-flavoured butter, and boiled ox-blood— these were staple foods, and reared big-boned men and round-bosomed women.

At the end of eating the old man went fumbling in a corner, and came back with a cow's horn full of a pale liquid. He proffered it to me. "There is no harm in it," he told me. "'Tis mild and old."

It was usquebaugh, flavoured with wild honey, and, though old, it had retained the fire of youth. It made throat and eye smart, but I took my share as required by ritual, and the old fellow left a bare mouthful at the bottom for the crone.

We went outside after food. The Gael tholes ill with indoors while the sun is above-ground, and that is why his dwelling is no more than a makeshift against night and weather. He is a tent-dweller, forced in this grey north to burrow in a clay bothy shaped not unlike a tent.

Now that I had broken bread, what men there were came out into the open. They were mostly old, and, after their habit, strolled to hear what news was going where my host and I leant on the wall of the pasture. And talk went back and forth.

One son of my host—"father of the clan back there," he said—had been levied on the Queen's side, and another, to escape that levy, had run off and joined Wat Tyrrell, O'Neill's ally, at Loch Ennil.

"If war is in it," said he, "two brothers will be at the killing, as has happened before now. If myself were young—" He fingered his slit ear.

"You got that in fight?" I put in.

"I did so—from a Scots bonnacht [1] of Sorley Boy MacDonnell's that time Shane O'Neill came down on the Maguires over beyond. A claymore he had, and the haft of my sparth-axe broken."

"A bad day for the Maguires," said another ancient. "Ye were well beat that day, Eoghan?"

"Ay, were we! But Hugh Maguire had the sound drop in him, and he came back in his own time. I was there that day too, Rick."

"If you were on Maguire's side now," I said hintingly, "you would be on O'Neill's side too."

He never turned head to me, but answered cryptic-

[1] Hired soldier.

ally. "That is the side I would be on, surely—and whatever side I might be on I might be on the same side as yourself, tall man."

"You might." I was cryptic too. "While the truce lasts I am paying a visit to my cousin, O'Cahan of Dungiven."

"Ay! I thought you had the northern Gaelic. A namely clan. 'Tis said young Donal Ballagh led three hundred gallowglasses at Clontibret."

"The slow road you are taking," put in the old fellow called Rick, who had a sharp-set tongue.

"It suits me well." I looked at my old host. "What road would you take yourself?"

"Well, now"—he rubbed his chin—"'tis like enough I would take the road yourself is on—if I was wanting to see a sept of O'Neill and he a friend of mine." He pointed a finger. "Over there is Drogheda, and up there is Dundalk, and nearer here is Ardee and Donamain, and if the soldiers did not rob you the Stokes would be putting you puzzling questions—and the lie not always handy."

"And to-morrow and next day?"

"I will tell you. Over there, north by west, is MacMahon country—a pleasant place and a pleasant people, given to drinking *coirm* ale, but bogged in the marshes you would be on the road. Here, now, you are on the height of ground and only small streams to cross, and straight north from here are small townships of O'Duffys and O'Nuallans, who would be for hurting no one and he rightly inclined. That's the road till you cross the Blackwater into O'Neill's country, where no one at all troubles a stranger who would be a cousin to O'Cahan."

And that is the road I took, taking my time to it.

I rode circumspectly, and was careful of my little mare, and made acquaintance with the people of the soil. I ate with them, slept with them, held converse with them, and found them sib. No man did me hurt or sought to, for I was one of their own, passing through on his own business and taking, as a matter of course, the share that was due to him. I met no English soldier on that road. The power of the English Queen did not reach in here. Indeed, it did not touch me until I had crossed the Blackwater and thought myself safe in O'Neill's country.

V

I crossed the Blackwater within a mile of the mud fort of Portmore, at that time held precariously for the Queen by one Captain Williams, a tough-grained man of Wales. I did not waste any time looking for an easy crossing, for away on my right I could make out the low green mounds of the outer earthworks of the fort. The country was level thereabouts, and the garrison had cut down the woods to guard against surprise. I was in plain view of anyone who might be on the watch, and many an escape had been frustrated a mile or more on the side of seeming safety. So I gave Benmee rein across the open, the first she had got since Life side, and she stretched herself out at her gallantest pace. In a matter of ten minutes we were into a scattered plantation of pine and out of it again on a rolling dry heathland.

Now I was surely safe in Ulster, with Dungannon, the stronghold of O'Neill, scarcely a day's ride away. I drew Benmee down to a walk, rode in between two round knowes, ambled round a curve—and there,

not more than a hundred paces away, were two horsemen riding towards me!

I pulled Benmee in so sharply that she swerved half
round, and then the horsemen saw me and came
spurring. In the Highlands no man turns back if he
wants luck on his road, and turning back now meant
facing the border. I hesitated, and while I hesitated
the riders came nearer, and with a sudden stound of
heart I recognised them. They were Sir Francis
Vaughan and his man Pybus. The right thing to
have done then was to go galloping back round the
belly of the curve and take to slanting northwards
when I had the chance. Benmee had it in her to show
clean heels to the big English horses, and there was
no sense in risking capture so near safety. Yet some
dourness of spirit held me there, some deep-down
distaste of turning my back on this Englishman of
mettle, who was never unfair and for whom I had a
respect. So I squared Benmee round to them and
waited. All I could do was to throw back my long
cloak, so that Vaughan could see I carried a long sword,
but had not yet touched hilt of it. They pulled up
before me at honest distance, Pybus behind his master.

"Well met," cried Vaughan pleasantly. "You
have been long on the road."

"Thanks to you, Sir Francis Vaughan," I gave back.

He laughed. "I ask your pardon. Three thick-
pates made a poor compliment, and I am sorry you
did not cut the thickest off at the neck."

I saw Tom Pybus grin, an honest and faithful man;
and in memory of that day by the Life Ford he kept
his beast tight-reined with one hand, and held the
other across his waist, close to his hilt. He rode a
wide Flanders gelding, and on the crupper of the

saddle before him was strapped a hawking-frame, whereon were perched a brace of goshawks, hooded and tasselled. Sir Francis himself carried a gerfalcon on his gauntleted wrist and wore the green hawking-tunic and plumed cap of the cult. His only weapon was a small sword aswing at thigh, while Pybus wore his trooper's clumsy blade. All this I took in at once, and at the same time made sure that no other riders were in the reach of valley behind them. This meeting, then, was a chance one, and my luck might hold. And yet a wave of chagrin came over me that luck should play me this prankish trick at this juncture.

"Are you not on the wrong side of the Blackwater, Master Gordon?" Vaughan inquired banteringly, yet bitingly.

"And you too, Sir Francis?"

"No! My Queen owns all this Ireland. In her name might I invite you back to Portmore."

He was making play with me now, and the Gael in me did not like it.

"I am on my way to visit cousins of mine up north," said I, "and I would like them to be with me when I visit you at Portmore."

"How many?" asked he, with understanding.

"A thousand," said I, "and maybe one or two more."

"One or two too many," he said, and laughed, and then he grew serious and his eye firmed on mine. "So you have made your choice at last—or was it your choice from the beginning?"

"No," said I. "I had made no choice, until your friend, Captain Cosby——"

"No friend of mine," he stopped me quickly. "Perdition to him!"

There was silence then. This soldier and courtier was never so slow of speech. I think that he was perplexed, for his eyes frowned and his hand came up and stroked the hooded head of his falcon. Somehow he had a feeling for me, and it did not suit well with his loyalty to his Queen. Myself was growing restless inside. I was too near Portmore, and two of the enemy were more than enough. At last he lifted his head.

"David Gordon," said he seriously, "will you keep a truce with me?"

"Gladly."

"Go your road, then, but plight me your honour that you will say no word of what you have seen or heard at Bristol or Dublin."

I did not take two breaths to consider that.

"No," I said, "I will not pledge honour to that."

"Then you are finally against my Queen." His voice hardened. "And I must ask you to come back with me to Portmore."

"Your reason is a poor one——"

"The reason of two against one! You have no choice, and I do not want to draw sword on you."

"I know that," said I, "but here is your excuse for you."

And there was the blue-gleaming shine of my sword as it took the sun and the small keen tone of its song.

Vaughan was a quicker man than his servant. The gerfalcon fluttered down on the heather, and the small sword was out as soon as the Ferrara.

"This is folly," I said, in a final effort to be pacific. "Let us go our own roads."

For answer he drove his big charger at me, his light weapon at point. Now, a small sword on horseback is a childish weapon against even a raw swordsman with a Ferrara blade. He had to get home with his first thrust or have his guard smashed through. Pybus was still tugging out his stiff blade as Vaughan came in, lunging cleanly like a swordsman. I swerved handy Benmee aside with a knee, and as he recovered his blade, shore it clean off at the hilt. And there was Sir Francis Vaughan reining back his horse and my point at his throat, and his eyes steeled for the prick. But I recovered blade to the salute, and—"Look to yourself!" he warned. *Fair and a man of honour*

Pybus was coming down on me with intent to kill, his teeth bare, fury in his eyes—and dismay too, for he thought his master already dead. He launched the full swing of his blade at me, a terrific head-shearing blow. But I saw it coming from away behind his shoulder and glanced it carefully over my bonnet feather, and as he went past, bent flat over empty hawking-frame by his own violence, I gave him his deserts. I used the flat as I had at Life Ford, but I let him have the full weight of it across buff shoulders, so that he fell on his horse's neck, and the next bound of the beast somersaulted him into the heather.

And then I did what I should have done in the beginning. I gave Benmee her head, and we went belly-to-earth northwards up the curve of the valley. At the turn I swung in the saddle for a look. Pybus, at a stout trot, was trundling away after his gelding, and Vaughan sat still in his saddle and looked after me. I lifted my sword to him, and he threw up his broken blade in a gesture of farewell and salutation. A gallant man of the English.

CHAPTER V

I

HERE at last was Dungannon, the hub of the northern power, and it was not even a walled town. O'Neill himself had burned it down the previous year as a drastic measure against the sudden advance of the English from Dundalk, that advance that had ended at stark Clontibret field. And now there was the big stone keep with its walled bailey and, so far as I could see, not another stone building in the place. It was a wide-scattered disarray of clay, wattled, and wooden houses. Some of the houses had gardens, some were enclosed by an earthen rampart, some hedged with the whitethorn in full bloom, and other lowly ones clustered in a close with a post-gate at the end. Many of the wooden buildings were commodious and well constructed, with steep-pitched roofs, stone chimneys, carved doorways, and walls painted in bright colours.

There was no regular street or paved way in the town. Here a width of as much as fifty paces lay between the houses, and there two gable-ends left scant room for a couple of horsemen abreast. Luckily the weather had been dry, and the clay-road, packed hard, made easy going. There were dogs everywhere, big wolf-hounds, lighter greyhounds, and a squat blue-grey beast of the otter-hound breed—and all of them that were in sight came barking at me in no unfriendly spirit.

I was taken with Dungannon. It was sunny and

63

airy, and by no means dirty. Used as I was to Flanders towns, where the tall houses are cooped within walls, and the air has that sour muskiness that the plague left behind, this open careless place, with the sun shining and the big stone keep towering above the medley, was a pleasant change. It was more a camp than a town, for, though women looked at me over cut-down doors and children pranked in the open, there were soldiers everywhere. Many of the large wooden houses within their raths served as barracks, and big, clean-faced fighting-men moved about here and there in the lazy, good-natured way of their class. Within one rath I saw the bonnets and philabegs of Highlandmen, and was half-tempted to turn back to the unbarred gate, but when I looked into the next rath, there were more and still more of my country-men. So I rode on. I did not know then that O'Neill's Bonnachts—his regular troops—were many of them mercenary soldiers from the Western Highlands.

I made my very best show that day. I had groomed Benmee, plaited her mane, flossed out her flowing tail; of her I need not be ashamed. I had ridden her judiciously all the way from Dublin, and now she was in sleekly hard condition, carrying her head and mincing her steps in this strange town like the vain little lady she was. Myself had shaved freshly that morning over a still pool, tried to smooth down the back wave of sullen red hair, re-set my blackcock's-tail plume, and now I rode back straight and head up, my thrown-back cloak showing its lining of smooth fur and the polished hilt of Andrea Ferrara winking in the sun.

I moved along slowly, Benmee's neck arched to the rein, and though my head was still, my eyes roved.

The thought in my mind was that it must be eleven of the clock and near time for dinner, and that this was not Ireland if someone did not offer it to me. Better leave it to chance, and keep trending towards the dun of O'Neill. Even now, from that airt, the odour of cooking meat came to me and made mouth water.

Many men saluted me frankly as we passed; all of them looked knowingly at the clean legs of the mare; no man at all hindered or questioned me. This was a free town. And then as I opened the wide space before the dun I overtook two men strolling easily, and they moved aside to let me pass. I drew in Benmee and lifted a hand, half in salute and half in query.

One of them sported a bonnet the marrow of my own, but instead of philabeg he wore horseman-buff with a black steel back-and-breast. A lantern-jawed man he was, with a long Scots nose. The other was a slim, swack young fellow, with no covering on his notable yellow mane of hair. His short cloak was lined with rose-hued silk, and there were red selvages to his bleached-linen tunic; a gallant lad, with a reckless blue eye and a smile about his mouth.

"Ho, man o' Scotland!" said the lantern-jawed man in the clipped Gaelic of Strathclyde. "What clan?"

"Gordon," I told him.

"So! Mary Stewart's Highland hawks! Not many of them stray this road. I am a Crawford out of Carrick-Kennedy country."

The young Irishman was running his eye over me and over Benmee. "Man, Hugh!" he cried. "Do they breed darlings like that mare in the Antrim glens?" He looked at me with query in his eyes.

65

"They do not," said I.

"Maybe in Claneboy?"

"If you want to know, I come from Dublin."

"Dublin!" exclaimed Hugh Crawford the Scot, interest alight in his eye. "With message for O'Neill from the new Lord Deputy?"

"I am on my way to visit O'Cahan of Dungiven. Is he by any chance in this place?"

"Donal Ballagh?" cried the Irishman. "He is not here—nor at Dungiven. Do you not know? He is truce hostage with Bingham in Galway."

And there was my luck gone awry once again. This custom of hostage was usual in Irish truces. In the present one with the English the Ulster leaders had yielded as hostages six young chiefs of note.

"Galway!" I repeated the word after him.

"Ay, Galway! sixty leagues from here, and there he will be—having the fine times—while the truce lasts.'

I was once again thinking bitterly of Dame Luck. All the way from Dublin—all the way from Arras— had I come to see this cousin O'Cahan, and he was beyond reach at the other side of Ireland. Blood is thicker than water, and the family tie is a close one amongst us. I had looked forward to offering my services to a chief of my own blood, knowing that he would be understanding with my shortcomings. Now I was only a stranger amongst strangers—one Scots fighting-man among the many—and, tall as I was and strong as I was, I had not much to offer: a blood-less sword, a sour experience of life, and no experience at all of war. Very well, then!

I heard the young Irishman speaking. "Do not be minding that at dinner-time," he said lightly. "Come and eat with us, man of the Gordons."

Already I was beginning to feel aloof with my native dourness. "Let me not trouble you. The Ordinary——"

He laughed. "There is none. No man goes hungry in the dun of O'Neill. My name is Doncadh Donn Maguire."

Here, then, was one of O'Neill's young smiters, son of that great Maguire who had scattered the English at the Ford-of-Biscuits.

"Come on, lad!" said Crawford. "The O'Neill keeps open table."

No doubt, this tough and hard-headed Scots leader of mercenaries had been deciding in his own mind that a man who was come out of Dublin was worth questioning, and that the man to do the questioning was not far away.

"Thank you," said I then. "My name is David Gordon."

I slid off my saddle-pad, slung rein over arm, and the three of us walked across the wide exercise-ground towards the great keep. It was as stirring as a hive, this dun of O'Neill. Outside the big bailey were a score or more of Irish-bred shelts in care of ragged horse-boys, and Maguire called one of these to take charge of Benmee. We entered the bailey through a postern-gate in the rear wall, and found a multitude like a clan gathering—chiefs and retainers in full costume. Surely, O'Neill kept open house.

Hugh Roe O'Neill had been gently bred and nurtured, and this courtyard showed it. There was a great square of closely cut green lawn in the middle and beds of tulips flamed along the edges. Beyond rose the massive bulk of the keep, with an open door at the head of cut-stone steps, a black arch piercing the middle, and tall, glazed windows looking inwards. Along the sunny side of the bailey was a wide terrace under a light pent-roof, and in there scullions were busy laying immensely long tables. Groups of men lolled about on the grass, waiting for the dinner-hour: clan chiefs in their white and saffron tunics and silk-lined cloaks; gallowglass captains in steel. and buff; young men, bare-headed and clean-shaven; old men with long hair and beards; seannachies,[1] harpers, brehons—all the retainers of a royal Gaelic court. And there were ladies there too, tight-bosomed, flowing-kirtled, with lace and linen on their plaited hair.

Near mid-green was a large group round a garden-bench, whereon sat a man and two or three ladies.

"That is O'Neill taking his ease," Doncadh Donn Maguire informed me.

I was too far away to note more than that he was a man with a beard trained in the English mode.

Crawford murmured that he had a word to say to the chief, and hurried across the lawn. He looked back significantly at Maguire, and that lad, with a comradely freedom, put his hand within my arm and slanted me towards the dining-terrace.

"These fellows will be talking, dry as an old dyke— and keeping dinner late. See that white old rogue taking his seat by O'Neill? He is the greatest tyrant that ever lived enough years to grow grey."

"A relative of yours?" said I guardedly.

"My fine fellow! But for him I would be down beyond in Galway having the fun of the world with Donal Ballagh O'Cahan. That fellow is my father."

"He might be an understanding man," said I.

---

[1] Story-tellers.

"He might; but he was young himself once, though you would never be thinking it. You will be sorry missing Donal Ballagh?"

"I am."

"Thick as thieves we are—I never heard him speak of you."

"You would not."

"You know him well?"

"I do not know him at all."

We looked at each other and burst out laughing.

"*Mhuire!*"[1] he exclaimed. "You would be a good man to tell a secret to—and bury it safe. Ah! there's old Paudh going to blow the cow-horn."

That dinner of O'Neill's was an informal plenteous affair. As soon as the dinner-horn winded the multitude drifted easily towards the tables. There was no order, nor was there any hurry. The crowd circled round, found places, and set to work. The top cross-table was reserved for O'Neill, the ladies, and any of his older chiefs who might be visiting; that table was covered with damask and laid with plate, Dutch pottery, and Venetian glass; there were forks for the ladies and finger-bowls for who cared to use them. The other tables were of bare planed oak and furnished with beechen platters and methers, and drinking-horns edged with silver. Maguire bestowed me amongst fellows of his own at a table about half-way down, and it was surely the noisiest table there.

As I have said, the Irish were notable meat-eaters, and here was meat for any army: beef and pork, fowl and game, venison from the woods, salmon and eels out of Bann Flu, and for the first time since leaving Dublin I tasted wheaten bread. The drink was even

---

[1] Mary.

more plenteous than the meats; usquebaugh, mead and metheglin, a new English beer, Spanish wine in jars, and Garonne wine in flasks, and never a mug of water. And everyone ate hugely and drank copiously, and made talk and laughter without end—not like the forthright Saxon, who centres his mind on his meat, nor like the French, who are also gay talkers, but use extravagant gesture with knife and chicken-bone. And, above the noise and clatter, came the skirl of the pipes from where two tall fellows strutted back and forth on the gravel outside O'Neill's table and played ports [1] that I had heard in far Glenfiddich.

Some time towards the end of the dinner Maguire left my side, and returned in a matter of a couple of minutes. He placed his hand on my shoulder. "O'Neill would like a word—would like to make your acquaintance, David Gordon," he said.

I had been expecting that message.

II

I stood before O'Neill and his women and his chiefs, and I bowed to him and I bowed to the ladies. The one sitting by him was young and lovely, brown-haired and soft-eyed, and I felt big and awkward and ugly.

"Hugh Roe," said Doncadh Donn Maguire familiarly, "this is David Gordon out of Albann, riding up from Dublin to see Donal Ballagh O'Cahan."

There was but small formality in Gaeldom, where there was vast pride in race. Hugh Roe O'Neill was a queen's earl, but he was not feudal lord. He was chief of the clan, father, brother, friend, to be addressed frankly and called by his name—Hugh, Hugh Roe,

[1] Tunes.

Hugh O'Neill; but if one was called upon to be formal one used the proudest title that could be yielded— O'Neill.

He rose to his feet to me. "Gordon!" said he, and his voice rolled the word deeply. "To be sure. You are Donal Ballagh's cousin?"

And I again bowed.

"I knew it. I saw your father in this very dun when I was a boy. You are welcome to Dungannon, David Gordon. You are my cousin too—twice removed."

His hand clasped mine firmly, and his eyes met mine so keenly that I felt the shock of their scrutiny. Blue eyes they were, deep-set and close-set under brows, and they had a shock like ice or fire. He was a man of middle height, this great O'Neill, with good shoulders, notably long arms, and the slightly bowed legs of the horseman. He wore a silken tunic like his chiefs, went bareheaded like them, but, unlike them, he carried a trained spade-beard on his chin—a fair red beard, already flecked with grey.

He turned to the lovely, brown-haired woman. "Woman-of-the-house," said he, "this is our kinsman, David Gordon. His father, Iain, a black gerfalcon, stole my cousin, Nuala ni Cahan, from under her father's nose and off to Scotland with her."

The lady smiled to my salutation. "'Tis a bad habit men have," she said aptly, and drew brisk laughter, for she herself had been stolen by O'Neill from under the nose of her brother, the Marshal Henry Bagenal.

"Dhia!" [1] exclaimed Hugh Crawford, sitting across the table. "Do you never forget anything you ever saw or heard, O'Neill?"

[1] God.

"But that was a great ploy, Hugh, and she, Nuala—God rest her—the heart-breaker of the north.—And how is Iain Gordon standing the years, David?"

"He is dead, O'Neill," said I, speaking for the first time.

"God rest him! It is good to see one's kin in loneliness." He glanced at young Maguire. "Does David Gordon know about O'Cahan?"

"Hostage in Galway——"

"But not for long, I am thinking." He looked at me and smiled—a wonderfully taking smile, coming out from below his stern eyes, that made me understand why men and women liked him. "You will be welcome at Dungiven, I think—and you are welcome at Dungannon, I know. It is not forgotten that your father was on O'Neill's side that bad day in Antrim."

"And now," cried his lady, "you will be talking old times and old fights, and we will leave you to it."

III

The ladies left us, the pipers stopped playing and hurried to their meat, and O'Neill took my arm. "Sit down," he said, "and let us pledge each other in a horn of this wine. Crawford you know. This is Maguire of Fermanagh, who has not dowered a certain lad with much sense——"

"True for you, Hugh Roe," agreed Donn Maguire's father, a stern man with a white beard.

O'Neill sat me down by himself, and we touched drinking-cups. "A pleasant ride from Dublin you would have?" he said carelessly.

"Very pleasant, O'Neill," I replied.

"It is sometimes not easy these days to reach Dungannon from Dublin—but, of course, you would have a safe-conduct from the new Lord Deputy?"

Here was the deft half-query, the first of many that would winnow my news like corn from chaff. And I felt rise in me that strange national dourness that ever sullenly sets itself against winnowing. The men about me were silent, waiting for my answer, but, instead of answering, I put a half-question of my own.

"There was a friend of your cause, O'Neill, on the borders of the Pale—Colum O'More?"

"He and his clan."

"He is dead."

"Dead! Colum O'More dead?"

"Slain in Dublin by an English officer."

"What dog did it?" It was Donn Maguire cried that.

"One Captain Cosby of Cong."

"Cosby the Killer! They say he wears a mail shirt in his sleep."

O'More had been one of O'Neill's trusted chiefs. The word of his death was a shock to everyone who heard—except, it might be, to O'Neill himself. O'Neill had too much on his mind to be shocked by the death of one man, and, in his time, had helped to slay Irish chiefs to foster his single cause. "The man who killed O'More," he said quietly, "did disservice to his Queen. With Offaly and the Glens roused, Dublin will need a full garrison.—Well, David Gordon?"

"I was friendly with O'More," I went on. "I had to flee from Dublin——"

"You are safe from the Queen's men here," said O'Neill, a small touch of pride in his voice.

73

But that word safe nettled me. "I did not come for safety," I said, I fear ungraciously, "but to offer my services to my cousin."

"I am your cousin too, David Gordon," said O'Neill gently.

"I have little to offer you, O'Neill," I said glumly.

"Well said, Scot!" cried Crawford. "That is the hilt of an Andrea Ferrara you have there, and besides being a sword it is a good one."

"Look!" I cried then, so that I must be understood. "I had Cosby open to a plain lunge above the gorget, and I missed by three fingers. That is the kind of swordsman I am." Let me say now that the missing of that lunge had rankled in me. If my father had been alive he would never have forgiven me bungling that plain thrust.

O'Neill put his hand on my shoulder. "Swording is only an art," he said. "It is the man I look for."

"For what I am worth," I blurted out, glad to get it over.

His hand pressed. "You are mine," he said. "Leave it to me. Come out now in the sunlight— these boys are getting noisy."

IV

Many of his following were still at table, and the young ones were beginning to lift voices in song. O'Neill, Maguire, Crawford, and I went out on the grass.

We sat down on the garden-bench, and O'Neill was no longer indirect in his questioning. "What is your news out of Dublin, Cousin David?"

I knew what he meant. "De Burgh has brought

reinforcements of five thousand men, with culverin and mangonels," I told him.

"A pleasant peace-time force!" said old Maguire dryly.

O'Neill's eyes darkened and deepened. "What quality?" he asked me.

"Three thousand veteran troops and two thousand from the soutnern train-bands."

"The veterans are as good as the best," said Crawford judiciously, "but the youngsters do not like cold steel."

"Cold steel is better than hot lead from top of a wall, with a hard Scots head safe behind the same wall," said Maguire with stern humour. This was a half-jibe at Crawford, who was noted for the art he had acquired in the French wars of defending duns.

O'Neill took no notice. His eyes were on mine.

"I was only eight days in Dublin," I replied to that waiting look, "but already the train-bands were being drafted into the southern garrisons."

"And the veterans held in Dublin?"

"For the time. And the day before I left, de Burgh had a Council with his Connacht leaders."

"The Connacht leaders! The full leash! I thank you, cousin. You have already served me well."

"You may thank a dead man, O'Neill."

We were silent for a space, and O'Neill in a muse of his own. He lifted his head at last and looked at Crawford, his eyes crinkling. "What would you do, Hugh, if you were the English Lord Deputy?"

"God forgive us, O'Neill, but I would do something."

"The direct thing?"

"Ay so! If I had five thousand reinforcements I

75

would come straight at you and make you burn Dungannon a second time."

"And we would be giving you Clontibret over again —you bloody loyalist," said Maguire.

"What would yourself do, Maguire?"

"I would be thinking it out to myself," said Maguire cannily. "But I know what Hugh Roe O'Neill would be doing if he were in de Burgh's place."

"Go on, Prince of Ulster," mocked Crawford.

"He would wait till harvest, when the clans do be scattered in field and shieling, come down full force through the Gap-of-the-North, and put all Ulster under fire and sword."

"Surely," agreed O'Neill, "that is the wise plan. But note that Conyers Clifford in Connacht is also eager to come down on us through the western gap at Bellashanny."

"And Hugh Roe O'Donnell, my darling, will be saying a word or two to that," said Maguire with satisfaction.

"With his clan at the harvest? No." O'Neill turned to Crawford. "Hugh, we will put you behind a stone wall. I am going to lend you to O'Donnell— you and your Scots—with word that you are to garrison Bellashanny and the fords of Saimhor while the clans are in shieling. We shall be attacked on two fronts, as I see it, and if you lose Bellashanny you will let Clifford in on my rear."

"I will not let him if I can stop him," said Crawford mildly.

And then O'Neill turned to me. "I have work for you too, David Gordon. You are now sept to O'Neill, and O'Neill will have to thole the brunt of the coming fight. Your cousin, Donal Ballagh, is in Galway, and his foster-brother, Calvagh MacManus, holds Dungiven. There you will go with a written word from me. With Calvagh you will warn the clan and help to lead it when the onset comes." He slapped me on the shoulder. "And that is enough for one day. We will go to the ladies now and try that new ruby wine out of Lisbon, and hear the harpers play.—Come, brothers!"

Thus it was that the great O'Neill gave me work to do.

CHAPTER VI

I

THERE now was the O'Cahan stronghold of Dungiven
standing above the shallow clear waters of the Roe,
and there was I, David Gordon, riding down to it,
two days out of Dungannon, and the high moors
behind me.

I had stayed the best part of a week in O'Neill's
camp and had learned to value the force and prudence
of the great leader; and, despite myself, I had become
friendly with young Doncadh Donn Maguire. I was
his discovery, to be taken possession of in his own
impulsive way, with no minding my silence—or no
noticing it in the spate of his own talk. He took me
on a raid on quarter-grown wolf cubs into the fastnesses of Slieve Gallion; he took me eel-fishing on
Lough Neagh; he even tried, but failed, to get me
amongst the damsels of the house; and finally he
accompanied me on my road as far as the head of
Cairntogher Pass. He would have come all the way
to Dungiven if O'Neill had not strictly warned him
that he must be back among his own clan in three
days, and that warning he dared not disobey. He
told me a good deal about Donal Ballagh, my cousin:
that, though he was something younger than I was,
Donal had been made full chief of the O'Cahans on
the death of his father, my uncle, a year past; that he
had neither brother nor sister; that he was still un-
married . . .

"Not that he hates the fair ones," Doncadh said, "but there be too many to choose from, and one should be in no hurry. I hear the Galway lasses are bonny, with a certain dash of Spain to them. 'Tis amongst them I would be, with Donal, but for the old devil, my father. He advised Hugh Roe that the two of us would be aye in trouble and, maybe, cause blood and scandal. Did you ever hear the like?"

"I did."

"My sober fellow! A great pity Donal is not at home to teach you some things. Man, Dathi, you will like him. He is as tall as you are, but black in the hair, and he can sing a song and the mead to his thrapple—here—and fight! him laughing the whole tulzie and his broadsword shearing casques."

"He will have no cause to like me," said I. "I never shore a casque; all the love I ever saw was an ugly game; a crow and I sing much alike, and—yes! —twice already you have made my head buzz with metheglin."

"Wait you, my darling! if love comes as easy to you as lifting a piggin of beer, many the man will be jealous—and did I not see you touch Hughie Crawford twice in a minute yon play of swords we had?"

And now, here was I, facing Dungiven across the water, and I was at the end of my long road. A month ago I had left Arras and barren days, and though luck had played a quirky game with me all the way, yet had she led me onwards towards a life worth living. I had only my horse and sword and cloak, but the future was in my own hands.

Yet was I sorry, too, that my cousin Donal Ballagh was not at home. His absence made me feel of small account. Calvagh MacManus, his foster-brother, might be a good man, but he was not of my blood, and it might be that he would resent the incoming of a half-Scot with the authority of O'Neill in his pouch. That is why I hesitated and drew rein at the margin of the Roe, and looked across at the dun.

A sunny afternoon at the end of May, and everything was quiet and still! The blackbird's song was done and the thrush not ready for his evening trill, and there came to my ears only the soft and lonely murmur of the river—a small, apart, uncanny, quiet chuckle at something not human. It put a weight of childish loneliness on me and held me there in a thoughtless sort of gloom based outside all life.

Up a long, paved causeway beyond the ford was the grey-stone, squat, battlemented tower of the dun; a wing of wall ran either side of it with a guard-tower at each end, and it was pierced in the middle by an arch opening into darkness. The slope right and left of the causeway was of worn grass and clear of all habitation, but round the side of the northern corner-tower was a scattering of wooden and clay bothies—a whole hamlet. And then I heard children laugh, and my eyes followed the course of the stream to where a clan of them were wading knee-deep in the clear water, intent on a pursuit of eels under the flat slabs of mossy stone—a game I knew. It was a quiet and happy scene, and the gloom was only in myself.

By the side of the big arch a guarding kern sat on a block of wood, busy smooth-chafing the haft of an axe with a fragment of glass, and his long light sparth leaned on the wall close behind him. Very particularly he was giving his work the final touch, his hand moving in little stroking movements. He extended the haft at a slant, looked along it, one eye shut, and then his eye lifted in line and fixed on me, and the other eye remained shut for yet a draw of breath. Slowly he got to his feet, the glass fragment tinkling as it fell, and slowly his spare hand slipped back towards the grip of his sparth. At that I set Benmee at the ford and splashed across at a walk, and at a walk rode quietly up the causeway, throwing back my cloak to show my sword in sheath and no weapon in hand.

Two lengths away I checked Benmee, and the kern, a lean lathy lad, stepped in front of the arch. "Where your road, friend?" he inquired in friendly enough fashion.

"Calvagh MacManus with word from O'Neill."

"God save him! Calvagh MacManus? So—so! O'Neill would not be hearing the news yet. You are welcome, tall hero. Calvagh is within the court. I will take your horse."

He yelled in through the arch, and another kern came tumbling out of a side passage to help him.

II

I walked in under the gloom of the arch, and came out into the full sunlight of the bailey. It was not more than half the size of O'Neill's great one, and a glance showed that there was no wife or woman in this household. It was the stronghold of single men and soldiers. Penthouse buildings of weathered wood ran round three sides; one-half of it was paved with cobbles, the other was packed clay. In the middle was a big high-pitched building with walls of heavy oak, roof of rye thatch, and wide unglazed window openings; and the frames of windows and open door were intricately carved in scroll-work, and coloured red ochre; here and there, in corners, grass and weeds grew undisturbed.

Before this middle-house, on the packed earth, two young men were engaged in a putting contest with a smooth round stone, big as a child's head. One was a middle-sized powerful figure, naked to the waist, with a shag of red hair on chest and arms. The other was tall—very tall—and in a short-sleeved linen tunic. Nearly a score of men were looking on, and an old white-haired, long-bearded fellow was holding forth, while a black Austin friar made fun of him.

I walked slowly—and something stiffly after my long ride—towards them, my cloak thrown back on my shoulders. The tall young fellow was balancing for the putt, and, all eyes being fixed on him, none saw me. With smooth and easy power he pivoted from foot to foot, and the stone went sailing in a huge curve.

"Ho! Ho! Ho!" laughed the friar happily. "Beat that, if beating is in you, Calvagh, son of Manus."

The old white-beard lifted his voice—a most surprising volume of a voice. "A good cast—good enough! But the full spade short of his father's best— God rest him!"

"Ho! Ho! Ho!" the priest again laughed. "Was there ever a son to beat his father?"

The tall lad strode across and playfully shook a clenched hand in the old fellow's beard. "You big-paunched, bellowing old shield-striker!" he cried. "Two years ago you said the same thing of a cast a full spade short of that one."

The old fellow grinned unashamed and opened his mouth for retort—and thereupon his eyes fixed themselves on me. And there they widened and his mouth was no wider. Then he blinked rapidly, gathered his look close on me and hurriedly crossed himself. "Jesus of Mary!" he half-whispered, and even his half-whisper had volume. "Your father come back to life in all his might!"

The tall young man turned quickly, and we looked at each other. Who he was I did not guess, but I knew that he was not Calvagh MacManus. The broad red man was MacManus. This was no common man, I knew, but if his hair had been red-gold I might have taken him for the famous O'Donnell, ally of O'Neill. I think that that man there was the bonniest man I ever saw—I have ever seen. He was tall and supple like a spear, with a mass of black curls over a white square of brow; his face had a healthy pallor, and his keen dark-blue eyes were well set under black brows—a keen lean face with a fine salty humour to it. There and then he set alight in me that spark of liking that must come at the first glance or not at all.

We stood there a few strides apart and looked at each other, and all the others were still, too, except white-pow, who had his hand atug in his beard. The young chief made the first move. He came at me slowly, but directly, and placed his two hands gently down on my shoulders—and our eyes were level. "I know you," he said. "You are my cousin, David Gordon, out of Scotland."

"But——"

"I am Donal Ballagh O'Cahan."

"But——"

"I know. I got back from Galway yesterday."
His eyes crinkled. "And the devil never came faster!"

"I am David Gordon," said I then. "I am from
Arras in Picardy to see you—cousin."

His hands pressed my shoulders. "You are welcome
a thousand times." A little glow came behind his
eyes, and I knew that I was welcome.

For the first time in my life I felt that I was welcome
for myself—and a lump came up to my throat, and
I could not help my eyebrows twitching.

The white-beard seannachy was at my cousin's
shoulder. "I knew—I knew first," his great voice
proclaimed. "He is the dead spit of your father and
he young."

"God forbid!" said I, swallowing the lump. "He
was not the ugliest man in Ulster!"

"He was that," he boomed, "and the best man at
your right hand or at your left in the same place—and
the best caster of the heavy stone."

Donal Ballagh saw that I was touched. He swung
round to my side, his hand on my arm. "This young
fellow of four score or five," he presented, "is one
Turlough, son of Teaclan, and once on a time he used
sing a lay and pluck a harp string—and thinks he can
do both yet. And this is Father Senan of the Priory,
who says our prayers for us—and his own—when he
has time from the fishing."

The priest came forward. He was well past middle
years, but sturdy, and there was not a grey hair in
his strong brown beard. He wore the black frock of
the Austin friars, and his hair was close cut, in the

84

Celtic tonsure, from ear to ear. "I knew your father, David Gordon," he said. "This old fellow, Turlough —he was not so old then—the two of us rowed the young pair over Bann Flu the night they went from here." His blue-grey eyes searched me with a wistful look. "Is there anything of Nuala ni Cahan in you?"

"No," I said. "She was gentle and beautiful"; and I smiled to his look.

His eyes filled and his mouth quivered. "Ah!" he cried, "there she is—there she is now, deep down in you. Do I not remember her, and she smiling? I was young then, and I loved her myself, God forgive me! Your father was a better man. Is he well?"

"He is dead," I told him.

"His soul with God—and with her!"

"Amen," said Donal softly. "We are in like case, cousin." Then he lifted his voice. "Here, Calvagh —Calvagh MacManus, my foster-brother, who by his easy ways in this dun has put a month's work before me to thin the paunches of these fellows you see grinning."

The garrison gallowglasses laughed, and in that laughter was the admiring, confident note that showed that this stronghold was a happy place for men. MacManus had pulled his tunic over his head, and he came and took my hand with a murmured word of welcome. He had a square face, and a grim one for a man so young, and all feeling was now hid behind a grey eye. In after days, when we grew to know each other, he told me that he was filled with a passion of jealousy that first hour. That I can understand, knowing the closeness of the foster-tie.

My cousin was considerate of me to the end. He

drew me towards the door of the mid-house. "A long road behind you, my light! You will have a bite now and a sup, and we with you. Time enough for talk. Come, brothers!"

And so I was made welcome to Dungiven.

IV

The inside of the mid-house was one great high room. It had a stone chimney, a bare floor of hewn boards, a long oaken table on trestles, a scatter of straw-bottomed chairs and backless benches, and all round it were uncurtained alcoves wherein were wooden sleeping-benches. It was, in fact, the living-room of the dun, whose cold stone chambers were mostly used for stores and armaments. The Gael never could bide in a dungeon of stone.

In there they plied me with cold venison, barley-meal bread, and *coirm* ale, and jined me at the eating —Donal, Calvagh, Turlough, and the friar. And they talked, and presently I found myself talking too, giving a lame enough account of France, my father's death, and my journey as far as Dungannon. When I got myself as far as that place, I remembered for the first time that day that I had a written message from O'Neill. I fished it from my satchel—a folded scrap of vellum with the Red-Hand of O'Neill stamped on a splash of wax.

Donal Ballagh looked at the name on the outside and flicked it across to Calvagh MacManus. "It might be that Hugh Roe wishes to bestow a daughter on you, Calvagh. Take a look!"

Calvagh growled. "It could be that woman will trouble us soon enough in this dun," he said, and I

86

felt my cousin stir at my side. Calvagh looked over the writing and handed it back, and Donal read the formal Gaelic aloud.

Calvagh MacManus, friend. David Gordon bears this, cousin in the first degree to O'Cahan, and my kinsman as well and in my service.—"Ah ha! Red Earl—not servant but sept."—*He is a swordsman of skill*—"Not so!" said I, "but a bungler."—*But he lacks experience of war. I bestow him in your command.*—"The wise fox he is."—*Take heed now. The truce with the Sassenach they will break at the harvest time, and they will strike in on our front and on O'Donnell's front, I think. It will be hard fighting and our lack will be trained horse. I look to the O'Cahan clan for a mounted standard, and this my kinsman you will find useful to teach sword-play against the coming of your chieftain and your brother. At your service. O'Neill.*—"And that is that! A wise letter. Hugh knows."

Donal sat there staring at the scrap of vellum, and a far-away look came in his eyes. "War in the harvest time," he murmured. "War—war—war! June—July—August! three months—short enough and long enough—if word comes. . . ." He twisted the letter in his hands, still musing, and then, suddenly, threw off this introspection that had brought a touch of colour to his face. "Three months!" he cried, "and we with our work before us.—I am glad that you are here, David."

"I am glad too, Donal," said I.

And I was glad.

v

I was happy at Dungiven. Though I have known happiness many the day since then, and though a certain pair of eyes will read this writing, I will say in this place that never have I known more content than I knew at Dungiven that summer. I was among my own kin, was acquainted of their lives and the lively run of their thoughts, and I was accepted as a man amongst men. All that makes for the only living content there is, the only content that is necessary in any place under the sun.

And better than all, a close tie grew between my cousin and me. From the first minute I liked him, and from that minute his keen mind got below my unprepossessing surface. Strangely enough, I was his nearest male relation. The main stem of the O'Cahans was a thin one at that period, and, other than an old uncle living at Derry Columcill, he had no men relatives nearer than cousins once removed. Of these and more distant kin he had a multitude, for the O'Cahan was a long-tailed clan and could muster a thousand able-bodied fighting-men.

Donal Ballagh was full of life and eagerness, and life and eagerness were in me too, though they never showed in the face of day. He liked nothing better than good talk, good wit, the singing of songs, skilly fingering of chanter, the plucking of strings—ay! and in its place the downing of methers of *coirm*,[1] metheglin, and a heady Spanish wine. And for all my stolid front I too liked to hear good talk, and was a grand listener and a putter-in of a word on occasion to make sure that the argument stay on the road; and I could laugh at a sally—when I saw it—for all that I was a Scot; and I could hold down my own share of ale for being the same Scot; and on the big pipes, though I could not finger a pibroch, I knew a spring [2] or two that were new in Ciannachta.

[1] Ale.   [2] Tune.

We were great talkers in Dungiven. On my first coming we talked for three days back-and-fore, and after that, as they say, we began talking. That household of men was the grand place for dispute and discussion and wordy pleasant warfare. For I have noticed that men talk more than women when women are not of the company, and that men do not talk freely, even on free subjects, when women are in the house. Oh! but the good times we had within that dun on the Roe. As has been said, it was a man's house. Women from the township came in to cook and clean and wash, but no woman slept in dun or bailey. That was the custom, and no man thought of breaking it—except one.

At this minute I can shut my eyes and see that big room in the mid-house of a long summer evening. The low sun would be shining over the defending wall in through door and windows, and in a little while after that the room would be in a luminous shadow. Supper-time it would be and every bench and seat occupied by an easy brotherly company, not troubled by thought of rank or degree, yet not unaware of pride of race. The broad strength of the Gaelic would make a guttural boom and the high-pitched Gaelic laugh echo up amongst the collar-braces of the roof. Food and drink would be on the board in princely quantity and be partaken of hugely. Presently, from outside would come the heart-stirring shrill of the chanter and thrill of the drones as a couple or three pipers strutted and turned; or Turlough Mac an Teaclan would run his hooked fingers across the weird strings of the harp and make cold shivers run over us with those queer, plucking, rippling runs, and then he might declaim in his great voice an ode to some

dead O'Cahan, or dree a lament sadder than the long
waves of the sea, or sing a song with a refrain that we
all joined in—a song that could go on endlessly and
put a strange glamour on us; or I might finger a
spring, and some swack lad jump on the board to
dance a graceful and intricate step-dance from the
hips down; or when the ale began to bite someone
would strike up a gay sardonic air wedded to frankly
ribald words that no woman should hear. And then
the music would cease for a while, and, after a silence,
talk would again break forth and laughter ring. And
then the gloaming would deepen into the tremulous
half-dark of the summer night, and one by one men
would stroll away, or slip away, or stretch themselves
out on the sleeping-benches in the alcoves, and the
table would be left to the centre group of the household
—Donal, Calvagh, Turlough, Friar Senan, and me.
There we would talk of the coming campaign and
make plans for it, or deride made plans, drawing
example from fights of the past and men that fought
them; and then, when all were gone, it became a
custom for Donal and me to go out in the bailey, pace
up and down shoulder to shoulder, and speak of things
between ourselves.

In these walks together I told Donal all there was
to know of my past, which was little, and he told me
some of the many things he had seen and done. He
had been as far as Greenwich Court with O'Neill; he
had been to Lisbon and Cadiz in his uncle's ship out
of Derry Columcill; and, though he was younger
than I was, he had led his clan in half a score of stark
fights, notably at the Ford-of-Biscuits and Clontibret.

But there was one episode in his life that he could
not be got to dwell on: the recent breaking of hostage

at Galway. Every man—and every woman too—of the clan was curious to know the why and the how of that business, but all that he would say was that he had had a private quarrel with Rickard the Sassenach, Baron of Dunkellin, and that Governor Bingham had taken sides with the loyalist and put Donal himself behind bars, thus breaking the terms of hostage; whereupon Donal had broken prison and made his way home by secret roads he knew.

What the subject of the quarrel was no one in Dungiven was told, but I, for one, could make a near guess. Often and often in the midst of talk I had watched Donal go into that spell of day-dreaming where the face smiles and grows wistful. And sometimes, when we were alone, I might murmur: "Galway town and it far away!" Whereon he would start and flush, or even set on me with half-playful fury. Then would follow a tough wrestle, where neither of us held advantage unless I secured top grip and could use shoulder weight. And also among the maids of the clan—and of these there were many of his own blood and caste—he was no longer the frank trifler. Doubtless others saw as much as I did, or more, but after the manner of the breed, no one dared say a word till O'Cahan took it on himself to open the subject.

VI

After ten days or a fortnight in Dungiven, Donal took me on a round of visits to the scattered septs of his clan, and made sure that I became accepted as one entitled to all the rights of the blood. And as he progressed he arranged for a gathering at Dungiven of his chiefs and captains.

There for three days, in the intervals of terrific hurling matches and high feastings, were discussed the plans of the clan for harvest and the campaign. The crops were to be cut and lifted as they ripened, and the women and the old must do more than their share of the harvesting. This man, and that, and the other, by name and degree, had to equip ten, twenty, forty gallowglasses and so many kern, and hold them ready for the hosting. Such and such a one could mount three or six or ten horsemen. When—now? Next week? Fine, surely! Send them down to the dun, horse and man. Horse are needed and horse take time to train. . . . So it was that in a short time we had a squadron of fifty horse at Dungiven, and lively times with them. Donal, Calvagh, and I spent hours marshalling and drilling, and, with a new enthusiasm, I set about teaching sword-play on horseback: how to avoid the arm-wrench of the full lunge, how to draw the too-eager first swing and follow the parry with the deadly backhand cut, how to make sure that though your man overrode you, you left empty saddle behind.

But first, and for my own prestige, I had to prove to these smiters from all Ciannachta that I was fit to teach. Before them all one fine evening Donal tried me out. Donal was reputed an able sworder, had learned Scots play from Hugh Crawford, single sword practice from the Queen's O'Reilly of Breffni during a truce, and rapier tierce and carte that time he was in London. I had a full measure of nervousness that evening, for O'Neill's word had gone out that I was a skilled man, and, with this friendly critical crowd of blooded fighters looking on, I felt stiffer and clumsier than ever.

I started warily. I felt the ground with the flat of

my feet. I kept a lock on the blades to try for Donal's possible weakness of wrist—and did not find it. I parried carefully, kept solely to the lunges of ritual, and gave ground more than I might. Donal was wary too, for his accepted reputation was at stake. But our blood was young and in time it warmed up in spite of us. It warmed up more than it should, I fear, and in two minutes we had the men shouting.

That bout was as near the real thing as to make no matter. Luckily, wise old Turlough made us use Scots play with targes, or we would surely have drawn blood in our eagerness. Not that either of us lost temper, but we forgot, at the time, that our blades had killing edge and point. At no time did I feel that I held Donal at advantage, and at the best I did not attack as often as he did, though, later, he insisted that at the end my counter kept him wondering. A prick or a slash would have been the sure result if Father Senan, coming in from his fishing, after looking on for half a minute, had not thrust the butt of his salmon-rod between us. We drew back and panted, and Donal laughed, while I felt my head to see if I still wore it. Then my cousin threw his arm around me and I patted his shoulder, and I was accepted as a sworder; while for the rest of the evening the bout was discussed in all its aspects, some holding that in actual fight Donal would have taken me early on, and others that my patience and strength of wrist must win in the end.

There was one man in Dungiven who, I think, loved me better than he loved his chief. That man was Father Senan, the Austin friar. I was my mother's son, and he fathered me. He was a wise, kindly, sturdy old man, and if he had any fault it was an inordinate love of angling and a lack of patience if anyone dared to dispute with him on that art. From observation he had devised a new method, where his lure imitated the natural fly that brings the fish clean out of water in a bonny silver curve. No one mentioned garden-worm or maggot-gentle in his presence unless warfare was intended—and frequently it was. He took charge of me from the beginning; he taught me to fish in his own fashion, extolled the virtue of a small fly with a woodcock wing and a moth body, of another grey-brown one for early June, and a red-brown one for treacherous August. With all his quiet wisdom he set my feet on the road of understanding; in the confessional he used sit back and talk to me of things that had nothing to do with the shriving of sins, so that my friends twitted me on the grievous load that kept me so long on my knees; and when I smiled, as was not now so infrequent, his bearded face would light up, and then grow wistful, minding youth and love.

So I was happy at Dungiven.

CHAPTER VII

I

I come now to an evening in July. A fine clear evening, with the faint hum of midges in the air, after a cloudy week of thundery showers.

Looking back on that evening, I am wondering if this story should not have begun then, for all that I have written up to this is no more than a slow prelude to my real story—as will be seen.

Donal and I, with Father Senan, had spent the afternoon at the fishing down the full-flowing, amber reaches of the Roe, and the fishing had been good. With a silver and blue hackled lure tied for us by the old priest we had made spoil among a fresh run of salmon, round-girthed hen-fish, up from northern sea. Late in the evening, and hungry as hawks, we fared dunwards, our catch—at least a score—slung in panniers over the withers of a hill pony.

Ferdoragh, the gate-ward, came down to the ford to meet us. "A messenger here for you, Donal Ballagh O'Cahan," he shouted above the splash we made, the water up to our knees.

"From O'Neill?" Donal inquired quickly.

"All the way from Galway, he says."

Donal checked in ankle-depth of water, checked dead-still for one draw of breath, and then stepped out on dry ground. "We will see him," he said, carefully quiet. He made no hurry. He said no word to us—did not even look at us—but, where he and I might try a race uphill to the arch, he plodded with a steady stolidity that I had never before noticed in him. Father Senan looked across at me behind him, frowned half-smilingly, and shook his tonsured head.

The household was at supper when we got in, and the messenger from Galway was at home in that company. He was no townsman, but a big, black-bearded fellow of the gallowglass caste, with the hugest pair of hands I ever saw in a man. At the moment they were enveloping a wooden ale-piggin, and I did not see the piggin till he laid it down as he rose to his feet. "A writing for O'Cahan," he said, and fumbled in the breast of his rough crotal tunic.

"You are welcome, Tadg Ironhand," greeted Donal gently.

The messenger tendered the folded missive. It was stained with the sweat of his body, I saw, but also I saw that it was tied with a rose-red riband of silk, from which hung a small seal.

Donal took it, glanced at it quickly, and brought his eyes keenly to the man's face. "All well, Ironhand?" he inquired with significance.

"Well, surely, my heart—and bell-metal for soundness."

Donal looked all round the room, and every man there of us had his eye somewhere else. He looked at me, and I was loosing the thongs of my wet footgear. I had soon fallen into the homely fashion of going about all day hoseless in the easy rawhide brogans of the Gael. In the evening we used kick them off, or prise them off if we had been in water, bathe our feet in the run of the Roe, and for the rest of the time pad about barefoot in the soft dust that was pleasant and cool between our toes. These men of war were notably

clean of habit, and knew the worth of cleanliness in
hard campaigning. In that summer weather they
went about as nearly naked as they might in decency,
and in the warm nights slept stark naked on the sleeping-benches. Only in the chill of dawn would they
groan and reach blindly for war-cloak.

Donal did not hesitate for long. His fingers closing
tightly on his letter, he strode out of the room, across
the bailey, and within the door of the tower. Leaning
to my hide thongs, I could see, through a window, the
crenellated battlements of the keep, and presently his
black head ran like a bead among them. Up there
only the far-away sky, a half-moon still wan in the
light, and a sparrow-hawk asoar with fluttering pinion-
tips might look on as he read.

The room was silent and still all around me—not
as much as a breath lifted. I prised off my wet footgear, straightened up, and because of the tension
in and around me, let out a thundering bellow:
"Will no full-bellied son of a —— give us our
supper?"

Out of the sudden startle and clatter that followed
came the voice of the Galway Tadg. "My hand! I
would not like to be the man that would starve you
after that."

There was laughter then, and the tension broke.
For the first time I became aware that all these men
knew as well as I what had weighed on our chief's
mind.

II

I was still eating when Donal came back. He sat
down quietly at my side and ate with me. He ate
hungrily enough of what was before him, but I doubt

97

if he knew what he was eating, for he picked clean the bones of a coney, a food he despised. And he imbibed great draughts of *coirm*, and with it put away his silence, growing more than usually gay and light of tongue, and calling on Turlough Mac an Teaclan to play on his harp. And old Turlough ran his hand across the strings, and wistful lovely notes came about us, and deep true notes that made the heart stir. . . . And he sang, only above a whisper, but a whisper that filled the room, the lovely and tender love song of Bright Una.

> Girl, now that my eyes
> Again shall look long on you,
> Girl, now that my heart
> Is athirst in the drouth for you,
> Girl, now that my soul
> Yearns deep for the deeps in you,
> Now, while my life has a wing,
> Do I sing my song to you.
>
> Eyes, deep as the dark of the sky,
> Eyes, bright as the sheen of the sea,
> Face, pale with the pallor of dreams,
> Hair, flame of red bronze breeze-free—
> I am drowned in your eyes and your dreams,
> The flame of your hair is in me.
>
>   .   .   .   .
>
> Girl, if never my eyes
> Again might look long on you,
> Girl, if ever my heart
> Is drained dry for the drouth of you,
> Girl, if ever my soul
> Is lost for the loss of you,
> Still, though my life has no wing,
> Will I sing my song to you.
>
>   .   .   .   .

And Donal, head in hand, looked out of drugged eyes and forgot us all.

When the song was done the half-dark was about us

and men moved quietly away, so that in a short while we were alone, Donal and I. And after a time I got to my feet and went out alone and sadly under the moon and the thin stars, and as I walked I found Donal at my side. We paced up and down, as was our custom, but for long and long we said nothing.

Donal spoke first, after clearing his throat twice. "To-morrow," he said calmly, "I leave you in command."

"As you command, O'Cahan," said I formally.

"I will be away for a time."

I had no word to say to that, and after a pause he went on. "I am going down into Connacht—I suppose you know."

I had to help him. "I know you have a letter there," I blurted out, "twisting your heart-strings, and I know that it is the letter of a woman."

"Who will be my wife," he said softly.

"Oh, lucky woman!" I cried in spite of me, a sombre weight on my heart. I was losing this lad that I loved.

At that he put his hand within my arm and pulled my shoulder against his. "It is a pity that I did not tell you before now," he excused himself. "There is nothing that should be hidden between us, brother."

"Tell me nothing," I urged. "I do not know how love alters a man."

He chuckled softly, "You will know soon enough, greybeard."

"I will not," I said firmly—almost savagely.

And then he began to talk more freely, the half-dark hiding the colour in his face. Roundabout talk in the beginning. "You know hostage is held a pleasant custom . . . O'Neill and O'Donnell could find a score to take the yoke, and had to be wise as ten foxes to choose their six. Donn Maguire, our light-head, nearly came to cursing his father over it. The six of us, Garv O'Donnell, Bainne O'Neill, MacWilliam Oge, and the rest were without a care, free as air within the hostage law, and we were treated with the best. Great easy times we had! . . . Galway is a fine town, with Spanish ships in and out—and Corrib and Clifden water full of fish, the Joyces thick with deer, and Aran Isles over yonder and the hookers of Galway to sail out to them and see Hy-Brasil. . . . We jaunted up to Menlo, across to Athenree, down to Dunkellin— and as far as Cashlean-na-Kirka on Upper Corrib. Man, David! there is a dark-haired one at that place —Eithne, daughter of the great Bevinda O'Flaherty— would make your tough heart turn over——"

"Is that the one?" I stopped him.

"No, *the* one is Amy Burc, daughter of Rickard the Sassenach of Dunkellin."

"The man you quarrelled with?"

"And she the cause. I met—my lady—at a reception of Bingham's in Galway, and after at Cashlean-na-Kirka and at her home in Dunkellin—and other-wheres." He paused, as if thinking of all these meetings, and went on inadequately. "We came to think alike—and knew it. We did nothing underhand. I spoke her father, that long narrow man. He would have none of me for a son-in-law. He said so. He said it at great length. He is ten times more of the loyalist than the old dog-fox his father of Clanricard, and he gave me all his choice thoughts on us rebel dogs of the North. What he said I would stand from no other man, and will not stand from him again. He is nothing to me or to Amy any more. That was in Galway. . . .

We decided to wed and say nothing till the hostage time expired—she decided as much as I did. Foolish we were, maybe?"

"Maybe you were," said I.

"We failed, anyway. A spy was about us somewhere. The dawn we were to be wed I slipped out of my quarters straight into the waiting arms of Bingham's guard, and five-ten minutes after that I was behind iron bars. Amy, as I learned later, was whisked off to Athlone under the wardship of the Governor, Sir Conyers Clifford. What was I to do?"

"You came home."

"And broke prison and hostage at the same time. Not a hard task, either. No tight guard was kept on me; even a half-word came quietly that as soon as the father was back in Dunkellin hold and the daughter safe in Athlone, I might walk out into freedom and no one say a word. That might suit Bingham, as he it was who had broken the laws of hostage in another man's quarrel. But it did not go with my plans to put myself back under the yoke. . . . Tadg Ironhand slung me a long *sgian* through the bars a floor above ground—and my gaoler was not caring greatly for the point of it—so I walked out soft and easy, met Tadg and had a talk with him, and got home here a day before yourself. Easy as a drink of wine, David."

"Maybe it was easy enough for you," said I, "but not as easy as all that."

"Easy enough in truce time. But it was not so easy to hide my secret from all the old women that are in this dun, and one of them David Gordon. And yet it was good to me that you should feel my trouble—and my anxiety for word from Athlone. That word came to-day, a letter from my lady herself, by the hand of Tadg, her foster-father." He touched the breast of his tunic. "As long as she was in Clifford's ward inside the walls of Athlone nothing could be done, but now she is back with her father in a strong place he has down beside the Clare border. But not for long! Rickard does not trust me—or her. In ten days—a fortnight at most—he is taking her to Dublin and sending her from there to Greenwich Court in Ormonde's train. . . . And she says, 'I am ready now, Donal. Will you come?' "

The pride in his voice stirred me. "By God!" said I, "did she say that?"

"Her very words. And to-morrow I go."

"Alone?"

"Alone I would like to go, but alone I might miss the one chance. She is well guarded, and Dunkellin has a garrison of picked Sassenach in the place. I do hope to snatch her single-handed, but a sudden sally might be the only chance for us. I am taking ten of your horsemen—and Father Senan—the smallest force I dare trust for what may be needed."

"And Calvagh MacManus?"

"No. I leave Calvagh with you."

"In that case I come with you. It would not be a nice thing to put me in command over your foster-brother." There was ever a small jealousy there.

Donal peered in my face. "Is that why you would come?" he queried prickingly.

I did not answer that. "I might fail you in a fight—" I said.

He stopped me with his hand. "Listen, David! There is no risk in taking ten or twenty men to Dunkellin. The truce still lasts, and we could move hither and yon through clans not unfriendly. But once success—or failure—gives the alarm we shall be in the very nick of danger all that twisted road back to O'Donnell's Saimhor line. In ones and twos we must steal our way by roads we know—and you——"

"Look!" said I dourly. "Do you command me to stay?"

"I do not."

"Then I come."

"Come, then, pighead," he cried at me, and shook me with both his hands. "Man, David, I am foolish to let you, but I want you at my shoulder—in fight if fighting comes, and in peace when Senan speaks the words over my lady and me. You are my nearest kin—and nearest me too—and second in Dungiven whatever befalls. David, the thing I am doing will make no difference between us two? You know that?"

"I know that," I lied stoutly.

CHAPTER VIII

I

ALL through the night we had ridden hard, and the horses were dead weary. Even my own hardy Benmee faltered now and then. They were weary although, before making this last long burst, we had given them a four hours' rest in a hazel clump well back from, and looking down on, the Galway road. While we had lain in that clump a strung-out, careless cavalcade of men and ladies had ambled by citywards on the road below us.

"Bingham, very like, giving one of his routs—the gay old badger!" had said Donal, and frowned at a thought of his own.

The horses were spent because we had come all the long way from Dungiven at a breaking pace—down to the narrows of the Erne, where we had swum across into Breffni, round by Loch Gara through MacDermott and Costello country—and rough country at that—and so skirting the MacWilliam and MacTheobald lands, where at last we had to move warily. But luck had been with us all the road, and now, this fifth day, we were on the last long leg.

We had crossed the Galway road with the fall of night—a clear night with the moon near the full—and thereafter Tadg Ironhand had led the way and in a hurry. That country south of the Galway road was flat and heavily wooded, and among the woods were spreads of dangerous marshes dark under the moon. But Tadg knew his way. He kept trending westwards and still westwards under the curtain of the trees, and sometime before the lift of dark came down to the margin of a wide plain, a waste of heather that whispered sadly under the dawn wind. There we halted and gave our horses breathing space.

"We must be at the other side of this before the light comes." Tadg spoke hoarsely and swayed loosely in the saddle. "God! for the sleep I will be having then."

Donal placed a hand against his shoulder. "Tadg Ironhand, my jewel!" he said warmly.

This gallowglass must have iron in all of him as well as in his hands, for to our five he had ten weary days behind him.

That waste was luckily a dry heath, with here and there a low humplock of grass. The heather was old and stiff, in places up to our girths, and our horses went swishing through it at a steady half-walk, half-amble. Nimble they were and sure-footed after their breed, and only twice did one trip over a tussock and pitch its rider with a crash and a crackle of Gaelic malediction. I rode close behind Tadg, with Father Senan behind me; and Donal, away down the strung-out line, shepherded the rear.

In the break of dawn a black pine-ridge showed away in front, and in another quarter-hour we burst through a thick breast of sallies and came in amongst the trees. And there Tadg halted and we gathered round him. "We are here now, O'Cahan," he said, pride in his voice. "This is Esker Raida, and beyond in the vale is the dun. There is no good in me any more till I put sleep over me."

"Nor in any of us," said Donal. "Rest it is."

We found a trickle of water amongst the sallies, and in there we tethered the horses. Ourselves went into the brink of the Esker among the pines, where the ground was dry and sandy, with a fine mat of brown needles. There we lay down wearily. Our ration of provisions had run out in the night, and I was very empty, but stronger than hunger was the desire to sleep, and sleep I did under my long cloak.

Sometime in the morning I waked to hear a gallow-glass growl furious curses. He had lain down too near a big ant-heap, and the ants had found him and got stingingly under his tunic. I mind starting to chuckle, and then I must have fallen asleep again, for I was dreaming of running water that would not quench my thirst, though I poured down mether after mether.

It was high day when Donal shook me awake out of a league-deep sleep. Tadg bent over his shoulder and pointed to the ridge above.

"Come and see," whispered Donal, and the two turned and started to climb.

All the men were sound asleep, the hoods of their cloaks hiding their faces. Father Senan was lying at my side, his cowl fallen back, and in the light of day his bearded, gentle face was grey and cold. Quietly I spread my cloak over him and rose to my feet. The hard sand had numbed a hip-bone, and I had to stamp my feet to get the life back.

The Esker was very steep at this point, and I had to help myself upwards by the spindly trunks of the pines. Half-way up I heard a scrambling behind, and there was the old priest dragging himself over the crotch of a root. I waited for him.

"Could you not be staying in your bed?" I chided him.

"Could I not!" panted he, agrin; "and big Albannach [1] feet stamping all round me to wake the dead. Give me a small grip of you, boy."

So we went on together. We found Donal and Tadg lying on the crown of the ridge, and we lay down by them and looked out on as pleasant a scene as eyes ever saw after hard days.

II

We looked over the tops of trees to a green and pleasant vale, park-land clumped with orderly plantations, with here and there the brighter green of growing corn. In the middle distance a stream flowed and wimpled, and my eyes followed its course westwards, and there, not two miles away, was the lifting plane of the Atlantic Sea, the green waters of Galway Bay brilliant under the sun. Southwards of it tall cliffs lifted shoulders out of the green, and the sun was swallowed in the black fronts of them.

Donal elbowed me, and I followed his pointing finger. "There it is, now." His voice was low and deep.

It was our goal, the stronghold of Dunkellin, a mile away eastwards. It stood on a knoll above the stream, a strong square tower with a high mantling wall, and below it, near the water, was the usual scattered hamlet and the Norman tower of a church.

"And you to take that place with ten men!" said Father Senan.

"Fourteen counting yourself, holy man. What do you carry sparth-axe for? If we got within yon port I would not ask for more."

[1] Scots.

Tadg had been examining the vale with searching eyes, his big hands arched over his brows. Now he spoke. "I know that lad," he said. "Ruari, the herd! See him?"

We looked where he pointed. Out in the vale, some distance to the left, was a thick young plantation, edged with undergrowth, and at the brink of this, shaded from the sun, stood a herdsman, leaning on a spear and looking out towards the sheen of the sea. On the plain before him a scattered herd of black cattle grazed—cows, oxen, and young calves.

"Can ye make out his dog?" Tadg inquired anxiously. "He owns a white half-wolf bitch, Gnav, would kill a man. No sign of her I see."

We could see no sign of her either, but Tadg lay peering for many minutes to make sure that she was not hunting in the plantation. "Pups she will be having," he said at last. "Luck with us! Ruari is honest enough for a herd, and might be trusted, but I will not be trusting him a great deal all the same. Wait ye here, now, and keep an eye open. Veal for dinner is in this." He crawled along the ridge to the left and was lost to sight amongst the trees.

We waited and watched with interest. After what seemed a long time a magpie rose from the plantation behind the herd and flicked away with its protesting chg-chg-chg.

"One for sorrow," whispered Donal.

"And two for joy," said I, as a second magpie flushed.

The herd took no notice, but he would know that magpies were always on their short flights and always protesting about nothing. Still we waited, our eyes on the herd. We expected him at any moment to turn and look into the growth behind. But instead, and very suddenly, he stumbled, fell flat on his face, and, it seemed of his own volition, slid backwards into the underbrush.

"By the red MacSwyne!" swore Donal, chuckling. "Surely, Tadg, you are not putting much trust in him. Watch ye, now!"

After another wait the herd came weaponless from the grove and circled round a solitary calf, feeding some distance out. Deftly he edged it towards the plantation until, finding itself too close to the trees, it turned to face him, and at that proper moment Tadg burst from the undergrowth, clasped it body and legs in his great arms, and was back into hiding, quick as fox or weasel.

"My choice thou, Tadg a son!" cried Senan delightedly.

In another quarter-hour Tadg and the herd were with us below the crown of the ridge. The herd came first, a mat-haired kern, barefooted, stumbling under the weight of the dead calf across his shoulders. Tadg came behind, helping himself along with the lad's spear.

"Put it down there, Ruari boy, and rest yourself," Tadg said, and turned to Donal. "He has news—good or bad I am not sure. You can trust Ruari, but we can cut his windpipe if we like. He has heard of you."

"Your news, my young lad?" Donal came at once to the point, steel in his voice, and the kern sensed the prick.

"There is no one in the dun, my lord O'Cahan," he began hurriedly. "The servants and a handful of pikes only. . . . The Lord and Lady Amy are in Galway since ere yesterday to a feasting of the Governor's——"

"Hell to Bingham and his feasting!" cursed Donal feelingly. "I feared as much when the Athenree people went by us last evening.—When do they return, boy?"

"To-night, prince."

"Is knowledge at you?"

"It is surely." He pointed to the dead calf. "That one's mother, a young heifer calved too soon and spoiled for the milking, was beefed this morning to make a late supper for the lord."

"What?" cried Donal. "Does Rickard the Sassenach devour a whole beef for supper?"

"Maybe his fair daughter eats a bit once in a while," said Father Senan.

"A big tail of soldiers is with him as well," said the herd.

"Go on, Ruari," urged Tadg.

"Look, chief O'Cahan! Lord Rickard is full of suspicions—and well he might. Near a fortnight ago he missed Tadg, and him watching him since yon at Galway town. He put the wood-kerns to the searching, and they traced Tadg as far as Tuam and he making north. Enough that was. Threatened to hang him—ay, did he!" He rubbed his nose, that had a trace of blood from his fall. "From the top window of the dun at the end of a string——"

"Never mind me," growled Tadg.

"I would think small of hanging a lad myself, if put to it," hinted Donal bleakly.

That herd had a faculty of humour. "I know it," he said. "Between you and Rickard the Sassenach a loose head is with me this day, but I will be waiting for the hanging that is farthest off." He was finding his tongue and courage. "Mind you, one-and-all, if it was not for the Lady Amy, the darling one, dumb as fish would I be, for a shut mouth——"

"The thing you never had, Ruari mouth-open," derided Tadg, and turned to Donal. "This is the fork of the stick we are in, O'Cahan: Rickard the Sassenach has a guard of twenty trained men on the road with him—his Sassenach bodachs in steel and buff—and all mounted."

Donal considered that. "It is not the worst of news," he said at last. "It shows that in his mind was a march home in the night and the lady with him.— Is that all your news, herd?"

"Every word—but Tadg will hang if ever——"

"Come, then," Donal stopped him. "Work is before us that calls for a full belly."

III

During the meal Donal was deep in thought, and in no pleasant thought either, to judge by his drawn-down brows. And, indeed, I too was thinking seriously. This lady of his, in the midst of twenty soldiers, was the kernel of a nut not easy to crack. And crack it we must—or try to. More to myself than to him I spoke aside. "Twenty troopers! Heavy metal for our light horses!"

"That is not worrying me at all," Donal said. "You saw me pick these lads here, and I picked them well."

"Look you," I suggested, "if the dun is weakly held we might walk in at the gloaming—and there is our ambush."

Donal nodded. "It could be done. It is in my mind. But once in we might not get out that easy.

A servant slipping away on us, a soldier dropping over the wall—and Dunkellin would have two hundred men round us before dawn, and more coming."

"But an ambush out here——"

"I know. I do not like it. Fourteen of us—heavy men—driving down on them, all holds loose—and Amy, and it might be other ladies. . . . God!" He shrugged his shoulders to throw off the vision. "Ah well! risk is in it any way you look, and the risk we must take. If you are done eating—and time for you —we will look over the ground."

Father Senan and Tadg Ironhand went with us. Tadg led seawards for half a mile to where the Esker took a curve north and again west. Here we were out of sight of the dun, and went down to the outer edge of the trees, crossed over the bight, and came to the other angle of the ridge. And there was the Galway road. It came in a straight line side by side with the Esker and, at the angle, held straight out over the level until it curved out of sight round a plantation a quarter of a mile across the grass.

Donal looked up at the Esker, he looked along the Galway road, he looked over the sweep of pasture, and made up his mind, his jaws grinding. "Ambush it is," he said in his teeth, "and this is the spot. If Rickard the Sassenach looks for danger he will hardly look for it so near his own dun. Post our men up there in the fringe of the trees—that side of the point—and no one coming on the road can see them without turning to look. God be good to us—and to them a little and He judging them!"

At that word ambush I felt my heart tighten. Here, at last, the buttons were off the blades and the test had come for me. Ah well . . . !

We went over the ground particularly. There were some dozen lengths of steep grass slope, with a whin or two, from the edge of the trees to the road, just enough distance to gather breaking speed, but not enough to give the ambushed time to lock front or train arquebus. We paced it, we paced the space between tree and tree, we examined the ground to make sure that there were no coney burrows to break a leg, barked the backs of two trunks to mark the limit of our stance, and were finally satisfied that no more could be done at that time.

Father Senan, saying no word, had followed us about as we worked, and now he had a word to say, a glint in his eye. "My children, I see you are out for a shedding of blood, and I am a man of peace——"

"With a sparth-axe at his thigh and his tonsure under a casque!" said Donal derisively.

"A man of peace—an old friar who, belike, will be binding a marriage before morning. I strike no blow this night—unless I have to."

"You might strike a blow at Ruari, the herd, and you watching him back at the camp—and you at your prayers the same time."

"Prayers I will be at surely, but not in camp; and I will tie Ruari to a tree, a twist in his mouth. See that fine thick clump of growth out beyond. In there I will be, head under wing like a black chicken."

"What is in your mind, holy man?" Donal inquired.

"That Rickard the Sassenach of Dunkellin is no fool. At the onfall he will know what the onfall is for, and his highest endeavour will be to get his prize away. Ye, both hands full, might be too busy to call halt, but if I could summon up enough courage I might sally out and reason with him in a Christian spirit."

"And rid me of an unwilling father-in-law. No——"

"Silence, son! Would you gainsay the Church?" And at that we left it.

IV

It was dark there on the edge of the trees, and my nerves began to string themselves tightly. The waiting was beginning to tell. Eastwards, the moon had risen above the Esker, but our angle of the ridge was still in deep shadow except where a thinning of the trees showed a silver gleam among the trunks. The road below us was dark too, for the shadow of the trees still lay far out on the grass. The spread of parkland was a wavering grey shimmer, and the tree clumps lifted out of it like black islands. So bright was the moon that I could see the silver sheen of the sea and make out the black bulk of the cliffs of Clare beyond it. A most quiet and radiant scene under the summer sky—but here under the fringe of the trees were men strung for the killing.

A horse stamped on the hard ground, a girth creaked, a man whispered here and there to his mount, and then silence drew out thin and fine. No breath of air moved that we could feel, yet now and again the pine-tops above us soughed in a long breath of their own. Then far in the distance that same sighing breath would lift and move towards us, lift and move away till it died in the distance—a strange and lonely sigh concerned with some grief of its own not of this world.

I sat there in front of the line, and I envied the

hardened fighters behind me. They were used to this, the work of surprise and sally and shouting death so terrible to the English train-bands—and to veterans too. And I had never been in the press of fight. Yet Donal had made me captain of the charge and put full responsibility on me, himself taking left of the line. As he said, he must remain free for one thing only—getting to his lady's side and guarding her out of the press.

Time passed slowly. The shadow of the ridge lying on the grass narrowed and narrowed until now it was on the edge of the road. I do not know how near the breaking-point I got, but I found it difficult to sit still on Benmee's broad back, and I found something rising in my throat that if yielded to would be laughter. And then, somewhere in the woods far behind us, lifted the long howl of a wolf, the hunting-howl shaking through the night that causes the neck hairs to lift. I drew in my breath with a catch, and a man behind me moaned. That drawn sound steadied me somehow. I took comfort. Here was a man with nerves, too, and he a picked veteran. "Easy, brother, easy!" I soothed him.

And then out on the open before us lifted the shrill voice of a woman keening in her pain and laughing with the pain—a weird keen that rose high and high, broke into a hellish chuckle, and rose again. Gooseflesh ran over my thighs and loins.

"Chreesta!" gasped a voice behind me. "The Banshee!"

Donal's voice lifted in a steadying boom. "No! Only a vixen calling to her mate. See her flit out there."

Tadg Ironhand was away round the curve on the

115

Galway road watching for the first sign of the cavalcade. A gallowglass held his horse on the left of the line next Donal. We must be patient and wait his news. But he was a long time in coming, and now the road below us was full in the moon. In a short time we up here would be under its radiance too, and plain to be seen from the horn of the bight. Surely it must be that Dunkellin and his tail would not venture the road by night. The wise course! Rickard, by all accounts, was too seasoned a campaigner to risk a night ambush. Fools we were to think otherwise. I turned in my saddle to say as much to Donal, and stilled in that position.

There was no mistaking that sound. The clink of a shod hoof against stone! The road was mostly hard clay, but the sloughs of winter had been filled in with rounded pebbles from the shore—and at least one horse moved on the road far away. A hard breath was drawn in and held all down the line.

v

Someone was coming beyond a doubt, and in a short while it was certain that many came. There was the confused thud of many hooves and, now and then, the cadence of a voice lifted carelessly. I straightened in the saddle, flexed my knees, and slowly drew my Ferrara. It made no sound that time. There followed a slight rustle as each man got ready. We folded our cloaks over left arms and, bending forward, threw a corner over our horses' heads. I looked sideways along the ridge for Tadg. What could be keeping him? To me the tramp of hooves was just round the corner, though in truth it was still

116

a good way off. I cursed him mutely, and as I cursed he flitted under Benmee's head and placed his great hand on my knee. That hand shook—or my knee shook. "They come," he whispered tensely, and the whisper went down the line. "Not more than twenty *Sassum deargs* [1]—all in a bulk. Two ahead—one a lady —Dunkellin and my darling."

He was gone, and I heard him whisper to Donal, and then his saddle-girths creaked as he mounted.

The tramp was now indeed near. I was no longer a bundle of nerves. I seemed to grip all my feelings between my teeth, and I could see myself hurtling down the slope in a reckless mood. I kept my eyes at the end of the road and steadied my grip on hilt. . . .

And there was a horse's head, and there another. . . . Two riders came abreast—a lady on the inside swaying easily to the walk-amble of her horse, and beyond her a tall man, black-bearded. They went by and did not glance our way. My eyes did not follow them. For the head of their escort was coming round the curve, two and two riding abreast, slouched wearily in the saddle—riding carelessly at last. Their steel corselets took the gleam of the moon. Here and there a voice murmured, and one man whistled softly. They were so near home, danger behind, supper in front. Poor fighting-men! But I had no pity in me then. Instead, something snapped with a red spark in my head. I was in it now, and death and life were one. I eased back in the saddle, lifted my sword slowly, and waited. Down there on the road I marked the spot where the leading horse must be. . . . It was there.

I brought blade down with a cut that sang—the

[1] English soldiers.

agreed signal—struck Benmee with knee and heel, felt her jerk and spring, and there was I hurtling down at the head of the column. Thunder of hooves behind me, a startled clatter of hooves on the road, sudden shouts that rose into a shriek, and then Donal's voice like a clarion. "Amy! Amy! To me, Amy!" And then the slogan of the clan like a wolf's howl— "O'Cahawn! O'Cahawn!" No wonder men shrieked as we came out into the light of the moon.

Steel gleamed close to me. A horse reared aside in front. I gripped knees tight and struck it full, and horse and man fell sideways. I struck downwards and my shearing blade seemed to sing through empty air. I brought blade up in the swing, and there was a tall fellow in half-armour facing me, his long blade at the thrust. Close to the hilt I parried, and cut at the neck above the gorget. Deftly he warded the blade above his bent head. Here was a swordsman. And I had to kill him—or myself die. A horse bundled into me from behind and we were thrown close together. Quickly he shortened his blade and lunged furiously at my face, and I was just in time to catch the lunge in folded cloak. His face was close to mine now and I could see the gleam in his eyes and on his teeth, and forthwith I struck him terribly below the casque with the heavy guard of Andrea Ferrara. He fell under Benmee's feet, and Benmee plunged over him. I whirled her round, blade on guard, and—it was all over.

It was quick as that—quicker than that. Our first onfall had broken Dunkellin's guard beyond all rallying, swept them clean off the road, and the terrible sparth-axe had done its work. Dead men on the road, wounded men acrawl, men on foot running across the grass, scattered horsemen galloping furiously for the dun! It was all over.

Before I had time to think of Donal I heard the rallying blare of the curved bronze horn that had come down the clan for twenty generations. I kicked Benmee and galloped.

I came on him on the road near the first plantation, sitting finely upright on his horse, broadsword in hand. And by his side sat his lady, tall and slim in her saddle. On the road before them stood a lean man with a black beard, who still gripped the hilt of a broken sword, and by his side stood Father Senan, leaning on the long haft of his sparth-axe.

Men galloped to us from all airts, and I brought my mind to my duty. For the first time a surge of, I fear, savage content came over me. I had led men and not once thought of my own skin. My voice had a deeper note as I marshalled my lads and swung them across the road. We had won our lady and had Dunkellin himself in our net. And though two or three men had wounds, not a single man was missing.

I swung Benmee round and brought sword to salute. "All present, O'Cahan!"

Donal saluted back. "It is well. This is my lady."

Again I saluted, and the axe-blades swished to salute behind me. There was a disciplined silence.

The black-bearded Rickard stood up straight and tall enough, but his head was restless on his shoulders. He lifted his right arm and looked at his broken sword, and then threw the useless weapon furiously on the ground.

Donal spoke a quiet order. "Open ranks, there!" And then calmly to his enemy, "That is your road, Dunkellin."

"You had better kill me too," cried the other, a savage threat in his voice.

"Killing is done—this once," said Donal. "You are free to go."

Rickard the Sassenach threw a furious gesture towards the lady. "Come, daughter!" he ordered fiercely.

For answer she put her hand on Donal's arm, and though her voice trembled it was clear and strong. "This is my place now, father."

Still a moment he hesitated, struggling between ire and dignity. Then he swung round suddenly, sent Father Senan staggering, and strode away between the open ranks. There was that in his stride that told us he would start running as soon as he was out of sight. I heard the lady's voice lifted tremulously. "Let us go from here, Donal. He will loose all Connacht against us."

Donal laughed confidently and comfortingly. "Let him, Queen! We know the safe road, and in a week you will rule us in Dungiven.—Twos-about, David, and let us go."

CHAPTER IX

I

FULL dawn found us deep in the woods north of the Athenree road, and there we made our first halt where a tinkle of water ran under mosses near the ruins of an old Christian, or it might be pagan, shrine. We had camped at this place on the outward ride two nights before, and had hidden, in a hole under the brambles, a couple of skins of wine, a bundle of barley scones, and the cooked hind-quarters of a fallow-deer. Besides this provender we had the remnants of Ruari's calf, which reminds me to say that the herd had been untied from his tree before we left the Esker, and had made straight for the Clare Fastnesses as the only safe place for him.

Before we set teeth in food Father Senan did his great duty. He washed his hands and his face in the running water, extracted from his satchel a rumpled surplice, a broad purple ribbon, and a thin book with a ragged leather cover, and called his congregation together. And there in that little glade he wedded Donal and his lady. I stood up behind Donal's shoulder, and Tadg Ironhand, her foster-father, stood at Lady Amy's. And as I stood there I wondered at Donal and I wondered at myself. Here was I, a man of twenty-eight, and I knew nothing of love. Was there something missing in me—and for me? Was all my youth wasted? Here, now, was my cousin Donal, who, having trifled with love in his time, was at last daring death for himself and all of us for this one woman. What was woman that such should be? I looked aside wonderingly at this Amy Burc, for the first time at leisure to contemplate her.

She was beautiful, no doubt, with her poised head and delicate colouring, but to me she was not half so beautiful as my dear cousin, Donal Ballagh, with his black hair acurl on his white brow and that firm mouth that could laugh or grow stern. She was tall and slender in her riding-kirtle, and from the coif on her head had strayed a ringlet of copper-red hair, and on her white round neck a small pulse beat and beat. I could see the long lashes cover her eyes, and her eyelids were so thin and pure that I could swear her eyes were blue beneath. And then she turned to give Donal her hand, and she smiled for him. Dhia! would a woman ever smile that way for me, light in her eyes and tenderness about her lips? She looked over Donal's shoulder and saw my interest and my dourly-troubled gaze, and she smiled to me too—a little wistful and beseeching smile, as if saying, "Please think kindly of me, for I will be good to this man you love." But it was her first smile for her lover that made my heart turn over in my breast. . . . Alas! once in La Soye a poor trull had kissed my hand, and once a virago had scratched me when I had knocked the man that beat her into the kennel. And that was all I knew of women.

After the marriage the old priest said a longish prayer, and as I knelt on the long grass, damp with the night's dew, I felt myself go slack and drowsy and weighed down with weariness. I filled my lungs with a deep breath and looked round at the men. They too were asag, kneeling on one knee, elbow alean on the other, heads adroop. It was again some comfort to me that these tough men of war also felt the strain. But the comfort did not abide, for in that moment of low ebb my thoughts turned bleakly to the long and weary road that lay before us. Dungiven seemed woefully far away, and how might tired men and one gently-nurtured woman twist a safe course day after day through a land raised before them? All I wanted then was a long sleep, and that I could not yet have— perhaps never.

A good meal helped us all, and something of the old gay hardihood came back to the company. Donal, his wife, the priest, and I ate together, and for the first time we had leisure to talk. But we talked little. The lady looked at me out of shy eyes. I suppose the hatchet dourness of my Scots face made her think me stern and cold; whereas I was merely more shy than she was. Also, she might have heard some of the men talk wildly of my bloodthirstiness in fight. For, by way of praising my first foray with them, they credited me with things that never happened—or that I had no memory of. Donal, the newly-wed, was silent too, but his eyes were eloquent with love and hope—and a great fear as well; his happiness was in his hand, but not securely, and many days must go by before he dared look happiness in the face.

When we had finished eating, Donal called us all together. "Now, my clan and my children," he said, making a play of words in the Gaelic, "here is where the roads divide, to meet at Saimhor or at Roe, and God guide us, every one. Ye know the rule of old: scatter wide and avoid fight. A dead enemy ties a string to your feet. As we know, the wood-kerns will already be on the trail, and riders gone the open road to warn Cong and Tuam and Athenree. Let not more than two men keep together, for the meshes of the net are close; but ye have broken many a mesh before now, and will again, God aiding. Go, then, and remember, my heroes, that ye are hurrying to a wedding-feast at Dungiven, and that that feast will last a day for every day ye have ridden with me on this great venture. God with us!"

II

Each man in turn came leading his spent horse, saluted his chief, bent knee to his lady, and was gone. Tadg Ironhand came last, and the lady, with an impulsive gesture that I liked, clapped her soft hands each side of his great shaggy head and kissed him on the brow. "Tadg, my only father now," she whispered, and for a moment, like a child, he laid that great head down on her shoulder. Oh, but this was a kind and lovely woman!

I went to where Benmee hung her head, too weary to nibble the grass, and found Father Senan groaningly regirthing the heavily padded saddle on his own thick cob. I gave him a hand. "Tell me, fighting friar," I put to him, "would another sword be a help to those two back yonder?"

"Do you know the road?"

"Could you not be answering my question first?"

"I could if I liked, Albannach hot-head. Am I not hard at the thinking? Look you, son! If these poor beasts of ours were fresh, an extra sword—and a sparth as well—might help to break a road for yon two if we found it closed. But as we are, we are done, and them with us, if ever it comes to sword work—and four horses make a trail that the kerns can follow."

I led Benmee back to the glade where Donal and his bride waited, and Father Senan followed close behind.

"Wait, David," said Donal lightly. "We four are going together."

I was as light as he was. "Are we so? Here is a cunning old popish friar, and like a leech will I cling to him, and he a weasel in the woods. We meet at Dungiven."

Donal caught me at the shoulder and looked into my eyes. "No use wasting words on you," he said, and scowled at the old friar. "Bring him home, Senan, or—" He turned away.

Lady Amy reached me her hand, and I bent knee, and for the first time that I could remember my lips touched a woman. Her fingers pressed on mine, gently firm.

III

There, then, were old Father Senan and I setting out together for Dungiven, and we began by turning our faces from it.

"A cunning old popish friar, I heard you call one," he chided.

"Choice words."

"So! Cunning will I be, then. More cunning than fox or weasel—as men can be and are. Follow on, thou Albannach half-calvinist." He led away westwards without any northing, though Dungiven was north and by east, and I made no protest.

The sun was four hours high before ever he cried halt. We had come as fast as our tired horses could travel, but very circumspectly—deep in the woods, away from the bosky margins of marshes and pools, prying into open valleys before we crossed them, never once following a man-made track. Once we circled round a township of clay bothies, and once a herd's dogs barked at us as we disappeared into the trees. But no man accosted us, or, I think, put eyes on us.

We made our first halt at a woodland lochan—a bonny quiet pool deep in the wilderness. The wood-ridges came shelving down to it on all sides, and on three sides it was fringed with a thick belt of whins still patched with fairy gold and crackling softly in the summer heat. Tall and ancient whins were they, and rabbit-runs led deep under them in low dark arches. At one end was a level spread of good grass, with the four stone walls of some ancient ruin.

Our first duty was to the horses. We let them cool off, rubbed them down, and gave them water sparingly, after which we moved aside some dead bushes in the doorway of the ruin, tethered the beasts inside, and replaced the branches. Then, with swords and *sgian*, we cut for them two armfuls of the freshest grass, and hoped the juicy food would not gripe them.

"And now," said the old priest, "you and I will be a pair of buck coney. Come!"

He led the way along the wood-edge, treading carefully on firm ground that took no mark, until we were near the far end of the lochan. There he folded his cloak over head and shoulders, lay on his belly, and wriggled under an archway in the whins. I did likewise, and followed him deeper and deeper until at last we came out on a tiny island in that rustling sea—a wee patch of grey stiff grass with the twisted stems standing up all round it, and the air full of the mystic, dry, pleasant odour of the golden bloom.

"The secret chamber of our palace," he whispered pantingly. "Thanks to God, and to Him will we give thanks at last. We will now say one or, maybe, two rosaries in thanksgiving and petition."

We were on the westward side of the loch, and by getting our heads close to the whins our eyes were shaded from the strong sun. With my *sgian* I gouged out two divots for our hip-bones, and we spread our cloaks over them.

"Pray away, holy man," I agreed out of a yawn, wriggling into comfort.

He started valiantly, and valiantly I responded. The drone of his voice was not unpleasant. I found myself being soothed by it, and sometimes slurred the response. . . . It was the voice of Senan. . . . It was the voice of Turlough singing a new song. . . . It was the long sough of the sea. . . . It was only a whisper in a gathering silence. . . .

When I waked, long after, the old man was sound asleep, his face gentle, and his fingers were still and loose in the middle of the second decade of his beads.

That was a great sleep surely. It was evening then. I sat up and looked round me. The sun was down behind the western ridge, but the tree-tops across the lochan were a suffused red glory. I let the old man sleep on, clasped my hands over my knees, and watched the glory lift and fade. A saturnine mood, not unpleasant, came gently on me. I lost sensation of time and space. I had no desire to move from that place any more. Lapped in a quiet wilderness, safe in the heart of it, danger forever banned the ring of it, why trouble with the vain urges of head and heart? Why not be passive—like the whins—like the trees—like the cool loch water? What was life, then, but a little ripple in a great stillness . . . ?

IV

The old priest's voice roused me against my will. "Rain in that sunset," he said, "and it is we who will know it before morning." He was sitting up, his arms lifted in a great long yawn. "You let me sleep, Davy. I dreamt I hooked a four-foot salmon and he pulled me into the Pooka's Hole, where I swam better than he did, and raced him all the way to Limavady. Would you be telling me, now, what you appropriated out of that store of provisions back yonder?"

I felt for my satchel. "A shin-bone, it looked like."

"I saw you. Only a shin-bone! There was the bottom of a skin of wine, and a bit of haunch left over. Who got them?"

"They are not far away. I saw you, too."

He chuckled, climbed stiffly to his feet, and looked out over the loch. "Look at that, now," he cried delightedly. "A thousand thousand of them."

I jumped to my feet and looked. The day had been a still one, but now a small thin air was drifting down from amongst the trees, setting the old whin stems acreak and lightly rippling across the face of the water. But besides that faint ripple of the breeze the loch was ringed all over by the lift and dip of thousands of feeding trout. Most of the fish coming clean out of the water were small, but here and there a back fin cut the surface and a fat ripple ran as a broad fluke flicked over.

"On the take," said I sadly, "and nothing to take them with."

"'A cunning old friar!' said he, and cunningly the Albannach cleaved to him. Wait ye, my jewels!"

Forthwith, and in haste, he lopped off a four-foot length of tough whin stem, twisted and awkward, but pliable enough once he had trimmed it clean.

"Worms!" scoffed I. "Where will you get them this dry weather?"

He snorted at the word, and gave me a scornful eye. "I hoped I had taught you better than that," he said, and was busy emptying his satchel on the ground—venison, wine-skin, and priestly gear. At the bottom was a beautifully made, thin, wooden box, and this he snatched. It contained a dozen feathered lures of his own tying, a length of line woven of finest flax, and an assortment of tail-pieces plucked from a grey-horse brush. "What would you be saying now?" he questioned.

I looked over his shoulder. "That moth with the furry body."

He glanced at the sky. "Too clear a while yet. This scrap of tinsel and cock's plume—we will try them with that."

We forged a road down to the water and looked it over from behind the shelter of a whin. The drift of air went up the loch over our right shoulders, and the depth of the water close in was not less than a foot over a gravelly bottom.

"Look," he whispered—"a nice one cutting water. You try him, Davy."

But I respected the glisten in his eye, and pointed to the boil and ripple within reach of his makeshift engine. Head below the whins, he crept forward, and trailed his line in the water to straighten it. Even as he switched it out a small fish came to the fly and kicked itself free with a splatter. The short word the churchman said was of the church, but not reverent.

And then he started to fish. Ill-equipped though he was, he skilfully laid his lure like a kiss across the ripples. And he had all the world's luck. Like enough, that patch of lochan had never been fly-fished since time began, and the trout were greedy as pike. He caught five or six sizeable ones, then a half-pounder, and then lost a sturdy fighter. Thereafter came a lull, and he slipped off his horse-boots and waded into the water. There he caught another half-pounder, and luck finished with him. A monster took his fly, kicked angrily, and went straight away from that place with a yard of horse-tail as well as fly. Whereat the holy fisher said many words that were neither holy nor churchly.

"I am sorry, David son," he said humbly. "Wait till I tie on another fly for you."

"No!" I stopped him. "After you cursing every trout in the loch, seed, breed, and generation?"

So we went back to our horses, moving cautiously among the trees and looking in over the broken walls. We saw nothing to disturb us, and Benmee was glad to see me. They had finished their provender without hurt, and we cut them some more. Then, with flint and steel, we started a little hot ember of fire with dead furze roots, and cooked our fish on forked sticks, and the priest, searching his wonderful satchel, brought forth a small purse of dry salt.

"Trout," said he, his mouth full, "like all fish, eat best fresh, and our bit venison will come in handy the night that is before us. But—and mark this—I have known the bottom of a wine-skin to taint the liquor after long jolting."

"I take the first mouthful, then?"

"Surely! The Albannach be an honest race—and you keeping your palate in the hole at the bottom."

So we finished the trout, and thereafter finished the wine, and as we drank we discussed our plans.

"Not a stir will we stir out of this," said the priest, "till the moon tops the trees. We might be safer in the dark, but the lie of the land is not known to me, and the dark has many traps besides Sassenach soldiers on the Menlo road."

"When do we turn north?" I put to him.

"As soon as that way is safe. The first drive of pursuit will go that airt, and I am seeking to get outside the brunt of it. Since the days of Shane and the coming of the new church I have once or twice— ay! four or five times—been hunted—like a wolf— and I ever found it a good rule to follow behind the hounds nosing for me. To-night—and to-morrow— we will keep striking west and by north for the shores of Corrib, slip our way between Cong and Tuam, and make for O'Connor Roe country, where my tonsure might save your flaming head."

I ran my fingers through the upthrow of my red hair.

"No!" said he; "it is but a warm brown."

And I grinned at the lie.

When the moon showed through the trees we went out to the waterside to look and listen, and were mightily startled by the scurry of a herd of fallow-deer that had come down to drink where a small stream gurgled out of the loch.

"A good sign," said Father Senan, when he got his breath back. "The deer would not be here if men lurked in the woods. Let us to the road, son."

After the startle of the deer everything was very still and very peaceful too. The belt of whins was a grey shimmer and the woods a quiet blackness, and the water before us a shining silver shield, except where the topmost branches of the trees, with the moon behind them, cast a lacework of shadow. The quiet and peace of that lost small water abided with me the rest of that night.

v

All night we slowly worked our way north and by west. Our tough little horses had been freshened by the long rest, and we ourselves, after such a fine sleep and sound meal, were again restrung for the adventures of the road.

An hour after midnight the moon clouded over and the rain came sighing over the woods. That rain held steadily for three hours, and slowed our pace. The rain itself we did not mind. We but wrapped our long cloaks round us, pulled the hoods over head, and the oil-impregnated wool, with its skin lining, kept us dry and warm. Sometime near dawn we rested against a tree and ate the last of our provisions, and I shared a bannock with Benmee, that nibbled it daintily out of my fingers.

At full daylight we examined the country before us from the head of a slope. It lay below us, flat and heavily wooded, mile after mile, until at last and far away it lifted into a low ridge, bare of trees.

"Corrib Loch is at the other side of that drum," Father Senan told me. "There will be a township or two down there in the woods—which are not as thick as they look—and we must find an Eireannach and a Christian sometime to-day or starve. Shall we strike on for a piece?"

I agreed, and we went down into the plain. But before going the priest wrought a remarkable change in himself. Up to now no one would have discerned in him the churchman—his tonsure hidden under a leather morion with a steel rim; a war-cloak over his knee-long saffron tunic, that was belted with leather instead of the cord of his order; and his sparth-axe never to be mistaken for a crook. But now he hung his morion on the saddle-string and draped cloak over it, and there was the Celtic tonsure from ear to ear, filmed with a ten-days' growth of iron-grey, but plain enough. Somehow that tonsure gave his bearded face a certain mildness, not noticeable under the morion. He was not done yet. He unbelted his tunic, pulled it over his head, turned it inside out, and there was the habit of his order, short indeed, but of the proper black, with cowl flat on shoulders and cord sewn round waist. Now, truly, he was a friar and could never have been anything else. He reached me his sparth-axe.

"Sling it this side of your hip," he requested, "and if I have to snatch it—well and good."

"If we meet Bingham's riders now, you will burn," I warned him.

"And you hang. Where the difference? Let us on."

It was well on in the morning before we came on signs of a township. First we struck a pannier-track leading our way, and this we followed with due precaution, the friar moving ahead at each of its many twists and examining the track beyond before he signalled me to follow. For the better part of an hour we went thus, and then, at one wide curve, he checked and gestured me aside urgently.

Not far behind him was a low-growing hazel in full verdure, and I swerved Benmee into the shelter of this and peered through the branches at Father Senan's broad back. Beyond him I could see a few yards of the path before it curved out of sight, and on this presently appeared a barefoot Irish villager, a middle-aged man, with a dark lean face and a wild-cat-skin cap on his cropped head. He halted before the friar, took off his cap, and bent knee in a short quick bow to the Church's blessing. This portended well, and I listened with open ears.

"God and Mary's blessing with you, my son," said the priest in a mild fervour.

"God and Mary with you—and Saint Patrick," came the response.

"Where does this road lead to, my child?"

"To my township of Bellaghy, reverend father, a mile back from here in O'Flaherty country."

"Is there a priest with you in that place?"

"My grief! no, father. A true priest has not come our way these months."

"Alas! for our religion——"

"Are you looking our way, father?" he asked eagerly. "You will be a thousand times welcome."

"Is a Queen's priest with you?"

"Mary mother! No. We are poor, father, but you will be safe there. No *Sassun dearg* troubles us these days."

"Then I will come. But there is one with me—a young brother straight from France—not yet a holy man of Mother Church, but on the road."

"He will be welcome too, father."

So I came out from my screen of hazels and saw the surprise in the Eireannach's[1] eyes. What with my bulk below war-cloak, my equipment, my feathered bonnet, my days'-old scrub on chin and cheek, I must have looked anything but a man leaning to holiness. Afterwards the priest denied as much as a single small lie. His brother I was, as were all men; my celibate ways showed a churchly leaning; and out of France had I come, if not straight, not unseldom in a hurry.

The Eireannach, Murrigan O'Flaherty Dhu by name, led us back to his township, and he was a proud man of his find. We were indeed very welcome amongst these simple and primitive clansmen, and it was heart-warming to see their love and loyalty towards the wandering friar, and, in some reflected degree, towards his brother in disguise. They regaled us of their best, procured from somewhere a flagon of Spanish wine in addition to their own heady brew, piled fresh beds of bracken for us, and permitted no one in our vicinity while we rested.

And, indeed, Father Senan did not rest for long. He was a new man in his priestly calling. Weary and worn as he must have been, an old man who had borne the strain with tough fighting-men, he rose to do his duties finely and tirelessly in that hamlet of lowly

[1] Irishman's.

men. In that place that had been without a minister for so long there was much for him to do: children to be baptised, couples to wed or to have their bonds made regular, the last Sacrament to be administered to two or three who were sick, a new house to be blessed, and the shriving of many who believed themselves to be sinners. Poor sinners! There was not amongst them one sinner as I knew sinners.

CHAPTER X

I

A FINE fresh morning it was after that night of rain.
The sun was above the trees, and the sky, far and pale
and fragile, was without a cloud: and high up in it a
lark soared and sang. Here and there a thin smoke
of vapour rose off the wet grass, eddied, quivered,
and was gone. And a thrush, after his breakfast, sang
six notes of a song.

Above the thrush's singing I heard the sound of
running water, and, going that way, came to a dell
winding back into the woods with a strong stream
purling down it. I followed it up till I reached a
small cascade that made a nice pool below, and there
I did my toilet. The water was heavy after the rain,
but not muddy, and I stripped and plunged into the
brisk coolness of it. Thereafter I shaved by touch, as
I was accustomed to, put on a fresh linen under-tunic
that I carried in my satchel, washed the used one
under the runnel, and hung it to dry on a hawthorn.
I felt a new man now—skin aglow under fresh linen,
chin pleasantly smooth, energy new in me—and a
stomach clamouring for breakfast

After a fine meal we decided that we would leave
the township early in the evening, make for Corrib
side, and never cry halt till we were past the danger-
spot of Cong. But that choice was not long left to us.

There came a stir and flurry outside our door, and
in hurried Murrigan Dhu with one of the outposts.

These outposts had been set to watch the inlets to the villages, Mass being a heinous offence and punishable with death. This one had been stationed on the southern track and had a disturbing tale to tell.

He had met one Eoin, son of Gannon, from the township of Clounacaora, six miles south, and had learned that a troop of English horse had billeted in that township the previous night. Eoin had been out with the MacWilliams against the English before the truce, and in the night he had stolen away with his neck. The Sassenach were drawing a net through the woods, he said, for the stragglers of a terrible northern raid, while a body of light horse and kern had made a dash to block the Curlew passes. Two hundred of the O'Cahans from north of Tirowen, so the story went, had come like a flame on Dunkellin, put the garrison to the sword, cut out Rickard the Sassenach's tongue, burned down the dun, and were off to the north with the Baron's daughter, twenty maids, and six crocks of gold. Our poor little raid, that had looked so fine and bold, had grown prodigiously in the telling, and I began to think small of myself. We had but emptied a few saddles, stolen one calf, and abducted one willing maiden — nothing to boast about any more.

We did not tarry long in Bellaghy after that news. We made our churchly calling an excuse for haste, and the clansmen, whether they suspected us or not, did all they could to set us on our way. In less than a quarter-hour we were mounted, the priest had given his final blessing, and we were agallop out of the hamlet north and by west.

We had gone a mile when I called to mind a good

linder [1] I had washed and left hanging on a hawthorn bush near a waterfall. I cursed shortly.

"Curse away, fellow-soldier," said the friar. He had re-turned his tunic, and his bearded face was stern under its morion. "You see," he explained with grim humour, "if it comes to the bit, I would rather hang than burn."

And indeed we got overclose to a hanging that day.

We had ridden an hour at a speed to conserve our horses, but we were not as watchful of the road in front as we should have been. We looked for danger from the rear, and kept eyes backward wherever the ground gave us prospect. Thus it was, we came ambling down a brae, round a clump of briar, and out on a wide wagon-road. And there, not two hundred paces on our right, was half a troop of English horse advancing towards us at a foot pace.

II

Things happened quickly after that. We did not wait to count the enemy. The shout they gave seemed to act as a spur to our mounts, and we were across the road and into the trees at top speed before they had set hooves aclatter. The woods were open here, and the ground rising gently to the ridges hiding Corrib; but though we were in a tight place our strait was not yet desperate. Our horses were handy and quick, and the pursuers heavily mounted. Given an open way, an occasional marsh, a few clumps of undergrowth, and we might easily win clear. Already we had gained ground. The half-troop was spreading

[1] Undershirt.

out fan-shape, instead of making a direct push for us, and we thought that a foolish proceeding at the time. But we did not know that the country ahead was patrolled by the other half of the troop. We learned soon enough.

We rode full gallop up a long glade, swerved with it to the left, and there, full in our path, was a big man on a big horse, a giant fellow in buff with a peaked casque above his eyes.

"We're for it!" Andrea Ferrara grated and sang out of scabbard. I was riding half a length behind and holding Benmee in. Now I gave her knee and she was abreast. "I will take him," I shouted to the priest. "You keep on."

The trooper faced us solidly in the middle of the glade, and already his heavy sword was out. I was close to him before I saw who it was. Tom Pybus! the man I had drawn sword on twice already. "God!" was the thought in my head. "One of us will kill the other this time."

But neither of us did. I suppose the big fellow knew that he was slow with his weapon and that I over-matched him, or it might be that he had no mind to press me. Instead of using his weight to charge me down he reined his horse stiffly and, as I came at him, his blow was hesitating and loose-handed. I parried so fiercely that the hilt was jarred out of his grip, and there he was at my mercy. He swayed his head and shoulders away from me, and I had only to run him through the belly. I could not. Instead, I thrust foot under his and shot him clean out of the saddle. And he had not thudded on the ground before I had bundled by and was up with the priest, who had checked his horse and armed himself with sparth.

"*Mhuire!*" he cried; "you killed him."

"You could not kill that man."

I glanced over shoulder, and there once more was Tom Pybus trundling after his horse. I had to laugh.

"He fell like a sack of stones," called the priest. "Was it the hilt?"

I shook head. "Press on! Luck comes with him always."

But our luck did not overtake us yet. We laboured slantwise to the head of a long rise, and below us was a shallow valley, and beyond it a stiff brae jutted with black and coloured limestones. The bottom of the valley was a chain of thick clumps of blackthorn and bramble with a gleam of running water showing between. We raced down the slope, the air singing in our ears, broke between two clumps, and came to a racking halt on the brink of a brawling torrent, brown and swollen by the rain.

III

That torrent was not more than a dozen long paces wide, but it doomed us more surely than a great river. For the depth and rush of it between tilted slabs of stone made it wholly impassable—mounted or on foot.

To our right it slanted away from our pursuers, who were still over the ridge, and, in a last effort, we forced our horses that way through the undergrowth. In less than a minute we came to where it again curved back, and, midway in the curve, a great shelf of limestone shouldered out of the rush of water. It was some four yards out from the high bank on our side. Father Senan in after days computed it at six or maybe seven spades, and used to boast that while I jumped the whole way he jumped most of it. Between us and that slab the water ran deep and strong, but beyond to the shelving bank it appeared fordable. I looked at the torrent, and it was forbidding. I looked at the stone, and I liked it better. It offered a chance of escape, and we had no time to look for a safer one.

I hurled myself off Benmee and slapped her on the withers. "Good-bye, lassie! You carried me well." There was little time for farewell.

Father Senan was at my side. "I can never do it, David," he cried.

"Do it we must," I shouted above the rush of the waters. "Stand back!"

The undergrowth gave me two short paces. I twisted cloak under arm, gripped my sword-scabbard high, took the quick kick-and-jerk of the hop-step-and-leap—and leaped. The stone jarred me to the neck, my feet slipped into the water, but already my hands were secure on a jut of rock, and I pulled myself to security. Father Senan was on the brink, looking down on me and shaking his head.

"Throw me your axe," I shouted to him, and that he did. I grasped the jut of rock with one hand, grasped the socket of the axe with the other, and reached the four-foot handle as far as I was able. "Jump!" I dared him furiously. "Jump—and drown —or hang! Jump!"

Later, he said it was the fury in my eyes that compelled him. He pressed morion down on his head, gathered his cloak, and threw himself forward. He clutched all hands at the axe-haft and soused under.

The shock of his weight all but wrenched my fingers from axe and rock, but, luckily, the rush of water and my pull carried him round to the back-swirl behind the shelf, and there I held and hauled him, got a hold of his collar, and dragged him belly-down to precarious safety.

He spluttered through bearded lips, winked the water out of his eyes, and stared at me speechlessly. I gave him no time to get wind or tongue back, but caught him round the waist, cloak and all, and plunged feet first into the rush beyond the rock. We found bottom knee-deep; the water ridged up our thighs, but our solid weight withstood the pressure, and we made the other bank in one desperate splashing rush. And it was then we heard the shouting behind us; and there came a scutter of horsemen down the slope.

"David," cried my stout old warrior, "with axe and sword we can hold this against them."

"Not against arquebus. Come on!"

We faced the shelving bank and the rock-jutted brae above and started the slow climb. What risk or safety was beyond we did not know—nor care very much then. Our pace was tardy now. The old priest who, on horseback, had stood the strain with the best, was short of wind and limb, and was soon spent amongst those slippery bosses of sun-hot stone. He lagged, and I waited for him.

"Oh, Davy! Davy!" he panted. "I am old and done. Be not minding me. You are young—you make on——"

In reply I caught him at the belt and pulled him in front of me. Then, indeed, I should have thanked God for strength of body and lung. But I had no time, and I needed all that was in me for the work in hand.

In a little while the old man could do no more than keep feet under him, and I pushed him upwards like an unwieldy sack.

Three-quarter-way up I was forced to halt. Face-down over a rock, I struggled to get my breath, and never before in my life did I experience that terrible whooping indraw that fails to fill the lungs. I thought my heart would burst.

The priest lay against me, speechless, and gently patted my shoulder. "Look!" he whispered at last.

Down below us many horsemen were forcing a way along the torrent-side, looking for a crossing-place, but none had yet ventured our road. One man directly below us had dismounted and was busy over the priming of an arquebus. I filled my lungs once again, and resettled my grip. The old man groaned with the effort, and we resumed the climb—slowly and slowly. We were near the head of the brae when the waited-for bellow roared behind us and the lead spattered the rock at our side. We were over the top before another shot could be fired.

There we halted, drawing in the air open-mouthed, the blood hissing in my ears, my head dizzy, sweat salt on my lips; and, once open, our mouths stayed open, and our eyes stared in front of us. For there before us was the wide reach of Loch Corrib, the water we had been trending towards so eagerly for two days, and now it hemmed us in and betrayed us. We stood at one horn of a deep bay, and on our right hand, where we had hoped to hide in the woods, was a mile-wide stretch of deep water. We could not hope to get round the detour of that inlet before our pursuers found a road to us.

Corrib is a great expanse of inland sea, a good thirty miles in length and, at this point, some three miles across. The far shore lifted into a fine wooden ridge, gapped by the gash of an inlet going back into the breast of big hills—great purple masses of hill, peaceful and remote under the high summer sky. Over there was safety, here death was at our heels, and, between, Corrib waters shimmered in the sun.

"David, son," said my old friend, stilling his panting breath, "I am old and done, and this fate had to overtake me soon or late. But you are young. . . . Look! if you hurry now you might get round that horn and win clear. Never mind me—I can hold them a while."

I looked at him sullenly.

"Up or down they will find a road," he urged, "and why should two of us suffer? There is no more good in me."

A hot anger came over me. Had the old fool no sense? How could I face Dungiven and the soldierly men who held it, knowing that I had left the old priest to die?

"Oh, David—David!" he cried then, seeing the anger in my eyes. "I do not want to be the death of your mother's son—the woman that I loved—the only one."

That touched me. I put my arm round him. "Since you are the only father I have," said I, "I will not part with you this day. Come! We will work round by the trees close to the water."

So we went down the slope, linked together. And

we did not hurry. The old friar could not, and, since I was tied to him so irrevocably, a mood of desperate quietness came to me. No, not quietness! A strange satisfying humour that gave me a sense of pride in myself. By the goodness of God, if we were going to die we would die side by side, and my name and nation would not be a byword in the mouths of men.

So we came to the trees, went quietly through them, and came round a patch of wild raspberries above the fine gravel of the shore. And there a tall man, leaning to pick a berry, started upright and swore a sudden short oath.

V

We were startled too. I swung the priest aside and grasped at my hilt. And, grasping it, I had Andrea Ferrara out and on guard. For one glance told me who this man was.

He was Captain Sir William Cosby of Cong, the slayer of Colum O'More. Here now was death close to us—and to him. My mind leaped to the conclusion that he was here with his men and that the end had come for us.

"Draw!" I said in my throat. "I will kill you this day before I die. Draw, you swine!"

His hand was at his hip, but there was there only a dagger. He was not even in his soldier's dress, but wore a doublet and hose of black and red, and, instead of casque, a flat-topped slashed cap. As I came at him he snatched at his poor weapon, gave back a step, and crouched on guard, but in his eye was the knowledge that death was at his throat. It was

so easy to break through that guard. It was too easy.
I hesitated.

And as I hesitated a woman screamed at my left
hand. And though she screamed she was bold. She
came round the raspberry canes like the wind and,
unhesitatingly, drove between Cosby and me. My
flickering blade was not a hand's-breadth from her
shoulder. She looked from one to the other. "What
is it?" Her breath was drawn in sharply. "What is
it, Captain Cosby?"

A young maid she was, and bonny too. I could
note that even in the stress of passion. Not very tall,
with black hair waving and the good blood not yet
ebbed from her cheeks. Frightened she might be,
but not dismayed, though Father Senan says that my
ferocious mien should have dismayed Queen Maeve.

"What is it, Captain Cosby?" she asked again.
"Who is this man?"

"A rebel outlaw," said Cosby, swallowing his palate.

But I was no longer paying attention to man or
maid. They were of no interest any more. For,
glancing by her shoulder, my eyes saw something that
made my heart jump. Down at the edge of the water
was a small coble—a lovely, shapely, God-sent small
boat, painted green and white. There it was. I
blinked my eyes to make sure of it.

I glanced at the priest. His eyes were on it too. I
bellowed at him. "Go on! She is ours."

Life had come back to my old Trojan. He hesitated
not at all. He scurried. He clattered on the gravel,
shoved the boat's head off, fell over the bow, scrambled
to a thwart, grasped oars, and with a practised flick
had her stern on to the shore. "Come on, my hero!"
he roared, a fine vigour in his voice. "Ours she is."

Cosby growled like a hound, and would have been at the old man, but in two long strides I half-circled the maid and was between him and the boat. My sword was at his throat. "Move, you dog, and die," I threatened. "Move. Oh, move!"

The flaxen moustache that bushed up over his cheeks twitched, and his teeth showed. But he did not move. Step by step I went backwards to the gravel. I was taking no risks now.

And again this young woman flew lightly between us, and now, instead of fright, there was the flare of battle in her eye. "You hulking red savage," she cried, "that boat is mine!"

I retreated steadily, and she faced close to me.

"Dare you steal it?"

I was on the gravel now.

"You will hang——"

"Without it," I finished for her.

She must have seen that I was past moving, and, for the first time, she showed dismay. She threw her hands out in an impulsive gesture and her eyes widened.

"But I must be home."

"Walk," said I.

"To the other shore?"

A long walk surely.

"You brute!" Anger and dismay in her tone. "I must be home. My mother——" She wrung her hands and half-turned from me.

My heels splashed in the water, and I paused before I swung for the boat. I paused because, before she turned away, I saw virginal fear in that maid's eye, and something that was almost a prayer to Heaven— or to me. "Mother Mary!" I caught that desperate whisper.

And then and there I acted on impulse. Maybe it was not impulse after all, but a sudden knowledge that it was not right to leave the maid alone in this wilderness with a brute—and with rough soldiery on the hill behind. I strode at her, caught her round the waist with my left arm, lifted her high, pounded into the water, and dropped her without ceremony into the bow of the boat behind the priest.

"Home to your mother, vixen," I cried, "and keep better company."

I dragged at the gunwale and vaulted clean over the oar into the stern. That maid had not once screamed or struggled in my arm.

It was then that Cosby made a final essay. He rushed forward into the water, growling, dagger lifted, teeth bare, and, forthwith, I did my very utmost to get him. I put arm and shoulder behind that long lunge. He braked himself desperately, head thrown back, and the drag of the water on his feet helped. My point just reached him below the breast-bone, and steel jarred on steel. It was true, then, that he wore mail. The shock knocked him flat on his back with a great splash.

"Dhia! He is spitted," cried the priest.

"No! but he will be," I shouted, and then and there would have leapt back and pinned his throat to the gravel. But at that the oarsman tugged full strength, the boat shot out into the loch, and I fell breast down on the sternboard, my long blade trailing in the water.

The flurry and the fury were not yet finished. As I scrambled to my knees a great shout burst from the hill, and men on foot came pouring down to the lochside. Three were well ahead: two troopers armed with arquebus and, a tall officer carrying a naked sword. The foremost soldier plunged through the water till it reached his hips, levelled his piece, and pulled trigger. He had aimed low, for the bullet cut the water one side of the stern and went singing off into the air.

"Oh! Coward! coward!" cried Father Senan. "And a lady with us."

The second trooper pulled up on shore, looked at his priming, and brought his weapon to the level. I turned to the maid in the bow. "Down!" I ordered her, and she crouched her dark head to the gunwale. Some instinct brought me to my feet to draw the bullet high. But the bellow of the explosion never came. For the tall officer came bounding behind his man, struck him a mighty blow under the ear, and laid him flat on the gravel. I knew that tall officer. He was Sir Francis Vaughan.

A fine warmth surged in me. "A Vaughan! A Vaughan!" I cheered him, cap doffed. "My fine man of the English!"

He lifted his hand and waved to me.

CHAPTER XI

I

Back there on land there had been hot stress in plenty, and now we had snatched ourselves clean out of it and away from it. We were a distance from the shore, and suddenly, as it seemed, a great quietness had come about us. There was only the click and feather of the oars, and a soft gurgle at the bows, and all about us was the wide reach of Corrib rippling in the soft breeze and shimmering under the sun. I sat in the stern, and looked at the priest pulling, and he looked at me, some trouble in his eye. He had no word to say for a long time.

"Tell me, son," he questioned suddenly, "why were you so eager to kill that man, then?"

"He is Cosby—the slayer of Colum O'More."

He knew that part of my story, and at once brightened. "*Mhuire!* If I knew! Surely you pricked him."

"He wears steel."

The friar was a good oarsman, but his wet clothes hindered him. Moreover, his cheeks above beard were strangely pale and his breath blew through his lips. So I slipped off my cloak, and placing my hands over his, stopped the sway of his body. We changed places. As I sidled by him in that swaying little craft I glanced at the maid, who was now sitting up in the bow. She had uttered no word yet, and now she did not even glance at me. Her eyes were across the water to the group on the shore, a frown of some perplexity was on her brow, and a soft dark curl, darker than the frown, was on her brow too. I had to dispose of my long scabbard by her side, and she quickly moved her dress aside out of the way.

I was not so deft with my oars as Father Senan, but I had strength and again my wind, and I lifted the boat through the water at a fine surge direct for the Connemara shore. The sooner we got there the better, though our pursuers had a twenty-mile circuit to reach us.

The old man made himself comfortable in the stern, eased his heart with two or three deep breaths, and bethought himself of his calling. He looked up at the sun-full sky. "Glory to God and His Blessed Mother, and all the Saints," he gave thanks, "that saved our lives this day!"

"And a saint or two with us for a small while yet," I added prudently.

He smiled at me, his eyes wet. "And a small meed of thanks to one David Gordon too." He pulled off his close-fitting morion, and rubbed his hand over his steaming tonsure.

And at last the maid behind me spoke. "Why!" she cried, in some surprise; "you are a priest, after all."

"And a poor sinner as well," he said. And added, "You need have no fear, my daughter."

"I am not afraid," she denied. "I never was afraid." She said it proudly—too proudly for my taste.

"She was afraid to stay behind," I said out of my throat.

"Oh!" That was a little gasp of surprise, and then

came silence. Never before had I silenced a woman so completely. And, now that I come to think of it, I never have since.

"You will forgive us, my daughter," said my wise old man at last. "We had to do it. We were flying for our lives from the English soldiery——"

"Why? Because you are a priest?"

"There was another reason too—and if anything it was a better reason."

"But how should I know?" she made complaint. "This ruffler brandishing a sword before a man defenceless—if he had said but a word!"

I made the boat leap. Here was feminine malice.

But my old friend had a salty tongue too. "He is a very hasty young man, this young man, surely," he said mildly. "A great pity the four of us did not sit down to it—and the day so fine."

"But there was no call for swashbuckling," she gave back spiritedly. "And, though you may be a priest, a wolf sometimes puts on sheep's clothing— with his brother, the red wolf."

My sorrow! but she was quick as an adder that day.

"Our acts belie us, my daughter," said the priest quietly, "and we hope to prove that to you. If you tell us where you live, we will row you as near as we may with safety—and be thanking you a thousand times."

After a pause she told him. "That gap opening between Inish—between these two islands. In there."

I turned to look where she pointed, and saw the mouth of an inlet open between rocky bluffs. It was still a long mile away and some distance to my left, and I set the boat's head for it.

"Cashlean-na-Kirka, the dun of the great Captain Dame Bevinda O'Flaherty, is somewhere in there?" half-queried the priest.

"I am her daughter Eithne," said the maid.

"At your service, my lady," he gave back, a trifle blankly.

II

All Gaeldom had heard of Queen's Captain Dame Bevinda O'Flaherty of Cashlean-na-Kirka. A widowed great lady, with one daughter and a mind of her own. Because of some private quarrel with the MacWilliams and the O'Kellys she had armed her stronghold with a culverin or two, garrisoned it with a standard of ferocious O'Flahertys, and held it against all comers. And then she made petition to Elizabeth, the English Queen, for permission to do these things she had already done. "Bevinda!" said that Queen, reading out the strange name and swearing a customary oath; "'Sdeath! but these wild Irishmen have outlandish names. Bevinda! Still, the man is well disposed, and in our grace we will make him a Captain." So the Dame got her Captain's commission, and was more than equal to it. And though men laughed, there was no ridicule in their mirth, for Captain Bevinda was as good as any man of her clan, and the men of her clan knew themselves to be a shade better than the best.

And here now was her dark-haired daughter, whose boat we had pirated, whose body we had abducted, who was powerful enough to more than double the mounting dangers of the road—and we were rowing directly into the jaws of the tigress. I slowed down my rate of rowing, and was not at all happy in my mind.

154

For, however I looked at it, I could not see this insulted daughter do anything kindly towards one man she had lately called a hulking red savage and another she had but now hinted a wolf in sheep's clothing.

And then a fine memory struck me. Had I not heard someone say the name of this maid before? . . . I had. . . . And I had it. Donal Ballagh, that last night at Dungiven, had spoken of a visit to Cashlean-na-Kirka, where he met his lady, and where lived her dark-haired friend named Eithne ni Flaherty—who could make my tough heart turn over. Dark-haired she was, indeed, and this day my heart had turned over once or twice—but not for her. . . .

There was some way out of this, now, if only I could think of it.

I looked at Father Senan. Here was the man with the cunning, wise tongue. Let him resolve this instead of David Gordon of the Scots hard head—and the sullen face to spoil his work. I chose my words carefully.

"This lady," said I, looking at him intently, "is a friend of her who was Amy Burc."

He stared at me in a complete amazement, his face vacant of all but surprise. Before the import of my words could reach him the maid behind me spoke quickly, anxiously.

"Amy Burc—my friend—who was?"

Then he got it. His eyes beamed on me. "My darling fellow!" he cried. "My sound man! The rope is not made would hang us, nor the tree planted to make a faggot for our burning." He smiled at the maid over my shoulder. "Your friend is well, my lady," he told her. "But she is no longer Amy Burc."

At once she knew what he meant. "Oh!" she cried,

155

high and happily, and I heard her hands clap together. "Has she got her gallant O'Cahan?"

"She has surely—her own Donal Ballagh." He looked at me gratefully. "This, my friend, is David Gordon, his own cousin; and, in religion, my name is Senan. I married the young pair yesterday in the woods north of Athenree, and they are off north for Dungiven. It is a great tale."

"How splendid!" Her voice was warm and glad. I drew a deep breath of relief. I could feel the new mood that came about us. She was so eager that she forgot for the time the hulking red savage. "Why," she cried, "I was with Amy that morning our plans failed us—and I was with her two nights ago at Bingham's feast. Tell me, father."

He cleared his throat like the story-teller he was, and a wicked humour made me laugh at him. I glanced at the eager maid over my shoulder, and she caught my red eyes.

"A brief tale," said I, "and easily told. Two hundred men of the O'Cahans, as well as a red savage and an old done friar, raided down from Dungiven, put the Dunkellin garrison to the sword, cut out Rickard the Sassenach's tongue, burned his dun, and made off north with his daughter, twenty maids, and six crocks of gold. That is all."

"Oh!" breathed the lady weakly.

"Oh, surely!" said I, very pleased with myself. "Red gold and red-haired maids, every one."

"Would you add a dark-haired one for contrast?" She came back on the recover, and got within my guard.

The priest laughed. "Never mind what he says, Lady Eithne. He is only retelling some of the wild rumours that are already gone abroad. This is the true tale."

III

And there and then, as I drew steadily on the oars, he told the tale, and he told it well. He began it at Dungiven with the message that came for Donal, and he finished it at Corrib shore; and, like all good story-tellers, he added an inch here and there to stress the risk and the daring. But foolishly, and for no reason at all, he would dwell on what he called my leadership in the ambush—and lie shamelessly at that, until I could stand it no longer.

"Bah!" said I. "What saw you—and you hiding in your bush?"

"Head under wing—ay?"

"And tumbling Dunkellin off his horse."

"Fright that was. He rode over me."

But the lady was eager to hear, and hear it all. She did—and some besides. But at the very end she surprised the story-teller. "Oh!" she cried, pain in her voice. "The pity that ye should spoil it all for me at the end." She brought her palms together. "Why the threatening sword and the—the terrible words? If I—if you told me——"

"My dear daughter," placated the priest hastily, "before we saw you we saw this Captain Cosby— and we thought we were only deeper in the net with his soldiers all round us. And forget not, Lady Eithne, that though sword was drawn, no blood was spilt, thanks to God."

"But it might. This—your friend—was eager for blood. He said so! That lunge was made to kill."

Father Senan looked at me, and I could not or would

157

not help him. That lunge was meant to kill, and she knew it.

This business of the brute Cosby seemed to touch her very closely. She would not leave it. She put another question to the priest.

"Who was this man—this Colum O'More that was killed?"

"Of Offaly—a noble friend to the north."

"In fair fight?"

He looked at me troubledly.

"He was my friend."

"But a soldier has to fight," she cried, almost plaintively, "and—sometimes—to slay. Captain Cosby is a soldier—hard, but a great fighter for his Queen— and my—my mother's friend. Why this ugliness of killing?"

If Cosby was her friend, or her mother's friend, I would say nothing. My silence was too much for her. As I glanced over my shoulder to get a line on the approaching inlet I saw that her head was down in thought. And when next I glanced round she was sitting aside and looking at the shore, now close ahead. The arm of the loch opened between its guarding islands, and I straightened bow for it.

"No," she said quietly. "Your left oar. We take the shore channel."

I did as she bid, and came inside the rocky tip of an island. The channel was not more than arrow-flight wide and shoal water.

"Close inshore," she directed me. "We can be seen here."

I looked back up a deep inlet, and a mile away on the other shore was a tall, strong, grey tower standing above the water on a bare promontory. Behind it rose a wooded hill, and above that a brown ridge gashed by a corrie.

I pulled strongly for the land, here heavily wooded to the water's edge, and skirted along on the fringe of the trees. The strong tower was now hidden behind a nose of land, and on our rounding that it still remained hidden by another farther on. Between the two points a bonny inlet was thrust in among the hills.

"In here," said the lady shortly.

The thought came to me that in here we were on the wrong side of the main inlet to make good our escape. But I said nothing, and did as I was bid. At the head of the water a strong stream came down brawling from the hills—and a prime trout-stream by the look of it. The lady's hand directed me, and we grated to shore just outside the outward drive of the current. At once I jerked in the oars, stepped over the side into a few inches of water, and lifted the bow to the gravelly edge of the beach. I stood within hand-reach of the maid, but she looked past me at Father Senan, and spoke quietly to him: "Ye will be safer for the present this side of the loch—if ye trust me."

"With our lives—and in your hands they are, my lady."

"The—the soldiers will be looking for you on the other side. Sometime to-night they will come to Cashlean-na-Kirka and—" She paused, and smiled at the priest.

"My daughter," he smiled back, "any small lie you might tell has my absolution beforehand."

"Listen, then. You see this stream—the Glosha. There is your road. Follow it up into the hills—four miles it might be, and not a hard road. Half-way up you will strike the pannier-track from Cashlean—at

159

Glounamaol—and, following that, you will come to the deer-warden's bothy in the Glen of the Echo. Tell old Garrodh that I sent you. He lives alone with his hounds—and you will be safe with him. No one goes that road, and the stags still in velvet. And note this: he has never forgiven my mother for being known as a loyalist. Food he will have—it might be venison, for sometimes, he says, a hart breaks a leg slipping on the Linen Apron—which is a lie, I think. In the morning, at the latest, more will be sent—and the way may be open for you. Now you must hurry—and I must hurry too."

"Oh, kind one of the heart!" The old man's voice was vibrant. "Lucky the day we met you!"

He scrambled stiffly over the thwart, and I gave him shoulder and arm to the gravel. There he turned, took the lady's hand, and bent his kindly lips to the softness of it. "God and Mary with you, O Queen of Connacht! and may your love be as gallant as a Prince."

"Or your chief," she said prettily.

"I have two," he said strongly; "and if he is as gallant as one or the other he will do."

She flushed a little, lifted to her feet, slipped neatly on to the thwart and over it, and reached hands for the oars. The priest stamped across the gravel to the grassy shore, and I grated the boat out into the water. There she deftly swung the little craft stern round, and looked at me evenly for the first time. Her oars were lifted out of the water, and she leant forward, the handles under her young breasts.

And I drove myself to do the right thing.

I strode into the water knee-deep and took off my feathered bonnet. Some impulse of flight came on her at that, for she quickly straightened and dipped oars. I laid a holding hand on the stern. "My lady," said I, "I ask your forgiveness. I am sorry that I hurt you."

"You did me no hurt, sir." She was as quick as that.

"No!" said I then. "It is for my own hurt I ask forgiveness."

She looked at me puzzledly, and then smiled suddenly. "As for forgiveness, Master Gordon," she said, "I forgave you long ago." Then she leant forward and spoke in a low voice that the priest might not hear. "Your old friend, I think, will not be fit for travel for a day or two. A priest, he will be safe with us, but there is no need for you to stay."

I glowered at her from under sullen brows. Would she, too, have me forsake this, my old hero?

"For him there is no danger," she replied to that glower, "but for you there must be."

"Can I go, then?" I asked simply.

And then a warmth came into her eyes and her face, and a small thrill into her voice. "You may," said she; "but you will not, though you die."

The oars ridged the water, the stern slipped from under my hand, and she left me there watching her. Her lithe young body showed every curve as she leant back to the oars, and a vagrant dark curl played across her brow.

CHAPTER XII

I

WE took near on two hours to reach the deer-warden's bothy in the Glen of the Echo above Glounamaol, and this though the road was no rugged one. The old father had been pressed too hard, and, though he hid his weariness under a gay humour and all his many halts were to admire the bonny trout-pools and fishing-runs so plentiful along the stream, he made no remonstrance when I gave him a hand over the steeper bits.

A lovely glen it was, too, lifting slowly into the heart of the massive hills and deepening as it ascended, with graceful birch trees on the braes and dark-leaved rime [1] trees by the water. But at that time we were in no mood to appreciate. We just plodded wearily along within the dominion of the enemy, trusting to the word and kindness of a maid that we had not used too kindly.

In an hour we lifted over a steep tilt and struck the pony-track. It came up from the right in a narrow twist of glen and went on ahead of us above the water. Where we joined it we sat down in the heather for a rest, and looked back over the road we had come.

There below us, framed in the little hills, was the wide expanse of Loch Corrib, scattered with its lovely islands, wimpling brightly under the sun, serene as

[1] Alder.

the sky above it. Beyond it was the immense wooded
spread of the Galway plain, purpling, hazing, dimming
to the far horizon. Over there, under those trees, we
had slunk and fled for our lives, and nearly lost them—
how long ago? It seemed very long ago. But it could
not have been so long, for the sun was still high;
and so I started wondering at the fallacy of time. The
old priest roused me to go on.

With the coming of the pony-track the country
changed. There were no more trees; the stream ran
clear and clean over limestone in the bare bottom of
the valley, and the heather grew close down to the
water; on every hand big brown hills, with round
bald heads, lifted in sweeping curves; and where the
glen narrowed in front a great purple mountain looked
down over the horizon from miles and miles away.
Glounamaol! The Bald Glen—the name was a
fitting one.

In another hour we lifted out of the narrowing gut
of Glounamaol and came out above a surprising
hollow in the hills—a bowl-shaped, sunny small valley
with the lovely green of grass in the bottom of it,
furze bushes, yellow-blossomed, along the stream, and
the faint sigh of falling waters in our ears. The green
was dotted with the black of highland cattle and the
pale brown of mountain sheep. At the far end the
Glosha water came down from the far hills over wide
limestone aprons, and the rushing sheen of it was like
bleached linen. The path swept evenly high up on
the curve of the bowl, and following it with our eyes,
we saw the squat hunting-bothy just below the lip
and to one side of the cascade. Whoever lived there
would have the sough of water ever in his ears, and
must dream of green seas roaring.

The deer-warden was soon apprised of our coming. The approaching path was in view of the bothy for its whole length, and we had not taken a hundred strides on it before the boom of a great dog's barking filled the bowl.

"Give me back my sparth," cried the old warrior, who knew how savage hounds could be.

But these hounds were well trained. They stayed close by the house they guarded, and presently ceased barking. A man appeared outside the door of the bothy, looked long at us from under his hand, and turned back into the house. He did not stay long inside. In less than half a minute he was back in front of the door, his two dogs at his side. And there he waited for us.

"He is for taking no chances, this old fellow named Garrodh," said Father Senan. "Look at him."

We were near enough to see that he had armed himself with a long-bow taller than himself, and that it was ready strung, and that though he leant on it easily his feet were set in the archer straddle. And when we came nearer we saw the feathered end of an arrow peeping from his oxter.

"Faith! you are welcome to the sparth," whispered the priest. "What am I? Only an old done friar." He slipped open the front of his tunic to show the colour of his order, and, as I carried his cloak and morion, his priestly calling was in evidence.

We came slowly up the last rise to the bothy, and out on the level patch in front of it, a spread of short crisp grass with a deer-flenching gallows standing up in the middle of it. At one side was a fine bank of bell-heather, and the wild bees' hum was added to the drowsy sough of the waters. The great dogs, one dun and one brindled, slipped forward before their master, crouched back on their haunches, and from deep down in them came a sound, not so much a growl, as a note struck on a bass string. We halted side by side, and the deer-warden leant on his bow over against us and was in no hurry to talk.

An old man he was, but straight and not lean: with great hunches of shoulders, a sandy beard, and eyes washed clean of blue, so light were they. And his great hand grasping the bow was like a ham in size and colour.

"God and Mary with you, O son!" saluted the priest.

"And Saint Patrick with ye—father!" he responded in a surprisingly high voice. But he made no move to welcome us. After all, not every man with a shaven pate might be trusted, and shaven pate's companion did not look other than a wolf.

"You will be Garrodh, the deer-warden?"

"Garrodh, son of Garrodh, descendant of Eochy, who died on the field of Athenree."

"Rest his soul! A bad day yon for Connacht!"

"And for Edward the Bruce." He glanced at my Scots bonnet.

I could feel the astute Gaelic twist of my old friend's mind as it wrought over the problem. He began again, and this time more frankly. "I am one Senan of Arachty, and this is David Gordon, cousin to O'Cahan of Dungiven."

Old Garrodh's cold eyes leapt to mine, and it was as if some memory warmed them. "David Gordon!" said he. "Is it not the strange thing?" Then he went on in a spate. "Young Donal Ballagh I know. He was in this place a week before Christmas and shot a yeld [1] hind—a strong shaft to his ear, with this. No seven-times-damned arquebus with him! Look you, now! The man that would stalk the red gentlemen of the hills with a roaring bull throwing a lead ball this way and that way, no more, maybe, than breaking a leg and frightening all the Joyces—that man is face-set for the roasting red flags of hell. There was a Cosby of Cong——"

"That man will be roasted, if he is not careful," put in Father Senan. "And roasted he will be as well if he is careful—the Lord forgive me for judging him."

"You know him."

"Twice this day he and his *Sassun deargs* loosed arquebus on us."

"Lucky for you it was not me had you at the end of a shaft."

"Is Garrodh, descendant of Eochy, on the side of the Sassenach?"

"He is not," he flared, "whatever side Bevinda O'Flaherty is on—God give her sense."

"So said your young mistress, Lady Eithne, when she saved our lives in her white and green boat. 'Go to Garrodh, the deer-warden,' she said. 'There you will be safe.'"

Garrodh threw the strung bow over his arm. "Could you not say that before, holy man?" he cried, striding forward and tendering the hand of welcome. "Here you will be safe, or nowhere safe. Come away in."

II

The bothy was much bigger and more comfortable than the common hunting-bothy. It was built roughly

[1] Barren.

of stone slabs, clinched with clay and thatched with long heather. An open porch faced the pony-track, and in there was the hounds' sleeping-place. And, strange enough in a hill-bothy, the two small windows were glazed in green glass. During the hunting-season the chieftainess and her guests used it for days at a time, and this accounted for its size and fittings.

As I entered the front door behind the old hunter I saw the back door over his shoulder, and, as I looked, it closed the last few inches slowly—just as if someone had pulled it to carefully behind him.

Garrodh treated us in princely fashion, and by that time we needed his generosity. There was no venison, but there was mountain mutton, with oaten cakes, butter that had been cheese-seasoned in a peat-hag, and milk lashed with usquebaugh. And, eating done, he built up the fire of bog-pine and peat, and soon the old priest, busy at his tale, sat in an armed-chair before the glow, clad only in Garrodh's woollen cloak, while his own clothes were steaming at one side. Though my horse-boots had been water-filled more than once that day I did not yet remove them, and I kept sword behind my hip out of sight. The memory of that closing door stayed with me.

In time, with an excusing word, I got up and went out the front door. The two hounds were in the porch, and the dun one came and smelled my long boots. I flicked a finger, and he lifted massive head to my palm. "Come, lad," I invited, and he followed a few paces, thought better of it, and walked back to his post.

I went across the green under the deer-gallows, and looked down into the cup of the little valley. The sun was setting, and the hollow down there seemed deep and far away, and a thin band of haze, faintly pearl, lay along the course of the stream. The only sound was the slow sough of the water down the limestone aprons, and in that strange light that sound was like a sigh for something beyond all kenning. The setting sun poured its light on the curve-over of the down-rushing stream and made it alive, but below that the spray was so deadly white that it seemed touched with blue. The bald heads of the hills were a sad orange, and a single cloud above them was redder than red fire. And no bird sang.

I stood there, full of a great loneliness, a dreichness, a devastating knowledge of my littleness—that terrible evil of knowledge that knows that whatever one does leads nowhere for ever and ever. "That being so," I thought, "let one do what is to do and be done with it." I was in that mood where a man, shorn of all illusions, faces all things calmly.

Quietly I walked round the cow-crodh [1] and found that the back door of the bothy led into a deep fold that curved back over the rim of the valley. I went along this fold until it led out into thick heather, and there before me was the true wilderness. A wide, savage, sterile glen sloped up and up into the face of a great hill that was darker than purple, and the whole floor of the glen was a jumble of immense grey boulders. There an army might lie hidden, and if anyone had come out the back door he was safe from all searching.

I stood for a time, knee-deep in the tussocks, looking up that savage and lonely valley, and was about to turn away, when a movement in the heather caught my eye. No breath of air had moved, yet, over there a

---

[1] Byre.

little way, a tuft swayed aside just as if a hand had moved it to make a peep-hole.

That mood of calmness still on me, I hesitated not at all. I walked slowly forward, not even placing hand on hilt. "Up!" I spoke softly. "There is no fear." And the heather shook and a man scrambled to his feet.

"Cathal O'Dwyer!" I cried then. "My own friend!"

"Brother!" Wistfully welcome was his smile. "You have the hillman's eye."

Cathal O'Dwyer of the Glens it was, but a Cathal woefully changed. His fine mop of flaxen hair was tousled and lustreless, his face worn thin, his saffron tunic loose on the broad bone of his shoulders. His right arm was bandaged across his breast and the end of a wooden splint showed on the back of his hand.

I strode forward and placed my hand gently on his shoulder. "A long way from home, Cathal friend," said I, "but glad am I to see you."

"Far and far," said he, his voice shaken; "but where else would I be? Cosby the Killer still lives."

"You are hurt?"

"His work. He wears a chain shirt next his skin. I had him at *sgian*-point and broke blade on him—not far from here. I escaped into the woods, but he did this with a French pistol. This is a known refuge, and Garrodh set the bone. But I think that I was not in my own mind for many days. I am better now—and better seeing you, David Gordon."

But, indeed, he was not well. His shoulder was shaking under my hand. I took his sound arm. "Come! The man with me is a priest, and leal to the bone."

169

As we walked down the fold I was perplexed and troubled. This man, given a fair chance, would slay Cosby—and Cosby deserved slaying. Yet the Lady Eithne—or her mother—thought highly of him. How highly? Ah well! It was none of my business till I found that out. . . .

CHAPTER XIII

I

I SLEPT well, and did not dream of running water or green seas roaring. Senan and I lodged in the ben-room of the bothy, while Garrodh and O'Dwyer made beds of heather and their cloaks in the kitchen. Once or twice in the night I thought I heard the old priest groan at my side, but when I waked in the morning he was sound asleep, and I slipped off the couch without disturbing him.

The sun was pouring in through the green glass of the window and calling me outside, so I picked up satchel, flung cloak on shoulder, and slipped through the kitchen, where the others still slept. The dogs in the porch greeted me with wag of tail, and this time the dun one followed me down into the valley.

It was a splendid morning of light, and the weather at last felt settled. No longer was there the gloom of dying day to weigh one down. The sun, above the curve of the moor, sparkled on the cascade, and the clear run of the stream chuckled between green banks, where a golden blossom was still on the furze. And above the happy sough of the falling waters came the happier singing of a lark, the keen note of the mountain linnet, and the bright chirping of a pair of goldfinches, aflit from whin to whin. A gay morning, and was I not the poor fool ever to be dog-ridden? I slipped off cloak and plunged into a curling pool below the falls, and the sting of the limestone water made me bellow;

and after a run on the grass, a chase after an indignant mountain sheep, and a gambol with the hound, I slapped myself warm, and made ravenously for breakfast.

Garrodh and Cathal were up and busy at the new-lit fire, and a fine fragrance came from where burn trout were curling on a home-made grid.

"Pity you have not any for yourselves," I said, looking over the old warden's shoulder.

"You will let us have the tails, anyway," he chuckled. "Our holy man is still at the sleeping."

I found him lying on his back, but not sleeping, and there was a twist on his face this fine morning.

"Slugabed!" and my hand reached for his shoulder.

"No, lad!" and he winced. "My old enemy is on me, and I knew it would." And, seeing the concern in my face, he added hastily, "It is nothing—only a stitch that plagues me whenever I get wet all over or go angling too early of a spring."

"Where is it?"

"Here—below the small of the back and across—like a knife if I move—worse it has been often. . . . What is to eat in the house?"

This was better. "Trout," said I. "You will not be fit for your share?"

"*Mhuire!* you Albannach rogue! Not more than two, and pink in the flesh."

If he could be so choice in his diet there could not be much the matter beyond this painful muscle-seizure across the loins. Painful it was beyond a doubt, for as we propped him on the couch he groaned heartily and cursed us warmly.

"Ah ha!" said Garrodh. "It grips you. Well I

172

know the twist, but in this house is the thing will burn it out of you in three days."

"Burn! You——"

"Protect us all! It is only the first run of the still, and warmer than new wool. Wait you and see."

We fed him sparingly out of prudence, and then turned him, protesting furiously, on his face while Garrodh rubbed into his loins a cloudy liquid with a pungent odour. The great fleshy hand moved with a surprising gentleness, and, whether it was the soothing or the liquid, our patient was much relieved of his pain.

Safely on his back, he stopped a groan and smiled at me. "That is better. But, son, it will be the best part of a week before I can march."

"There is no hurry on ye, surely," said Garrodh hospitably.

"I know, a friend. But in the heart of Connacht there is always danger for a man of Ulster, and Cosby the Killer I do not trust. Look, Davy! As a priest I am safe, since Captain Dame Bevinda is loyal to the Church, but a young lad in a feathered bonnet, with a mile of sword at hip, is in the mouth of danger. You are used to the open, and oh! the long legs of you! In four days now you could make O'Donnell's line. That is sense—is it not, Garrodh?"

"Sound sense enough," admitted Garrodh; "but he is welcome here."

I shook fist under my old man's nose. "I will stay," said I, "and drown you in the first peat-hole we come to, so that I can tell Dungiven what fate took you."

Father Senan caught my hand and squeezed it.

"O dangerous fist!" He stopped and listened. "Who is coming?"

The sound that had come to us was the clink of a horse's hoof close at hand. Followed immediately the deep bay of a hound. Garrodh peered through the window and laughed. "My dear lass, Lady Eithne! Look!"

I looked, and saw no one. "Where?"

"There—that far curve of the track."

And, following his pointing finger, I saw in the distance, close to where the path came out of Glouna-maol, a lady on pony-back.

Old Garrodh laughed again at my surprise. "But this is the Glen of the Echo," he explained. "A strange thing and uncanny—but it makes this house a safe place. A word whispered, a stone turned at that point there—and at no other—and the sound travels to this one spot like it was whispered in your ear. Sometimes it frightens me. Yesterday, the holy man here was looking for his sparth-axe when the hound barked—and I in for my long-bow."

For a long time I looked through the glass and wondered. A groan from the bed made me turn. The priest lifted on an elbow and fell backwards, hot-worded. "My life!" he cried tartly. "If I was not crippled or had one here with decent manners, this darling one, that succoured us, would be met and welcomed on the road."

"She knows the road herself," said I sourly, and marched out of the room.

Cathal O'Dwyer was at the back door. "I go to my hole in the heather," he told me through door chink. "It is not good to give anyone too many secrets to keep."

I looked long at my bonnet lying on a bench. After a time I took it up and smoothed out the black-cock's feather, and after a longer time, turned and walked, slow-footed, into the open.

II

Eithne O'Flaherty came riding slowly—very slowly—and I met her half-way. She drew the pony to a halt, and I came to a halt myself, a good pace short of its nose. "Well, Master David Gordon," she cried gaily, "are you feeling less bloodthirsty this morning?"

Her laughter rippled and made me smile. I might have told her that her own biting mood of the day before had vanished very completely, but I was careful not to do so. She was in a happy humour, and small the use to prick her memory.

"A good morning to you, Lady Eithne," I saluted, bonnet off.

"Bloodthirsty? No! And in no mood either to run away with twenty red-haired maidens?"

This was pricking me hard. "Red or dark," said I, "I would liefer run from."

"But, being brave and courteous, you haste to meet one. Is that it?"

"Your kind-heartedness deserved——"

She laughed, her hand stopping me. "Poor—poor! Kind-heartedness is a poor compliment when one is young—so I am told. Why not turn me a neat compliment about Maeve of Connacht or Deirdre of your Ulster?"

"But that one had red hair."

"To be sure—to be sure! Red-gold for the Gael always!"

I think that she was hurt, and from us she deserved no hurt. "Dark hair is very beautiful too," I said bravely.

"Thanks for your second best, Master Gordon. But why tarry here? You will need your breakfast?"

"I have just had it, my lady."

"I am sorry. I bring you some—and am without mine—only a little."

"Mine was little too," I lied handsomely.

"Let us to more, then."

The pony went by me and I laid a hand on his haunch, and, as I walked, my head was level with the maid's shoulder. There was a pannier-straddle across the beast's shoulders, and she sat on a saddle-pad behind it, one foot in a leather loop. She wore a white coif on her hair, but that vagrant curl had escaped to play in the morning air. Her neck in the opening of her close-fitting riding-tunic was finer and whiter than a lily, warmer than the heart of rose. Indeed but she was bonny, with a wholesome flavour to her like good wine. And her lips were aye ready for smiling.

We talked little. She asked how the old priest was, and when I told her, she spoke quickly. "Then you will be here for many days?"

"If we inconvenience you, Lady Eithne——"

"No, no!" she said, in some vexation. "Do not think that." And she was silent in some mood of her own until Garrodh came out to us at the deer-gallows.

She went in at once to Father Senan, and commiserated him and comforted, and impressed on him that he was safe in the Glen of the Echo, and need be in no hurry leaving it. And she would see that proper dainties were provided him.

"He is after a hearty breakfast," said I at that.

"A splendid fine breakfast, surely," he agreed courteously, his warm eye on me.

"We are going to have some now," I hit him. "In these panniers, Lady Eithne?"

"At that side are a brace of cold fowl and a pasty, and at the other, some flagons of Bordeaux wine."

The old man gazed at me with solemn and unforgiving eye.

"Pasty—and he in his bed—never! The wing of a chicken at sundown, maybe! And wine—the dry wine of Bordeaux in particular—is too heating——"

"If it does not gripe you," he exploded uncontrollably, "I fail in my office." He jerked on the couch, and yelped at the twinge.

"Be not minding the tyrant, Father Senan," she soothed him. "Your share I will see to."

She turned to me, a light in her eyes. "Why, Master David," she cried, "you are not so solemnly serious after all."

III

Eithne O'Flaherty did not stay long with us that morning. She gave Garrodh some directions as to our care, made note of a few needs, talked a while with the priest, and got up to go. Whereupon that man commanded me, like father teaching unmannerly son: "David, lad, you will see Lady Eithne to the corner."

So I placed the wine flagon well out of his reach, and did as I was bid.

"That old man loves you," she said, as we went.

"I do not think he hates anyone."

"But he loves you—and you him."

177

"Love?"

"Ah! perhaps you keep that for your lady?"

I threw up my head and laughed. "Ladies will spare me."

"And why!"

"Need you ask?" said I, looking at her under sullen brow.

She looked at me puzzledly, and then smiled. "Did you not meet any darling ones?"

"No."

"None at all?"

"None to know."

I could have told her that I had seen some beautiful women that were proud, and many beautiful ones that were pitiful. The proud ones never saw me, and the pitiful ones—but, indeed, of them I have no hard word to say, for I do think they were pitiful because they were kind. But I did not tell her all that, and she remained in a muse of her own till we came to the mouth of Glounamaol.

"To-morrow—or next day," she told me, halting the pony, "I will send or bring more food, though, judging by your second breakfast, your appetite is small for your inches. I know! It was kind of you to pretend, when I was so hungry. . . . I think that I am sorry for all I said yesterday."

"A brute—a ruffler—a hulking red savage!"

"Oh!" she cried in dismay, her hand to her mouth.

"I deserved them."

"No, no! It was but the temper of the O'Flaherty. But you know that if ever you anger me again I shall call you dreadful names." She touched the pony with her heel, and called back, "But I shall not mean one of them—and you called me a vixen."

I stood watching her, bonnet off, and her live young shoulders swayed lissomly to the quick amble. A pleasant and happy maid, and likeable. Bonny she was too, and her eyes—yes! I liked her eyes best. They were dark, but, unlike many dark eyes, they had depth, and they had a way of growing small and crinkling at the corners when she smiled. . . . I could see her smiling now. Impish she was, and given to teasing—and hot-headed, as I knew, but behind all was a balance that held against waywardness. . . . But what knew I of woman—this kind of woman? Sir William Cosby was her friend—her mother's friend, she said. . . . Could she not see the brute at the core of him? Ah well! she might make a man of him. None of my business. I was done with him except in the chances of war. But Cathal O'Dwyer was not. Well, that was none of my business either—and let Cosby look to himself.

IV

It was Senan that brought up the matter of the fishing. In the afternoon he saw through the green window-pane a cloud shadow slip across the moor, and inquired the wind's airt. "Man!" said he, "the fish would be taking—if there be fish."

Old Garrodh cocked his ears. It appeared that he, too, was victim of the cult, and had fashioned himself a couple of poles of spliced ash sapling. He even offered to share with me a tangle of barred worms he kept amongst damp moss in an earthen jar.

"What!" Senan shouted at me. "After all I taught you! That is only urchins' play after rain."

"It is so, then, by the hound Bran!" Garrodh's

voice lifted. "Let me tell you, holy man, that there is worm fishing and worm fishing."

"Trout slaying—not angling."

"I will prove you——"

"Prove it, then," cried the other, starting up, yelping with pain, and falling back.

"I will prove it. The Glosha, mark you, is no yellow-flood water—a week's rain only ambers it— and using the worm in water like that is fine art. See that little fellow twisting—even he is on the big side the day that is in it. Below your fish you must be, and your touch soft as canna down——"

"David Gordon, where is my satchel? . . . Look, now! I will tie you a cast. See this little one with the snipe wing, and this with the cock's body feather. That will be enough. . . . And now, if you will be keeping that flaming head of yours out of sight—and you picking your run—you will have the sport of the world, and this foolish old fellow, with his dirty worm, can take himself where this back of mine should be—and that is the innermost hot corner of hell— ouch!"

And so, to please him, I was compelled to spend the afternoon at the very hardest angling; crouching behind whin bushes, crawling on my knees, peeping between rush clumps, cunningly drifting my lures on the air and letting them suck round the eddies about the out-jutting stones. The water was hopelessly clear for comfortable fishing, but, by sheer hard stalking and marking, I caught six nice trout before I cursed myself for a fool and called enough.

Garrodh, who had shared the water with me in all honesty, had ten. "Never thought you could do it," said he. "Man! it was bonny fishing, I must admit.

Look you, now, we must pacify our holy man, so put these two to your string."

When we came in at the door Garrodh's voice was lifted high. "It was good fishing surely—and maybe I should not have given you the first run of the water."

"How many, David boy?" came the priest's mild voice from the ben.

"Eight," I lied.

"Eight! Fair enough! And Garrodh?"

"Eight also," I called.

"Did you count them? Bring them here." He examined our strings and recounted them. "Eight, yes! Och, but these are the lovely ones—see the girth there?"

"Mine are a bit bigger, would you say?" suggested Garrodh mildly.

"That could be, then—with the big ugly cannibal heads to them. Wait you till this grip eases on me—you wait and I will show you."

"Maybe you will, then," said Garrodh, pleasantly doubtful.

CHAPTER XIV

I

THAT morning I did not wait for Senan's bidding to be escort, nor did I breakfast beforehand. I went down to the burn, bathed, and shaved too, kept an eye on the path in case anyone came, and when the lady appeared, took the brae at an easy slant and met her farther than half-way.

'Well, David Gordon," she called, her eyes acrinkle. "Is your breakfast with you this fine morning? Ah! pity that I had mine."

"And a fresh trout for you, Lady Eithne."

"But I had breakfast very early, and—but oh! ravisher! the tale of your doings has come to Cashlean-na-Kirka."

"Mine?"

"Were you the only reiver of your three hundred— the number of ye has grown to that, and your maidens to two score, not all red-haired, a drove of kine, and two pannier-loads of gold. Which poor maid did you seize in that accustomed way, ribs acrush, and no word said?"

"She was named Eithne," I gave her bravely. "And more than I bargained for, so I dropped her."

"I deserved that." She lifted her young neck and laughed, and kept me looking at her. "Like an empty sack you dropped her in the bottom of the boat, and she said a word to herself that she has already got a penance for. But my question! Were you the man of Ulster who wore a blackcock's feather in a Scots bonnet?—like the devil's horns, they said!"

"There it is."

"And did you slash a man's head off backhand?"

"I did not."

"And did you kill the captain of Rickard's guard with blow of hilt?"

"Knocked him off his horse only."

"He was Langdon Coote, and a famous swordsman."

"Better than I—and unlucky."

"Your Sir Francis Vaughan knows who Blackcock's Feather is. You know I have met your gallant man of the English." She paused, and then explained with some care: "That is how I was across Corrib that day. Sir Francis was coming to see my mother, and I—and Captain Cosby—went to bring him the short-cut. Ye gave him a long ride to Cong. He spent last night with us, and I told him the true tale of the raid on Dunkellin. He would scarce believe that ye were only half a score."

"Fourteen."

"Near enough. Sir Francis is a gallant gentleman and your friend."

"A gallant enemy."

"He thinks highly of you too. He said that four times you had a man at your mercy, with danger around you, and did not strike to kill—and that once he was the man."

This was rating me too highly. "But, Lady Eithne," I tried to explain, "one was but a cut-and-thrust trooper, and Vaughan had only a small sword against a heavy blade of Ferrara."

"But Captain Cosby you would have killed," she

hit quickly, "though he had only a dagger. There was death in your eye and in your arm."

"We were in a net and desperate."

"You called him a terrible name. You must have quarrelled bitterly—and he killed your friend. In fight?"

I had nothing to say.

"You know," she tried again, "my mother thinks highly of Captain Cosby. He is a notable leader and a notable man in his own country, where he has large estates in the shire of Derby."

"He would be safer back there," said I.

"Is that a threat?"

"No. A warning."

She let that subject be, and we went on silently for a space. I caught her dark, thoughtful eye watching me sideways, and looked straight ahead at the linen apron of the fall. Why could she not be looking at that bonny rush of water too, and not at my hatchet glower?

When next she spoke the teasing imp was in her voice. "When I told Sir Francis Vaughan about your cousin Donal and his lady he was pleased, and vowed that he would take his soldiers back to Athenree, where he commands, and leave a free road . . . and he wondered how I got one David Gordon to talk so much that short while across Corrib!"

I laughed with her, but I did not say that I had small chance of talking in her company.

"And oh!" she said, her glance sidelong, "he warned me very seriously."

"He was brave," said I; "but it could be that you needed the warning."

"Do you think so?" she inquired demurely. "He

warned me that what one cousin did do, another might dare."

"No fear of that, Lady Eithne," I cried quickly.

"No fear at all, Master Gordon," she agreed, and touched pony with her heel.

II

The deer-warden met us on the green.

"Garrodh," said the lady, "I told my mother, who has eyes, that I was riding up to look over your ground to see if the wolves were amongst our young ones. A good excuse?"

"Surely, my heart! And no need to make a lie of it either. A grand day for the heather is in it."

"If Father Senan can be left alone for a small while." She looked at me, her eyes crinkling in that smile.

"Left alone he will be, anyway," said I.

So the three of us took the two hounds, and a pony loaded with our dinner, and set out. I came behind the maid through the fold in the valley. Cathal O'Dwyer lifted head out of his nest of heather and waved a friendly hand. My poor Cathal!

We skirted the desolate glen of stones and the mountain beyond it, and so came out among the slopes and stony peaks of Connemara. We circled many herds of fine hart and scattered hinds aloof with young, marked down the burrows of the mountain fox, looked for signs of the forest wolves, and climbed the great hill of Maam for the view: the tumbled Pins, stark and blue, the bulk of Muilrea, the far loom of Croagh Patrick, and the green Atlantic sea bare of all sail, washing the stony headlands of Inishmaan.

And in a valley turned to the sun we had our dinner

companionably together, and talked of deer-craft as practised here and in the Highlands. All those hours among the hills Eithne O'Flaherty was no more and no less than an eager youth. She was no longer the subtle woman playing the one game. She proved to me that, apart from her sex and her beauty, she had an appeal that might outlast youth and mere sex. Oh, but she was the splendid fine companion!

Sometime in the afternoon we turned the shoulder of a hill, and there, far below us, was Cashlean-na-Kirka on its promontory, and beyond it Corrib water sending its far arms into the dark of Galway woods. There on the hill-side we parted from our lady, with a promise that she would come to the Glen of the Echo as soon as she might, and we stood and watched her winding downwards on the deer-track till a fold in the ground hid her.

III

Garrodh, on the long circle homewards, was mighty particular to keep the stags to windward, and occasionally crawled to the crown of a ridge for closer scanning. "Good heads all," he muttered to himself, "and some better than good." On the third or fourth time that he went through this business he gave a grunt of satisfaction. "Look!" he pointed cautiously. "See that second-season hart with only one prong, and it crooked. An old Monarch gave him that last back-fall—the puppy!"

"Maybe," said I, "that fellow will break a leg at the drinking-place."

"Hero! You know the game. To tell truth, there is nothing in the house but salt pig, and our holy man might like a change from speckled trout—and dainties."

He proffered me his bow. "Would you be drawing shaft on that fellow—running?"

"I? At fifty paces, standing, I might notch him."

"You are welcome to miss."

"And we needing venison—no!"

We were lying on the edge of tall heather on the head of a slope, and below us ran a long strip of young herbage where the ground had been burned. At the far end of this a clump of hart browsed, heads facing away from us against the drift of air, and amongst them the fated One-prong. We slid back into the hollow, and, while I held Branog, the dun hound, Garrodh gave the brindled bitch her instructions. He said no word, but his hands were eloquent. The great animal trembled and whimpered softly, and, at a final signal, went off full stretch along the bottom of the hollow. Then Garrodh leisurely strung his bow, chose an arrow carefully, and we crept back to our vantage-point, Branog at our heels.

"Watch you, now," the hunter whispered.

Nothing happened for a long time, and then a single hart lifted a head and looked against the wind. Garrodh nudged me. Yet the stags went on browsing, but their heads were now turned to us, and gradually they began to drift nearer. They were in no hurry. They walked a few smooth strides, nibbled daintily amongst the young heather, and again moved forward.

"A wise bitch, Breacan," whispered Garrodh. "She is crawling back there, not showing an ear-tip."

The whole business was very simple and very sound, like all good work. The deer drifted along until they were level with us, and it might be forty paces out. Then Garrodh got to his feet, quietly—not hurriedly, and the stags threw up their startled heads, took one look, and away like the very wind. But before ever they took the first bound came a twang clear as a note of music, and One-prong pitched forward, scrambled to his feet, and fell again.

"Too far back in the belly," shouted Garrodh, starting forward.

The wounded beast rose and staggered, and then Branog was on him, and he was ours.

And we had fresh venison for supper.

CHAPTER XV

I

I DID not put off my breakfast this morning. Suddenly it came to me that my courtesies might be misread, and I had not courage enough to be thought a fool.

I had my morning plunge, and went straight back to the bothy, where I helped the one-handed Cathal with the platters and Garrodh at rubbing spirit into our sick man's loins. And, the work done, I strolled into the open with Branog, dropped into the valley, and strolled down the course of the stream. Indeed, I was not watching where my feet took me and was somewhat surprised to find myself on the pony-track at the top of the Bald Glen.

There I lay on my back in the cushion of heather, and, with half-shut eyes, stared up into the fragile morning sky. The lark's song came to me and the busy chirp of a stonechat, but these only touched the edges of my mind, for I was wondering to myself on the strange charm of our perilous safety in this fastness of the moors. It was like a valley out of a great dreaming. It was like a serene island in dangerous seas. We were bewitched in it and in content. In content! Ah! but the dangers that lurked without must be faced sometime. Sometime? Soon now . . .

There in an hour — or in two hours — Eithne O'Flaherty found me. The pony shied as I sat up, and she slipped to the ground on her two feet.

"I have no purse, highwayman," she cried. "You must take myself."

I was about to scramble to my feet, when she stopped me. "Stay," she commanded. "I will sit and rest." She let the pony move along the path, and came and sat on a heather-tussock below me.

And there I sat, and was surprised to find that she was beautiful, with lovely colour in her face, and her eyes deep and lightful. Bonny I knew she was, and bonny she had been in my mind's eye as I had lain there thinking, but, somehow, the mind's eye recalls colour and spirit but dimly, and there before me, now, in the flesh she was a lovely woman, with some tenderness of air about her that made my thick blood run warm.

"Sorry I wakened you," she said. "What were you dreaming?"

"A fool's paradise."

"And who was in it with you?"

"You were—for one."

"And were we happy?"

"I was."

"And it was a fool's paradise?"

"I was doomed to the outer wilderness."

"And I too?"

"No."

"I was left alone?"

"No."

"But I might be lonely."

"Why should you be?"

"Why, indeed? But one cannot help loneliness." She spoke in that low soft way she sometimes had, and then quickly shook her dark curls. "Ah! but let us not think too much of to-morrow," she cried.

"This is my day, and I am Queen over this my valley, and you are—what you are, I do not know. To-day is ours, and to-day I am in no hurry. My soldier mother is away to Galway with Sir Francis and Captain Cosby to council with Governor Bingham. So, instead of breakfast, you will give me dinner, and you will show me how trout may be caught with a bird's feather."

And all that day we had together.

II

We went fishing in the afternoon.

But we did not catch many fish—only two, and these at the beginning. Truth to tell, I am ever inclined to close my mind down on the business in hand and ignore all other things. When my lady saw me crawl behind a whin, and then a second whin, and waft my fly over a rising trout, and hook my fish and land him workmanlike, she was surprised and pleased, and applauded my skill. But when I merely glanced her way and did the same trick over again at the next run, she realised that her presence was of no importance to this business, and quietly took the proper steps.

When I saw with satisfaction a nice fish break water at the tail of a pool, and had worked my way into position, she came and lifted her head over my shoulder, and moved it about better to see what was doing. I did not rise the trout. Nor the next—nor any more. Patient I was, and patiently told her what not to do— and patiently she did it.

"Woman!" I boomed at last. "Are we here to catch trout?"

She chuckled happily. "Why, no! Now that I have seen you do it, it no longer interests me."

"Well, then?"

"I think that I would like to sit down here in the sound of running water and the linnet's singing and watch the kine grazing—and listen to you, and you talking."

So we sat in the grass at the stream edge, our feet on the gravel.

"Talk away, then, Queen of the Bald Glen," said I.

"But I want you to do that."

"About what?"

"Yourself, surely."

And I was silent as a stone.

"Well?" she demanded.

"Do you not hear me saying all there is to say?"

She turned her face to me, smiling out of her dark and deep eyes. "You are my subject in this my dominion, and I must know all of you before I reward you."

And she did get me to talk about myself. It was mostly a matter of question and answer, for there was not much that I would tell freely, and some things that could not be told, but I was as frank as I might be. Yet it could be that my meagreness gave her an impression that I had depths beyond her plumbing, and that would touch the woman in her.

"You are a loyal man, David," she said at last, "and you have been very lonely. You make friends very slowly. See! I count them on one hand."

She did that, and had a slender small finger to spare.

"Eithne O'Flaherty for that one," said I boldly.

She gave me a sudden quick look. "I am not sure," she said softly. "So I question you. And now that we are done with the past—your father, and your Mary Queen, and your loneliness—we will talk of the future."

"Yes."

"Your future."

"But it is hidden."

"You have thought about it?"

"My sorrow! High foolish dreaming!"

I turned over on my face at her side, propped chin on hands, and watched the clear water check and streak over bright gravel.

"Let me see," she speculated, "what qualities you have for that future. Loyalty—yes!" And then she teased me. "Are there others?"

"Plenty," said I. "I play a port out of tune, dance a spring unspringily, wrestle a man fairly, swing a *caman* [1] dangerously, point blade clumsily——"

"Soldierly arts these."

"The arts of a plain soldier."

She was wearing a light scarf of grass-green silk, and the soft summer air blew it softly across my face. I caught it in my fingers and held it under my chin, and that tie between us made me strangely talkative. "Wait, my Queen," said I. "Let me get this clear to myself and you—so that my reward shall not be too high—nor too low. A plain soldier! There is my career. Never to lead armies but in dreams. A standard of foot, a squadron of horse—it is in me to command so many, and be careful of man and horse. That is the art I am now learning, and this the land to teach me."

"But if the truce lasts?"

"It will break."

[1] Shinty stick. *Hurley*

193

"And will the north win?"

"The English are hard to beat."

"They have been beaten." The Gael spoke quickly in her.

"And will again, but besides being good men in war they have the arts of the Greeks, and will keep the clans divided. That much I have noted. But I see, too, that the English will never subdue the Gael as long as mothers bear sons. Yet in my view will the north be beaten—this time."

"And then?"

"Many of us—those who come out of it—will be forced to fly, and there is a colonel of pikes—now in Arras—who would welcome me with a tail of gallow-glasses."

"And then?"

"Then I die."

"Die?"

"So, my Sovereign for a day. I am, this bright hour, making that clear to myself. A leader of gallow-glasses cannot expect to draw old breath. This year—next year—it might be ten years—we die—a plain soldier's fate. We grasp it, and there is an end to all foolish thinking."

"But romance?"

"None for me."

"Yet you are young!"

"Young enough, surely." I turned head and smiled wonderingly at her under my brows. This lady was making me talk. And why not? It was a good thing to put clearly this thing called life before myself and before her. "Indeed I am young," said I, "and fine, fine dreams I hold inside my ugly head."

"Dreams only?"

"Dreams will be all. Dreams will be better."

"Dreams of what, David?"

I did not look at her. "Telling dreams spoils them. Look! there is a rise. Let us try for that one." I jumped to my feet, caught up my pole, and crouched along the bank.

"David Gordon," she cried hotly, "you are no friend of mine."

"I am," said I.

"You are not. What I will make you I do not know—I do not know—but you will not catch that trout."

I did not.

That evening I saw my Sovereign Queen to where the pony-track slanted off Glounamaol, and watched her to the first turn. Suddenly a thought struck me and I cried after her, "Queen, Queen, you forgot my reward." And she put her hand to her mouth and called back, "Already it is yours."

I did not know what she meant.

CHAPTER XVI

I

So . . . Ten days we stayed in the Glen of the Echo, and I know now that there was no need on us to stay longer than half that time. Whether it was the salving with raw spirit or his eagerness to be at the fishing, brave Senan was hobbling about on the third day, fishing on the fourth, and fishing every day after that; and he and Garrodh failed to convince the other as to the superior merit of lure or worm. In my opinion Garrodh was the more adept on his own water, but I did not say so.

After the fifth day my old friend had a shamefaced eye when I caught it, and, now and then, a side glance showed that he was aye watching me with a speculative look. And oh! but his back would keep troubling him. He used to scramble painfully up the brae of an evening, grumbling, "The fool I am! The old fool I am! To-morrow I will be on my back again." But to-morrow he was out with his fishing-pole, bright and early, and kept his grumbling for the evening.

Cathal O'Dwyer was in that small kingdom of the glen, but, indeed, he was not of our company. He, that was once the light of heart, lustrous of eye, was but a ghost, a shadow. He was quiet and gentle, no trouble in the world, so little needing or demanding notice that he did not smit us with his own woe of the spirit. When our lady was not in the glen he liked, somehow, to be near me. It could be that my natural quietness was in tune with him, or that his bodily weakness drew on my bodily strength. We used sit in the heather long and long, looking up the desolate glen of Carrigdhu, or stand in a daze watching the white water down the linen apron, and I cannot mind one word we said to each other in those hours.

Ten days! And nine of them the finest days that fine summer. The nine finest days in all my life—up to that time. And our lady came to see us every day. And every day I met her on the way and went part of the way homewards with her, a little farther every day, until soon I did not leave her till the turn of Glounamaol. Beyond that she would not let me go, for safety's sake.

We used to go back into the moors together, we fished—a little—together, we sat and talked endlessly. Friends and comrades we became. Quite frankly now she called me David, and sometimes, when I was eager to show her something—late nestlings full fledged, moor-fowl head-peeping, a fine head on a hart—I whispered Eithne—and hoped she did not notice. God His Glory! she was a lovely one and unspoiled, gay and pleasantly wayward, in love with the open and with life, full of vigour and clean health, and with a mind—as well as a body—to thank God for.

Old Garrodh, I think, could say his prayers to her —his heart, his light, his brightness of the world. O'Dwyer used watch her dumbly out of his own subdued and ghostly world; the good priest wondered how such a one could be born on top of rude earth, and how, being born, grew in sweetness yet became noble, and being so noble could be so full of charity to hunted men. Not one word did he say to me to show that he looked on us as man and maid together. A wise old man and fine of mind.

And so came the ninth day and the end of this our kingdom.

That day Eithne did not come in the morning, and I was weary listening for the warning from Echo-point. Nor did she come at noon or in the afternoon. But when the sun was already reddening she came hurrying. We heard her at Echo-point, and Garrodh, looking through the window, stopped me with his great hand as I moved to the door.

"Look, a friend! She is taking it out of the garran. There is hurry behind her—and maybe hurry on us too."

He and Senan gathered our few chattels into a bundle, so that, if necessary, we could retreat into Carrigdhu and leave no sign. But there was no need. When she reached the edge of the green there was no one on the track behind her; and I met her outside the door. There was some ebb of colour from her face and her eyes had a dark glow, but gay and gallant were her head and her voice.

"My reign, alas! is coming to an end," she cried; "and this my kingdom perishes. A lost glen—a stony valley—water singing to itself alone."

Like fine singing that was, and my throat filled.

"Where is my holy man?" she asked then.

"Here, my Queen," said he, coming out of the door.

"Are you fit for the road, Father?"

"Any road—or the one to the World's End."

"To-morrow night must it be, then." She spoke

quickly. "My mother talks of coming to see Garrodh, and I think that she has a suspicion. I have been careless, I fear, and she knows that I am in this glen every day. That she would know, for nothing can be hidden in her own house. Someone followed me yesterday, and what was seen I do not know. But do not fear. She is frank, and noble too, and will do nothing by stealth. To-morrow—to-night, if she questions me there is nothing I can or would hide, but you must be ready. She takes the raid on Rickard the Sassenach lightly, and says he deserved what befell him—that he is not worthy of alliance with O'Cahan blood. Listen, now. David, you will meet me to-morrow—an hour after dawn—at the mouth of the Glosha. I will row the boat across, and we will hide it under the bushes. Then at the first dark of the evening you will go down, and Garrodh—are you there, Garrodh? You will row then to the north side —to the spring of Tubberglass. You know it?"

"Well I know it, my heart."

"There and nowhere else. Now I will have to hurry. I could not get away till my mother was at the milking bawn, and I fear she will miss me. No, David, you must not come. I will ride hard all the way."

I lifted her on the pony at the edge of the green, and she grasped my hand in a hand that was strangely cold. "In the morning at the Glosha," she whispered, and was gone.

I stood watching till she was round the curve into Glounamaol, and then I went and looked down into our happy valley. But it was now deep and far away in the light of the gloaming, with a wan mist along the stream, and it was lonely, lonely. And I looked at the rush of the linen apron, and it was deadly white and deadly lonely. And I looked at the moors rolling under their orange glory, and they were lonelier still.

III

The larks were up as I went down the track in the morning, up in the sunlight above the crown of the moors, though where I walked was still in shadow; and when I got amongst the trees in the lower glen the thrushes were singing. A pleasant morning, but I was in poor tune with it. I was facing out into the world again, and taking with me an experience that had stirred the roots of my life. Evermore now would I see things from a new angle; evermore now would my best days be touched greyly, my spirit a little more lonely, life a little bleaker. But I would be more a man too, and understand men better. And one had to go on living.

When I got in sight of Glosha mouth I saw the white and green boat resting its nose near a thick clump of water-willow. Eithne I did not see, but she would not be far away. In a short while now I would be saying "a blessing-with-you," and I must harden dour face and keep watch on slow tongue.

I hurried on to the boat. The oars lay across the gunwale and still dripped water. I turned and scanned the slope of grass and the few bushes along the shore, but my lady remained hidden. Then I whistled softly, and at that the water-willow rustled and a cloaked woman came round the side of it. But she was not Eithne O'Flaherty!

A tall woman with a hunting-cap, eagle-plumed. on her dark hair, the long Irish cloak on her shoulders,

200

and a hazel staff in her hand. There was no mistaking who that woman was. There could be only one woman with a face like this face in these parts; a harsh and weathered face, but the face of a great lady. That long nose and long chin proved the obstinate breed of her, and the dark eyes, deepset under level brows, showed fire kept in place by strength. This surely was the Captain Dame Bevinda O'Flaherty.

And I was neatly in her trap.

She walked across the grass and halted before me on the edge of the gravel. Her lower lip, not thin but finely chiselled, was pressed firmly against the upper; and she slowly looked me up and down.

"Shelterer behind a maiden's skirts!" she said, in a slow musing voice. There was no cut in that strong voice, yet I felt a cut. "You are one David Gordon—the man they call Blackcock's Feather?"

I took off bonnet and bowed.

"Cousin of O'Cahan?"

And again I bowed.

She took her time, and I waited. Her eyes were on my face, and it was not a face to win me grace. I was entirely at her mercy here on the shore of Corrib. My old priest, indeed, was safe in the Glen of the Echo. We were neatly parted, and, no doubt, her fighting-men guarded the pass—and a score of them hiding in these bushes. I could face back there and die on the road, or I could die fighting here—or I could make essay to seize this white and green boat and die on the water, boats all round me.

"Go on, sir," she said, reading my thoughts uncannily. "I am only a woman."

"Play on, Bevinda of the O'Flaherty," I said then.

"Play, sir?"

"Surely. You can kill or let me go in your own time."

"Kill you! Why?" There was the bite.

But I was minded to bite too. "I expect no mercy from the Sassenach."

"Sassenach!" Out came the blood of her. "I am Captain Bevinda O'Flaherty, and I make allies where I choose." She calmed herself with firmness. "You were with O'Cahan? Who is with you here? Oh! I know your story. A priest? He has been ill?"

"And is well now."

"Why did you stay in danger?"

I could not tell her. I could not tell myself.

"Did you think to copy your cousin?" Cuttingly smooth the question.

"You do not know your own daughter, Dame O'Flaherty," was all I said.

"No? But I know a romantic little fool," she cried smartly, and was again calm, her eyes intent on mine. "Your attention, Master Gordon. I will let you go from here in safety if you make me one promise—on you honour, which I will grant, as an O'Cahan."

"And a Gordon."

"So! Promise that you will not seek to see my daughter again."

I had that much in me to answer on her last word. "I will not promise," said I.

"It would be a promise easy to keep," she urged calmly. "You are little likely to see her again. She is betrothed to Sir William Cosby, and she is crossing the Irish Sea at Advent—when she marries him. Well?"

"I will not promise," I repeated dourly.

She looked at me long and steadily, and then she smiled, and I knew whose mother she was. "No," she said half-musingly, "it is not a promise that Blackcock's Feather would make—nor any man. I will not press it. The O'Flahertys can take care of their own, and bite hard in doing it."

I waited for her final word, steeling myself not to glance at the bushes on the shore.

"Listen, now, David Gordon," she said. "I do not harry hunted men. This boat will be here for you and the priest at the fall of night. Garrodh, the false one, will row you to a place of safety; and tell you your old friar to keep wide of Cong, and cross Moytura waste in the dark. That is all."

She turned from me, and walked directly to the little boat. And I came behind and held the bow. Her hand rested on my shoulder for a moment as she stepped over the gunwale. "You are a foolish man," she said, "but you are strong."

"And ugly."

"No—not ugly—obstinate. That is why I am not afraid of you. Men like you do not know how much to dare."

She reached me her hand, and I bent over it.

"O great Lady!"

"I am sorry," she murmured. But for what I did not know at all.

I stood there watching her handle the boat surely as a man, and, though there was a strange want at my heart, there was in it, too, a pride that the hunted David Gordon had found a woman noble.

IV

In the gloaming we crossed to the north side of Corrib, and left Cathal O'Dwyer behind and lonely in the Glen of the Echo. His wasted face was set to hide the grief of parting, and his grey eye avoided mine. Before we left I took him aside and placed hand across shoulder, a habit of mine. "Come with us, brother," I reasoned with him. "There will be work for you in the north, and it may lead this road. Come!"

"Where Cosby is, there I stay," he said, gloomily firm.

"Must you kill the man?"

"Need you ask?"

"I need. Look! The lady that saved our lives—do you know that she is plighted——"

"By her mother?"

"I know not."

"Her mother, surely." He looked at me closely. "I will kill him, David Gordon."

"Or he you."

"My luck." He caught my arm in a firm grip. "And then?"

To that I said nothing, but I knew in the marrow of my bones that if Cosby slew this man I would slay Cosby.

Very quietly we slipped through the quiet water that gleamed palely to the darkness of the shore, and no word broke the soft lapping ripple at the bow of the little boat. We felt subdued, pressed under by the weight of these outer skies. We were like foreign men coming out of a known and homely land into a strange place in which strange things lurked.

In the half-dark of the summer night Garrodh, rowing softly, brought us to shore amongst a jumble of rocks, where a spring ran down over green mosses and tinkled murmuringly as it fell. There was deep water close in, and I was able to land on a flat boulder, while the old friar, sighing to himself, stumbled against the gunwale, and handed me out our well-stored satchels. Then I helped him ashore, and we buckled ourselves for the road. Garrodh was leaning at the bow, holding the rock, and there the priest gave him his final blessing, and I bent down and took his great hand silently.

"Ye will go in safety," he whispered. "In my bones I feel it—and I know too that you will come this way again and you not hiding."

His words heartened me. I straightened up and turned away, and goose-flesh shivered over me. For a hooded woman was there before us, and she had made no sound. Eithne O'Flaherty! Well I knew her, though her face was only a pale oval in the half-light.

"Come!" she whispered to us, and leant towards the boat.

"Garrodh, wait for me." She caught the priest's sleeve. "There is need to hurry now."

She led the way on a path amongst the rocks, and we kept close behind. Beyond was a bare patch, and then a copse of hazel with the beginning of a track winding up a brae towards the open. And bridle-tethered to the hazel branches were two horses.

"You know them?" she whispered.

One was the priest's thick garran. The other was my own bonny mare, Benmee. She knew me before I spoke. As I untied the reins she snorted softly into my face and nuzzled my breast with her small shapely head.

"Lassie—lassichie!" I greeted her. "You the darling!" And rubbed between her ears.

Eithne laughed lowly. "Oh, but you can make love too, David," she said. "Your gallant enemy, Sir Francis, brought her to Cashlean—our spoil he said; but it might be that he guessed ye were not far away. . . . But you must go now. My mother is waiting for me at the next point, and I promised—I promised not to be long."

"She is a noble lady," said the priest, and taking her two hands, he bent over them and drew her close to whisper: "We three will meet again, my dear one. This is not the end." He turned to his horse, with my knee for stirrup heaved himself to his saddle, and moved away round the hazels.

Eithne and I were alone in the gloaming. She was gallant and kind to the end. "Good-bye, comrade," she said, a throb in her voice, and reached me her hand.

I took it and held it, a firm, dry, small hand. I chose my words slowly. "You Queen, I subject— that always. Your need is mine—alive or dead."

"Will you know my need?"

"I will, by the goodness of God."

"For that I will pray then," she said.

I looked into her face. It was a delicate white oval in the black frame of her cloak, and her eyes were black pools—and her hand trembled in mine. "But I will be very lonely," she whispered.

I did not even kiss her hand. I but held it in my two for a moment, let it go gently, turned and sprang on Benmee, and went driving head-down through the hazels. I never looked back.

CHAPTER XVII

I

BEFORE I finish this, the first part of my narrative, I am impelled to say something of our homecoming to Dungiven. It was the first homecoming in all my life, the first time I realised that here was a home where I would be welcome for myself alone. Surely it was that knowledge that finally brought me into the fine fellowship of men.

It was on a still, sleepy, slumbrous afternoon that Senan and I rode up the glen to the brink of the ford below Dungiven. Our enduring small horses were spent and thin, and we draggled and weary. We had taken the full week on the hidden twisted road from Corrib, and most of the days and all of the nights had rained on us—a warm rain, but a wetting one. That was the only discomfort that befell us. Our boots and cloaks were miréd, our faces stubble-bearded, our eyes weary for undisturbed rest. My blackcock's tail was the only jaunty thing about us. And here at last was the haven of Dungiven; and Dungiven, that grey old dun, seemed a castle of the dead. No one moved about it, no one moved in the township on its flank. It lay there, slumbering and aloof in the haze of heat, and had no welcome for us. Not even a bird sang—and one bee went humming by sleepily. Our hearts went heavy in our breasts, and a great heaviness and lonesomeness came down on top of us.

"All of them," spoke up Senan bravely, "men,

women, and children, will be down the strath hay-making, and the garrison having a sleep to itself—same as Ferdoragh above."

Ferdoragh, guard of the gate, sat on his stone by the dark of the arch, his head down on his breast and his lean shanks spread abroad. He did not hear our horses splash knee-deep across the ford, he did not hear the hooves on the causeway; our shadows were on him before he lifted his head, stumbled hastily to his feet, and blinked rapidly. His mouth opened and shut with a click. "Great God!" he swore. "Is it ye?"

"It is," said the priest bitterly. "And why would not I be cutting your goat's head off with the sparth?"

"Holy Mother of God!" cried Ferdoragh, his eyes alight. "Is it not grand to hear you, and ye back to us again!"

"Are we the last?"

"And the long last. Ye are all home now. A house of the dead this was, instead of a wedding-house—and the chief going about cursing a holy friar—and his lovely one at the weeping. Go on in, now, my darling fellows! Go on in, now, and 'tis I will let them know the great day is in it."

We rode under the gloom of the arch, and he yelled after us, "Horo! the wedding-feast, and it lasting till Lady's Day."

And as we rode out into sunlight of the wide court-yard the great bell in the tower began to boom. Ferdoragh was leaping on the rope, and the brazen clang roared and roared.

That bell was only rung for a great feasting or a deadly alarm, and so it now waked the dun with a hum and a clamour. Out from the big living-house, from the penthouses, from shady corners men came tumbling, half-naked and barefooted, grasping sparth or sword or spear—anything that had blow in it. And then they saw us, and the stark note of fierce alarm paused and broke queerly, and changed into the high and terrible note of the slogan. That high peal with the note of triumph in it made my hair stand up. And the thudding boom of the bell was inside my head.

And all at once they came down on us in one mad rush, mouths open and arms tossing. Our horses reared in panic, and I was in a panic too and stared round me for a refuge. Between a notch of the parapets above I saw Donal Ballagh's head turned down on us, and a red crown, shining in the sun, was at his shoulder. I swung Benmee for the door of the tower, but next instant I was lifted bodily out of the saddle and whirled here and there about the bailey. Great hands clapped me, strong arms clasped me, voices roared and laughed all around me. I saw old Turlough Mac an Teaclan with the tears running down on his white beard. Calvagh MacManus shouted in my ear: "To-morrow we were out at the searching—I needed you." Tadg Ironhand, his mouth red in his black beard, roared heartily: "Now will my little one be happy."

Presently the press about us was shorn through impetuously and Donal Ballagh had an arm round each of us. His eyes were flaming in a white face, and he kept repeating, as if to himself, "Well—well—well!" Until, suddenly, he shouted, "Laggards! Laggards! Ye will pay for the fright on us."

My ribs bent under the crush of his grip, and I threw an arm across his shoulder. He was my own blood-cousin and we liked each other. I felt a tightness in my throat and my eyes stung.

The bell had stopped booming now and quiet came suddenly; I could feel the feet shuffling in the dust. The men made room about the three of us, and the lovely young wife, Amy, came through. Her blue eyes were swimming in tears and her mouth was quivering as she smiled on us. She caught the old priest's hands and kissed them, and faced me, a quick shyness in her look.

"There she is for you," said Donal, shoving me forward. "Will you salute her?"

I tugged off my bonnet, bent knee, and lifted her fingers to my lips. And as I straightened up she placed her hands softly on my shoulders and kissed me on the rough cheek. "You are welcome home, cousin," she whispered. "We were so unhappy."

My face flamed to her flush, and I could scarcely let her hand go. That was the finest of our welcome. But the welcoming was not yet over.

Donal was again holding us, and swung us towards the door of the keep. "There are a couple of words to be said," he threatened. "Come this way!"

At that old Turlough lifted his great voice. "Justice!" he bawled. "The clan will have justice."

Donal turned to him. "Who withholds it, bellower?"

"I warn you, Donal Ballagh O'Cahan. There might be good telling in this, and the first of it is the clan's due. Ah! look at my old rogue and the gleam in his eye."

"There is a tale, surely," said the priest, clearing throat in anticipation, "and if we had a bite and a sup . . ."

Behold us, then, sitting at the long table in the mid-house and a mood of high feasting all round us. I sat between Donal and his queen, with Senan at her other side, and the board was weighty before us and all down its length. Those who could not reach the table ate and drank standing, and all the time the turmoil grew. For the boom of the bell had roused to hurry all who had heard it. Men—old and young —working in the fields, had grasped any weapon to hand and come in at the full stretch on pony or on foot; in couples and threes they streamed in, and, as they arrived, Ferdoragh shouted the news, and fresh cheers broke forth and a fresh press of welcome came about us.

There was a lump in my throat and the meat choked me, but I took two deep gulps of Garonne wine, and that steadied me. Now I knew I was one of the clan, and that the coming home of Senan and me had put the great finish to a great adventure. In truth our raid into Connacht was a notable affair and a marvel in all the north and west. Men would tell in wonder how O'Cahan and his cousin, with ten men, bearded one of the great Sassenach barons at his own door, broke his guard, stole his daughter, and twisted home through fifty leagues of raised country without losing a man.

All the fine lads who had been on that great ride made their own adventures and ours warp and woof of the one saga, and they stood about us now, drinking great methers and talking and retalking of the exploits that were done, so that jumbled scraps of shouted words deafened me: "Hit the stallion on the nose and down the both went—NO! not that way—backhand, same as you would flick a thistle—was I not behind, and a spatter blinded my eye?—sword in two halves—like a thistle-head, I tell you, and I kick it across the road—choking him he was till the chief stopped him—like a hare, and my spear held under his oxter—and two notches I made in it that same night—in his cloak—and I heard the jawbone crack—and the girths broke, and he over the horse's tail—in a hop, step, and a jump, and they took the dun in the jump without seeing it—was I not behind him and the blood in my eye?"

Father Senan, done with eating, took a long draught of ale and cleared his throat loudly. At that signal silence settled down slowly, and here and there a man clapped hand over neighbour's open mouth. Feet shuffled, benches grated on the floor, and the clan settled itself to hear great story-telling. For the priest was indeed a great story-teller: though Turlough, with professional jealousy, would ever insist that he had a bad habit of certain ironic exaggeration. Not that Turlough himself was free from that fault, but his exaggerations were in the artistic grand manner. Now as I looked aside at the old bard I saw jealousy as well as interest in his eye; but as the tale unfolded the jealousy was ousted by the craftsman's admiration for craftsmanship. He held his hand-harp on his knee, and every now and then he would pluck a little run of notes and lean down to listen, and, every time, a tingle of coldness ran down my spine. To-morrow or next day this Turlough would sing us a great lay and put our deeds in the memory of men as long as harping lasted.

"I am home now," began Senan artfully, "and I am glad of it, and though I set out on the sly and easy road, thinking to have the grand times to myself on the flank of danger, I blundered into the bottom of the net, pulled the meshes all round me, and gave David Gordon the task of hauling me out again. Oh ho! canny I was and cunning I was, and boasting to myself how I would head away from pursuit to Corrib side, skirt Moytura waste, make friends among the O'Kellys and O'Connors, and get to O'Donnell's border in easy and full-fed stages—bringing this poor young Albannach behind me and him praising me, head and belly. Ay! And all the time he saying to himself: 'You old bag of bones! Home I will bring you in spite of yourself, the devil, and all the *Sassun deargs* of Connacht!' And that he did, and every bone in the bag knows it. For look you, my children, sometimes he treated me like a bag of malt, and sometimes like a sea-pig in the water, and once or twice like a Christian man . . ."

And so he set out to mould the mood of his listeners and deftly put contrast over against contrast. Thus he got the room tense with our alarm at Bellaghy, and brought the English horse to the very brink of the village as we galloped out at the other end, and then he had them roaring at the pother I made about losing my fine linder.

When we did encounter the Sassenach we encountered them astoundingly in numbers and ferocity. Thundering down on us they were, with one man and two men and three men guarding every gap—and the man that faced us was like Finn or Cuchulain: a mighty warrior, wide as a door, on a gigantic horse, his head under his helmet like a black pot and his sword above the tree-tops. Poor Tom Pybus! And there was David Gordon, the little fellow, his black-cock's feather slanting in the wind and his legs twisted round his kittle mare's belly, and his sword like a wisp. And the big fellow fell to shake the mountains. . . . We were through, we were safe—and the Sassenach—all the garrison of Connacht—trailing after us.

He brought us to the torrent suddenly and had his listeners agape with the depth and rush of it; and forever the enemy coming down on us from the hill. And there was that small jut of rock out of the foam at the grim last moment, and I in the air like a stag, and himself sousing and being emptied ignominiously, and dragged and pushed and buffeted to safety up a brae that was a cliff, while the lead dunted the black stones.

He had us safe over the top at long last, and the gentle woman at my side sighed with relief. Ah! but it was then we were in the trap worse than ever, and no atom of hope for us in all the world. He made that sure. There were the three miles of Corrib on one hand and a mile-wide arm of it on the other, and we there in the bight with the Sassenach crossing the torrent behind us.

"Thunder of God!" swore Donal, feeling my arm. "But ye got out of it? Ye are here with us."

"We got out of it," said Senan quietly, "thanks to God and a lady — young and lovely as sloe blossom."

Amy turned her face to me, but, very carefully, I was not looking at her.

"Now we are at the heart of it," cried Donal.

"And who the lady?" queried his wife.

And he told her.

"Eithne!" she cried, and grasped my arm. "My dear one!"

"And a long brute with her."

"Cosby of Cong?"

"The same."

"Did you kill him, David?" Donal leant across to me.

"He did not," said the priest. "A shirt of mail saved him, but the dunt of the point flattened him on the edge of the water. But myself was cunning, for while this fellow was making himself polite I up and stole the boat."

"The boat?" The whole company seemed to shout the word.

"Surely. A darling small boat painted white and green, and two oars in it. There we were meshed, and there was the boat, and there was the finger of God pointing. What else could I do but steal her?"

And he went on with his tale. When he described how I seized Eithne and dropped her in the bow like a pigling into a pannier for Derry Columcill Fair the lady clapped her hands. "That was how to take the little rogue! Go on, father!"

"That was the end of our troubles, my lady," he said. "Nothing could befall us after that." And no longer the fervid story-teller, he went quietly to the end, giving credit where credit was due, but never stressing the companionship between Eithne and me. A wise and thoughtful old hero.

At only one point did he warm again: when he came to the fishing with Garrodh. "A good man, Garrodh," he admitted, "and a true man, but about angling he holds notions I would give him penance for. His branded worm!—I showed him, did I not, David?"

"You did not," said I.

"What? And the trout I nourished you with!"

"I never want to see a trout again as long as I live," I told the whole table.

All the time the tale stayed in the Glen of the Echo I felt the lady's eye on me, and now and then her hand was laid gently on my arm. I drank draughts of red wine, kept my eyes on the table, and schooled my face to steadiness. But well I knew that this fine woman was already busy at surmises and conclusions, and that in the days to come I would have to bear with questionings framed to hide questions. Ah well! this was no longer a bachelor house, and we would have to pay for our chief's happiness.

PART II: ATHENREE

CHAPTER I

I

DONAL BALLAGH O'CAHAN, Amy his wife, and myself
leant on the ramparts of Dungiven and looked idly
up the Glen of the Roe. The valley was a routh of
greens and browns, and the thin, hot haze of autumn
lay like a veil on the quiet face of it. The croon of
the river came to us sleepily up the causeway; the
warm air lulled us, heather-scented from the south;
peace lay on the broad of the world; and there was
no choice for a man but to be either happy or melan-
cholic.

Donal and his lovely red-haired wife leant close
together, and I fear that I was the melancholy one.
They were so happy—and I—well, I had small reason
to be otherwise, but the hazed sunlight, the croon of
the Roe, the stillness and the peace put their strange
wistfulness on me and set my thoughts on far roads.
I fear that I sighed. And Donal straightened up and
heartlessly laughed at me. "Surely," said he. "Connacht, and it far away!"

Amy looked across at me, and her woman's eyes
were gentle. "He is finding Dungiven lonely, I think,"
she said. "We are not the best of hosts, husband."

"Ye are not," I growled, "but ye are the best I can
get."

It was a month since my return to the dun, and in
that time this lady had squeezed me dry in her own
gentle way, so that I was scarcely aware of it and thus

217

did not resent it. Besides being a handsome wife this red-haired lady was a wise one. She made no high-handed essay to change the habits of the dun, but she set out to make a pleasant domain of her own that would woo man and maid to it. The great bailey, with its penthouses and mid-house, she left alone for the present. These were the men's quarters, and the men were grateful for not being disturbed. But at the west side of the dun, where there was a postern, she was already planning a terraced garden, and even now the masons were building the outer wall to it. "If this war comes," she said, "it will keep the old men and myself busy, and ye will see green lawns and flowers and a lily pool where that packed clay is —and ye will learn to tread gently and doff bonnet and practise fine manners. And, David, do you know who will visit me there?"

"I do not," I lied.

"Eithne ni Flaherty, and—and, yes! I think I will offer her your heart."

"It is yours," said I, "and the only thing I have."

"My fine fellow!" cried Donal, who was listening. "Your mother's portion is yours, and maybe you will be noticing how our Uncle Conn over at Derry Columcill wants you to stay with him. He has two ships in the Spanish trade and no one for them. When will you try the merchanting?"

"When you kick me out."

"A small while yet. But all the same, we three will spend a week with him soon. I would like a ship myself."

"We cannot," said I. "There are twenty men here to learn the arquebus." This same Uncle Conn had brought us from Spain a score of a new-pattern weapon with an improved lock, and I was busy training the men to it.

Up on the ramparts now I turned away from the lady's eyes, that had the power to bring the blood to my face, and looked along the white of the road that twisted west down the glen. "Look!" I said suddenly. "Mounted——"

Donal turned quickly, palm above his eyes, and stared intently down the valley road. "From the O'Neill, think you?" he put me quietly, but his feet shifted restlessly.

"From someone—and that hurry on him."

Donal looked down at his wife, and she, seeing the trouble in his eyes, pressed close to him. "Not yet," she whispered, half to herself. "The truce still holds."

We leant over the ramparts and watched the rider, a saffron-clad kern with spear hip-slung and heels in his horse's flanks. He was pressing his mount hard, and would be at the ford in half a minute. Already we could hear the thud of unshod hooves and see the blurred shadows flit on the sun-baked road.

"He might be from O'Donnell," said I, and felt a pulse beat. For a messenger from O'Donnell, riding in haste, might mean a campaign Corrib way—and more besides.

The rider splashed across the ford, and there came faintly the high challenge of Ferdoragh.

"We will wait here," said Donal quietly, holding his wife's arm. She gazed at him, and he smiled down at her. A steadfast man when the pinch came.

We had not long to wait. In a minute, strangely drawn out, we heard a shuffling on the stone stairs, and the red head of Calvagh MacManus rose into the frame of the turret doorway. "Rider from O'Donnell," he shouted at once, excitement in his voice; and my heart gave one dunt.

The kern stumbled into the light and swayed on his feet. He was covered with dust; even his black glib was powdered white; and his face was grey and haggard. Behind him came old Father Senan, puffing after the long spiral.

"O'Cahan?" inquired the man hoarsely, blinking from one to the other of us.

"At your service, a friend," said Donal.

The kern saluted and cleared his throat, and Donal looked with reprimand at his foster-brother.

"He would take nothing till he said his word to you," Calvagh excused himself.

The man wetted his cracked lips with his tongue and began the speech that he must have committed to memory on the weary road. "Hugh Roe O'Donnell sends brother's greeting to O'Cahan and seeks his help."

"The Sassenach?"

"The Sassenach—a red wind blast them! Listen, chief. This is what I am to say: The great fighting-man, Sir Conyers Clifford, with the loyalist dogs of Clanricard and O'Connor Roe, two nights ago came down on the fords of the Saimhor and tried to storm the dun of Bellashanny. They failed that time, but are in a ring round it, and Hugh Roe O'Donnell is gathering help from the four winds."

"Hugh Roe used to be strong enough to guard his own borders," growled Calvagh.

The kern stiffened. "Hugh Roe can do more than that, as the world knows, but Clifford, the wily one, picked his time well—when the clans were in shieling and the dun with a bare garrison. Thirty standards of foot, ten squadrons of horse, a ship from Galway with engines landed to batter down the walls—and over against them in the dun a handful of bonnachts under Hugh Crawford out of Albann. Chief, I was bid say to you that this is no small foray. If Clifford wins Bellashanny he holds one gap of the north, and O'Cahan is no safer than O'Donnell. Hugh Roe asks your help. That is my word." He threw out his hands in a sudden sharp gesture and pulled himself up to hear the answer. And he got that answer on his last word.

"O'Donnell shall have O'Cahan's help," said Donal quietly.

"That was known, great O'Cahan," cried the messenger, and suddenly went limp. He staggered, and Calvagh put a holding hand on him.

"See to him, brother," ordered Donal. "He is of the true breed."

Calvagh and the O'Donnell clansman disappeared down the dark curve of the stairs, and we stood silent, listening to the shuffle of the feet on the stones. The young wife turned her head aside from her husband and looked across the ramparts at the brown side of the glen beyond the river.

Donal did not look at her. He stood up very straight and held her arm firmly within his. "It is on us—the big blow," he said, "and we must look to our plans."

"Your plans are made," said the priest.

"We have but decided to send help to Bellashanny. This is only the beginning. Remember O'Neill's warning? De Burgh, Kildare, and the Pale will come down full force on Dungannon, and there the full brunt will be. That is what we must prepare for."

"Then your place is here," said Father Senan.

"Well?"

"The thing to do is the thing I see in your mind."

"And it?"

"Send all the horse you can spare to Bellashanny—with a good man to lead them."

"And who would that man be, I am wondering?" Donal smiled, his eye away from me.

"There is a middling good man that I have in mind," said Senan.

The two laughed, but I saw nothing to laugh at in this serious business. I turned sullenly enough to Donal, and he clapped me on the shoulder. "David, brother! Your two-score horse must be at the Saimhor to-morrow before nightfall. You lead, with Calvagh as your second. What are you standing there for and time pressing?"

I heard Amy's sigh of relief. Here was respite—and de Burgh might never strike. Alas! In a week Dungannon became an armed camp with all roads leading to it. But sure, an hour gained is precious to lovers.

CHAPTER II

I

THAT was a strenuous ride through a wild and lonely land. Our road led us across vast moors, purple with heather, where the pilibeen flapped, calling wearily, and the grey plover piped plaintively along the slopes; by black tarns where bog-lilies floated and dry reeds shivered in the wind; down into quiet valleys where small streams gurgled and corn-patches yellowed in the sun; and up long stone-ribbed braes grown with yellow whins, that crackled in the autumn heat and breathed their mystic odour into the air.

The haze of the fall was over all the land; there was a stale feel in the keening wind; high in a pale sky the yellow-tinged clouds sluggishly drifted. It was like riding through the land of a dream. Ride an hour in it and you had ridden a year, and so might ride for evermore.

And it was a land emptied of men. In the corn-fields women bent to the hook and stooked the sheaves; in the wattled townships women came to the doors and watched us out of calm eyes; in the upland shielings women herded the black kine. They spoke little to us riding through. Quiet they were as their own hills, patient as their dumb earth. "Bring our men home to us," cried one young one. "Laggards, laggards!" taunted an old hag.

But surely we did not tarry on that road. Our first night's camp was in a pine-wood near a hamlet with a stone dun, where the women brought us oatcakes and curds, and an ancient seannachy,[1] fighting done, hobbled to our fire and gabbled of old raids into Tirowen in the days of Shane. Before the fall of the second night we had reached the Saimhor.

The wind, blowing to us, brought the hum of the siege long before we sighted it, and told us that we were still in time. Every four or five minutes the deep thunder of the culverins shook the air, and in between a rattle of arquebus crackled and spat. And at last, topping a slope, we saw the dust and smoke lift and roll, and yonder across a mile of plain was the stubborn dun of Bellashanny standing above the Falls of Assaroe. It was dim in the pother of dust, and to the right smoke rolled up where the culverins thundered on the breast of a round hill. On that hill we could distinguish the straggling lines of an entrenched camp, and on the plain below a yet larger camp—a huge camp this, curving from the river and ringing hill and dun. The Saimhor lay below us like a carelessly dropped ribbon, with wimpled stretches where the fords were, and at each ford were armed men.

"Let us down to it," cried Calvagh eagerly, at my side.

"Down with us, then! Twos, in good order."

But we were already late for any of that day's work. The fight sallies were dying with the sun and the culverins were now silent, while the smoke-cloud slowly lifted and rolled away.

We rode straight for the camp, keeping the curve of the river on our left and making a string to its bow. Midway on the string the guards at one of the fords

---

[1] Story-teller.

saw our array, and a single horseman galloped across to us.

"Young Maguire," shouted Calvagh, riding up from the rear. "See the yellow mane to him."

It was, indeed, Doncadh Donn Maguire, my gay lad of Dungannon: bareheaded, with a hawk's feather in his splendid hair and a black corselet carelessly buckled at the shoulders. At first he did not know me. "Ye come late," he shouted. "From where?"

"Dungiven," I called back.

"O'Cahan's lads! Ah! and is it David Gordon, by the High Powers? Blackcock's Feather! Oh-ho for it! And there is Calvagh himself." He galloped and swerved to my side, eye and hand welcoming. "And where is Donal Ballagh?" he inquired.

"Waiting the word from O'Neill."

"Same as my father. Once on a day Donal could not be held from a rally like this."

"Two-score of his best here," said Calvagh.

"To be sure! It could be that a new-wed man has small stomach for blows. My choice! but yon was a great play ye made in Connacht, David Gordon. Why did ye not call for me after ye crossed Erne? Is it true that you knocked off the head of Langdon Coote, the swordsman, with a blow of the basket?"

"It is not."

"It is said, and he is a dead man anyway. You will be wanting to report to Hugh Roe?"

"If we find him."

"My camp is yonder by the ford, and an ox roasting. Send your men across. They know my lads—they were all at Clontibret together. I know where O'Donnell has his quarters near the Abbey, and we two will ride over to him."

225

It would have suited me fine to ride up to Red Hugh, forty trained men at my back, but here was the wise and kindly word, so I swallowed my vanity and gave Calvagh his orders.

Maguire and I backed away and watched the men swing off in rank. "Work you put into them heroes," he commended. "Let us on."

II

"Fine talker," said I, "have you any word of this siege?"

"A hundred thousand! Faith! there are two sieges and hot as hell on Easter Monday: the Sassenach at the dun, and we at the Sassenach. Clifford, the fox, in a trap of his own setting! Friday in the night he sallied up from Sligo, surprised the fords at the dawn, and hoped to surprise the dun. But my bold Crawford, Hugh the Albannach—you met him at Dungannon—jerked the drawbridge in his face and settled down like a badger, every tooth with a bite to it. So siege it had to be—or retreat, and tough Clifford took his chance. He planned the game neat as a bout of chess, but foolish to make plans and forget how Hugh Roe O'Donnell might tumble the board. And that is what Hugh did. Not waiting to marshal the clan, he swooped down with the men he had handy, beaconed all the hills from here to Innisowen, struck here and struck there like a flash, and struck harder as his strength grew. In tens and twenties came his clan, angry as the red bees, and from over the border the Maguires, the O'Ruarcs—and now yourself. By noon, Monday, he had forty companies on the Sassenach flanks, and yon is how we have them now."

226

He gestured widely from river to castle, and I envied him his fine roll of words.

"On Saturday the Sassenach held all the fords as far as Devenish, now he holds only one—the Path-of-the-Heroes above the falls, and he has a collar-and-elbow grip on that, his only road. My lads behind wor the ford we hold—a bonny fight—to our bellies in water and hitting overhand, and when a man went under he stayed under. To-morrow, and God is good, we will put the Sassenach in the trap and the *gouloge* [1] down. The Sassenach! Ay, and all the royalist dogs of Connacht—O'Connor Roe, Clanricard, and his son Rickard the Sassenach. Is it true you cut out Rickard's tongue?"

"It is not. Can Crawford hold the dun?"

"That fellow! Tough Hugh! with eighty Scots bonnachts and ten days' food! That badger will not be drawn.—We turn right here—Hugh Roe will be down by the Abbey."

The sun was behind the high square tower of the dun, that stood out black and sharp against a warm sky. The smoke had blown away, the rival camps had ceased their worrying, and instead of gun-peal and slogan a great and peaceful hum rose from plain and hill. The Irish camp that we skirted was a medley of hastily erected shelters, and it was as full and busy as a hive. Here and there fanned fires began to flame cheerily, little spirals of smoke twisted, and groups of men were busy round the cooking-pits.

"A hard and merry day," said Maguire. "That smell makes me hungry. Let us hurry. Siege and counter, attack and sortie, skirmish of horse and tulzie [2] of pike—from dawn to dusk. We were not

[1] Forked stick.   [2] Struggle.

227

strong enough to carry their trenches by open assault, 'and the dun defied them in spite of all their arts. They battered at it with their culverin, tried to set a mine in the arch, made essay to bridge the moat! Blazes! but you should have seen the mailed fellows tumble in the ditch when Crawford set their wooden tower afire. Yon, now, are O'Donnell's quarters."

We had swung round the north edge of the camp to where the Abbey of Assaroe looked across at Innis Saimhor. Between the Abbey and the island we could see the clean green of the sea, golden tracked by the sun, with an anchored ship swinging black against the gold.

"There is Hugh himself," said Maguire. "The, young lad with the red hair. The small fellow is O'Gallagher of the Gallowglasses, and the big black lad MacSwyne of the Axes."

O'Donnell's quarters were in the stone guest-house of the Abbey, but the young eagle stayed outside in the open air. With the two notable chiefs named he sat on a bench before the door, looking out along the track of the sun. Our approach made him turn his head, and, seeing us, he lifted to his feet.

I looked at him with interest, for this man's fame was overseas. I knew he was not old in years, but I had expected him to be war-hardened and grim. And he was only a lad: a young, lithe, swank lad with finely-red hair, a delicately smooth face, and grey, wide-set eyes. He looked at me, and then I knew the force that was in him. For his eyes had the hooded-eagle set under the wide brow, and he had a way of leaning forward from the hips like an eagle ready to stoop—and aye ready was he. "Is it you, Donn?" he called, high and clear. "Keep you a tight grip yonder?"

"A double hold, Hugh, with forty men just in from O'Cahan. This is Donal's cousin, David Gordon, who leads."

O'Donnell looked at me with quick interest. "You are welcome, David Gordon," he said. "Your name is known. My mother—God rest her—was a Scot too."

"A sword hand to him, by all accounts," said O'Gallagher, who had remained seated, one knee across the other.

"Horse or foot?" inquired O'Donnell.

"Horse, O'Donnell," I replied.

"Drilled men too," amplified Maguire; "half of them with the flint-lock."

The young leader's eye lit up, and it was only when they lit that one knew how the Gaelic gloom lay behind them. "It is kindly thought of the O'Cahan," he said warmly. "Horse we need. You will camp with Maguire for the night. To-morrow the fight will be for the Path-of-the-Heroes, and your horse will have good share in it. Luck with ye."

"Were I trapped like yon," rumbled the heavy voice of the black MacSwyne, "I know what I would do."

"So do I," mocked the small leader of the gallow-glasses, "and it would be the wrong thing."

"Would it so?"

"It would, for out you would be sallying with your big hired axes—and we would bury you with your head under your oxter. Now, I know what I would do."

"What would you do?" inquired O'Donnell with interest.

"I would dare the Falls of Assaroe in the dark, and make a bid for Sligo walls."

"In the dark across Assaroe?"

"I would so," said O'Gallagher, and there was a
hard daring in his eyes that did not belie him.

"Conyers Clifford is a good man too," said O'Donnell
musingly. And then he shrugged his shoulders. "Ah
well! we must wait the morrow."

III

We rode back to the river by the skirt of the camp,
where the fires were now bright and the men at food,
and splashed across the ford to where our men were
settled amidst clumps of willows. My lads were
already at home amongst the clansmen of Maguire,
and as noisy around the cooking-fires as the owners
of them. There was talk and laughter everywhere,
as was the way of these Eireannach fighting-men.

With Calvagh and Tadg Ironhand I looked over
the horses. They had been watered and well picketed
amongst the willows, and the men had found a trampled corn-field and had cut the heads off the ripe corn
for a fine pile of forage. And then Donn Maguire,
Calvagh, and I sat on our cloaks by the brink of the
Saimhor, ate roast ox, and talked of the morrow.

Twilight was darkening round us, the camp-fires,
far and wide, twinkled brighter, a drone as of bees
drifted with the lazy air; behind us a gallowglass
laughed, at our feet the river gurgled. Overhead the
sky was high and deep, with little grey cloud-islands
floating amongst the faint stars; a great peace folded
us in; we seemed to be far and far removed from war
and death; we stopped talking of battle and its
chances. Then the day's long ride came home to me
and I yawned.

"Blast me!" swore Donn Maguire, "I forgot. Let us be taking a fine sleep to ourselves, in the name of God."

I pulled my new mail shirt over my head and lay on my back, folded in war-cloak, but sleep did not come to me for yet a while. I stared into the deepening blue between the stars and thought of many things. Now at last was I soldier and leading my squadron of horse, and men, who were good men, talked of me as Blackcock's Feather. And Advent was still two months distant, and luck coming my way. For with the Sassenach and the loyalists trapped on the Saimhor, Connacht was open to us, and the great O'Donnell would not hesitate in sweeping it from end to end. And what then? And what then? Queen's Captain Bevinda O'Flaherty, who could bite hard in her own cause, might be careful with a man who could bite and had bitten. And Eithne? the kind one who had looked at me out of the deeps of her eyes . . . And who would be lonely—lonely . . . And so I drifted into sleep and dreamt of dark curls on a white brow—but I could not see her eyes.

My awakening was rude.

CHAPTER III

I

My awakening was desperately rude. A hand gripped my shoulder and bit, and Donn Maguire's voice shouted in my ear. "Gordon! David! The fight is on."

The daze of sleep on me, I caught his hand fiercely. "What is it?"

"Listen to yon." His hand tugged at mine and lifted me to my feet, cloak about my knees.

I shook my head, as if the turmoil was in it, and looked towards the dun. Down there red flashes cut across the dark, arquebuses cracked, fierce yells rang through the night.

"A sally on the camp," cried Maguire, and at that O'Gallagher's words came to me.

"The Ford of Assaroe!" I exclaimed.

"Never the Path-of-the-Heroes in the dark?"

Calvagh was at my shoulder. "Let us get the men horsed," he bellowed in my ear.

There followed a nerve-dragging time of blind feeling for straps and buckles, of the shouting and movement of men, the tugging and rearing of startled horses, and a scrambling and pushing into some kind of order. When at last, with shirt of mail settled on my shoulders and sword in hand, I sat on Benmee aquiver at Maguire's side, facing the ford, I drew a long breath of relief. The horse were arrayed behind us in double line, and the gallowglasses crouched, fully armed, amongst the sallies at either hand.

The night had changed while we slept. A clouded sky hung over us; big drops of rain spattered now and then on my mailed shoulders; the air was thick and hot. Yet the night was not dead black, for, somewhere southwards, the moonlight suffused greyly through the cloud-pall and showed us the waters wimpling with uncanny gurglings down the ford.

"A finger for a blink of light!" cried Maguire. "It is hotter down below."

It was, though the arquebuses no longer crackled. Steel clanged, men shouted, the night was in travail. And we at the ford, not knowing what to do, waited for the birth. We had not long to wait. A horseman came clattering out of the dark beyond the ford and racketed to a standstill at the edge of the water. "Dogs! Dogs!" he yelled. "Are ye up?"

"Who rides?" thundered Maguire.

"O'Donnell's word. To the ford—to Assaroe." Frenzy must be swaying him in the saddle. "The Sassenach are crossing. Down on them and hold them till the clan musters. Up with ye!" He swerved his horse away and was gone up the river towards the fords of Devenish.

"It is so, then, David Gordon," said Donn Maguire, suddenly calm. "Let us down and push them over the fall."

The gallowglasses came breaking through the sallies. I manœuvred my men out into the open, behind the clumps, and, with Calvagh and Tadg keeping touch on the wings, we pricked forward on that desperate venture.

The English, without doubt, were making good their escape from the trap. Sir Conyers Clifford, hardy man of war, was playing dice with death—a bold game, boldly played. North side of Saimhor was failure and death, south of it the bare chance of getting his force behind the distant walls of Sligo. And he took that chance to save his men and his province. Leaving guns and stores as spoil, he, in the heart of the night, marshalled his men down to Assaroe, and, squadron by squadron, marched them shoulder-locked through the rush of waters above the falls—the Ford-of-the-Heroes, and every man a hero that night. Behind their leaders, O'Connor Roe, Clanricard, Dunkellin, Vaughan, Cosby, Wingfield, they marched in good order, and if, here and there, a man lost his feet, the thunder of the falls drowned his last cry. Half, two-thirds were safe across, when a Scots sentinel on an outwork of the dun caught the glimmer of moving steel in a vanishing ray of moonlight, and guessed its import. His alarm roused the garrison, who lit a bonfire on the ramparts and themselves sallied out, firing their arquebuses.

O'Donnell, roused out of sleep, did all he could, but he could never hope to array his wide-flung clan in time to bring the enemy to bay. The more fight-lusty of his men, half-naked from their sleep, grasped sparth and spear, and came yelling their slogans on the English rear. But they came too late, charging on a stubborn rearguard, all steel and buff, that took minutes to die and gave the main force time to marshal its columns on the left bank and begin its orderly retreat. O'Donnell's men, dammed back by that stubborn rearguard, flowed upstream to the next ford, and with this scattered body our gallowglasses intermingled as they blundered along in the dark. Calvagh, Tadg, and I kept our lads out on the flank of this jumble.

I have never met any man who could tell clearly the story of that night. All that any man can say is that there never was the like of that running fight from Saimhor to the gates of Sligo. It was one long-drawn-out rallying and worrying of maddened men in the dark.

The English foot kept in close column, hugging the sea; the English horse, split into squadrons, flickered around it, front and rear. They were fighting for life, and no better fight was ever made. Time and again the clans, half-naked, gathered force and stormed down on that massive column; time and again they were met doggedly by hedge of steel; time and again a squadron of horse stemmed those yelling rushes, were surrounded as with a flood, and drove a way through—a remnant, captain and trooper knee to knee. Men died, and dying, were trampled under foot; riderless horses bucketed out of the press; yells of hate and rage, triumph and challenge, rent the night; steel rang on steel, thudded dully on buff, went silent through warm flesh. But that iron column, rallying and mending its rents, held doggedly on its way.

And down above that trailing fight was the gloom of the low sky and the rain drumming in off the grey sea. Here were cliffs, dropping sheer and black to the restless lift of the waves, and here were long wet strands with the tide creeping and a stain on the edge of it; and at long last came the pale dawn stealing, and over there in the distance were the towered walls of Sligo.

I, who led them, will say that my forty men did their share that night. My post as leader steadied me, and, until the very end, I was not concerned with my own part in the fight. Once I mind a pike dunting on my mailed shirt and nearly lifting me out of the saddle; once I was in a staggering mêlée on the brow of a cliff and heard the waves boom between the shouts; and once I exchanged blows with a halberdier knee-deep in the tide. But my whole mind was bent on nursing and still nursing my troop, and using it where we had a chance to do our share. No foolish attempt did we make to stem a charge of the heavy Sassenach horse. Twice, indeed, we charged on a broken remnant and emptied many a saddle, but mostly we skirmished across the front of the column on our light and hardy horses and tried to retard the retreat. Time and again, avoiding the full charge, we swooped out of the dark slantwise at the head of the column, forced it to set itself in a pike-hedge, and swept by just outside the points. When the final rally came I still had thirty men behind me, but by then our horses could hardly raise a trot. Calvagh was still with me, but Tadg had been dismounted somewhere in the dark.

Dawn came and saw us surging against the walls of Sligo. We had failed to hold or break the enemy. His dead were strewn along the coast, his horse were only a remnant, but still he faced us as stubborn as ever. And Sligo was now ready to receive and save him—and save Connacht.

It has been argued that if Sligo had been a mile farther away none of the English force would have escaped. It could well be. O'Donnell's men, scattered from Devenish to the sea, had not been ready for a night attack, and, eagle though Hugh Roe was,

236

he necessarily took a long time to get his heavy-armed gallowglasses into action. All night long, away in the rear, he had been mustering his scattered men and sending them forward, but it was only now in the dawn that he, with his main force, came down on the English flank. He was too late. With Sligo walls in front he had no room to swing forward and cut the enemy off. But, even so, he very nearly succeeded in winning Sligo.

The east port was open; the portcullis had creaked up; the head of the Sassenach column was pressing through the arch, when O'Donnell made his last desperate effort. And this time my men charged home with the clans. The remnant of Clifford's horse tried to stem us, but we flooded round them and, one by one, they were dragged down to death. And there too—sad day!—I lost my great mare, Benmee. A big pikeman, teeth agrin, thrust her through the breast, and she sank under me. If my feet had been in stirrup nothing could have saved me. As I was falling forward under the pike of the soldier, a fierce grip pulled me to my feet, and there was the great foam-flecked beard of Tadg Ironhand at my shoulder. At once the press was round us, and we were only two units in the storm.

We bore down, shoulder-linked, on the Sassenach rear and drove in with it to the gate. The rear broke, and we intermingled with it, still driving forward. That was a tense minute—Eireannach and Sassenach in one swaying mass—hacking sideways and yelling into each other's faces. We reached the gateway. Nothing could stay us. Already a score or more of us were in the gloom of the archway—and then!—Then the portcullis clanked down, pinned a halberdier as if he were a fly, and snapped that press of men in two. Half a standard of Sassenach were left to die without, and our score were trapped in the arch.

I was one of that score.

A minute ago I was one of four thousand harrying a beaten enemy, now I was one of a score trapped and doomed. For yet a minute I did not realise it. Then, above the din, a voice cried in my ear, "We are in it now." It was Calvagh MacManus at my shoulder.

"And hard dying," boomed a voice at my other shoulder, and there was the flaring beard and blood-shot eyes of Tadg Ironhand.

And as I twisted head to look back at the massive grill of the portcullis there was Doncadh Donn Maguire, his back against the bars, his golden hair atoss and his eyes gleaming. Why not? We four had been in the front of that last charge, and we were big enough and strong enough to keep our places.

"Let us kill," roared a big gallowglass of the Maguires, his voice high above the worrying of the clans dammed against the portcullis.

But there was little space there to kill or be killed. Our score, mostly together, faced inward. What few of the enemy were amongst us were already dead and held upright only by the pressure. I stood breast to breast with a tall halberdier, whose weapon was broken above the axe, and by the grin in his teeth I knew he was the man that had killed Benmee. "Dog!" he cried into my face. "If I had a hand free——"

With a sudden side-thrust of the shoulder he made

an inch of room and jerked his halberd-arm out of the crush. "I have you now." But at that a look of shocked surprise came into his face and his lifted weapon fell behind his shoulder. "You've done for me," he whispered, and his face twisted.

It was Tadg. At the small of my waist he had driven his great hand forward, and his *sgian* had gone home.

It was not pleasant to see the man die. I strained back and let him slip to the ground, and his room gave my sword-arm room—"Let us die in the open."

And we had our way. For the first time that night the English broke before us. They were safe within their walls and, now, they did not want to die. They turned and strove inwards, and we drove them. And when they reached the open they did not at once wheel round on us, but scurried away right and left, and gave us an open space below the big gate-tower. In a little time they would rally and turn, and then the end would not be long. That great cobbled space was crowded with men, and beyond them was a street of wooden-joisted houses running down hill into a grey sky behind the grey roofs.

But we did not die just yet. We were a panting clump of men just outside the arch, and, suddenly, Doncadh Donn Maguire, with a great shout, whirled me round. "Look!" he cried.

The tower, north of the gate, was buttressed by a dozen stone steps, and at the head of the steps was a wide-open door. No doubt the tower was garrisoned and the portcullis room full of soldiers, but here was a chance we could not lose.

"Up! Up! Up with ye!" roared Maguire, bundling the nearest man forward.

"Let me die in the open, chief," prayed desperately one of his own gallowglasses.

"Like a wolf? Be badger now, Ulic, and sell your life dearly."

As we made for the steps the nerve of the Sassenach returned. A yelp, as from a pack, and their long front surged on us.

"Steady, brothers, steady!" It was Calvagh, cool as at drill. "Two at a time, and we are all in."

At the head of the steps Donn and I turned at bay. Leaping at the head of the English was a big fellow in fluted half-armour, a bloody sword in his hand. Here, now, was a man that I must kill. Back through the night my arm had ached from gripping hilt, but now I felt no ache as I brought blade up and went down a step.

"Here is the weapon for him," cried Donn. "Leave him to me."

Maguire had broken his sword sometime in the night and was now armed with the long-handled axe— the terrible weapon of the gallowglass. He made no pother at all about this killing. The big fellow came leaping up at us. "Have at you!" he cried. And Donn swung his axe. That was all. It shore through guard, dunted on steel morion, and the big fellow crumpled and rolled down under the feet of his men.

Donn yelled clear and high, threw up his axe, and next moment I had him by the belt and through the doorway. Calvagh banged the door shut, and Tadg shot the big bar into its slot as the weight from outside burst against it. The tough oak strained and held.

"That was a clout I hit," shouted Donn happily.

The room we were in was the main guardroom, but we did not pause to examine it. Every man there had only one thought—the portcullis chamber above our heads. If we could win that before the walls of Sligo were manned and lift the portcullis, Sligo might still be ours. The men were already at the turret stairs and crushing upwards on each other's heels. There was no hanging back for these fine fellows in that crisis of death.

And alas! death it was. Maguire and I were not half-way up the dark curve of the stairs before the fight broke out above us. The portcullis chamber was fully manned, and here was our last fight.

It was a great window-slitted chamber, covering the whole floor of the tower, and there was plenty of sword-room. The heavy top-bar of the portcullis stood six inches out of the floor, and there was the heart of the fight. Though the guard outnumbered us, our first charge swept them across the room, and Calvagh got the holding-pin free and two men in the chains before they rallied and charged back. And this time reinforcements came pouring in to them. For another stair led up from the south tower, and by this the soldiers came and came and came.

It was about that time that I let the grip on myself go. All the night long I had been the careful and anxious leader of my troop, and at no time had the lust of battle swept me. Now I was to die, and, from somewhere, it came suddenly to me that never had I fought care-free. By Heaven! I would try myself out now, knowing it to be the last chance.

I was not sorry for myself. I surely was not unhappy. If I could describe my feeling at all I would call it exultation. I was no longer the silent, dour Scot. I laughed, I rallied the men cheerfully, I shouted the sword-song of Gillian the Black:

I am the Sword—hammered and wrought
    By Gillian, for Gillian.
Where, now, the swank men, lean men who fought
    By Gillian, for Gillian?
Dust in the wind, clay in the rain,
    Like Gillian. Ho! Gillian!
Still am I clean, blade without stain—
    Dead Gillian, dust Gillian!

I was pleased with myself. I was tall, with heavy shoulders and strong wrist, and I moved lightly on long legs. I used the point mostly, and I knew that my father, in the face of God, would not call me clumsy. The power came from somewhere inside myself. Men faced me and parried, and I drove right through them. I raged in a fine gaiety across the floor and back, and the men followed and died round me—but the end was certain.

IV

There we were, now, at the foot of the next flight of the turret stairs—all that was left of us. There was a drift of hot steam in the room and the flagged floor was slippery. Donn Maguire was there, un-wounded, though the corselet was torn from his shoulders; there was the rug-headed, big gallowglass called Ulic, covered with blood not his own; Calvagh MacManus, bleeding at neck and shoulder; and Tadg Ironhead, leaning against the lintel, blood running down his great hairy thigh.

"Up to the next floor," I roared. "We can hold them there. On, Maguire!"

Ulic and Maguire disappeared backwards, Calvagh

and I were shoulder to shoulder in front of Tadg. And then a man in front of us—no Sassenach, but a traitor gallowglass of Clanricard—dropped suddenly on one knee and got home with his *sgian* below Calvagh's guard, "Done, now!" he cried, and fell.

The killer lifted his head close below me, and I smashed it savagely flat with my hilt. A pikeman, about to dash in, flinched back, and I was in the doorway.

Tadg was at my side, leaning on the jamb. Fiercely I cursed him for tarrying. "Hamstrung!" he cried in my ear.

"To my shoulder!" And, still facing forward, I succeeded in hitching him to the first tread of the stairs.

Then Maguire's voice came from above. "I have him," and the big fellow's weight was lifted off me. It was time.

A small lithe fellow in officer's armour was facing me, and he was a swordsman—better than I was, now that I was driven to defence. The pikeman was trying to edge in at his shoulder and the sworder snarled at him, and, as he snarled, my blade scored his neck. He came at me again, and, as I took the second tread of the stairs, his point pinged upon my mail-coat. And then I had him at vantage. That spiral stairway was made for defence, since it forced the attacker to use his left hand. He saw that I was escaping him, and showed a fatal hardihood. He sprang inwards to the foot of the stairs and tried me with the upward lunge to the groin. I swerved away round the corbel, his blade searing my hip-bone, and then countered him overhand above the gorget. He staggered, and fell clear of the doorway, but no other took his place. The game was too desperate.

Maguire and big Ulic supported Tadg at the head of the stairs. We were in a low-arched sleeping-room with a four-poster bed in one corner and tapestries on the wall. Through the window-slit I caught a glimpse of a hill far away, and the young sun made a glow behind it. It seemed a glimpse of another world.

"Us against all Hell," said Donn, gay to the end. "Is it not the pity of the world that no one will be left to tell the things were done in this tower?"

"Dhia!" said the big gallowglass huskily, "I could drink Loch Erne dry."

And there was the chink in our armour.

Tadg Ironhand was my man, and I took him in my arms across to the couch, while the others watched the stairs. He had a clean cut slantwise across the thigh, and I tried to staunch the bleeding. There is one thing that every clansman takes to war: a pouch of dry moss—the same healing moss that the great Dalcassians used to staunch their wounds that time they fought their way home from Clontarf. I applied a great pad of this, and bound it with strips torn from the couch covering.

"Small use now," he whispered, and as I bent over him he touched my shoulder with his great hand. "You led us well, a Gordon!" he said. "We were your children. The clan will know." And after a pause: "Pity this is the end for you."

"Not yet, brother," said I.

"No. It would be fine to die under the sky." He turned his head to where the light came through the window-slit.

"We will do that," I told him.

Again I took him in my arms, and went across to where a curtain hid the last up-flight of stone steps. "Let us to the open," I called to Donn, leaning like a cat at the stairhead.

"That will be best," he agreed, after a pause.

"This is the place for me while I have a tooth left," said big Ulic.

"Stay and kill, then," said Donn, his hand against my back on the stairs.

Up on the battlements we drew clean breath once more. I laid Tadg down in a corner by the turret tower and straightened up. The smooth flags of the roof spread before us a score of paces—a square floor shut in with notched parapets and roofed by the sky —and the clean wind of morning blew across it and stirred life in us afresh.

With Donn I leaned against the open door, looking down into the gloom of the twisted stair. Down there, where had been so much turmoil, was no sound at all now. No sound at all for a long time, and then a great voice roared, "Here is for you, dead man."

The thunderous bang of a petronel shut on the last word, and the crash of a fall followed. Then came a sudden clamour, and a voice of authority broke out above it. "Back! Back! Some are still above." Ensued a scuffling and growling, and clank of arms against stone.

"And there went Ulic Mor," said Donn. "Our turn now."

But our turn was long in coming. Everything was again still, and in time it was no longer seemly to crouch above a hole and wait for a head to slash at. I was glutted with fight, and a great weariness came on

245

me. Without a word I turned and strode across to the parapet, leaned breast on it, and looked down and away.

In the distance were the fine sheen of water and the bulk of hills, dark with woods, where a trail of cloud floated. A fresh autumn morning for one not sodden with death! I looked away from it to the plain below, and there were the clans drawing off from the fight. They were in complete disarray, and mounted men galloped across their rear, urging them away out of gunshot. And who, I wondered dully, was to gather what was left of my two-score horsemen? It did not matter. I was only fifty feet above them, but all life lay between us. Never now would I ride at the head of two-score men to the gates of Cashlean-na-Kirka. Never now would I see the light in the dark eyes of a maid. Never now—never now . . .

Donn Maguire's low whistle called me, and I walked across to his side. He held his great axe ready and looked at me out of wild deadly eyes. "They come," he whispered. "Listen."

I heard nothing. I laid my hand on his arm. "Donn," I said, "let the last rally be here in the open."

I drew him back from the doorway, and willingly he came. "Let it be so, long man," he murmured, oddly resigned.

The man who came, came quietly, and we let him come. Almost before we knew, his morioned head appeared out of the dark spiral. It stayed moveless there, looking at us.

"Come on," I cried. "Two at a time, and no quarter."

At that he came up and stood still in the doorway. And he was Sir Francis Vaughan.

But a very different Sir Françis Vaughan. No courtier this. This man was haggard and grim and strong—and very cool: his eyes steady in black-rimmed deep sockets, grim battle writ all over him. He carried broadsword in one hand and petronel in the other. I was sorry that I had to fight this man.

He thrust petronel in belt and dropped the point of his sword. "Enough killing," he said quietly. "You are my prisoners."

"Never—never," cried Donn Maguire hoarsely, throwing up his axe. "I will never surrender to hang in a Sassenach gibbet."

"David Gordon," said Vaughan, "tell your friend that ye are my prisoners and will be honourably treated."

Maguire looked wildly at me, and I held his arm. "A man of finest honour, Donn," I told him.

And Donn drew his hand across his eyes.

CHAPTER IV

I

THE half-town of Athenree was a medley of stone, wood, and wattled houses, straggling within four stone walls, and garrisoned by four Sassenach standards, as well as by some clan levies from Dunkellin and Clanricard. The road from Athlone came in below the Castle at one side, and the road to Galway ran out between barbicans at the other. It was the main loyalist stronghold south of Cong, but its Governor, Sir Francis Vaughan, had few good words to say of its security.

"This fort of Athenree," said he, "is proof against attack on all sides save that on which we look for it; this sunken North Wall would tempt a beldam to launch a sally at it."

He, Don Maguire, and I were leaning on the shelter-parapet, looking across the pasture grounds to the distant woods.

"It is well masked," said Donn, "with your barbican and corner towers commanding it."

"And a fine deep ditch," said I.

"Ay! a dry ditch easy enough to fill. If O'Donnell brought half a grove of mangonels and a couple of testudos——"

Donn laughed. "The red lad does not crawl on his belly with such engines."

"No, but, nevertheless, I will mount six culverins between tower and barbican. I respect the fighting qualities of your red lad."

"Where in all the world," wondered Donn ironically, "did you find cause to say that?" And the three of us laughed.

"David Gordon, here, will bear me out that once I warned him that this was no land for fortune-seekers, but for blows aplenty," Vaughan upheld himself. "And yet at that time I was not so sure about the blows. That sometimes-fickle Queen of mine sent me over, saying: "Francis, show you my rebel Irish how this game of war is played in the Lowlands." And over came I, thinking it but poor sport to chase half-naked Irishry from bog to bog. But mark you, they were no wiser in Dublin town."

"'Tis the man afraid belittles his enemies," said Donn.

"Well said, Maguire! When I got back by the Gap-of-the-North from Portmore my brother-in-law, de Burgh, had a new task for me. Said he: "Take these despatches to Clifford at Athlone, and rouse him to action. Body of me! to think that the terror of the Spanish Main is letting the young O'Donnell and his kerns threaten our border. Press him to follow the instructions here writ and we will meet at Dungannon within a month." So I rode across to Athlone, hoping for a slash at Wat Tyrrell on the way."

"Lucky for you you did not meet him or O'Connor," put in Donn.

"Like enough. But I was told that a steel coat struck terror into the wild Irish in their saffron, and, not meeting any, I thought that was truth. I remember how Conyers Clifford smiled, reading his orders. "We shall see, we shall see!" was all he said. And up we marched to Sligo, two thousand of us, sure that no force in the north could withstand us. We were all eagerness to cross the Erne, and there was my calm, steel-grey Clifford hanging back in Sligo till Clanricard and O'Connor Roe brought up their levies. "Conyers, let us on," I pressed him, "or de Burgh will tire waiting for us at Dungannon." He laughed at me. "At Dungannon," said he, eyebrow lifted, "there is a keen gentleman named O'Neill, as de Burgh will find out—and over here is a red lad O'Donnell that, some day, I hope to see the heels of —next week, I pray." And in a week we marched— and in the night too, like Welsh border raiders, whereat we cursed Clifford most heartily. Could we not take Bellashanny in a fine afternoon, smite O'Donnell hip and thigh within a week, in a fortnight be down on O'Neill's rear and drive him into de Burgh's net?— and there was a neat finish to the business. Ye know what befell then."

"Stout fellows!" commended Donn. "Better fighting I never saw."

"The only thing left to do. Myself never thought to come out of that trap, till our tough buccaneer found a road for us. But I am no longer a fool." Vaughan placed a hand on my shoulder. "Where do these fighting-men come out of, David Gordon? I have ridden this island north and west, and it is all a wilderness—woods and marshes and bare hills, and clay hamlets hidden in corners—and ragged peasants walking after the tail of black oxen; yet we send trained troops into that wilderness and they come out not at all, or they come out broken. Where come the smiters from?"

"From the soil," said I, "wherefrom all fighting-men come."

Maguire clapped Vaughan's shoulder in his friendly impulsive way. "If ever England beats us," he cried, "it is men like you and Clifford will do it."

"England will beat you in the end, Maguire," said Vaughan confidently.

"In the end!" I wondered. "Where is the end?"

"Let that be. But I know that if I face O'Donnell again, ye will see me with an advance guard, a rear guard, a strong reserve, and an open road behind."

"We will not see any of these things, jailer," put in Donn, laughing ruefully. "You keep the devil's own grip on us."

And that was plain truth. Maguire and I had confidently looked forward to an escape on the march down from Sligo, but Vaughan had kept us under such strict guard that we never got the faintest chance. Tadg Ironhand with his wound he had bestowed in a safe place in Sligo out of Dunkellin's reach, and of him no word had reached us, though we learned later that he had made good his escape.

Now we had been three weeks in Athenree, and Vaughan's grip was surer than ever. He had treated us fairly and very wisely. He had taken us down to the dungeons of the keep and chosen the best one for us, one of the few that had light from outside. It had a stone floor and stone walls, and a stone arch for a roof, an iron-clamped door, and a barred slit of window level with the fosse. And outside the door was a dark stone passage and stone steps leading up to the main guard, with another strong door at the head of them.

"Ye are dangerous men," he told us, "and I will hold ye with might and main!"

"My soul to perdition! but you will so," said Donn sadly, looking round him in the grey light.

"Ye can have these quarters," went on Vaughan, "or ye can pass me word of honour."

"What is that?" asked Donn eagerly.

"It is this, and I pray you to accept it: plight me word that for one week ye will not seek to escape, and at the end of that time renew it if ye see fit. Meantime, you will have full freedom within Athenree, and without the walls if accompanied by me or an officer deputed."

"My fine hero!" cried Donn heartily. "I plight my honour this minute."

It was the only thing to do at that time. There was no hope, yet, of an invasion out of the north, and there would be no heroism in immuring ourselves in a stone cell. And now for three weeks we had renewed our word, and we had nothing whereof to complain. Sir Francis was kind. Wishful to give us as much freedom as was possible, he did not quarter us in the Castle, where the hours were disciplined, but lodged us in a wooden-joisted house below his doubtful North Wall. In this he showed his trust, for in the rear of the house was a drying-green sloping up to the glacis, and to escape any dark night we had only to risk a ten-foot drop into the dry ditch. In these quarters we were wholly free, and our landlady, a woman out of Wales, widow of a camp-surgeon, was careful of our needs and our comfort.

II

Doncadh Donn Maguire, always gay of heart, was enjoying life to the full, and, indeed, but for a certain irk of mind, I too had no cause to complain. Donn's father, the great old Hugh Maguire, was ever a stern and serious man, and had never yielded anything but reprimand and restraint to his son's levity of spirit, but now the lad was free, though I kept some sort of hold on him, and he found congenial companions amongst the garrison officers. These were of the new train-bands, young fellows all, not yet soured by war, coming mostly from the wide country of Devon, and so in habit of mind and pursuit of sport very kin to the Irish without the Pale. Donn knew the English tongue, and had been to England in O'Neill's train, and so was at home amongst them. He was to be found in their quarters most of his waking hours. He threw them at dice; he matched them at rapier foil; borrowed a horse and went hunting and racing with them; bought, borrowed, or stole a gamecock of high breed, and fought mains all over south Galway as far as the Clare passes—and was rival with them for the favour of the few ladies in the garrison.

I was of the quieter breed and not made for easy friendships. That ugly, set face of mine was against that, as well as the reputation that rumour had falsely tied on me. The young fellows shied away and held me in something like awe. Some of them had seen the quarrel in the "Pied Horse" in Dublin; all had heard exaggeratedly of the raid on Rickard the Sassenach; two or three had been at the harrying of myself and Father Senan at Corrib; and the fight in Sligo gate-tower was known to all. None of these adventures, one might say, was of my own seeking or habit; I no more than happened to be drawn into them, and chance had centred on me and on my blackcock's feather. Belike it was that unique plume that called attention to me and gave me a dangerous name.

Though Donn Maguire was of my own age he never treated me as such. Rather was I the gruff, but not too difficult, uncle. He confided in me, never took my advice, made fun of me in his gay way, and looked to me to get him out of small scrapes. He borrowed and spent the last of my coins, and then, through the agency of the Galway merchants, raised credit in his father's name, and came to me clinking a full purse. Whereupon I laid him on his back, took it away from him, and doled him out coins painfully when his need grew clamorous.

With only two of the English officers was I actually on easy terms. One was Vaughan himself, a sterling man, who improved on acquaintance. He had seen life in camp and court, and could sail in all winds. A keen, satiric man, veiling a strong core. My habit was to visit him at the Castle in the forenoon, take a cup of wine with him, and listen to his talk of three courts—wild tales sometimes; and on occasion he visited us in our quarters.

The other was Ned Billing, Captain of the North Gate, a ruddy, grizzle-headed veteran, very fond of a dry French wine, and an expert in the chase. He had spent so many years in Connacht that he was grown Irish in habit and very largely in sympathy. He was one of the few English that spoke Gaelic fluently. "Old am I for changing," he told me, "and stiff in the bone for night work, or with Wat Tyrrell I might be." This Walter Tyrrell was an Englishman, and a very notable leader of forays on the Irish side.

Ned was indeed a great lover of the chase, and had himself bred two fine hounds named Satan and Urith Ban. He knew every covert from Suck to Oranmore, and was not guiltless of running another man's stag— as I found out in our expeditions into Dunkellin woods.

CHAPTER V

I

I was having supper with Vaughan in the upper hall when he broached his subject. He leaned back in his chair and yawned. "I am tired of this Athenree," he said.

"I was tired three weeks ago."

"Your luck will better itself, mayhap. Never a blade is out in al' Connacht, and what your northern smiters are at I know not. Conyers Clifford would seem to have forgotten me—not a word from Athlone these ten days. So will I forget him. Know what I am doing to-morrow?"

"Coming out with Ned Billing to kill Clanricard's deer."

"No. I am riding into Galway to see Dick Bingham. Care to ride with me?"

"If I might."

"Bingham is starting his Wednesday receptions," he said, giving me a careless shrewd eye. "It might be worth while looking over his Spanish-blooded beauties."

He kept watching me out of the side of an eye, and I looked at my plate.

"There is a dark-haired, rose-cheeked beauty from the head of Corrib that I would like to see again. Belike, she will be there—with her mother and long Cosby."

I made no remark.

"You know her, I think?"

"Do I?"

"The last time I saw you with her you had a right hearty grip of the maid. A hot-spirited beauty, and noble too. You must have spoken her fairly while crossing Corrib?"

"The old priest did."

"Yet it was your deeds she boasted. She knew so many aspects of your exploit that, I think, for a whole week I could have put hand on you."

"I know that, Sir Francis."

"It was no affair of mine. Well, we may renew our acquaintance to-morrow. But as regards Cosby—" He looked his question.

"I am done with him, unless he forces me."

"I will see that he does not." He got up from the table to snuff a tall candle, and spoke carelessly. "It might be that you will best him in another fashion. And, by the way, if you have a spare doublet——"

"Donn Maguire will buy me one in the square."

"Shall we take him?"

"That—or the dungeon."

"He is good company. I shall be ready after dinner-hour."

I was in bed, but not asleep, when Donn came in from the officers' messroom. He had taken his share of a heady wine of Portugal and was singing a love-song. He sat on the side of his bed across the room and his voice was muffled as he pulled tunic over head.

"Pity," I said, "that you have not a decent doublet to your back."

"Buy me one, leather shoulders."

"If you had, Vaughan and I might take you to Galway with us."

"God's blood!" He had acquired the English oaths to help out his many in the Gaelic. "Have you not a full purse of mine hidden away somewhere?" He gazed all round the room. "It is not in this house, for where is the chink I have not searched?"

"It is lean enough now, and only enough to equip one of us—and that one is not wild Doncadh."

"Our credit is good—and when we get to Galway——"

"Galway! You will spend the day in the dungeon."

Before I could guard he had me sprawling on the floor, and it took me ten minutes to master him and roll him helplessly in his bed covering.

II

Shortly after noon—a wonderful warm day for the last week of September—Donn and I, freshly arrayed, were about to set out for the Castle, when Tom Pybus, Vaughan's body-servant, came clumping to our door. A queer dumb fellow, this big trooper. Here in Athenree he had always avoided me, and if ever I caught his pale blue eye there was something sheepish and abashed in it. That I could understand. I had treated him roughly and something contemptuously, and no soldier could forget such treatment.

Now he was excited in a lowering sort of way, and saluted us stiffly as he came into our quarters. "The Governor's compliments," he said. "He is not riding into Galway to-day."

Donn swore a great Gaelic oath.

"My master bade me say that he will call on you later," said Pybus, and strode out of the room.

"Messages from Athlone?" I called after him.

He turned. "Yes, sir."

"Any news?"

He hesitated. "There is a rumour——"

"Out with it, Thomaus, old dog-face," cried Donn.

"Fighting with O'Neill near Armagh——"

"My soul! and ye running."

"It is said the rebels beat the Lord de Burgh in two fights."

Donn's hand came clump on the table. "And what else would the rebels be doing, blast you? And the Maguires would be there too, by the High God!"

Pybus strode away, and Donn made for the door.

"Where to?" I called.

"To get the news at first hand." He spoke over his shoulder, his eyes flashing. Then he stopped, and came slowly back to the table where I was sitting.

"Remember we are prisoners here, Maguire," I said.

He sat down heavily. "Do I not know that now? And, David Gordon, it is only now that I know it. God! Think of what we are missing."

After a silence he spoke musingly. "But they are nice boys, the Sassenach, and—you are right, sober fellow—one should not go cocking bonnet among them in the time of their bad news. Hard words there might be, and I might have to stick one—or maybe two of them—through the gizzard.

259

Let us be waiting awhile!" He got up suddenly and paced up and down the room. "That dungeon! That dungeon! It is like a stone coffin to get out of."

"One of us inside and the other outside——"

"By the great wind! A bright thought! My fine man! You could be getting down in the ditch and pulling a bar out of the grid."

"The grid is too narrow. A friendly fellow like you might bribe a jailer on the outside."

"The best way to bribe one of these is to clout him over the sconce, and devil the hardier fellow than yourself——"

"And my head on a pike a short time after."

And all afternoon we discussed and rediscussed half in play, half in earnest, our chances of escape. In the end we decided that if O'Donnell came south of the Cong line one of us would lodge in the dungeon, while the other, from the outside, must seek by guile or force to effect a rescue.

"Vaughan is wise and wily," said Donn doubtfully, "and will see what is in our mind. Like enough he will pop you in to keep me company."

And so the discussion circled round once more.

III

It was evening when Vaughan came to see us. He was wearing military dress, and his face was set to hide his thoughts. I pulled a chair in for him without a word, and he sat, his arms on the board, while Donn filled out a stoup of wine and moved it before him.

He took it and smiled to us. "Your good health,

260

my enemies!" he said, and emptied it at a draught. "I thank you for your nice sensibility to-day."

"Bad news, Sir Francis?" I put to him.

"Bad news, indeed." His voice was quiet. "But good news ye would call it, and ye may. Your O'Neill and O'Donnell have given us another lesson in strategy, and a double stroke to drive it home."

Across the table I saw the light leap in Maguire's eyes, and his yellow mane seemed to lift. Yet he said no word, and did no more than move the flagon in front of Vaughan.

Vaughan helped himself, and looked at me. "Last night I made complaint that Clifford had forgotten me, and at the time his rider was on the way. I would that he had forgotten me a little longer or had better news. Ye are eager to know?"

"What you are pleased to tell."

"Not pleased, my friends. But I will tell ye, as Clifford has written. Ye are aware that the Lord Deputy's design was to strike from Connacht and through the Gap-of-the-North by Armagh. Ye know what befell the first stroke—and the second was no luckier. At the very beginning young Trimblestown and a thousand men were cut to pieces at a bog-pass in upper Meath by Tyrrell and O'Connor."

"That is the way the two have," murmured Donn.

"But the main attack on O'Neill was under de Burgh himself. He rebuilt the fort of Portmore, and tried to wile O'Neill into the open out of his strong places round Dungannon. O'Neill gave wile for wile. He kept his main force masked, and set his horse and light-armed men to watch and harry the Queen's forces. Both leaders were playing for time: O'Neill waiting to hear from O'Donnell before risking open fight, and de Burgh waiting for Clifford's flanking movement before he drove O'Neill into the trap. And then came Clifford's failure, and O'Donnell with a picked force came hastening to his ally. After that was no more biding time. De Burgh found himself face to face, for the first time, with heavy-armed soldiers—gallowglasses, you call them—and men trained to the arquebus. Twice he essayed fight, and twice was he beaten, and now the remnants of his force are scattered from Dundalk to Dublin, and Portmore is close beleaguered by the north. That is the tale."

"It was great fighting," said Donn, a muscle twitching in his cheek. He was holding himself in very well.

"The north has given us a big debt to repay," said Vaughan. "But there is something that cannot be restored to us. William de Burgh, who was husband to my sister, was sore wounded at Drumfluich, and this day lies under the sod at Armagh."

"It is good to die in war," said Donn. "God rest him."

"Amen," said I.

"He was a good soldier," said Vaughan, "and honest—no courtier, but believed men as they spoke. A malison on the ruffling boasters of Dublin! They made him belittle his enemy, and stayed safe within walls while he went out to die."

A silence followed. We all sat thinking our own thoughts, and these in time came to the same groove.

"I am sorry," said Vaughan, "but I must hold you."

"The devil's tight hold too," said Donn chagrinedly.

"And our intended ride to Galway must be postponed for many weeks."

"That does not matter."

"I fear that a dull time is before you—but, belike, a right lively one for us. Clifford is taking no risks. He assumes that O'Donnell will make a descent on Connacht before winter. If he breaks the Sligo line there is nothing to hold him between there and here, and it is here that we shall hold him—Galway, Athlone, Athenree. I pray God that he will venture so far."

"If Hugh Roe comes," said Donn slowly, "you will, maybe, not thank God for answering your prayer."

Vaughan laughed for the first time. "At least we shall welcome him warmly," he said, and turned to me. "Cong and Tuam are being abandoned, and we are to be strengthened by the Cong garrison." He looked from one to the other of us. "I can trust you two soldiers not to quarrel with the new men?"

"Faith no!" Donn promised. "If the clans come south of Cong we will take to your dungeon and bribe your jailer."

He nodded understanding. "Until then I pray you to leave things as they are. There is no need to immure yourselves within walls, for I assure you that escape is impossible."

We left it at that for the time.

CHAPTER VI

I

IT was on a dank afternoon in October that the reinforcements from Cong arrived.

At the time I happened to be alone on the sunken North Wall in the rear of our quarters. There was a moist feel in the air and a thin mist hung low over the sweep of plain that I could see over the head of the slope outside the wall. I was gazing idly over the grey level, dotted with kine and, here and there, a spear-armed herdsman on a rough garran, when the long line of the Cong garrison crawled out of the woods on to the north road: first a troop of horse, then a column of foot, a disorderly array of townspeople, a medley of ox-drawn wagons, a park of culverin one behind the other, more ordered foot, and the rear brought up by another troop of horse. They crawled slowly across the plain, and I watched with some interest until the bastion hid them from my eyes. Then I went down to my quarters, and, in tune with the dull weather, speculated dispiritedly on the future.

We were doomed to be prisoners within these walls for how long? A throw of dice, a main of cocks, a scraping of foils—boys' playthings! A little hunting, it might be! but no adventuring to Galway. Nothing but idling amongst soldierly enemies, with a careful watch on tongue and manner, while Sir Francis Vaughan prepared a warm reception for our friends. Was there nothing we could do? Nothing!

Donn was slow in getting back from his usual visit to the Castle, and I think I dozed for a while and dreamt that I was deep underground with someone knocking over my head.

It was Tom Pybus at the door. It was evening then, and I was hungry. I cursed Donn before calling Pybus to come in. "Sir Francis begs your presence at the Castle, sir," he told me.

"Was that the Cong garrison?"

"Yes, master, and Cong town with it."

I thought I understood Vaughan's message. He wanted me to meet Cosby in his presence, and make sure that no sword-work would ensue. There was no danger of that now—on my part—but Vaughan had better have his surety. I donned my best tunic, smoothed out my blackcock's feather, left sword and *sgian* behind, and followed Pybus. As I slanted through the square at the heart of the town, the Cong garrison was taking up quarters in the wooden shelters that Vaughan had hastily built for it.

There was a group of officers round the peat and bog-pine fire in the great hall of the Castle—some, my acquaintances of the garrison, others of the newly arrived force—and the scullions were laying the table for supper.

Ned Billing of the North Gate called to me down the length of the hall as I strode towards the turret stairs, and I waited for him. "Blazes!" cried he, "but we have the full house, and some of the sweetest maidens in Connacht. Come away up and look at them."

"Old fool!" said I.

"Not me. But look you, the mind is at me to cut the yellow head off young Maguire."

"What has he done?"

"A little friend of mine—Duvesa MacTheobald, who else?—and he already whispering in her ear. Son, the loveliest dove hair——"

"Bah!" I cried, "a finger-snap for your dove hair."

"Surely, surely! There is a head of black curls would suit me just as well."

And to this day I wonder why my heart, that must have known, was not dunting in my side.

I pulled aside the curtain at the stairhead and stepped into the upper hall. It was finely lit with new, heavy waxen candles, and the tapestry stirred gently in some draught of air. About the cavernous fireplace were scattered fully a score of people, men and ladies. Donn Maguire was there for sure, and Vaughan, and big Cosby with his upright head and light hair, and talking to him a tall dame whose back was turned.

And facing me down the length of the hall was Eithne, the lady of my dreams.

II

I stopped for a single instant and my heart gave an empty leap. And then my feet took me up the hall. There was nothing else they could do. Easy, now, easy, David Gordon! Your ugly hatchet face is a fine shield, and many eyes will be looking at you. Take your cap in your hand, and you will be getting through this somehow.

I walked directly to Vaughan. "Your pleasure, Governor?" said I.

"You were slow in coming, David," he greeted me, with easy familiarity.

The tall dame turned. She was Dame Bevinda O'Flaherty, that noble lady—the long chin, the long nose, and the deep eyes under the brow.

"Captain Dame Bevinda," introduced Vaughan, "let me present David Gordon."

Her eyes held mine, and she gave me her hand frankly. "Ah! Blackcock's Feather," she said, and smiled. "Connacht has heard of you, and Connacht has been unkind to you."

"Not always, Dame," said I, bowing deeply.

"And this is the Lady Eithne," went on Vaughan.

Alas! we were far away from the Glen of the Echo and the mood that was easy on us then. Our eyes met. She curtsied, and I bowed. That was all. But while there was a flush of warmth on her cheeks there was an odd transparent pallor as of excitement about her mouth, and her dark eyes shone deeply under the lovely dark curve of her brows.

Vaughan put his hand on my arm and kept it there. "Captain Cosby," he said, "this is my friend, David Gordon."

We stood up to our full heights and looked at each other. He was tall as I was, and his eyes, that used to be bosses of pale stone, were now yellow like a lion's. This was my enemy. I knew that now. More than that, I was his enemy. I knew that too. Vaughan was wise in bringing us together in this company, for if I had met Cosby anywhere else my hand would have sought hilt at a whisper.

"I have met Captain Cosby," said I, and could not bend my stiff neck.

"And will again, by the devil's grace," he said in his strong voice, his head upright and his neck like a pillar below his powerful jaw.

"Which side his majesty?" said Vaughan. And then quickly, "But let that be, gentlemen."

"At your service, Governor," said Cosby. "He is your prisoner."

He turned his shoulder to me and spoke to Eithne, and I saw her shoulders lift in a long breath of relief.

Dame Bevinda was now speaking to Vaughan. It seemed that he had placed his upper chambers at the disposal of the Dame and her party, and she was insisting that they must keep the disciplined hours of the Castle. She asked him the supper-hour, and he told her seven of the clock. "A proper time," she commented. "If we might, we will go to my woman, Breadh, till then." She turned to me again and smiled. "There will be great talking between you and me, Master Gordon."

Vaughan and Cosby accompanied them to the turret stairs. Eithne gave me one quick look and one quick smile, and that was all. No word had passed between us that used to talk so freely. A great strangeness had come down upon us, and our old mood seemed gone beyond recalling.

I was alone on the floor, and here and there curious eyes were on me. I looked round for Donn. There he was, under a wall-light, Ned Billing and himself making talk and laughter with a bonny fair-haired woman. I went towards them.

Donn caught my arm. "Lady Duvesa Mac-Theobald," he introduced. And to the lady, "This is David Gordon of the blackcock's feather you wanted to meet, Lady Duvesa."

The lady's merry, grey, black-lashed eyes went over me closely, and I hoped that, having had their fill of my dour face, they would need no more. "I am glad to meet the great David Gordon," she said in her silver tinkling voice. "All Connacht speaks of him and his feather."

"He did his share," said Donn, "when he was well watched."

"And I hear that he can make pretty speeches too."

"Mother o' God!" cried Donn in surprise. "Whoever heard him make one?"

"He had much practice by Corrib shore," said she, her eyes looking at me under lashes.

"All he did by Corrib," said Donn, "was to run like a hare."

"That hare had a lovely form," said the lady, making play on the word.

Only I understood. Donn and Ned had heard nothing of my sheltering in the Glen of the Echo. This young lady had, and I could make a close guess where she had got her knowledge. Before she might indulge in further banter the bugle went for supper, and there was a movement towards the great hall. Bold Donn edged off with his Duvesa, and left Billing and me to follow in the ruck.

We found a seat well below the salt, and Ned hunched over a great round of beef and carved for both of us. "One good thing," said he, "this alarm of war has given us the pick of the beeves of Hymany—besides the darling ones."

"Beef for me."

"I saw you being presented to the lovely Eithne."

"You know her?"

"Know her! With all Connacht I respect the mother and love the daughter. Let me be thinking, now, of all the times I laid my heart at her feet only

269

this last winter. But where the good? She but made play with me, so I turned to fair-hair—and look! here am I carving beef for an Albannach gallowglass-leader while fair-hair listens to an addle-pated Eireannach with a yellow mane."

"Try raven locks again."

"That I will. Though bluff Cosby has the pull of me there." He looked up the table and grew serious. "The shame of hell to see her wasted on that chuff![1] I suspect the mother. A wise lady, that Bevinda, for all her boldness. Note you that she draws no steel in this war. Your Red Hugh, in his swoops, gets no stable hold on Connacht, and until he does she leans to the power that leaves Cashlean-na-Kirka an unburned roof. But she is Eireannach at heart, and not ill-pleased to see us Sassenach get our belly-full of hard knocks. You will be knowing why she chose Athenree instead of Galway as winter quarters?"

"I do not."

"Because Cosby is here. The maid and he are plighted, and the wedding is to be here on All Saints'."

So that was it.

I looked up the length of the table. Her beauty under her black hair was like a light. No longer now was she demure, but talking lightsomely with Vaughan. And Vaughan himself was changed, with a gallant flash in his eye and a touch of colour in his face. Cosby at the other side was busy with his platter. He took no part in the word-bandying, but ate his supper stolidly, as much as if saying, "Let the maid talk! I have her leashed." My gaze was still on her musingly, when she glanced down the table, and our

[1] Boor.

eyes locked. She looked at me long and steadily, a keen look with something puzzled in it, and something wistful, and something else that I could not define. My underbrowed look at last made her eyes waver and sink.

"The little rogue! The little rogue!" chuckled Billing. "Did you get yon? The woman's wiles of her, letting the eye drop shyly and swithering the heart of you. With that shy trick she won all the hearts in Galway last winter. Amy of Dunkellin—that ye robbers stole from us—and herself shared the palm at the Governor's routs. Even plain old Dick Bingham shaved his chin in the Eireannach fashion to please her. But she was not to be captured. She played us deftly, one against the other, winning hearts and reserving favour; spurning the too bold, encouraging the shy, tempering the despair of the fallen. Faith! I know the whole gamut. Was I not through it?— and will again, by Jupiter!"

"You forget Cosby."

"Beelzebub's bowels! but I did. She is no longer the free maid. The false step she has taken. After playing aye so gently and kindly with our hearts she has yielded her own to as blustering a chuff as ever crossed the Irish Sea—even if he is lord of a baron's hall in Derby. But mark you, Davy boy, I suspect the mother and her liking for that safe baronial hall in middle England."

After that I did not pay much heed to the veteran's babbling.

III

I went across the square, where a big camp-fire blazed before the wooden shielings, and down East

Lane to our quarters below the North Wall. But I did not stay indoors. I stumbled across the slope of drying-green at the rear and from there climbed on the wall. The sentinel, coming down towards me, challenged loudly, but knew my voice in reply, and paced back towards the corner bastion.

I leaned my elbows on the shelter-wall and looked across the night. It was black and quiet, and a jack o' lanthorn flickered and jumped in the marshes beyond the Galway road. Eastwards of the bastion the night fires of the kerns made a yellow glow, and no sound came out of the darkness other than small puffs of air sighing fitfully over the grass.

A fool and a dreamer! These were David Gordon. I had been living on dreams many a week, and now I knew their emptiness. Because a maid had saved my life by Corrib and treated me with a great kindness I had built a bower for her—and she had many bowers to choose from, and was not like to choose mine. After all, I was, myself, to blame. I was only an adventurer flying for life, and for me she had done a fine thing finely. All the rest was in my own fancy. Ah well! I was used to disappointment. And I had no cause to complain. Since coming to this Ireland, life had moved for me, and would keep moving, God willing. This dispelling of a dream was only an episode in the life of one whose first fine ideal of youth had been shattered by eight years of sordid living. Again had I to gird my loins—and I would. This imprisonment would not last for ever, and already my name was known. A home and life waited me at Dungiven or at Derry Columcill. But, dear God! I was lonely—lonely. . . . And she had said that she would be lonely too. . . . And that would pass. Be not sorry for yourself.

I threw up head and laughed. And a voice below hailed me.

"My gay fellow! Who have you up there in the dark?" It was Donn.

"Bad company," I told him.

"The devil has the best stories," said he. "Let me share the laugh."

"Laugh at yourself, then."

"And welcome! 'Laugh at yourself,' says Mealachy Beg, 'and you will be sure that no one else will!' There's a man in the house looking for you."

I knew who that man was. I scrambled down into the drying-green at Donn's side. "You are late home."

"Late! Sure it is no hour at all, but that old firebrand, Bevinda of the O'Flaherty, took the ladies off under her wing. Tell me, my long boy, did Donal Ballagh ever say a word about the lovely Duvesa MacTheobald?"

"He did not."

"I always knew that fellow had no eyes in his head."

"He had, for one of the two finest in Connacht."

"Let that stand. I know the first."

"Maybe you do," said I.

The man I saw leaning on the table in the wavering light of the candle within our room was Cathal O'Dwyer of the Glens. "You are welcome, Cathal O'Dwyer," I greeted him.

"Am I, David Gordon?" he asked wistfully, his face aquiver.

"A friend! my own brother! Rest you. This is Doncadh Donn Maguire of Fermanagh."

"Namely son of a namely father—Breastplate of the North," acknowledged Cathal.

"And a heart in him harder than the breastplate," said Donn.

In the Glen of the Echo, Cathal, recovering from his wound, had been in weakly health, but, now that his wound was healed, a more terrible blight had fallen on him. He was thin and haggard, his shoulders fallen in and an angry red flush high up on his cheek-bones.

"Is Garrodh here with you?" I asked him.

"He is not. I came in with the O'Flaherty tail."

"And your lodging?"

He hesitated. "The kerns are kind."

"But I, your brother, should be kinder. There is an airy attic up under the roof, and out in our green you will get all the sun that is going."

He demurred faintly, and I kept patting his shoulder. I was woefully grieved for this, my friend. There was a terrible fatal light in his eyes that I could have wept to see. Indeed, he was near tears himself and his face quivered. Donn poured him out a fine mether of wine, and he drank it slowly and daintily. And then Donn, with an excuse, left us. He knew O'Dwyer's story.

"God is good," said O'Dwyer. "The fine friends one meets when the need is the sorest—finer than I deserve."

"What you deserve from me," I comforted him, "is everything. You and your foster-brother, God rest him, set my feet on a man's road."

"And it brought you here?"

"And will lead again from here. And here, too, there may be work for me."

He looked at me closely. "There may be, surely." He threw his hands wide. "But look at me," he said, "and the strength gone from me—a blast on me—and my work undone."

"Is it still on you?"

"I cannot help it. Mark you, David Gordon, it is easy enough to kill Cosby the Killer. A throw of spear or pull of bow and it is done. But I want to see him face to face and see the knowledge of doom in his eyes. And I am only a withered branch—a withered branch." He looked long at me. "I know," he said. "I know. I will not put it on you, my friend."

I looked on the ground and spoke between my teeth. "Whatever you put on me," I said, "I will do it before the face of God."

"Then I can rest," he said.

And I knew if Cosby killed this man I would pursue Cosby to the gates of hell.

Why must I hate Cosby so?

CHAPTER VII

I

NEXT morning, after breakfast, I took Cathal into the drying-green, where the sun was warm; and there I left him, wrapped in his long cloak. When I got back to our room, Donn Maguire had disappeared. Myself slung on shoulder-sash, and, instead of Andrea Ferrara, thrust black-*sgian* at hip. Carefully I brushed bonnet and re-set feather, and, throwing short day-cloak on shoulder, made my way towards the Castle, where the renewal of my word was due to the Governor.

Crossing the square, I saw Cosby directing the completion of the wooden shelters for his men. He saw me, too, and strutted across boldly, his basnet jauntily set on his upright head. He faced in front of me, and I had, perforce, to halt. "Gordon," said he, his face cold stone, "we are ill friends, and will remain so."

"Ill friends, no!" said I. "I am your enemy."

He sneered his cheerless grin. "My enemy! A rebel hired-fighting-man: If Sir Francis Vaughan, who governs here, had not forbidden it, I might show you how we chastise rebels. But there is one warning I will give you: presume not on your acquaintance with the Lady Eithne O'Flaherty."

"I am on my way to thank her," said I, "for once saving my life."

His eyes yellowed. "You had better move carefully."

276

"I will be very careful."

For a moment he forbore my eye, and then, swinging on his heel, stalked away.

The great hall of the Castle was empty, except for the halberdmen on guard. The sergeant told me that the Governor was in the town, and, on this, I ventured to the upper private hall, where I found a middle-aged tire-woman building birch logs about a new-lit fire. She was a stranger to me.

"A terrible thing," said I into the air, "to waste the fine morning at the sleeping."

"Is that the way, tall young hero?" said she, merrily aware of my meaning. "The young ones are about this hour and more, and maybe could be found for the looking."

"I came to see the Governor," I told her, "and will wait for him on the East Wall."

"It is a good place to be at the waiting, surely," said she pleasantly.

At the left of the hall was a door giving on the East Wall, a favourite exercise-ground of Vaughan's and mine. I lifted the latch and stepped out, and there was Eithne herself, strolling down towards the bastion at the corner. She was not alone. Duvesa MacTheobald was with her, and on that maiden's left hand, on the edge of the glacis, strutted the bold Doncadh Donn Maguire. Their backs were to me, and I was minded to slink back within the doorway before they turned. But I hesitated too long, and they swung round at the corner and saw me. So I walked up the wall with something of the pikeman in my parade. And, with a pang, memory recalled the quiet Glen of the Echo, and the days I used to go down to meet a maid at Echo-point.

It was a rare morning, with a high clear sky full of austere autumn sun, and a clean breeze out of the west. And this young lass, walking straight and lissome in the sun, with a black curl blown across her brow, was born of the sun and the wind. She welcomed me with a smile, a warm, somehow half-shy, half-mocking smile, her head a little bent and her eyes looking at me from under her bent brows. Donn and his lady welcomed me too, but not so much for my company as for my convenience.

"I was telling the ladies," Donn cried, "that this was our favourite stroll of a morning, and that we would maybe not permit them to share it."

It was Vaughan's and my exercise-ground, not Donn's, but I let it go.

"This morning we will take, then," cried Eithne. Frankly she came to me and took my arm. "I want to talk to you, David Gordon," she said. "Be off, young ones!"

II

And so, in couples, we walked the East Wall from Castle to bastion and back again. Below, the glacis sloped to the open space behind a street of low houses; at her shoulder was the parapeted shelter-wall, and beyond it the grey-green plain spreading to the woods, with smoke from the shieling fires blowing across it and mounted kerns driving cattle to the grazing.

"And now, David Gordon," she said, "you will tell me everything about Dungiven and my darling Amy, wife of your cousin."

"She is very happy."

"And her husband at war?"

278

"Then she may be sad too."

"Tell me about her. How does she carry herself?"

"She is very kind and very wise."

"Go on, please! What is she doing in that place of men?"

"She is creating her own domain—building a sunken garden, with a fish pond, and a lily pond, and a walk of the box tree."

"And does she ever speak of one, poor Eithne ni Flaherty?"

"At great length. Of her impish ways and her love affairs—and her great ferocity."

"But she, indeed, might. Oh! but I would love to see her, and she happy!"

"And she would like that lady to visit her in her garden when it blooms," said I.

"Said she so? That would delight me." She let go my arm and clapped her hands, happiness in her voice.

"Yet I think that you will never visit that garden in bloom," said I, who could not let her be happy.

"Why do you think that?" she cried quickly, a little startle in her eyes.

"You will be very far away."

She threw up her head and looked at me. "That is a poor reason—that is a poor reason." There was pain in her voice, and then she was calm again and spoke even-toned. "If Amy asks me I will come— even if I be far away."

"You will be welcome," said I.

"And, I wonder, who will welcome me?" And then she was silent, which was strange, for never had

I known this maid to be lacking in speech. We met Donn and his fair-haired Duvesa once, twice, before another word passed between us, and then she changed the subject. "How is my old priest?"

"Well. And is not done speaking of your splendid goodness."

"Goodness, no! Happiness, yes! Was I not a queen then?"

"With your wise man—and your fool." Why was I so bitter?

"But we were happy."

"Surely. It were churlish to regret folly."

"Oh!" she cried. "Were you the foolish one?"

"Who else, lady?"

"Why, I was beginning to think, that I—but never mind. Since we are at Corrib, let us go on. Ye got home safely?"

"We did."

"And you came back to Saimhor leading a troop of horse?"

"A troop of bonny men."

"And lost them in Sligo tower?"

"Left most of them outside—alive, I hope."

"And twenty of you held the gate-tower against odds?"

"For a little only."

"They speak of a man who sang the sword-song of Black Gillian, and was more terrible than Conal Cearnach or Cuchulain. . . . He wore a bonnet with a blackcock's feather. . . . And he came a prisoner to Athenree. Men say that a man like that man could not be kept behind stone walls unless the walls suited him—for a reason."

This was hitting with bare steel.

"He was but a plain soldier—and foolish," said I.

"Still foolish."

"Still the same folly, my lady.—Here is one, now, that is no fool."

"And there speaks folly. But I like your first folly best." She laughed, not unhappily now.

Cosby came striding along and stopped before us, his light, insolent eyes on me. "Said your thanks?" he inquired shortly.

"They will keep till to-morrow," said I carelessly.

"Eithne!" he cried, "if this prisoner is importunate, a word to me or Sir Francis——"

She laughed merrily. "David Gordon," she said, "was most entertaining, and I look forward to to-morrow." She looked at me with smiling eyes. "I shall not be lonely any more—but I was."

"At your service, lady." I lifted bonnet and marched by Cosby, my shoulder stiffened in case he barred the way. But he forbore that push.

III

Within the hall I came face to face with Captain Dame Bevinda. She smiled at me, and then shook her head. "You have been taking the air with my daughter, David Gordon?" she said bluntly.

"I have, Dame."

"Was that wise, stubborn man?"

"It was not, Dame."

"You know she is wedding Sir William Cosby at All Saints'?"

"It is said, Dame."

"And I say it now. Let me advise you for your

good. But why? You will go your own gait, I know, but where will it lead you?"

"Where it will, Dame."

She looked at me steadily under her brows—her daughter's very look. "I wonder what you would dare, David Gordon," she half-mused. "Ah! daring is easy for men, but men such as you are never sure how much to dare. Can you read that, Blackcock's Feather?"

"I will think it over, Dame."

"Do that, then, David Gordon." And she turned and left me.

In the bailey of the Castle I met Vaughan hurrying in from his defences. "You are in haste," said he.

"And you too, Lord Governor."

He laughed his light laugh. "To perdition with dull duty! I was hasting to share the favours of a darkly-fair damosel. Hast seen her this morning?"

"On the East Wall."

"Lucky rogue!" Then he grew serious. "Art aware that her marriage with Cosby is set for All Saints'? You are. Then what is to be done about it?"

"Ask Captain the Dame that."

"Rather would I ask the daughter. I fear that she is wasted on our Cosby, and I would venture the guess that she knows it. If I help to spoil Cosby's sport I look to you to do your part. Where is he now?"

"With her on the East Wall."

"Then here goes spoil-sport," he cried, and hurried away.

But I think that the lady had already put her glamour on him, and that he was eager to be something more than spoil-sport.

Donn Maguire overtook me at the square, and thrust his arm within mine. "You will listen to a few words from me, shut-mouth," he said.

"These four weeks——"

"You never told me you knew Eithne ni Flaherty."

"Nothing to tell."

"No? Tell me, now. For a fortnight you saw her every day?"

"Ten days only."

"But you two became great friends?"

"Well?"

"And it might be a little more?"

"You forget long Cosby."

"I do not. Duvesa MacTheobald——"

"Let us speak of that one."

"I like her," said Donn simply, and very seriously.

"A small saying for you."

"Just that. But wait you! Duvesa thinks—she more than thinks—that this affair with Cosby is of the mother's planning, and that if you——"

"A kind clan of busybodies ye all are," I stopped him sourly.

"To hell with you, then!" he cried hotly, and threw my arm away.

But I caught his arm back.

"Mother o' God!" he cried warmly. "Would I not give my right hand to help?"

"We are prisoners here, and can do nothing."

"Something must be done. Take you to the dungeon, and O'Dwyer and I will get you out of it in spite of hell. Remember you are cousin to Donal Ballagh, and what he did——"

But I was set in a hard mood, and stopped him. "When O'Donnell gets south of Cong you or I will take to that dungeon. Let the rest be."

Whereon Donn cursed me fluently.

CHAPTER VIII

I

I WILL not chronicle closely the smooth-running course
of the next eight or ten days. They were uneventful
days in Athenree, but from outside it, away up north,
news of stirring happenings came thick and fast.

For O'Donnell donned his eagle wings, swooped
down on Clifford's northern line, and smashed it
utterly. Sligo fell, and the O'Connor Roe was sore
punished for his English leanings; Ballymote was
abandoned; Boyle surrendered; Tulsk was burned
to the ground; and the clans rolled south, gathering
strength as they came. The MacFirbis, the O'Dowds,
the MacWilliams, the O'Haras, the MacDonaghs, the
O'Kellys, the MacDermott, the O'Costello threw off
the loyalist yoke and flocked to the northern standard.
Nothing could withstand that advance, and any day
now Cong and Tuam might be occupied.

Donn and I waited the word, and no word came.
Suddenly all news of the advance ceased. It was as
if the clans sank into the ground. They might have
swerved east to Athlone or west to Galway, or, for all
we knew, marched back with their immense booty to
the Saimhor.

Athenree was full as a hive with the loyalist refugees
pouring in to the safety of its walls. Clanricard and
Dunkellin in our rear were marshalling their unwilling
clans; Clifford at Athlone wrote urgently to Ormonde
for reinforcements; Bingham of Galway hurried

Londonwards on like business; and Vaughan, bent on holding Athenree, strengthened his North Wall with half a score of culverin, filled his granaries, and salted down his beeves. Notwithstanding the many a lesson, the English forgot that the Eagle of the North seldom came the expected road. They were but circling themselves for another onfall.

Donn and I now held ourselves aloof from the garrison and the loyalist lordlings. We looked on these latter as traitors to the blood that ran in them, and that view of ours they sensed and were bitter about. We owed it to Vaughan to take no part in bickerings, and if we sought the crowded company in the Castle there is no doubt but the hot-headed Maguire would have blade out of scabbard before a day.

II

But though we no longer visited the Castle of an evening, there was one thing we never failed to do. Each early forenoon we sought the East Wall between Castle and bastion, and there walked an hour with Eithne and her friend. That hour's walk was the accepted routine, accepted by the two ladies, and by Vaughan, and strangely enough by Dame Bevinda, and not disturbed by Cosby, whom now I saw only at a distance.

These were wholly pleasant walks for Donn, but for me there was a pain at heart to mar the pleasantness. For my lady was very kind and very sweet— and very happy. And I could not quite forgive her the happiness. She was once more the light-hearted, kindly maid who carried the sunlight all about her and was dowered with the unteachable art of winning

286

hearts. And she talked as only she could talk, and got me to talk too, recalling the days we had spent together by Corrib; and discussing her friend Amy, wife of Donal, and the ploys we would have when she came visiting the garden in bloom; and wondering about the conduct of the war, and whether Donal Ballagh would not surely be with Hugh Roe and come down and rescue us; and what we would do when we were so rescued. To that last point she came often and often, and I could not tell her, whereon she twitted me, and made queer subtle small suggestions, the drift of which I did not see. Oh! we, indeed, talked of many things, and ever since then, whenever I recall those days, I am angry with myself that I was not all happy. And always she came back wistfully to the great loneliness that was in her kingdom of Echo Glen when we were gone from it, and how great Maam and wide Corrib were lonesome under the sun.

With Dame Bevinda I became strangely friendly, and I often sat with her in the upper hall and talked of many things—but not again of her daughter. For some reason I could not fathom, she showed a liking for my company and my short answers, and I liked her straightforwardness and her steadfast purpose.

CHAPTER IX

I

ALL SAINTS' was due to fall on a Saturday. Came Monday of that week and a great hunt. Under Dame Bevinda's and Cosby's arranging everything seemed to be in good train for the wedding, and already the great hall and the upper hall were being decked for the feast.

"The pick of the beeves we have surely," said Ned Billing to Vaughan, "and a rough diet for a wedding."

"What would you have, old gourmand?"

"It is not too early for a yeld [1] hind in the south woods."

"With O'Donnell gone to earth there is no reason against your trying. Make it a hunt, and for my soul's sake, get some of these lordlings and their ladies out of town for a day."

And so the great hunt. Full threescore rode out of Athenree that Monday morning and streamed south towards the beech woods, and amongst them were close on a dozen ladies, including Eithne O'Flaherty and Duvesa MacTheobald. Billing persuaded Donn and me to be of the company, and while Donn hung back amongst the damsels, I, mounted on a big black horse of Vaughan's, rode close behind the Italian gaze and sleuth hounds with Ned and the huntsmen.

"A brave day for sight and scent," commented

[1] Barren.

288

Billing, lord in this his own domain, "but yon flare of red in the east looks like wind later in the day." He turned in his creaking saddle and surveyed the straggling, careless crowd, from which came laughter of maid and gallant. "Body of me!" he grumbled, after the fashion of the skilful veteran. "Look at them! Think of that noisy pack tracking a wary hind in her own coverts. Like enough, the shy beauties are this minute belly-to-earth for the Clare border. Lucky we'll be if we get enough venison for Saturday —and I pray old Beelzebub that it choke Cosby."

Much to his own chagrin his forebodings came to be true. The hunters were unruly, pressing amongst the dogs at scent or trying a gallop on their own down the glades, and the hunted were few and shy. Once we lost sight and scent in thick covert, and once a fine fat, fallow-doe broke safe away before the hounds could be laid on. By noon we had not a single head to our credit. Till then the company had not strayed far apart, and a single dining-wind on the horn brought them all together in an open glade near a brook.

"See them come to heel, now!" cried Billing sourly. "God be with the days when dinner depended on good hunting!" A juicy collop, new-killed, is worth the whole fee-and-fife of these dainty viands, that it takes one-two pack ponies to carry." Yet he spoke with his mouth full and busy, and kept a round-bellied quartern of muscadine hid within the bend of knee. "Davy, lad," he whispered, "when this gorging is done you and I will whistle off Satan and Urith Ban to a covert or two I ken."

After a look where Eithne sat at the other side of a hamper from Cosby I assented.

Billing and I had little difficulty in slipping away after eating. A word to the huntsmen, and we were soon agallop down a narrow wood-alley, the two famous hounds at heel. At the end of a quarter-mile this alley swung to the right, and, as I took the turn, I glanced behind. For a moment I thought I saw the flutter of a riding-kirtle round the bole of a beech, but my next stride took me out of view.

"'Ware followers!" I cried to Billing, just ahead.

"Let us be churlish, then." And he pressed on.

We did not slacken rein for a mile or more, and now we had the woods to ourselves. We cast two blank coverts, and then rode south a couple of long miles to where the land trended gently upwards. Here spruce and pine grew amongst the beeches, the ground had in places a carpet of fine needles, and the coverts were fewer between the long aisles of the trees. And here luck came suddenly. A deer broke from a clump of stunted hazel, and the great hounds at once sighted it, and, baying gloriously, laid on full pelt.

"A barren hind, by Christopher!" shouted the delighted Ned. "Well coated and strong in the haunch. This will test us."

The hunt led us first south and then a little east through open woods, and all the time the hind was in full view. I was never much enamoured of a blind following of slot [1] hounds, but here was a pleasant excitement in a plain running down of our quarry. Good it was to gallop loose-reined and feel the spring of a horse knowing the game; good to hear the whistle

[1] Track, trail.

of the wind and the unchecked thud of hooves; good to see the hounds at full stretch and cheer them on as they bayed; and, at the end, greatly exciting to judge from the white scut of the quarry the slow drawing in to the first bay.

That hind did not give us a span in the first mile, and when at last we began to wear her down we were well within Dunkellin woods. At long last, after it might be a full hour, Satan, leading white Urith by some lengths, brought the quarry to bay at the foot of a short steep brae. With rearing and trampling forelegs she held the hounds off until we raced near, and then she broke away, the hounds on her haunches. Twice more she was brought to bay before the hounds could hold her by a fallen tree near a wood pool.

Billing, riding some stones lighter, got there first and did not wait for me. Not deigning to set foot against an untyned [1] quarry, he charged close in, and, as the hind reared at him, brought her down with a neat back-handed slash of hanger below the ears. "That is how to do it, my bully," he cried, throwing leg over saddle-bow and kicking off the dogs.

I reined in my blown horse and looked down at the fallen hind. "That will not choke Cosby," I said.

We gralloched the hind, and slung her over Billing's crupper. And then we looked about us for our bearings. "By thunder!" he cried, "that was a hunt— and all to ourselves. A cold supper for us this night! This is somewhere in the direction of Clanish Pool, and there is Fonagh Ard lifting over in the east. Up there lies Athenree, north and a little west. Let us

---

[1] Without antlers.

be on our way. There is a blowy evening in front of us."

We mounted, reined round to the north, and set out at a steady half-walk, half-amble, the now quiet dogs at our heels.

That ride sticks in my memory. Before we were half-roads the still day died in an evening of rising gale. Ragged clouds blew across a dun sky, and the great woods began to sigh in the kiss of the wind. Sun there was none, but a weird luminous half-light that came low down amongst the trees, and made the columned trunks stretch out into strange and solemn distances. Ever and again a scurry of fallen leaves rustled about the horses' hooves and whispered away amongst the trees; and above that scurrying whisper was the booming note of the wind, with now and again the cold cry of a whirlwind tossing up the dead leaves in a swaying spiral dance.

"A night I would not care to spend in here," said Billing. "This wind will keep rising—or I a poor judge—and there will be ruin in the woods before morning. Let us put a span to our going."

Twilight was deepening when, breaking between thin coverts, we came out on a wide open, bare of all but a ragged grass. On the far side was the black wall of spruce woods. I knew my whereabouts for the first time. "Esker Parc this," I said.

"And there be some of the hunt," cried Billing, pointing, "and dismounted."

Near the middle of the open I saw a small party. "Ladies amongst them," I decided, my heart warning me.

They were Eithne, Duvesa MacTheobald, and Doncadh Donn Maguire.

Billing lifted in his stirrups and gave the long hunt-ing hal-hallo, and the answer came back so clear and high that the dogs bayed in answer. I knew that voice.

"She has the note of a bugle," said Ned. "I wager yellow-nob has lost his way."

The two ladies were mightily pleased to see us as we came up and dismounted. So, I think, was Donn, though he took us matter-of-factly, and would not acknowledge being out on his point for home.

Eithne had lost her hunting-cap, her riding-kirtle was briar-torn, and there were clay stains on her right arm and shoulder. But she took her mishap gallantly, and the wind blowing across the level tossed her black curls bravely.

Maid Duvesa was in a tearful mood of thankfulness. "It was all your fault, Eithne," she insisted. "You would hold that some of the hunt had ridden this way."

"And here they are, ninny," Eithne gave back.

I caught Donn's eye, and he winked at me. "Gave us the slip, too," he said, "and had sport of their own."

"And what a chase!" gloated Billing. "An hour —an hour and a half—and four bays."

I brushed dried clay off Eithne's shoulders. "A fall? You are not hurt?"

"No. My horse tripped in a coney burrow. I fear its shoulder is out."

"You were in such a hurry," said Duvesa.

Billing led the hurt pony a few limping paces,

and felt its shoulder with knowing fingers. "Ay! A bad wrench. It will not see Athenree to-night with any weight on it. Better strip it and let it make its own way."

"But Eithne?" cried her friend.

"A fine black horse of Vaughan's to carry double," Billing called carelessly, his hands at the girths.

I stripped the English saddle off my charger and put the lady's one in its place. Meantime Ned tied my saddle behind the dead hind.

"Now, Lady Eithne," I said.

"But you?"

"I will show you. Come!"

Without further demur she placed foot in the hand-stirrup I made for her and was in the saddle like a bird. She grasped the reins, and settled her kirtle, and looked down at me. "And now?" she wondered.

The horse stood all sixteen hands, and I did a feat I had learned as a boy. I balanced on one leg, hopped on the other, and vaulted astride behind the saddle. Used all my life to riding stirrupless, for me the broad roach of horse was a good enough seat. I whipped my cloak round me. "Home!" said I.

"By the hounds of Finn!" swore Donn.

III

Behold us, then, riding home to Athenree; Billing, who best knew the road, ahead, Duvesa and her swain close behind, and Eithne and I in the rear—and losing ground. There was no reason why we should lose ground, but Eithne did not press the horse beyond a walk, and I urged nothing. She sat aside on the saddle, and now and then smiled at me sweetly--very gently—across her shoulder. "If we go too fast," she said, "you will surely fall off."

"Surely," I agreed.

I sat, legs awag, leaning well back, and there was still enough light to see the pink shell of her ear and a dark curl playing against the rose of her cheek.

Presently she spoke. "My hands are cold," she said. Yet she wore gauntlets.

"They might be," said I. "Give me the reins."

I straightened up and took them from her in my left hand. My arm lay along her waist, and the steady swing of the horse swayed her gently against it and brought her shoulders touching my breast.

She was silent for a while now. "The wind is growing," she said at last; and then in a whisper, "it is a cold wind too."

"It will be colder," said I, and she glanced at me quickly and away.

Presently she spoke again. "I am cold," she whispered, and gave a small shiver.

"And the remedy here," said I, who had the thought of it already in my mind.

The Irish war-cloak is full length, and it is as wide as it is long. I unloosed it at my neck, and was about to swing it off my shoulders, when she stopped me. "No; my share only. You were long about it."

So I drew half the cloak round her. "Hold it there," said I.

And we rode on. It was dark now, and we could not see those ahead, but I gave the horse reins and he held his pace smoothly. The keening wind cried all about us; the black copses shut us in; the dead leaves whirled by, pattering and sighing. We were alone in the dark of the world.

"This is our tent," she whispered.

After a while the cloak edges slipped from her grasp and blew free. "Butter fingers!" I chided, and resettled it round her.

"My fingers are numb," she said. "You hold it."

"I will do that."

And so both my arms were round her, and she could do no other than lean against me. It was a fine, keen, cruel situation. A middling good man of his hands on the back of a big, black war-horse, the pick of all maids on the saddle before him, and the wide dark world in his front. It was bitter and it was sweet. I held her in my arms, and that was honey sweet; but she was wedding another, and that was gall bitter.

And so we rode, the horse swinging smoothly and the wind mocking me. A maid in my arms and— have I never said it before?—and I loving her. She leaned frankly against me now, and frankly I held her, and in spite of any will of mine my right arm was close about her. Her dear dark head was under my chin and her curls sometimes whipped my lips. Every stride of the horse swayed us gently, and her heart beat and beat against my left arm below her breast.

The wind lulled a little and a cold rain came driving down on us. I resettled the great folds of the cloak and pulled the hood over her head, shutting out the night for her. I heard her voice saying the words of an old song: "I am blind in your arms."

In time, I do not know how long, for I did nothing to shorten the ride, we won clear of the woods, and over there across the windswept level were the lit window-slits of the Castle of Athenree.

The maid under the hood did not see them. She

turned face up and I saw the dark pools of her eyes. "You are very strong and very gentle," she whispered.

"I am very strong indeed," I agreed, "but I have no name for gentleness."

"You have a terrible name in war, Blackcock's Feather; but no one, no one at all but Eithne ni Flaherty knows how gentle you are."

My heart turned over. Athenree was very near.

"If you lose your way?" she half-suggested.

"Then we will ride north all night."

"And that would be splendid too. When would we reach Dungiven?"

"Alas! my Queen, at the other side of the new moon. Here is the gate of Athenree."

She sat up, and I drew the cloak off her. "O Mother Mary!" she whispered, in some strange chiding regret that was almost anguish. "O Mother Mary! why did you not answer my prayer?"

There was nothing I could say. There was no time to say anything. The drawbridge was down and torches blazed in the arch. There was her mother, there was Cosby, there was Vaughan—waiting, perhaps wondering. We clanked over the drawbridge and under the echoing hollow of the arch, and, though the torches blazed bright, I looked at no one. I swung off the horse and reached my hands up to my lady. She slipped into them and was on the ground, her eyes on mine and a glow in them. I took her hand then, and, bowing deeply over it, kissed the fingers that tightened for a moment. And then I straightened up and, taking no notice of anyone, walked firmly out into the dark of the street.

Donn overtook me on the way, but, contrary to his habit, not a word came from him. He slapped his riding-switch against his leather buskins and strode stubbornly a pace ahead of me. Even when we got within our room, where Cathal waited, he remained silent, and would keep stamping up and down the floor, his head up near the ceiling. Cathal regarded this new Donn Maguire with wonder.

As he paced Donn cast furious side-glances at me, but I refused to meet his eye. Though I well knew the only thing there was for me to do, I found it hard to broach the subject, and waited for Donn to make an opening. Presently our landlady came in with our supper of cold pasty and light ale, and I turned to the table as an excuse, but appetite was very far away from me."

"Supper, Donn?"

"To the pit of hell with you and your supper!" he roared at that. And for all of five minutes he used every oath he could remember in Gaelic and English, and they were many. Cathal stared from one to the other of us, dismay in his face that we two should have come to this pass.

At last Donn quieted down and, with sudden resolution, came to the other side of the table and leaned across to me. "What are you going to do, full-mouth?"

There was nothing in my mouth but a slow tongue.

My silence set him off again. "Oh, Great Michael's sword!—Look at him, O'Dwyer, and All Saints on top of us! I will be spitted by the devil's prong before a maid like that one is wasted on a Sassenach shield-striker.—What are you going to do? I asked you!"

I looked him in the eye then. "What are you going to do yourself? Your right is equal to mine."

"Ah! were you thinking of me?" he said softly. And then fiercely, "It would be finer of you to think of the woe that will come to an Irish maiden. Well?"

"By Heaven! Maguire, you are right," I cried. "To-morrow my sword goes back to Vaughan."

"And by the mother that reared me!" swore Donn, "if we fail to get you out of your stone coffin in four days I will break word myself and snatch Eithne ni Flaherty to a safe place." He straightened up and ran his fingers through his yellow mane. "By Angus of the Birds!" he said cheerfully, "I got that done easier than I expected. Fine man, reach me that pasty and I will be trying your share and mine."

CHAPTER X

I

DONN MAGUIRE had me up with the sun next morning, and, after a hurried breakfast, helped me on with mail shirt and sword-sash. Cathal O'Dwyer came down from his attic to see us go, and smiled gravely out of his wasted face.

"We will meet again, brother," I promised, my arm on him.

"If God is kind, *lochain*," [1] he murmured quietly.

And we did meet once again.

In the great hall of the Castle the halberdmen were already at morning duty, and at the head of it, near a new wood fire, Sir Francis Vaughan sat with a thigh over a corner of the table and waited for his morning drink. As we strode up to him he looked at me and my war-dress curiously. "Will ye try a cullis [2] of hotch-potch with me?" he invited pleasantly.

I slipped off shoulder-sash and laid the scabbarded sword beside him on the table. He quietly placed his hand on it. "Has it come, then?" he said gravely. "You withdraw your word?"

"I do, Sir Francis."

"If you must, you must." He turned to Donn, his eyes narrowing contemplatively. "And you, Maguire?"

"One fool at a time is enough," said Donn cheerfully.

[1] Friend of my heart.   [2] Broth.

300

Vaughan smiled cynically. "Hold it not in your mind that I am that fool."

"The sorry day for me!" said Donn.

For a space Vaughan looked musingly on the floor, his hand on my sword and a toe-point tapping quietly on the flags. At the end he drew a long breath.

"Let it be," he said. "We cannot suffer you to escape—and I will not." He called down the hall to his sergeant and gave him his orders. One man was sent for the warden, two others set to guard me, the others to guard the door. He was taking no risks.

And then Donn spoke up in a careless tone: "I think I will see the lad into his cage—if you do not mind, my Governor?"

"Not in the least, Maguire," said Vaughan ironically; "but set you one foot inside the outer dungeon door and within it you will stay. Please yourself."

"I will do that," cried Donn, "and it will be to take myself off, lest worse befall me." He came and clasped my hand, and his bold eye flashed into mine. "Good luck with you, a Gordon—and life to Erin O." And with a brisk salute he swung on his heel and marched high and proud out into the day.

The warden, an old key-weighted man, came and led us down the hall and through the arch into the main-guard at the other side. At the far end of this he unlocked a heavy door and led down a steep flight of stone steps to a grey-lighted cold-smelling passage, running right and left. I had been here before. But the door the warden now unlocked was not the door of the dungeon we had seen that time, but one at the opposite end of the passage. My friend, the enemy, was taking every care to hold me.

My guards stepped back to let me through, and Vaughan followed me in. He pulled the door to behind him, and we were alone in a low wide cell with a damp stone floor, a groined stone roof, and walls sweating cold from every stone; it was dim-lit by a horizontal slit in the far wall; there was a three-legged stool overturned on the floor, a wooden stretcher on squat trestles against the wall, and nothing more—except a black rat, that scurried as we entered.

"It is the best I can offer," said Vaughan. "I am sorry it is not better."

"Wide enough and high enough—and strong enough. What more?"

"I am indeed grieved—my friend—grieved to be compelled to this. I would give a hand——"

"There is mine for you," I stopped him. "You are a true man."

We grasped hands firmly, and without another word he turned and left me.

The door shut, the lock grated, bolts shot home, and at last I was a prisoner within four walls.

II

I sat on the three-legged stool and looked round me, but I had already seen all there was to see. So I put elbows on knees, head between hands, and, hunched up on that low seat, gazed down on the stone flags for a long time. I contemplated the slowing down of life, the terrible immobility that a man must breed within himself to go on existing in a dungeon, concentrating all his mind down to a single point, subduing his thoughts to one level above nothingness, becoming so little the medium of sensation, drawing so little out of his store, that, like the tortoise, he lives to an extremity of years. Would I, too, learn that woeful art of doling out the thin stuff of life? Time enough might be mine to acquire it. Four days! and Vaughan watchful. Four weeks—four months—four . . . God Almighty! no!

I started to my feet—the three-legged stool fell over—and began a-pacing of my domain: six paces from door to window-slit and five across. Standing on tiptoe, I could touch the point of the groined roof; the door was steel-clamped black oak; the window-slit was chin-high, and barely a span wide, and the mortar binding the cut stones that framed it was iron-hard. By looking at a certain angle I could see a narrow band of sky above the tip of the fosse, but, that day, the sky was greyly drear, and, though I watched a long time, there was never a rift of blue or gleam of sun to reward me.

That day was Tuesday. It passed slowly, but not yet draggingly, for there was much to think about and one or two things to avoid dwelling on. Food in plenty was brought me from Vaughan's own table, as well as a couple of skins for night covering. Two tall halberdiers of the guard were my warders. One stood fully armed at the door while the other attended to my wants, and they made no attempt to open discourse with me. I was adjudged a man of desperate daring, for no good reason, and the rumour of my name and deeds had grown foolishly monstrous.

Slowly the light drained out of my cell, and I followed it to the window-slit and watched the sad darkening of the sky. When I turned away at last I looked into a black darkness that, yet, seemed to flow in waves, and the rats were getting bold. With an effort I refrained from stamping foot and hissing them still, for I knew that I must grow accustomed to the pattering sound of these light feet.

For a time I sat on the edge of the trestle-bed, hoping that someone would visit me. But no one came. There was only the dark, and the feet of the rats, and the sough of a rising wind down the gut of the fosse. So I pulled off my steel over-shirt and lay down under the skins, hoping that sleep would come. But sleep, that fickle one, stood off from me, and thoughts that had been at bay all day broke in and would not be denied. What I feared to contemplate was the failure of rescue, the failure of O'Donnell, the long winter in this house of stone, and the gradual sinking into that lethargy that alone makes slow confinement bearable. And these I contemplated now.

Patience, David Gordon! Be not a child fearing the dark and the cold and the rats. Give your friends —your splendid and leal friends—a chance to show their worth. In these you have been lucky—luckier than in your love. No! You have loved a quick gentleness, a wayward sweetness, a frank nobility. Enough for any man. And though you lose them they shall remain with you always. But, indeed, they are not yet lost, desperate though the gamble is, for your friends are busy, and they are bold and eager. Give them a little time. Nothing can happen this night, nor, it may be, to-morrow night; but on the third night—surely on the third night?—some plan will be desperately evolved and desperately put to the test. For that you must be prepared in thew and brain. Be patient, then, and say your prayers—and sleep will come.

And in time sleep came.

CHAPTER XI

I

I DID not sleep long—an hour—it could not be two hours. It was the slow grate of the lock that waked me. I lifted to an elbow and looked at the door, and there was a faint gleam of light through the keyhole. A pause then, and the bolts were slowly levered back and the hinges squeaked. I saw a lanthorn in the opening and the big bulk of a man above it. That bulk slipped through and the door shut behind it.

"Who is it?" I had one knee drawn up and my weight balanced.

He fumbled at the lanthorn door and the light diffused itself through the cell. The man was Tom Pybus. I sank back on my elbow.

"From the Governor?"

He hesitated, and then, "No, master—my own business and yours."

I again stiffened elbow. Here was an East Saxon, man of a tribe I did not ken. What things might touch him deeply was a mystery to the Gael in me. To outward seeming he was quiet and stolid, stupid rather than placid; but it could be that fires of resentment burned deep down in him. Three times in the past I might have killed him, yet did not; but his life had been spared with something of a contempt that must rankle bitterly—and rankling bitterly . . .? In the hooded light I could not read his face, but in his hand he carried what looked like a sword. I was watchful. This fellow in handgrips would be strong as a bull.

"Sit," I invited. "The stool is there."

"No, master. There is hurry." But, hurry or none, he was slow to begin, and I could not help him. "Master," he said at last, "you have a great name as a swordsman."

"The name only."

"More. I saw you fight in Sligo gate, and you killed men like flies. But look! Three times you had me and let me go. Why?"

He asked the question simply, and frankly I had to answer. "You were too easy to kill. Do you resent it?"

"How? You were in danger and took time to be merciful. That is what I remember, master—my life three times."

Here was a surprising Tom Pybus. Suddenly he sat down on the stool, shuffled his feet, and made a great effort to be articulate to himself and to me. "I am only a common soldier, but I am not blind to—to the things that be going on. Master, this be no affair of war or sogering, and fair play is what I like—and you cannot have that behind a locked door. Master, whether I be doing right or wrong, I am doing what I must. I bring back your sword. Here!" And there was the hilt thrust into my hand and my fingers acurl round the familiar grip. "You will know what to do with it," he said meaningly.

Without another word he grasped his lanthorn and made for the door. I heard it close softly behind him, and waited ears on the stretch. Silence only. There was no sound of lock or bolt.

I lay there for a time, remaking my notions of this

plain soldier, who grasped fair play as he saw it and was not troubled by any other loyalties. He had given me my sword, left me with an open door, and put the rest of the problem into my own keeping. Here was Finn's fair play and a challenge at the same time. It behoved me to stir myself.

I did not don my mail shirt, since the weight of it might slow me, but slipped sash over shoulder, folded cloak over arm, drew my sword, and moved in the dark towards the door. I groped and found it, and it yielded to my touch with a long protesting squeak. I looked into the blackness of the passage and listened. Not a sound but my own blood in my ears. Even the rats were quiet.

On tiptoe I moved across the passage till I touched the other wall, and then, right arm advanced, went forward step by step till my shoulder, that had been touching the dark stones, slipped into vacancy. Here was the well of the stairs, and again I paused, looking up into the darkness. The stairhead door into the mainguard was evidently shut. I felt with a foot for the bottom tread of the stairs, found it, and, my back to the side wall, sidled upwards. One—two—six— ten stone steps and my outstretched sword-point touched the wood of the door above me. Slight though that touch was, it set the door moving noiselessly, and before I might crouch I was looking up the long length of the guardroom. I drew in a long breath and sank down until my eyes were just above the level of the threshold.

II

There was little to see, and everything there was to see, at the same time. Just the dim-lit length of the

308

great room, and a group of soldiers round a rough table by the fireside at the far end; and all but one of the group were bent over the board engaged in throwing dice with the death-and-life interest of the gambler. The man standing upright was Tom Pybus, his broad back to me and his hands clasped easily behind him. Directly above the table a cruisie-lamp hung at the end of a chain, and this with the red glow of the peats was the only light in the room. Where I crouched was but the faintest glimmer.

The wavering smoke-tipped light gleamed on the angles of hard and eager faces, shadows sprawled and leaped as men bent forward to count the throws, and the outlines of legs were picked out to the last curve against the glow of the fire on the hearth.

I had to get out of that room. There were two doors to choose between. One was the door into the bailey, full in the light of the hanging cruisie, and I knew that a sentinel walked the stone platform outside it. The other was directly behind the dicers, but, instead of wooden door, it was hung with a heavy curtain. Within that curtain, I knew, was a twist of stair leading up to the armoury and to the portcullis pent beyond, and, from the portcullis pent, a short flight of steps led down to the upper hall, which, as has been said, gave on the East Wall by a side door. There was my road.

I followed that road in my mind's eye and, as I did so, big Tom Pybus moved a pace to the right so that his broad back was between the dicers and the curtain. Here was the plain hint. I looked across the floor. It was clear of impediment or scatter of rushes. Would I crawl on my knees or slink along by the wall? I did neither. I walked slowly and on tiptoe, holding my breath, and ready at a lift of head to bound into action and drive a way through. And as I walked I heard the dicers talk and growl and laugh. They were baiting one man out of luck, and he was not hiding his chagrin.

"Hell's bowels!" He swore. "Double-bice again."

"The luck you deserve, yellow-belly."

"Say that again, pig-mouth!"

"No. You might be wiser to take his supper to Blackcock's Feather—six shillings wiser."

"Not a slit windpipe wiser, my fine——"

I moved the curtain softly aside from the jamb and slipped through, and as the curtain settled behind me a bench fell over with a startling clang. I had been seen! Now for action.

I clambered up the wind of the stairs, no longer moving quietly, bruised a shoulder against the pillar of the spiral, and bundled through another curtain at the stairhead—straight into the arms of a soldier who carried a tallow dip alight above his head. I had forgotten the night guard on the portcullis.

The curtain had bellied into his face and he had not yet had time to recognise me, but if his eyes were slow his tongue was not. "Hog! What joke is this?"

My sword must have missed him only by a touch. The hilt was against his ribs. My left arm was folded in my cloak, but my hand was free, and, as he grappled me, I drove clenched fist fiercely below his breastbone. The grunt he gave was the last gasp of his driven wind, the lighted dip fell behind him, and he sank down between my knees and rolled over. I strode over him—and paused.

No steps came clambering on the turret stairs; from there came only the distant sound of voices and laughter. Then I understood. The unlucky gambler, tired of ill-luck and baiting, had only started up from the table—and started me hurrying. A lucky chance. Otherwise I must have met this fellow, now kicking on the flags, on mid-stairs and at a grave disadvantage.

Strangely enough the light had not been put out by its fall. It shivered, a faint glow, in some current of air across the flags, and I picked it up hastily, cupping it in my hand against the draught. The man on the floor was now on his back, and I peered into his face. It was horribly atwist and his eyes were white balls. When his wind came back to him I must be well out of his reach.

Facing me, in the steel-cumbered wall of the armoury, was the door to the portcullis pent. I strode to it and up four short steps into a long and narrow chamber. The heavy top-bar of the grid ran along the floor, the windlass was at my hand, chains ran up into the darkness, and a cold air came up from below, and had a smell of the outside. At the other end of the chamber was mate of the door I stood within, and I made my way along the portcullis bar, drew the bolt, and looked down a straight flight of stone steps to a heavy black curtain.

I crushed out the taper under heel, and darkness closed in on me, but at the foot of the steps there was a chink of light at the side of the curtain. I felt my way down, widened the chink carefully with one finger, peeped through—and straightway forgot the danger behind me.

There was the upper hall. The wall lights were not burning, but a branch of three waxen candles was alight on a small table near the fireplace. The arras was decked with laurel and holly, and the polished leaves glistened in the candle gleam. A room decked for the wedding-feast! And yonder the bride. Eithne ní Flaherty sat at the table-end.

She sat as still as a carved figure, an elbow on the board and her chin in her cupped hand, and her lovely dark eyes stared unwinkingly before her. A dark curl lay on her white brow, and there was ebb of colour from her cheek. But in that pallor was not the coldness of marble, but some tender waxen transparency showing the magic of flesh and spirit. Here was no impish, merry lass, but a woman grown, contemplating something in her mind that made her eyes sombre.

She was not alone. Dame Bevinda, her mother, sat near her at the table-head, a tambour-frame before her on the board below the light, and she was engaged in making careful stitches on some white circle of embroidery. So she had some of the arts of woman as well as of captain. Every now and then she glanced aside at her daughter, but her daughter never looked at her. Both were silent.

I could not stand watching there for ever. The man in the armoury, recovering wind, would be urgent to discover the hog that rid him of it; the alarm might be expected any moment now. My only road led through this upper hall and through the bolted door behind the ladies' backs. Take it while there is time, David Gordon, and risk the Dame's alarm. So I drew in a deep breath, drew the curtain aside, and stepped softly within.

I was half-way down and within the circle of light when Eithne saw me. She did not start, but her eyes widened and narrowed and again widened, and she rose from her chair, as if lifted by a force outside herself. "David!" she whispered, and her lips remained apart.

Dame Bevinda hid her surprise. She did not even rise from her chair, but leaned her hands on her tambour-frame and waited till I halted before them. "And why the long blade, Master David?" she inquired calmly.

I glanced down at my naked sword, and for the first time it looked a silly long weapon. I smiled at it, and sheathed it quickly, and shook cloak loose on my arm.

"That is more seemly, surely. Did you break through your locked door? How many dead men are behind you, Blackcock's Feather?"

"None yet, Dame."

"And now?"

"I will take that door behind you, with your favour."

"And without it?"

"Then I must take it without, Dame."

She laughed, not unkindly. "You know," she said, "I will be sorry to see the last of you."

"Your sorrow may be long in coming, Dame," I gave her back.

Eithne had been watching me with all her eyes, and now she did a thing that surprised me. She jerked back her chair and ran light-footed up the long room to the head of the stairs leading down to the main hall. She leaned there listening, her dark head turned aside, and the mother and I watched her.

"You grow in daring, Master David," the Dame mused, her eyes not turning to me. "Shall I look for you before Saturday?"

"Or after it, Dame."

"Then you will be late."

"No, by God!" I was driven to say—"as long as a sword can cut a knot."

"A threat?"

"Take it so."

"I take your dare, Blackcock's Feather."

Suddenly Eithne started, looked towards us, hesitated, leaned again to listen, and then came flying to us, an arm extended to me. "Fly, David!" Urgent the whisper. "They come."

And, in turn, her mother surprised me. She started up from her chair. "Silly girl!" she cried. "Could you not think?" She threw a word to me over her shoulder: "Quick!" and, long-striding, went up the hall and stepped within the stair door. We heard her voice: "Your pardon, Sir Francis. I was seeking a flagon of your sweet muscadine."

We did not catch the reply. We did not wait for it. Eithne had my arm and was dragging me towards the side door, too fast for dignity. "Hurry, hurry, David!" Her strong young hands were quicker on the bolt than mine, and the cold air beat in on us through the open door.

I caught her two hands in mine. "I will be back, Queen. Listen, now! Trust Donn Maguire—and his friend named O'Dwyer—to the death."

"I know—I know! Go now."

Sudden and warm she pulled my hands forward and pressed them against her breast. Then she pushed me quickly out in the dark and shut the door softly in my face.

CHAPTER XII

I

I LEANED against the parapet wall by the side door and gathered wits together. They needed gathering. A moment ago my hands felt my lady's heart beat, and now I was out in the cold and unfriendly night.

Unfriendly? No. A fine night for a venture like mine, dark but not dead black, with faint stars in the rents of a sky ragged before a north wind; a bleak, windy, October night, with, now and then, a cold spit of rain in the wind's mouth. There below me was Athenree, dark and still, before me in the dimness stretched the parapeted head of the East Wall, and all I had to do was to bend head below parapet and make for the corner bastion and the North Wall.

There at last was the loom of the bastion close ahead, and I paused to peer and listen for the sentinel before venturing round by the glacis platform. The only sound was the sough of the wind in the teeth of the parapet, and I was about to slip round the body of the tower, when a yellow spark of light appeared far down the North Wall. It swung a little from side to side and came nearer as it swung, and as it came nearer the tramp of footsteps came with it. The night patrol changing guard. Many a wakeful night I had lain in my quarters and listened to it tramping by every couple of hours, and watched the lanthorn gleam run along the ceiling. I slipped in behind the tower and waited for the sentinel's challenge, but his challenge, when it came, startled me. For it came from less than a score of feet away round the curve of the wall. Very like, the careless fellow had been sheltering from the wind in the angle of the bastion, and it was my luck—and his too—that the patrol had halted me.

I listened anxiously. If Ned Billing was on his nightly round he might, as was not unusual, circle the tower and seek the Castle for a last drink. And I would not care to set Ned's loyalty and his friendship over against each other. But when the patrol halted at the other side of the bastion it was the sergeant's voice that was lifted. After that followed a murmuring and a shuffling, then a brisk order, the quick stamp of trained feet, and the patrol moved away towards the North Gate.

No sound once more but the piping of the wind, yet still I waited and listened—and in the end jumped too quickly to an explanation. "The sentinel," I told myself, "is gone up the wall behind the patrol; now for it!" And forthwith I darted round the tower —straight into his arms.

Luck, the trickster, once again!

"Who goes——"

He got no further. My cloak smothered him, and his arquebus dropped between us. I had not time to be gentle and apologetic. He was a thick, short fellow, but already I had his head down in a notch of the parapet, a hand on his throat, my weight on his chest, and a knee across his thighs. A little jerk of pressure to warn him how easily his neck would snap, and he went limp under me. I pulled up his head then and put mouth to his ear. "Silence, or I kill!"

I threw the cloak off his face, and he must have caught my feathered bonnet against the sky. "Black-cock's Feather!" whispered his strangled voice. —

I was thinking rapidly and closely. My plan to drop from the wall into my old quarters and have word with Donn and Cathal would be possible only if I killed this man. And, cold-blooded, I could not kill him. Donn would have word soon enough, and would understand. The only thing that remained was a drop into the ditch—and a sufficiency of the fear of death into the sentinel to give me time to get out of reach.

"Attend!" said I in a deep growl, and the slack tremor of him under my hands showed that he would welcome mercy, but did not expect it. "You will march up the wall to the second culverin and there count two hundred—slowly. Come back then, and your arquebus will be here. One small outcry, and I will throw your weapon into the ditch—and you can explain how you lost it before they hang you. Suit yourself. March!"

And he marched. He had not gone fifty paces before I grasped the pointed edge of the parapet, vaulted over, let myself drop to full length, thrust feet against the stones, and leaped blindly. I struck ground with a jar, and went hands and knees amongst the dying weeds in the bottom of the ditch. There were nettles too, I knew by the sting. On my feet again, I groped forward to the back of the ditch. It was a slope of stiff clay, and I kicked in a toe-hold, clambered to the top, and faced round to Athenree.

There it lay, hid in the night, holding my one jewel, fateful place of kings, fatal field of Connacht, blown over by the wind, showing neither tower nor roof, deeming itself safe against surprise. And here was its doom looking in over its toothed, sunken North Wall.

II

The wind blew steadily out of the north, and I could not go astray by holding in the teeth of it. Before me was the empty spread of pastureland, and beyond that, beech woods to the marshes of Suck; and beyond Suck I must be before morning.

So, grasping cloak and sword under an arm, I struck the long, loping, hillman gait, the hunter's lope that eats the miles. The keen wind sharpened me, the thin rain freshened me, the dark was a friend of mine. A strange new gaiety came over me. It was splendid to be free again. But an hour ago had I stared into the horror of being captive, and only now did I know how abasing to the soul is even the easiest of captivity. Here, now, was freedom and a purpose with it. Sometime to-morrow I might strike the outposts of O'Donnell, gone to earth somewhere south of Cong, and the words I had to say would surely bring the eagle of the north swooping on Athenree. And then—and then?

The wall of the woods loomed before me. In there was safety. And then, somehow, of no will of my own, my voice lifted in one cheer for freedom—the long howl of the wolf on the run. The trees echoed back that howl.

Soon I was forcing through thickets of bramble and hazel that fringed the open beech glades. The branches brushed wetly against my hands up to guard my eyes, briar trailers caught at my knees, grass tussocks were treacherous under my feet, but I pressed

steadily forward, and at last won through to the leaf-
carpeted open.

And there something caught my feet that was no
briar, and I fell full-length on my face. Sudden hands
caught my shoulder, a heavy body threw itself across
my legs, a bent knee was in my back.

"Gay lad, we will put a stop to your howling!"

III

Caught! A moment ago free, with knowledge of the
splendour of freedom—and now flat as a toad and as
helpless.

A toad? No! a tod! For, surely, if freedom was
such a splendid thing it was worth fighting for—and
dying for. Now! this minute!

"Quiet as a rabbit he is," said a deep voice above
me, and hands slackened for an instant.

At that I jerked my shoulders free, embraced a hairy
limb, and sent a body toppling. The man on my back
fell over, and I elbowed him fiercely in the ribs.
"Chreesta!" he swore. "Manus, you pig, where are
you?" But for the man on my legs I might have torn
clear, but before I could kick him off the other two
pounced back on me.

Hands clawed, feet twined, blows clouted, and
striking, kicking, twisting, I heaved myself up, tangled
in my cloak, sword between my legs. Twice I reached
my knees, once my feet, and my hand on my hilt,
but my attackers were as dourly determined as I was
and again swarmed me down. Before I fell that last
time I somersaulted a man over my shoulder, fell on
him, and held him under me to die.

"Chief," roared a straining voice. "Will I prick

him—or Ferdoragh is a dead man? By the throat
he has him."

"Hands off *sgian*!" commanded a voice outside
the vortex. "Would ye spoil our night? Three of
ye to one man! Ye sons of *bodachs*![1] Give me
room!"

At his first words I stopped struggling. My fingers
loosed from the man's neck, and I allowed myself to
be dragged clear of him.

"Grip him, Manus, you bastard," panted the deep
voice, "or he is on us again. The mad wolf!
Ferdoragh's windpipe is broken, anyway."

"And what were your big paws doing, Tadg?"
upbraided the chief's voice. "Put him on his feet,
babes, and let me rest hand on him."

One of the men holding me suddenly caught me
round the body and swung me upright. "There he
is, then, and the devil is in it if he breaks this hold."

But my fury was burned out. In the reaction and
relief laughter came up in my throat.

"Bloody wars! The tears are at him," said an
amazed growl at my shoulder. And at that I broke
into a bark of laughter.

A tall figure loomed before me and a firm hand
caught my shoulder. "Who laughs at death, fine
fellow?"

"Time you asked," I said calmly.

"God!" His face came close. "Who is it?"

"A pleasant welcome, cousin Donal," said I.

"Davy! Is it you, my darling?" His hands fell
about my shoulders and ran up to my hair. I could
feel the caress in them; I was amongst my own again.
"It is yourself," he whispered. "God is good."

[1] Old men.

Tadg Ironhand loosed his clutch, but, before he did, I felt his great palm press over my heart. "The hurt of hell to us!" he cursed. "There are a couple skelps [1] out of me, anyway." And then came a note of satisfaction into his voice: "And Ferdoragh is choked dead, glory be to God!"

"He was near that same," said the Ferdoragh from the ground. "Mhuire! but I saw the gates of hell in front of me."

We all laughed, and the throat-filling tension eased. Donal Ballagh's arm was round me now. "A miracle under the stars," he said. "Senan will say it was his prayers. He is behind in the woods half a mile."

"But how are ye here?" I began to wonder.

"Looking for you, my light; what else? We knew where you were held. Where is Doncadh Donn?"

"Back there in Athenree—and playing his part. A long story, cousin."

"Let us to where it can be told, then—and the night before us."

And so we went back to Donal's camp amongst the beeches, and waked Father Senan from his nest in the root crotches. And, frankly, he wept over me, and could not speak for a long time.

IV

"If only Amy could know," said Donal with longing, when I had told my tale and heard all the news, "and she getting ready her fine garden."

Donal, the priest, and I were seated against a tree

[1] Pieces, splinters.

321

trunk, and the priest leaned over and touched me. "Davy," he asked me softly, "will no one be visiting our lady in that fine garden?"

"How do I know? There are stone walls between."

"We came down to look over the same walls," said Donal, "and, maybe, look inside them too."

"With how many men? Remember what fell in Sligo, when I lost my bonny troop."

"Five only—God rest them—and Tadg here with a small limp."

"It was worth it," said Tadg, lying on the ground before us.

"I have two hundred of our own lads in these woods," said Donal. "Enough?"

"Two hundred! A thousand——"

He caught my arm. "Listen, my heart o' corn! We are the spearhead only. Hugh Roe has three times your thousand strung out and across behind us—all moving softly and all pointing this way—waiting for the home-thrust. Enough?"

I felt an excitement surge in me. "Donal," I cried, "if O'Donnell is bold as they say, he could storm Athenree this night."

"Bold! Athenree is ours. Hugh Roe is not a mile behind. Let us back and talk to him."

CHAPTER XIII

I

EVERYONE has heard of the great sack of Athenree
and of the fight that lasted from dawn to high noon.
Hugh Roe O'Donnell deservedly gets fame for the
exploit, but Hugh Roe himself gave Donal and me
our full meed.

We had drawn up to the sunken North Wall in the
dark hour before the dawn, a spearhead of fifty men;
and ten times that number lay strung out on the plain
before the North Gate. Our forlorn hope of fifty was
to make a surprise sally on the wall and on the gate-
tower, with the intent of lifting the portcullis and letting
the five hundred in; and the five hundred, once in,
would secure a hold on Athenree that might not be
broken before the heavy-armed gallowglasses came up
from the camp beyond the marshes. After that
nothing could save that stronghold to the English.

Behold me, then, in the dark hour creeping to the
brink of the ditch and looking in over the sunken wall.
At my shoulder, his hand in my belt, was Donal
Ballagh, and stretched out and linked behind us was
a chain of fifty men. Each man carried on his shoulders
a great *barth* [1] of grass and faggots. I had led that
burdened chain across the plain from the woods, and
it had been a most nerve-tightening task. For I had
nothing to guide me but the wind, and one small shift
in that would throw me wide of Athenree. Somehow,

[1] Bundle.

I felt the hardest of my task over when the gate-tower loomed out of the darkness.

Donal and I crouched on the brink of the ditch and listened. There were no sounds but our breaths, our heart-thuds, and the wind piping as it had always piped, careless of man and his affairs.

"We will be quiet," whispered Donal, "as long as the watch lets us."

I slipped into the ditch, and Donal followed after a word to the man behind. And then we built our bridge of faggots, each man passing his bundle up the line and Tadg Ironhand throwing it down to us.

The sentinel gave no sign while the work proceeded. He gave no sign when at last Donal, Tadg, and I crouched within the parapet close to a mounted culverin.

"They use a shelter-post in the corner of the bastion down there," I explained.

"Wait ye here," whispered back Tadg. "It would be a fine thing to keep him quiet," and he crept up the wall.

We waited. No sound came out of the dark, but in less than five minutes Tadg himself came crouching.

"He was asleep for himself," Tadg told us simply. "So I gave him one small dunt and tied his belt in his teeth. Let us to it."

Donal and Tadg sat astride, each in a notch of the parapet, and, one by one, the even flow of men was helped over into my hands. Our bridge gradually sank, and the last few men had to be hauled up from their own height below the wall. My part was to array the men in a close line along the shelter-wall towards the gate. No word was spoken; the men came silently into my hands; silently I led them into place; and silently patted each man on the shoulder for a comrade. They were my own men, and ready for any game.

The North Wall was ours. And Athenree, confident of its strength, was in its last dawn sleep. Not yet was there the clang of steel, the yell of slogan, anything at all to warn it of its doom. The wind only, weary and never weary, cried with a mournful sameness.

Now I was moving forward, drawn sword in my left hand, my right touching, now the parapet, now the chill flank of a culverin. Donal came close behind, his hand again in my belt, and, behind him, the linked line followed. The big mass of the gate-tower loomed above. My hand touched cold stone in front, and then the cut lintel of the guardroom door and, groping softly over wood, found the iron latch-guard. "Ready!" I whispered, and that small whisper sighed down the line.

The latch clicked, the door swung in, and, quietly as a friendly visitor, I stepped out of the dark into the murky light of the guardroom of the North Gate.

I changed hilt to right hand.

II

The North Gate of Athenree was defended by keep, drawbridge, and portcullis; and portcullis and drawbridge were controlled from the guardroom wherein I now stood. This was a great chamber covering the whole floor of the keep; east and west were doors giving on the wall head; a row of window-slits looked in on Athenree; and opposite these was the windlass, with chains running through loop-holes in the wall.

In a far corner was the door of the turret stairs leading up to Ned Billing's quarters.

I strode in at the east door and got the whole scene at a glance: the red smoulder of the peats in the big fireplace, the smoky glow of the lanthorns on the wall, the grotesque shadows aleap into the darkness of the arched roof, the guard scattered at ease. The men—twenty or so—were at the hearth end, and many of them asleep or dozing, lying asprawl on the wooden settles, leaning forward on the trestle-tables, lolling in the inglenook, unhelmeted, careless, dreaming no danger. And pouring in on them out of the dark a stream of fierce northern men, a gleam in their eyes and no worse gleam on the blades of the axes.

One moment quietness and, then—then we were amongst them. Someone lifted a head and cried shrilly—a bench fell crashing—a clamour lifted and was closed with the bellow of an arquebus—and steel rang on steel. Quick and short that fight! The guard was surprised, and our men were trained for hand-to-hand work. The press closed in, clanged, circled, broke asunder, scattered, and there was no more resistance.

Donal and I did not need to strike a single blow. The moment the fight broke, Donal and half a dozen picked men flung themselves on the windlasses, and the blows were still dunting when the chains of draw-bridge and portcullis began to creak. For my own part, I was busy looking for Ned Billing, and swinging clear of the heart of the fight, made for the turret door. And I had almost reached it when it was jerked open and Ned burst through. He was mazed and barely awake, and his head, without casque, was round and nearly bald; his tunic was unlaced and his broad hairy chest showed through his linen; and he carried his drawn sword in his right hand.

Just as he appeared, lean Ferdoragh, handy as a terrier, back-heeled a tall soldier before the turret door, and had *sgian* drawn back and down for the groin stroke. Billing with a roar swung up his blade and slashed furiously downwards at the clansman's head, but I took the blow close to the hilt and jarred the sword out of his hand. Forthwith I strode over Ferdoragh, got my forearm across Ned's throat, and forced him back into the doorway. Ferdoragh was behind me, yelling, "The *sgian*, hero! Give him the *sgian*." His short red blade dancing and darting.

I looked at him over my shoulder. "Follow me," I shouted.

I had little time to spare, but that time could not be better spent than in saving this veteran's life. I made full use of my strength. I caught Billing round the small of the back, and with one furious burst of energy bore him up the stair and into his own sleeping-room. There I thrust him backwards and brought blade to the point. Ferdoragh, bundling in behind me, I collared left-handed.

Ned was still dazed. "David!" he cried. "What is it?"

"The sack of Athenree," I told him. "You are my prisoner."

He struck his breast with clenched fist. "God! why did you not let me die?"

"Die!" I bellowed. "Enough will die this day. Gather your wits, man." I glanced down at Ferdoragh, now quiet under my hand. "Ferdoragh, this man has befriended me greatly," I said quietly.

"And me too, then," cried Ferdoragh, and then

grinned happily after the manner of his breed. "And he after trying to knock a hole in the poll of me."

"You will guard him here—with your life."

"With my life, surely," said Ferdoragh soberly.

I turned and leaped for the door. "Do not be an old fool, Ned!" I threw over my shoulder.

I heard the echoing slogan of the clans in the arch.

III

High noon in Athenree and the fight in a dead-lock.

A long and swaying fight since the dawn, and at high noon that dawn seemed far away. It had been a dawn that came slowly. Slowly the wan day had lifted and broadened, showing pointed gables in one flat perspective with the great keep of the Castle towering above, the grey of the stone walls, the black squares of windows, men lurking, soldiers running, smoke curling—and the fight worrying and thudding through it all.

Fearfassa O'Clery, the Bard, made a song of the Sack of Athenree, and I have heard Turlough Mac an Teaclan sing it to the clairseach [1] to bring the whole red fight back to one. He put into it the whirlwind onslaught of the clans, the high-breasted stand of the Sassenach, the stamp and sway and tongueless yelling of men, the shiver and gleam of steel, the first bright lift of the blade and the second dulled with killing, and behind all, the great surging note of triumph. It is a grand song, and women hate it.

Let it be said here that the English and loyalist Irish met our onslaught with a fierceness worthy of all great fights. Hurriedly mustered out of barrack

[1] Harp.

and bothy, they uprose behind walls, leaped down on us from embrasures, leaned to fire from window and roof, manned here and there a hurried barricade, and, in the end, held us in lock before half the town was won.

My part in that fight was that of all the others of my breed; breast to breast, driving inwards shoulder to shoulder, eager and determined unto death to secure a hold on Athenree that could not be broken till the gallowglasses came. We had won East Lane and the whole length of the North Wall, and had come up starkly against an iron resistance along the square at the heart of the town. A score of us had won across a lane making two triangles of Athenree, and were attacking a stone house strongly held. We flanked it down a narrow alley between head-high walls, and Tadg Ironhand, who had fought shoulder to shoulder with me all that morning, gave me a heel-lift to the crown of the wall on the right. As I bent to tug him up the whole world crashed to blackness before my eyes; a clang, a flash, and I fell and fell into darkness. It was that sudden bending sideways that had saved my life; for as I bent an arquebus ball grazed above my ear and laid me senseless outside the wall.

CHAPTER XIV

I

IT had been a sore clout on a hard Scots head, and it was long and long before my senses returned to their citadel. Consciousness came out of the well of blackness, trembled on the edge, dipped back and came again. I looked up, and men who were strange bent over me, and I wondered where and who I was. It was night-time, I knew, for candles burned on the wall where the arras was torn and branches of laurel and holly glistened here and there. It was the branches of evergreen that, queerly enough, brought memory back. This was the upper hall of Athenree Castle, decked for the feast—but why were the green leaves draggled and the arras torn? And a smell of smoke and burning was in my nostrils.

"Eithne!" said I aloud, and my voice was only a croak.

"Give him drink," said a voice I knew, and I looked at the men around me. They were strangers no longer. Father Senan sat on the edge of the stretcher-couch whereon I lay on my back; Donal Ballagh and Tadg bent over his shoulder, and Ned Billing stood at the other side, a flagon cupped in his hand.

"Father!" said I.

"Son!" said the priest, and his hand was cool on mine.

Tadg's bearded face crinkled up as if tears would

flow, but, instead, he laughed. "Christ alive!" said he warmly. "You could not kill him!"

"Not with a stone head," said Ned Billing.

Donal Ballagh drew his hand downwards from brow to chin, and his face, that had been white and strained, was now smiling. He could not say a word, but his eyes told me.

And then I knew the dull throb of an ache above my right ear and felt the tightness of a bandage across my brow. I brought a hand up to feel, and swore at the twinge.

"Fine!" said Donal with satisfaction. "Good and fine! Now we know that you are back to us."

They gave me the drink that I needed. Tadg wanted to give me ale as the only safe drink to quench a grown man's thirst, but the old friar knew enough of wounds and medicines to insist on cool water. After that I was able to turn on my side and get an elbow under me, though the room rocked. "Did anyone see my good bonnet?" I asked.

"Here it is," said Donal, "with the devil's horns still on it—and the dint in the steel mesh that saved you."

I looked around the hall. There was no one in it but ourselves. "Athenree——"

"Is ours. It is so! When the gallowglasses came we burned down the wooden doors and in on them."

"Prisoners?"

"A few. Your Sir Francis Vaughan with a broken thigh-bone—and this officer you left with Ferdoragh."

I looked at Ned Billing, and reached him my hand. "Donal," said I, "this is Captain Ned Billing and my friend."

"We knew that. We hope he will like a winter at Dungiven!"

331

I looked up at Donal, but Donal would not look at me. It was Senan that told me, still holding my hand. "The Governor sent the women out to safety before the gallowglasses came—to Athlone, we think. She is not in town, David—nor is Donn Maguire, dead or alive."

I lay back on the stretcher. There was no more I wanted to know. My bright bird, so near my hand, had flown away or been caged away, and the winning of Athenree was only an empty boast. I was weak and weary and aching. Life was too low in me to feel the stab. I shut my eyes and was dumb—dumb as a fish and as cold.

II

That night in the upper hall of Athenree was a thousand years long. And in time I was no longer cold. My head grew hot and throbbing, and disjointed fragments of dreams came and went tormentingly. Then the darkness began to tremor all round me and a strange sensation of size yet lightness came over me. My head seemed to grow and grow, and be too immense for any neck to bear; some mystic inward vision had an illusion of looking on a smooth snow-white ocean that moved evenly at first, then broke into chaos across the width of the world; every least sound was magnified and full of horror; my breathing filled the bowl of the sky; the rustle of the torn arras was more terrible than thunder; great weights fell and rolled, great seas swept and broke, and made no sound; a weird radiance that came from neither sun nor moon threw no shadow; and I was alone in that chaos where some unnamable disaster had overcome earth and sky and the kingdom of God. There was no time any more, and I was so lost in my doom of nothingness that I had forgotten the memory of men. And yet, through it all, I knew that I lay in the upper hall of Athenree suffering only from a child's nightmare of eternity.

And then, suddenly, came quietness, and someone was speaking close to me—a hoarse voice gabbling words I could not catch. I listened intently and the voice stopped, and, with a shock, I realised that myself was the speaker. Father Senan's arm was under my shoulder and his flagon of cool water at my lips.

"Fine you will be the morn, small son," murmured the gentle rumble of his voice.

"The grey morn," wondered I—"must it always come?"

"And the sun with it—God bless us all. Lie quiet now, Datheen."

Donal and Tadg, great strong men, weary after the long fight, slept leagues deep on the floor near me; but the old friar who, not fighting, had been busy all day at his own high work among the dying, did not sleep at all. If I groaned, if I dreamed aloud, if I flung restlessly he was at my side, wetting my dry lips, moistening the bandages on my brow, crooning over me the words that a mother croons to her sick child.

In the grey dawn he washed out the gash above my ear with sour wine and put on a fresh bandage, and then gave me a long drink that had in it a thin lacing of Bordeaux wine. And after that, peace came, and I drifted into sleep, drifted deep and deep, and had no dreams.

It was high day when I waked, and a bar of
sunlight lay across the cloak that covered me. The
heat and ache were out of my bones, and only a
small dull ache in my head—and I was hungry.
I turned over and lifted on my elbow. "Will anyone give me my yesterday's breakfast?" I wanted to
know sourly. And a fine peal of laughter went up to
the arches.

Hugh Roe O'Donnell, our great leader, stood at my
side with Donal and the priest. Slim and fine he
was, a clean silken tunic on his supple shoulders
and his red hair smooth above the clean pallor
of his face. And a smile hid the dream-gloom in
his grey eyes. "Breakfast it is," he cried, "or I go
without."

I felt embarrassed and had no word to say.

"He will take what he gets," said Senan, "and it
will be fat enough for him."

The prince put his hand on my shoulder and I felt
the warmth of his fingers. "David Gordon," said he,
"the north owes you a victory." I moved my heavy
head slowly, and he bent and, looking into my eyes,
smiled wistfully. "I know—I know, *lochain*!" he said
slowly. "I cannot help you. What you want you
must take with your own hands. My fine lad! my
poor lad! But what is O'Donnell's is yours always."
He touched me softly on the shoulder, turned and
walked away slowly, his hands behind him and
his head forward—a young but very lonely man.
And we all were silent till he passed through the
door.

I put a long leg out of the bed. "If you think——"

Donal put me back with one hand. "Here comes your breakfast, red fellow."

Tadg came with a mazer of porridge—gruel it was, and steaming, with a horn spoon in it and a bare lick of honey on it.

"No!" I roared, and looked at Senan. "Is this all I am getting, bald pate?"

"Just that." His eye was obdurate, and I looked at Donal, who kept a serious face.

I took the mazer roughly from Tadg's great hands, looked at it with disgust, and: "Very well so," I growled. "I may as well try it." And they laughed at me.

The spoon was angry against the bottom of the bowl. "Give me a drink," I commanded, and they hurried me a full flagon of milk.

"There is water in this," I complained in the middle.

"No, a childeen!" protested the priest. "Only the poor Connacht cows."

Again I put a leg over the side, and this time the priest stopped me: "Let me see that cut, son."

He was pleased with it; there was little poison there, he said, and he bandaged it afresh. Tadg shaved off my red stubble, and I grumbled when he rasped me. Donal sat silently at the end of the stretcher and waited till my face was dry, and then he looked into my eyes, felt my hand, and nodded. "David," said he then, "there is a dying man wants word with you."

"Not Donn——"

"No—no! Donn is whipped off to Athlone, I doubt. A man in your lodging——"

335

"Cathal O'Dwyer?"

"It could be. He has the Leinster tongue. He is dying, I fear."

"Dying?"

"Shot through the body."

"Who did it?"

"He will not say. All he will say is: 'Bring me David Gordon—I will see David Gordon'—and he is holding his life with his two hands."

"Is Cosby of Cong here?"

"No—not in Athenree, dead or alive."

My poor Cathal! He had failed in his vengeance, and now, dying, it still possessed him, and he would bequeath it to me. Cosby, no doubt, had guarded the women to Athlone. I was tired of Cosby. I had no desire any more to hold him at sword-point. But O'Dwyer was my true friend and must be seen. And whatever task he might put on me, that would I do —or die.

I was staggering on long unstable legs, and Donal had an arm round me. "I will see him," I insisted.

"Surely, brother, but not shamelessly."

They helped me on with my clothes, and we went out on the East Wall, Donal on the glacis-side and holding my arm, Tadg and the priest behind. It was again a fine, brisk October morning, with the sun in a high frail sky and an east wind blowing the smoke away from us. Athenree was still smouldering. Here and there a stone house stood, but all the clay and wooden bothies were burned down to fragments of walls and smoking litter. The kerns were busy searching out spoil, but the main force of gallowglasses was camped in the plain outside the Castle, and a great

336

drove of cattle was being already herded northwards towards the woods. The houses below the North Wall, where the culverin had been heaved into the ditch, were still whole, this part of the place having been taken in the first onfall, and the house of the Welshwoman, our landlady, had not even been looted.

She came hurrying down from the attic and was glad to see me. She, too, had grown fond of Cathal O'Dwyer—he was so quiet and gentle, she said, and gave no trouble. "He is dying, Master Gordon," she told me. "There is no more blood in him."

Donal helped me to his door and left me, and, as one should do in a chamber of death, I took off my bonnet as I entered.

IV

Cathal was lying under his cloak on the trestle-bed, and I thought he was already dead. There was no colour in him, not even on his lips, and the bones of his face stood out against the drawn skin. But that face was set austerely, invincibly, in some proud calm of its own, stronger than death's calm; and those steadfast eyes could not be blinded by the blank stare of death. Whatever was behind that unhuman calm was secure beyond all doubt, held more firmly than by stone walls. His hands clasped each other across his breast, and the knuckle-bones stood out like strong bosses.

I tiptoed to the bedside, and then his eyes moved and turned on me, and, though his face never changed,

337

his eyes smiled. I sank down beside him on my knees. "Cathal, Cathal, my brother," I whispered. "Who hurt you?"

"Brother too." His lips formed the words, and I held my ears close. "Be not minding that now." Every word was quietly slow and drawn carefully. "All is well with me at last. My heart broke in me that day in Dublin—and Cathal O'Dwyer was only a dead man, not resting. I want you to listen to me now, for there is not much time, and I am keeping Colum waiting for me over there." His eyes sought the foot of the bed, and my hair lifted.

"Listen, David. Donn Maguire was taken to the Castle last night, and this is the message that he sent to me for you by a woman Breadh: "The one you know will be waiting for you in the Glen of the Echo, and a message will be waiting for you in the township of Bellaghy." Say that after me. "The one you know——"

I said it, word for word, and content warmed his cold eyes.

"My work is done at last," he whispered.

"No, Cathal, no! Who did this to you?"

"Searching for you, he found me here——"

"Cosby?"

"But it was the good turn he did me—me, a dead man walking. Listen now again, brother. All that seeking of mine was folly. Let it stop with me. I take back your word. Do not you be minding Cosby. He and you and I are in the hands of God, and let us not be struggling in that nest. Are you heeding me?"

"I am." But, indeed, I was not.

He looked at me long. "Ah well! I can do no

338

more." His voice came strong. "I will come now, O'More."

His hands loosed, and one of them sought mine. It was colder than clay, but the fingers pressed mine firmly. And then he died. The life he had held so calmly strong went out of him quieter than a breath. I did not know that he was dead yet awhile. His face did not change, his breath made no sound, his eyes were as calm as the sky. Then his lips parted and his fingers loosed, and I knew that he was gone.

I stood looking down at him, and his death possessed me. For all the advice that he had given me my mind was set on him, on the bitterness of his days and the pity of his death. He was better at rest. Surely his heart was broken that day in Dublin, and he had been no more than a ghost driven by an urge that in the end failed. I felt extraordinarily bitter. This man had been treated unfairly—by Fate and by man. By man! by one man. In my mind's eye I saw the tossed flaxen hair of Cosby and his pale eyes and his mouth laughing without humour. And with that face in mind my teeth grated and I had no prayer to say.

I walked out of the room and found my three friends at the head of the stairs, and the Welshwoman on the steps below them.

"He is dead," I told them through shut teeth.

The woman threw her hands wide and opened her mouth to keen.

"Be quiet, woman!" I stopped her savagely. "He is happier than you are, who will have no house over your head the morn."

That stopped her. Her mouth remained open and it was no wider than her eyes.

"Be not worrying, woman-of-the-house," Donal comforted her. "This house and all in it will be safe."

The old priest was watching me with anxious looks. "I am sorry, Senan," I said to him. "There was not time."

"I saw him this morning early," said he. "Did you get his word?"

"It can wait," said I shortly, and went down the stairs.

v

But up on the crown of the wall the three of them came round me so that I could not move. They were very gentle and firm, as good men are with a sick child. Fine they knew that the dead man's word concerned me closely, and they knew that, in my then state, I was not fit to handle it.

"What is it, cousin?" Donal asked, his hand on me.

"Will any of you tell me where I can find Cosby?" I asked back. I am not an obstinate man, nor am I a vindictive one, but the clout on the head must have been working on me. It set all my humour on one road and closed down on that.

"Did your message concern Cosby?" the priest queried quickly.

"He is my concern now. I will find him under the mountains at the World's End."

"Then what was the word you had, my light?"

And, strangely enough, I found it difficult to recall to mind the message that should have stirred me like a trumpet. I ran my hand over my bandaged brow and a change of mood came over me. "I am sorry,

340

friends of my heart. Ye should not be troubling about me. Why are ye so patient?—but—but I will be better to-morrow."

"What did the dead man say to you, jewel of my heart?"

I looked at the old man and said my piece carefully as I remembered it: "The word was from Donn Maguire, and it was that a message would be waiting for me in the township of Bellaghy, and that one I know would be waiting for me in the Glen of the Echo."

"Christ, and Him risen!" cried the priest. "I knew it."

After that the three of them took no notice of me for a while. I might not have been there. They closed in and talked, and I stood leaning against the shelter-wall, my eyes on the ground, and little fumes of hot mist curling across my sight. And I paid but little heed to what they said about a man that, somehow, was a stranger to me.

The thing that had to be done had to be done at once—Donal was certain of that. If Ormonde in Dublin had sent an army to Clifford or a fleet came round to Galway, Hugh Roe would avoid that scissors-hold and fall back on the north. There was no time to lose, and to-day there was an open road. Then take your two hundred—this was Tadg—and the O'Flaherty will not be ferocious. Father Senan was wiser. That would be a waste of time. A big force must go round head of Corrib, and there was no need for fighting. The way was open across the loch, and a few men moving boldly would be credited with strength behind them. A few men! The fewer the better, said Donal and that few here—but would the man be fit to ride?

341

Fit as he would be for a week—and a week was a year
—and a man with a head like that was not a child to
be killed. . . .

But I was thinking thoughts of my own, and
suddenly cried out. "If ye will not tell me,
Vaughan will. I will go to Vaughan."

They had to give me my way that far.

We found Vaughan in his own quarters above the
arch, lying comfortably enough on his own bed.
Ned Billing opened the door to us. A skilly bone-
setter of O'Donnell's had joined the broken bones, and
one leg was a thick packet of splints and linen strips.
Vaughan's face was pale and weary, but the sound
strong bones of cheek and jaw had not weakened. He
greeted me with a smile as I bent close and looked into
his eyes. "Out of the wilderness ye again smote us!"
he murmured.

"Tell me, fine man of the English," I put to him,
"why would you and I be always hurting each other?"

"Because one of us was on the wrong side, my
friend. It is our luck, and luck is a woman—and
for a woman, though not the same, we both fight."
He caught my sleeve and drew me nearer. "I missed
your Ferrara early in the evening. Tom Pybus was
killed in the fight."

"Ah—ah! I was the death of him the fourth time.
Will God judge him kindly?"

"His meed." He drew me still closer. "There
is something I should like you to know. Dame Bevinda
is not gone to Athlone. She has taken herself and her
tail back to Corrib. You will know——"

"I know nothing now till I find the man Cosby.
Where is he?"

He did not answer me for a long time.

"A friend," said I, "if you know, you will not hide it from me this hour."

"Where your lady is he will not be far away."

"Is it so, then?" I turned to Donal behind me. "I will come with ye now, Cousin. Where is my sword?"

CHAPTER XV

I

I HAVE no clear memory of that second ride to Corrib, for I was out of my head all that day and some of the next. First I made a pother because they mounted me on a strange horse instead of on my own mare Benmee, and they had to be very patient in persuading me that she had been killed before Sligo.

"Sligo! but that was a long time ago," I wondered. "I was there, and Tadg here was singing a fine song."

"I was so," agreed Tadg, "and I wearing a black-cock's feather."

"Were you, now?" I felt my own. "Am I Tadg, or are you?"

"Brothers, surely."

"Let that stand."

So I mounted the strange horse, and off we set, the four of us, Father Senan leading, and Donal and Tadg at either side of my crupper.

They tell me that I said no word all that ride till we came to the township of Bellaghy; that I let my reins hang loose so that Donal had to touch my horse occasionally to keep it on the road, and that over and over, endlessly, I kept whistling a small piece of a gay port [1] that they had never heard before, but that I could never get the turn of it right—until, at last, Donal found himself whistling with me and lifting to the turn and going off the tune in the same way.

[1] Tune.

344

It was near dark when we came to Bellaghy hamlet, but no man waited there for us with a message. They decided to stay there that night, and Murrigan O'Flaherty Dhu gave us a kindly welcome. He knew who we were by now, and his hospitality was no less because of that. It appears that the first words I said were: "Man, Flaherty oge,[1] I left a fine new linder on a bush in this place five or ten years ago." And he flushed in some discomfort, whereon I put my hand round his shoulders: "Fine man, you are welcome —it is over the kindest heart within the four seas."

All I remember clearly of Bellaghy is that I did not sleep in it that night. Still I had sense enough to lie quiet in the dark and not trouble the old friar, who lay near me. Twice in the night I felt his hand on me, and once he put on a cool, fresh bandage. In the dawn, when he was sleeping, I went out into the morning, but my head was too heavy and dazed to be cleared, even by the fresh dawn wind.

As I stood barelegged out in the open a dog barked and a man in a hurry came in at the other end of the village, a mountain man without cloak or head-covering. I waited for him, but he stopped a good ten paces away, as was only natural considering my appearance. "Is one David Gordon in this place?" he called.

"David Gordon! I do think that the ugly man is here somewhere—there was a message for him."

"It is with me."

"Wait, now, and I will see."

I turned, and there was Father Senan in the door. "There is a message for David Gordon," I explained. "Where . . .? Oh! But am I not that fellow?"

[1] Young.

The mountain man was frightened and doubtful. "God be good to us all!" he prayed.

"All is well, my son," the priest encouraged him. "What is your message?"

"There is a boat waiting, and I am to take ye to the mouth of the Glosha—and after that ye will go where ye know. There is a hurry."

"We will go, then," said the priest.

II

So we crossed the loch, a sheen of silver in that still fall day, but I had no eyes for the lovely islanded wide reaches of the bay of Cong. They were fixed downwards on the hide bottom of the coracle, and I kept dully wondering if this stream of Glosha we were seeking flowed down out of Glen Rinnes—no! Glounamaol—but where, then, was the Glen of the Echo that I had in my dreams?

Going up the burn-side, I was sore puzzled. "Why am I here?" I wondered aloud. "This way leads to a land of youth hid in the wilderness—and that is no place for a man in torment—nor for a cheerless laugher. Cosby is never in this place. This place is for quiet, not for drawn swords and the chill song of them. I was here aforetime with one I know—and there was a man fine-hearted who thought he could fish——"

"True for you, a son," murmured the priest. "He only thought it."

"That is he speaking, Senan, fisher of men."

"God bring us luck at the end of this road," prayed he troubledly, "or someone will be in the dark valley."

346

"The valley of stones," said I. "It is beyond there
—Carrigdhu, where no birds sing."

In time we came up over the tilt of Glounamaol
into the mouth of the Glen of the Echo, and there the
priest put his shoulder back against my breast, halting
me, and Donal and Tadg bunched close to us. "A
wasps' bike we are landed in," he cried. "See the
crowd at the bothy?"

"Not more than half a score," said Tadg of the long
sight.

But I could not see all that distance. The great
slopes of hill shimmered and danced before my eyes;
above the purple hump of Maam the loop of a rainbow
twisted and twined tormentingly across the sky, and
ribbons of hot vapour curled up out of the valley, where
the singing of the water was sadder than dreams.

"We should not be here," I whispered, "but let
us on. There is a valley of stones beyond that will
suit us better—where we can hide till brain burns cold.
Hush! here is the Echo-point, and the happy people
might hear us."

"Up with us!" cried Donal in his indomitable
clarion voice. "Let us remember our clan and our
name. We carry this thing through—or die. March
on!"

We marched on, and made no pause till we came up
on the green level before the bothy. There we halted.

Dame Bevinda was there, and with her Duvesa
MacTheobald of the dove hair, and ten men of the
O'Flaherty clan. The deer-flenching gallows had
been knocked over and riven apart, and the men were
gathered round one of its limbs; they were about to
use it as a ram to batter down the bothy door.

But at that time I did not see the Dame or Duvesa,

347

or the men about their ram. All I saw was Cosby.
He was there.

III

I turned to Donal, and placed a hand against his
breast. "Donal," said I, "do not let anybody stop me."

He says my eyes that used be brown had turned
yellow deep under brow and that the bosses of my
cheeks had become hard marble.

"Cousin dear," I said again, "do not let anybody
stop me."

"No one under the sky," he said, iron in his voice.

"You were my own always," I said in my throat.

I swung away from him, and Andrea Ferrara came
out in the light of the sun. Someone had cleaned it
after the sack of Athenree, and now it shone with a
blue happy wickedness, and it whimpered shrill as it
came from scabbard. Oh! but the cold song of it
made me strong. I spurned the ground; when my
feet lifted they did not want to come to earth again.
Donal tells me that, in truth, I swayed from knee to
shoulder and moved forward like a man weary and
in no hurry, but that my face and the look in my eyes
would frighten the Fianne [1]; that men shrank aside
from me, and no hand went to blade. And there was
Dame Bevinda O'Flaherty before me.

"Would you dare to the end, a Gordon?" said she.

"Woman of the great heart," said I, "this thing
had to be. Forgive me, now."

Gently I put her aside with one hand, and there
was Cosby facing me, and his sword still in sheath.

"We meet for the last time, Captain Sir William
Cosby," I said, giving him his full title. "It was

[1] Ancient fighting troops of Erin.

348

meant from the day you slew my friend. Draw your sword."

He stood looking at me out of his light eyes, his teeth showing mirthlessly.

"Oh, cheerless laugher!" I cried. "Laugh now. This is the end of all roads. Make your peace with Colum O'More and Cathal O'Dwyer. With me you make no peace on top of earth. Draw!"

It happened very quickly. He saw me there, swaying on my feet, head bandaged, face dead white, sword lax in my hand. Now was his time to kill. They say his blade came out in one mighty sweep and, in the same motion, slashed like a streak at my neck. But to me that blade was slow as sway of a branch in the wind and as soft as the stroke of a reed. I had to wait for it until it came from behind his shoulder. And there my blade locked on it, twisted over and under it, and leaped forward in one clean shoulder-driven lunge—through open mouth and through spine. The guard jarred against his teeth. He fell backwards. I recovered blade with a single wrench, and swung on the O'Flaherty men.

"Who dies now?"

No one made the smallest move. It was all over.

I waited. A great weakness flowed over me; the world rocked; hilt slipped from loosed fingers; I should have fallen. But it was as if a clean strong wind came about me to hold me up. A rustle of skirts, a cry, a pair of strong young arms, and there was my Eithne holding me.

"David—David!"

I placed arm round her shoulder and leaned on her.

"Eithne," I cried, "I was needing you. It is

you I am needing. Do not let them hurt me any more."

"No more, dear. No one—no one will hurt you any more."

Dame Bevinda had the last word.

"Sad day!" she cried. "Sad day when the O'Flahertys are dared on their own ground. They need a man. Let it be."